DEATH
TAKES
THE
STAGE

Stonewall Inn Editions

Michael Denneny, General Editor

DEATH TAKES THE STAGE

DONALD WARD

ST. MARTIN'S PRESS
NEW YORK

Design by Glen M. Edelstein

Library of Congress Cataloging-in-Publication Data

Ward, Donald.
      Death takes the stage / Donald Ward.
           p.   cm. — (Stonewall Inn editions)
     ISBN 0-312-03474-1
     I. Title.   II. Series.
   [PS3573.A728D44   1989]
   813'.54—dc20   89-34857
                                              CIP

To Dad,
with love and gratitude

DEATH
TAKES
THE
STAGE

One

Arnie flexed the stiffness out of his back, kept his eyes on the
road, and allowed two large teardrops to fall, plop, plop, on
the front of his clean white T-shirt. In front of him, puddles of
heat mirage retreated endlessly south in an arrow-straight line to the
horizon while, on either side of Interstate 5, monotonous fields of
staked grapevines, or occasionally cotton, stretched off into the haze.
Inside the International trailer cab, the muffled roar of the diesel engine blended with a soft rush of conditioned air; and, on the built-in
stereo cassette player, Mimi lay dying in an unheated Parisian garret.

Arnie shifted uneasily in his seat and wondered if it would be cheating to push the Stop button before the opera ended. Bobbie wanted
him to use his driving time to absorb culture and learn about things,
but Arnie had already absorbed *La Bohème* three times between Los
Angeles and Vancouver, plus two more between Vancouver and the
San Joaquin valley, through which he was now passing on the way
back, and he didn't know if he could take the sad ending again. Not
that he could understand the Italian they sang in, or even remember
much of what Bobbie had told him about the plot, but it didn't take
much to know that when the girl started singing in a gaspy, faraway
voice she wasn't going to hold out for too much longer. And then her
friends would start whispering, almost talking, which was strangely
upsetting when they should be singing, and then her boyfriend would

come in and call her name and start crying and Arnie would start crying too—

Quickly, Arnie pressed the Fast Forward button and let the tape whiz through to the end. Those poor guys sure led a lousy life, he thought, blowing his nose. Of course, they didn't know any better. If someone had told poor old Mimi about eating right and jogging, she'd probably be skipping around today. On the whole, Arnie preferred the German operas. When those guys died, they sounded like they still had it in them to run a few miles before breakfast, and when the time came for them to go they went without bawling and getting everybody all upset about it.

Arnie, who had a tender heart, was particularly susceptible to crying, and ashamed of the fact. It didn't fit the image of someone who stood six foot nine in his socks, weighed two hundred seventy pounds stripped, spent full days at the gym whenever he could and, ten years ago, had almost made it to Mr. Teenage America—and would have, too, if only he'd worked on his neck a bit more, and maybe his calves. Still, things had worked out pretty good so far. He'd got into trucking, which he loved, and a few years after that he'd met Bobbie, whom he loved even more. Arnie could recall in every detail the afternoon they had met on Santa Monica Pier. He had noticed Bobbie right away, the prettiest thing he had ever seen in his life: tight little shorts, sandals, mini T-shirt, blond curls like a flower, just a hint of makeup, and standing no higher than the overdeveloped pectoral muscles that Arnie had kept flexing until their eyes had met and Bobbie had smiled and come over and said hi and Arnie had smiled and said hi and . . .

Here Arnie began to get turned on and, in an attempt to redirect his thoughts to safer channels, he put another cassette into the machine. A pleasant well-modulated voice addressed him. "Where is the nearest golf course?" it asked. *"Où est le terrain de golf le plus prochain?"* A pause, then, *"Oui. Où est le terrain de golf le plus prochain.* Can one rent golf clubs? *Peut-on louer des crosses. . . ?"* Arnie tuned out but let the tape run on. He had long ago given up any hope of ever getting his tongue around a foreign language, but he liked the sound of it and he knew Bobbie wanted him to try, to be ready for their big trip to Europe, where Mimi and all those other weepers came from. Although who knew when that would be. First they had to save enough so he could buy a rig of his own and become an independent operator. That

2

was the plan Bobbie had come up with just after they had started living together. First a rig of his own, then a few years driving it under the wing of an established firm, then, finally, their own company: A&B Trucking. It had a real good sound to it.

But that wouldn't be for a while yet. Bobbie's acting didn't bring in much—usually nothing, what with working on those showcase productions or helping out backstage for free—and altogether they had only a little over four thousand dollars in the bank, almost all of it contributed by Arnie, which was only fair since he was the one who was going to end up driving the shiny new eighteen-wheeler with maybe a custom-built Kenworth cab and a special paint job and lots of chromium-plated trim and a CB and a TV and a big bunk in case Bobbie wanted to ride along sometimes. It was a beautiful vision, and only sixty-five, seventy-five thousand bucks to go. Arnie sighed. No doubt about it, he was going to have to work harder, which would mean more nights away from home, but that couldn't be helped. And maybe he wouldn't have to get all the money up front. Maybe he could borrow. He would have to ask Bobbie about it. Bobbie was the one who knew about money and business and things like that.

Suddenly hungry, Arnie reached back into a soft traveling bag and withdrew a plastic-wrapped sandwich, the last of a generous supply presented to him early yesterday morning as he left the small commercial hotel where he always spent the night on his trips north. Arnie had a special fondness for this admittedly unprepossessing establishment because he and Bobbie had discovered it together on what they both liked to think of as their honeymoon. Actually, it was practical Bobbie who had insisted that they save money at a cheap no-frills hotel; and once they were installed at the Hastings Arms, it was Bobbie who had won the heart of its amiable Asian proprietress, persuading her to take Arnie on as a regular customer at a reduced rate. Now the incongruously-named Mrs. McLeod treated Arnie like one of her own sons (Ian, Andrew and James) and always included a kind message to Bobbie with the parting bag of chicken sandwiches. Arnie smiled. Bobbie could charm the birds off the trees without even trying.

Santa Monica seemed very far away. The highway still ran straight as a ruler into the mixture of heat haze and smog that seemed to be distributed in greater or lesser amounts over the whole West Coast of the United States. Even the coastal mountains, far to Arnie's right,

3

could be discerned only as faint shadows, smoky blue beyond the dull yellow fields. Arnie tried not to look at the dashboard clock because that always made the time pass even more slowly, but his eyes moved faster than his thoughts. Ten past one; not bad. He'd told Bobbie that dinner at seven would be okay and it looked as if he'd make it with time to spare. If it worked out that way, Arnie planned to stop off at one of those big bright corner shops and buy some flowers. Bobbie liked flowers.

There was a problem, however. Bobbie set great store by color coordination all over the apartment and wouldn't be happy with anything that clashed. Arnie frowned and tried to remember the living room walls. White? Sandy, like the passing vines outside? The upholstered furniture—blue, or maybe green? Arnie gave up. As long as there were places to sit and sleep, he was happy. But the flowers. Arnie's brow cleared: he'd just buy one of those big mixed bunches that offered every color of the rainbow, at least some of which were bound to be right.

He wanted everything to be right, because tonight would be special, as it always was when he got back from a long trip, starting with what Bobbie called a "gourmet meal," put together from a vast collection of cookbooks and filed recipe clippings that stretched wall to wall along one of the kitchen counters. Cooking was one of Bobbie's many accomplishments that Arnie, who had trouble adding the right amount of milk to his breakfast cereal, regarded with awe. Left to himself, he would exist happily on cottage cheese, canned tuna, raw vegetables, chalky high-protein drinks and the occasional burnt steak. But Bobbie's beautiful creations, looking like photographs in magazine advertisements, never ceased to amaze him, and he ate large quantities in appreciative, dedicated silence.

What had he ever done to luck out on such a great setup? What could someone so small and beautiful and clever see in someone so big and clumsy and stupid? Arnie could never figure it out. Early on, he had resigned himself to the fact that, although his body could probably get him all the one-night stands he wanted, the chances of anyone sticking around for a relationship after were pretty slim. And yet from almost that first day three years ago on the Santa Monica Pier, he had had just that, like a regular married man. Against all odds he, Arnie Siganski, no genius and no beauty, had found someone who loved him, cooked for him, washed and ironed his clothes, packed and un-packed his overnight gear, managed his finances, entertained him, and made his life interesting. Somewhere along the line he must have done something right.

Fighting a tendency to become unduly sentimental, Arnie ruthlessly tailgated a small blue Volkswagen until it nervously skittered off into another lane. He didn't want to be late getting home, because although he understood nothing about the mysteries of the kitchen, he knew that Bobbie hated having to keep things warm in the oven. Once Bobbie had scolded him for getting home late. It was done in a funny manner, but Arnie got the message.

"God knows I don't ask for much," Bobbie had shrilled, staggering out of the kitchen in a frilly apron and a saucepan hat, "slogging back and forth to the market, trying to think up something new to please you, peeling and chopping and cutting, hours sweating over a hot stove. And all I ask is for you to come home on time. I know what it is: you don't love me anymore. I've turned into an old slag, worn out before my time. And you've found some fresh young thing who can't even boil an egg."

Then Bobbie had untied the frilly apron from around his chest, pulled the saucepan off his head, and laughed his wonderful laugh that made Arnie go weak at the knees and begin to sweat with desire.

Just as drops were beginning to bead on his forehead and his thighs were starting to tremble, Arnie's attention was caught by a familiar gray shape forming out of the haze in front of him. Somehow the coastal mountains had slid quietly around and were now planted squarely across the highway. And on the other side of the mountains lay Los Angeles. And Santa Monica. And Covina Place. And Bobbie.

Two

Jake Weissman sat in his office and brooded about life. Life, at the moment, was not good. Life was like his office: brown, dusty and short on illumination. Life was living at the bottom of a dim air shaft, looking across at the offices of Klein, Klein, and Brown, Attorneys at Law, where from time to time the younger Klein had brisk sex with one of the secretaries, and where once a year a shaft of sunlight passed in the front window, out the rear window and across the shaft to enter Jake's office, tired, pale orange and very much secondhand.

Jake brooded about the symbolism of having to live one's life in someone else's used light and gazed across his desk at the wall where on that mystic day of next spring an exhausted sunbeam would once again briefly sweep over his small collection of framed posters advertising the various entertainments in which one or another of his clients had managed to croak out a line or otherwise flash past an audience's line of sight. He brooded about his clients, an ungrateful lot who hounded him mercilessly to get them employment and then, on those rare occasions when he succeeded in doing so, bitterly resented the ten-percent commission he extracted before forwarding their few and, Jake felt, ill-earned, dollars. Just one winner, thought Jake, one real winner with a real part in a real series paying real money and everything would fall into line. Other winners would follow. The ten percents would add up. And as the sun sank slowly in the west, he, Jake Weissman, theatrical agent extraordinaire, would bid farewell to twilit days, Klein, Klein, and Brown, and the fusty smell sent up by the decomposing debris that accumulated year by year on the asphalt-covered area beneath his window. Farewell without regret, thought Jake, and just watch me head for those good old Beverly Hills.

But all that was for the future. For now, he was stuck on Vine Street, too far from Hollywood Boulevard and Capitol Records to count, with not nearly enough work to give him an appearance of doing something. He envied Consuela, who sat in the outer office and placidly filled her hours of nonemployment by changing the color of her nail polish, conducting endless telephone conversations with her numerous friends and family, and reading passionate paperback romances. If pressed, she would interrupt these activities to answer the telephone, type up a contract, or make coffee. Jake decided to call for coffee and pushed the appropriate intercom button.

"Hello," said a voice, not Consuela's.

"Consuela?" Maybe she had a cold.

"She not here. What you want?"

"Who is this?"

"Congratulations. You got new secretary."

"What happened to the old one? Where's Consuela?"

No answer. Jake gave the intercom button a couple of pokes and tried again.

"Hello? Hello?"

The door of his office swung open.

"Hello yourself," said his new secretary, smartly attired for a day at the office in skintight black satin pants, a pink angora crossover sweater that crossed over a bare two inches above her navel, platform sandals with four-inch heels, and approximately half a tube of lipstick. She had enormous brown eyes, dark hair down to below her shoulders, and tits, thought Jake, to drown in.

His new secretary spoke again.

"You don't blink, you gonna get two sore eyes," she said. "Or maybe two black ones," she added.

"Where—" Jake stopped and lowered his voice an octave to its natural level. "Where is Consuela?"

"She go to New York."

Jake felt hurt. "She might have said something before she went. Like good-bye."

"She bet you never notice I take her place. She say you break her heart."

7

"That's crazy," Jake exclaimed. "I never touched her."

"She say that too. Whatsa matter—you gay?"

"I don't mix office work with my private life." Jake neglected to mention that, until now, there had never been any temptation to do so. Consuela and her predecessors had been remarkable only for their plainness.

"Okay by me," said his new secretary cheerfully. "You not so hot anyhow. Where you get all that curly hair—some beauty parlor?"

"It's natural," lied Jake.

"And why you wear all those gold chains?"

"Business. If you're going to be a Hollywood agent, you have to look like a Hollywood agent."

"You look like you got a string of girls in some back room."

"I wish I had. They might bring in some money. Now could we talk a little about you, Miss . . . Miss. . . ?" Jake floundered to a halt.

"I wonder when you gonna ask. Miss Morphy. Maria Morphy."

"Morphy?"

"With a u. I call myself that to fool immigration people. Nobody think to look for a wetback called Morphy."

Jake's blood pressure, already a little high, skipped off the chart.

"Miss Murphy. If you're an illegal alien, you can't work for me. I've got enough troubles without taking on the Department of Immigration."

"That's what Consuela say too. So all you gotta do is let me stay here, keep you mouth shut, and I don't tell them you pay somebody to carry me across Río Grande and then keep me in this dump for fifty dollar a week. And you can call me Morphy."

The office walls started closing in on Jake. "What happens if they find out about you on their own?"

Miss Murphy gave him a winning smile. "Then I say my cousin Consuela hire me and you just stupid jerk who don't know nothing. Okay?"

Jake's blood pressure began to subside. "I guess so," he conceded. "What did you do before you left Mexico?"

"Lots of things." Miss Murphy wiggled an eyebrow at him. "But don't worry. I make good secretary."

"I suppose you wouldn't consider going to New York with your cousin," Jake ventured hopefully.

The suggestion was received with contempt. "I don't go noplace where it snow," Miss Murphy stated firmly. "I don't like snow. I don't like rain. I like son."

Jake pointed out that the sun shone on New York too.

"Not enough. I like to take off the clothes and lie out all day." Miss Murphy moved a little closer to Jake's desk. "You like to take off the clothes and lie out all day?" she asked.

"Not much. No."

"Ah, you miss something so good. Son, he make the skin all brown and smooth and hot. Then all the pretty girl they want to touch you, run fingers through you hair, pull pretty gold chains, go to bed—"

"Murphy!" Jake knew he was turning bright red and hated himself for it. "Drop the subject. I don't want to hear any more about it."

Miss Murphy eyed the leather sofa in the corner. "You like to do?" she suggested.

"No!" Jake exclaimed quickly, thinking of young Klein across the way. Because if Jake could see him, then he could—"No," he said again. "Let's begin as we intend to go on. I don't do that in the office."

"Okay. So you take me out tonight."

"No, not tonight. Or ever. Anyhow, tonight I'm going to a Greer Garson retrospective. The movies. With my . . ." He searched for a word. "My friend," he concluded lamely, waving at Clare's photograph on his desk. Not for the first time, he wished it wasn't so damn accurate. Clare really should try just a little makeup.

Miss Murphy turned her luminous gaze toward the photograph. "Oh, yeah," she sneered. "Consuela tell me about her. She look like she need a good fock."

"Murphy!"

"And that go for you, too."

The door slammed behind her.

Jake took off the rimless glasses recommended by his optometrist as being so very today and rubbed his eyes. This was surely not happening. Maybe he had dreamed it all. If he pushed the intercom button again, maybe nice, plain, uncomplicated Consuela would answer and bring him his coffee. He pushed the button.

"What?"

Forget Consuela.

9

"Murphy, I'd like a cup of coffee. You'll find the coffee maker in the alcove."

"You find it," said the disembodied Miss Murphy. "I don't do coffee."

So it was going to be a power play. Well, he could show her a thing or two about that!

"If you work for me, you make coffee," said Jake in his most authoritative manner, the one he hoped to use one day on a representative of Universal Pictures, or CBS, or the Shubert Brothers. "I want it hot, strong, black and now. So get moving."

Once again, Jake's door opened and Miss Murphy stamped in.

"Look, Mr. Big Hollywood Agents," she fumed. "I come here as secretary. I type and I file and I take the dictation. I don't do coffee and I don't do windows and I don't do shoppings for little presents for the boss to give his . . ." She cast a scornful look at Clare's photograph, which appeared to be growing paler by the minute. "His friend! You got that? Good!"

She was gone. Fifteen seconds later she was back.

"You got a visitor," she reported.

"Who?" Jake had some trouble finding his voice.

"Some funny name. You handle Jolly Green Giant?"

"He's green?" faltered Jake, who was beginning to feel that this was a day when anything could happen.

"No, big. You wanna see him?"

"Why not?" Jake was past caring. "Send him in."

"I think he just stop crying," said Miss Murphy, as she left. "He say go in," Jake heard her announce.

My God, he thought a moment later, it is a giant! For, filling his doorway from side to side and almost from top to bottom was the largest human being he had ever encountered. He was dressed in a T-shirt, baseball jacket, work boots and jeans, with a bunch of keys clipped to a belt loop over his left hip. His hair lay short and flat on a round skull, and he gazed at Jake sadly through round, red-rimmed eyes.

Jake swallowed. "Come in," he said. "Sit down."

The giant jingled in and fitted himself, with much dangerous creaking, into one of the office's two vinyl-covered client chairs.

"What can I do for you?" Jake asked.

"Mr. Weissman," said Arnie, "you gotta find who killed my Bobbie."

10

Three

Jake, although ready for almost anything, was not ready for that. It was obviously a time to keep cool and go slow. Jake decided that it would be easier to begin with the latter.

"First of all," he said, in his best office manner, "maybe you could tell me who you are."

Arnie became flustered. "Gee, I'm sorry, Mr. Weissman. I'm Arnie Siganski." He got up and offered Jake his hand. "I thought that actress out there told you."

"That was no actress, that was my secretary," said Jake, surprised and relieved at the firm but gentle pressure applied to his hand by one twice its size. "And please call me Jake."

"How ya doin', Jake." Arnie sat down again. "My real name's Arnold, but I stopped usin' it so people wouldn't mix up me and Schwarzenegger. I don't compete no more, but I guess I'm stuck with Arnie. You remember my Bobbie?"

"I'm not sure," lied Jake, who definitely didn't. "What was his last name again?"

"Lang," said Arnie. "He said you was his agent, so I want you to find the shit who killed him so's I can kill the shit who killed him."

Cool and slow. Jake rearranged some papers on his desk. "Arnie," he said, choosing his words carefully, "you're making a mistake here. I'm not that kind of agent. I'm not with the police or the FBI. I'm a theatrical agent. I find jobs for actors and I talk with producers about their salaries—their money—and I help draw up their contracts. I don't know anything about finding murderers. I can't help you."

Arnie thought about this. "You never got Bobbie no job," he said, "or no money. He never got paid to act since he moved in with me."

This was more familiar territory.

"Show business is a very uncertain profession," began Jake, switching over to his set speech. "There are far more people wanting to get in than there are jobs available. Particularly now, when costs are so high and the difficulties of putting together a movie deal or getting a property onto the stage are so enormous. Even people with a good track record can't be sure of working regularly these days, and as for people without a track record—well, if Bobbie's on my list of clients he must have done something once, but it must have been a long time ago. And there was never any guarantee that he would do anything again," he finished lamely.

During his lecture, Jake had looked hard into Arnie's eyes, the better to convey the depth and sincerity of his message. Try as he might, however, he could penetrate no farther than their slightly glazed outer surface. He wondered whether anything at all had got through. Arnie didn't keep him wondering long.

"So," said Arnie, "are you gonna help me find the shit who killed my Bobbie?"

"Arnie, I can't," Jake began to plead. "I'm not qualified. You have to leave it to the police. Or a private detective," he added as an afterthought.

"I don't want no detective," said Arnie stubbornly. "I don't want no police. I want somebody who knowed and loved my Bobbie like I did."

"Arnie . . ." If only he could remember one thing about this Bobbie.

"Anyhow," continued Arnie, paying no attention to Jake's feeble interruption, "I been to the police. After I seen about Bobbie on television. They asked me some questions, but they didn't care. Just another dead fag who got unlucky with a pickup. But Bobbie wasn't like that. He never played around. He loved me like I loved him. Especially he wouldn't—"Arnie's face began to crumple up. "He wouldn't—" Arnie stopped and blew his nose into a large white handkerchief. "Please, you gotta help me. You din't see Bobbie like I did. Before they killed him they hurt him. They . . . they . . . oh—" And Arnie hid his doleful face in his big hands and broke down into loud, painful sobs.

Jake was horrified. Tears were not unknown in his office. They had been shed many times, discreetly, moderately and, above all, decoratively by many a disappointed aspirant to a plum part or even a lucrative commercial. But nothing like this. If he touched the sobbing giant, might the move be misinterpreted? Deciding to risk it, he got up, walked around the desk, and put his hand on Arnie's heaving shoulder. It was like trying to hold down a small earthquake.

"Arnie," he began, and faltered. "Arnie, please . . ."

At this moment Miss Murphy made a brisk entrance into the office bearing a filing folder in one hand and a large mug of coffee in the other. She slammed the file into Jake's chest and held the mug out where Arnie might see and smell it through his fingers.

"Here, *muchachón*," she said. Arnie took a shuddering breath and looked up at her. Miss Murphy smiled encouragingly. "You drink this," she went on, "and don't cry no more. Mr. Weissman and me, we gonna help you. Everything turn out all right, you see."

Arnie took the mug and tried to smile back at her.

"That's a good boy." Miss Murphy patted him on the shoulder. Then, turning to Jake, she whispered, "You got file there for Lang, Robert. Use it!"

"Did you—?" Jake began indignantly.

"Yeah," interrupted Miss Murphy. "I listen on intercom. I also check engagement book. Empty. And answering service. *Nada*. You got only one person who need you—right here. So help him."

"But he's—"

"Not so dumb as he look. At least he smart enough to see when someone got what it take to be actress."

With her parting shot effectively delivered, Miss Murphy exited in a twinkle of black satin and a light flurry of angora fluff.

Arnie, having stopped crying, swallowed some coffee and looked hopefully at Jake with moist expectant eyes.

Oh, God, thought Jake, all he needs is a keg of brandy under his chin. He pulled himself together. "I'll think about it," he told Arnie. "I really will. Leave your name, address and telephone number with Miss Murphy, and if I can figure out anything I can do to help, I'll give you a call tomorrow morning. Will you be in?"

"Yeah," said Arnie. "I ain't workin' right now. It's my birthday end of next week, and me and Bobbie was goin' to spend some time in La Jolla, just the two of us. So I ain't got no jobs lined up. I'll be around if

13

you want me." He got up, started for the door, then stopped and turned back, blushing. "Mr. Weissman," he added, "I don't expect you to do this for free. I got four thousand dollars in the bank. I can pay."

Overdue credit card payments. Overdue bills. Office and apartment rents coming up. It was definitely time for cool. "We'll talk," said Jake, coolly. "Don't forget to leave your number with Miss Murphy."

"So—you gonna help him?" asked Miss Murphy, appearing in the doorway five minutes later.

"I don't know," said Jake. "I told him to go to a detective, but he wants me. What do I know about solving a murder? I could end up dead, like Bobbie. I'm out of condition. I can't even get through a game of handball."

Miss Murphy moved into the office and sat down on the corner of Jake's desk. Her perfume, although applied a little too liberally, was expensive and pleasing. Jake found himself wondering if it would do for Clare what it most certainly did for Miss Murphy, who was now gazing deeply into his eyes.

"Look," she said in a low, confidential voice, "you no get hurt just to look around, see police, ask questions. Maybe you find something, maybe no. But you try, because that poor big guy, he got nobody now but you. Anyhow," she continued more briskly, "I look through books and you need moneys. Also exercise. What age you got—thirty-five? Thirty-eight?"

Jake mumbled something and turned to look out the window behind him. But Miss Murphy was not to be put off so easily.

"Speak up. I no hear you."

"Thirty-two." The number came out rather too loudly.

"You no look it. You too fat." Miss Murphy leaned forward and breathed into his ear. "But cute, like teddy bears," she murmured, lightly ruffling his hair. "So you get out and run around and lose the weights and then you live longer. Trust me. And don't worry about office. I look after." She picked up Bobbie's file and dropped it into Jake's lap. "Now, Mr. Private Eyes, you want coffee?"

Jake twirled around from the window. "You bet!"

"You got!"

Miss Murphy tapped out of the office on her spike heels, and Jake, satisfied that he had won a small victory, leaned back in his chair, placed his feet on his desk, and opened Bobbie's file.

14

Four

The file on Lang, Robert, was thin to the point of anemia, but it served to remind Jake that four years ago Bobbie had managed to get an understudy role in a touring company of *A Chorus Line*. He needed an agent, and an actor friend had put him in touch with Jake, who was just setting up in business for himself and therefore willing to sign up any performer with an Equity card and a paying job. A year later, after many calls from a now unemployed Bobbie, Jake had placed him in a soft drink commercial, where he appeared as a dancing juvenile in the back row. The last entry in the file showed that Bobbie had then taken an unpaid job at the Quest Theatre, a ninety-nine-seat establishment on Melrose Avenue, and never contacted him again.

It was not much to go on. In fact, thought Jake, it was far too little to send him on a wild and possibly dangerous goose chase asking questions about a dead person whom he could not remember and whom he had, strictly speaking, represented only once, a long time ago. To hell with it, he decided as he guided his fire-engine-red Thunderbird home along the freeway later that evening, just ahead of Clare's silver-gray Cadillac Seville. There must be better, safer ways to liven up a life. And, anyhow, he had enough worries of his own to contend with, the most immediate being whether or not he was going to get Clare into a sexually responsive mood when they got back to his apartment.

The evening had, so far, not proved a great success, and Jake was forced to admit that the Greer Garson retrospective had not been a good idea. In the first place, Clare was not a film fan. She existed solely for her interior decorating business and would consent to go to a movie only if persuaded that its action moved rapidly from one inspiring interior to another. Therefore, in the second place, they should have got out of the theater when it was announced that, owing to the unavailability of *Pride and Prejudice*— "You'll love the Regency decor, Clare"—the first feature was now going to be *Tobacco Road*. And in the third place, even with the promise of *Mrs. Miniver* to follow, he should definitely have taken her home when a voice just behind his right ear whispered, "Hello, Teddy Bears."

Realizing that the greeting would only be repeated in a louder voice if he pretended not to have heard it, Jake turned around. Miss Murphy was seated directly behind him, dressed for her night at the movies in a white off-the-shoulder blouse with many embroidered frills, no midriff and a considerable amount of artificial flowers that extended up into an upswept hairdo. Jake found the effect not unpleasing, and the disloyal thought flashed through his mind that if only he had known Miss Murphy last month, it would have been fun to take her to the 20th Century-Fox musical retrospective, rather than Clare, who was only mildly enthusiastic about all the overstuffed banquettes in the restaurant scenes.

Miss Murphy beamed at Jake and wiggled the fingers of one hand at him. With the other hand, she clutched the arm of her escort, who was seated behind Clare. Turning his attention to the escort, Jake noticed that he, too, sported an upswept hairstyle, which rose to an impossible height before cascading down his forehead into a neat point that ended somewhere just above the bridge of his nose. The gloss on this confection only slightly exceeded the shine on its owner's black leather jacket, which was tastefully decorated with chromium-plated chains and star-shaped studs, the whole ensemble being topped off by a pair of mirrored glasses, behind which the wearer might easily have been fast asleep. As if to prove otherwise, Miss Murphy's companion slouched down onto his spine and deposited one large black-booted foot on each side of the back of Clare's seat. Jake turned around hastily and riveted his attention on the earthy doings of Jeeter Lester and his family.

"You never told me you wanted Carmen Miranda for a secretary," said Clare as they stood outside the theater between features.

"I didn't," replied Jake. "My ex-secretary hired her."

Clare put on her ironic smile. "She must have been carrying a grudge. What did you do to her?"

"Nothing," said Jake quickly. "I never laid a hand on her. That, apparently, was the trouble," he added smugly.

"Well, she certainly got her revenge. Miss Gonzales was no beauty, Lord knows, but this one looks like a streetwalker. She probably does her shopping at Frederick's of Hollywood." Clare herself favored tailored suits in gray or blue, low-heeled shoes to minimize her height, matching handbags and a geometric haircut that ended in two sharp points, one on either side of her determined jaw. "Can she type?"

The appearance of Miss Murphy at that moment saved Jake from having to answer. His relief was short-lived, however. Miss Murphy planted a large, and, Jake suspected, red, kiss on his cheek.

"Some surprise," she burbled brightly. "We go out to same place!" She turned to fix Clare with a wide smile. "Rotten movies, no?"

Jake knew when he was outmaneuvered. "Uh, Clare, this is Miss Murphy," he mumbled. "Murphy, Miss Watson."

"I recognize right away," said Miss Murphy with meaning. "She look just like her pictures. Teddy Bears," she continued, "I lose my boyfriend Baron in men's room. You go get him and we talk here till you get back."

"Well . . ." Jake hesitated.

"Right in there." Miss Murphy waved a heavily braceleted arm in the general direction of the theater entrance. "You go now, before picture start."

Jake went. The door of the men's room was locked, and so, having tried rattling the knob, he knocked.

"Who's there?" asked a voice from within.

"Me," said Jake.

"Teddy Bears?"

Jake sighed. "I guess so."

The bolt shot, the door opened, and a black-gloved hand emerged. Jake found himself securely gripped by the front of his jacket, lifted bodily across the threshold, and then backed up against the now closed door. Uncomfortably aware of the smallness of the room and the discomfort of two pointed studs and a chain being dug into his chest, Jake looked up into Baron's sunglasses with as much assurance

17

as he could muster. It was like being eye to eye with a bee. Finally Baron spoke.

"My girlfriend likes you," he growled.

Jake smiled modestly.

"I don't like it when other guys start chasin' after my girlfriend."

"I wasn't—"

"Shuddup. Now, when other guys start chasin' after my girlfriend I can play it two ways. I can be nice and tell them to lay off or I can get rough. So what do you think I'm gonna do?"

"How about—"

"Shuddup. I'll tell you what I'm gonna do. I got somethin' here just for you."

The crush against Jake's chest relaxed and was replaced by a more concentrated pressure in the pit of his stomach. On lowering his gaze, Jake found himself jammed against the butt of a small snub-nosed automatic, the blue-black sheen of which echoed the highlights on the black glove holding it.

At that moment, the blood level in Jake's head seemed to sink to somewhere in the region of his shoulders. He felt faint, but was kept standing by the thought that if he moved a muscle Baron might pull the trigger.

"Y-you c-can't . . ." he stammered.

"Sure I can. Who's gonna know?"

"All those people out there."

"So what? I'm not gonna tell them, and you sure as hell won't." Here Baron permitted himself the ghost of a smile.

"But I haven't *done* anything!"

"Good. Then I'm doin' this at just the right time. Anyhow, let's get it over with. I don't wanna miss the next movie."

Jake closed his eyes and tried to summon up a short prayer. The only word that came to mind was *Help*.

"Well," said Baron, "are you gonna take it or not?"

Jake opened his eyes.

"Murphy says you're after a murderer and you should have some protection, so this here's the best I can do. It's a Walther PPK. German. Takes a nine-millimeter short cartridge. Now when you wanna load . . ."

The ensuing demonstration mingled in Jake's mind with conflicting desires to burst into tears and start laughing very loudly. Only the fact that he could see very little through his sunglasses prevented Baron from noticing that his lesson was not being assimilated.

"So that's it," he concluded. "Any questions?"

"I can't take it," said Jake weakly. "I haven't a license."

This time Baron managed a full-blown smile. "Don't let it bother you. Neither have I."

"Yes, but—"

"Look, Teddy Bears." Baron began to sound weary. "You got a choice here. You can end up maybe in a little trouble with the police or you can end up maybe dead. Which do you like?"

Jake opened his mouth and then closed it again.

"Yeah, I thought so. Now take the gun"—Baron dropped it deftly into the side pocket of Jake's jacket—"and beat it. I don't want people thinkin' I been makin' out in here with some creep in a polyester suit."

At this, Baron turned away from Jake and became enraptured with his own reflection in the mirror over the washbasin. A logo carried out in studs on the back of his jacket informed the world that he was a member of the Death Riders.

Jake considered that his ordeal permitted him the dignity of an exit line. He paused at the door.

"It's not polyester," he announced. "It's a sixty-forty blend."

Baron teased a stray hair back into the fold with a long-handled comb. "So you're a sixty-forty creep," he said. "Scram. And lay off my girlfriend," he added in a louder voice as Jake closed the door behind him.

The ladies were waiting in the lobby, Clare looking somewhat dazed and Miss Murphy as ebullient as ever.

"Well," she caroled, as Jake emerged from the men's room. "I hope you like what my boyfriend give you in there."

Heads turned and Jake fled with Clare back into the auditorium, where he sat tensely through the next feature as Miss Murphy amused herself by alternately toying with a curl at the back of his neck and running a sharp fingernail up and down behind his ear. Between enjoying these unaccustomed sensations and worrying about the consequences should either Baron or Clare notice what was causing them, Jake speculated on his chances of getting Clare back with him for the night.

At the moment, his chances looked dim. Clare responded favorably to such invitations only under the most ideal circumstances, and it had to be admitted that the events of the last few hours seemed unlikely to meet her requirements. But since Jake had never been able to discover any consistent pattern in those requirements on those rare occasions when they had apparently been met, he had evolved an operating philosophy roughly based on the premise that it never hurt to ask.

On this occasion, much to his surprise, he was accepted, and after Miss Murphy and Baron had roared off in a cloud of motorcycle exhaust, Jake and Clare climbed into their respective automobiles and set off for Jake's apartment in a discreet motorcade of two.

Five

S o it was that Jake headed home that night with a smile on his lips, lust in his heart and a Walther PPK in his pocket. He had already made up his mind to return the gun to Miss Murphy in the morning and put Arnie into the hands of a reliable private detective who, for a fee, could get to know and love the unfortunate Bobbie to a degree far in excess of anything Jake could manage. With this matter disposed of, he turned his thoughts toward planning a strategy for his coming encounter with Clare.

It wouldn't be easy. From long experience in playing the spider to her fly, Jake had learned that Clare wooed was not necessarily Clare won and most certainly not Clare melting and compliant to his every whim. Even when lured into bed, Clare had the distressing habit of turning over at crucial moments with a "Don't be silly, Jake" and falling fast asleep, leaving Jake, rattled and wide awake, to wonder if the conveniences of a one-to-one relationship were really worth the drawbacks. At such times, he allowed himself to flirt with the possibility of returning to the singles bar circuit, but his rosy imaginings of possible conquests there always gave way to more realistic memories of crowded rooms, unwanted drinks, unsatisfactory shouted conversations and, in the end, a less than impressive scoring average.

Also, it suited him to preserve a relationship that both parties had agreed from the outset would remain forever open and uncommitted, or, as Jake liked to think of it, permanently temporary. Under its rules, he and Clare kept their original status as unfettered spirits, free at all times to follow their inner voices and soar away on their own individual winds of change whenever the mood struck. The fact that neither of them had so far shown the slightest tendency to become airborne in no way diminished the value of the arrangement. Free was free, and if it had to be paid for from time to time with frustration, or even boredom, then so be it. No relationship was perfect, and, in Jake's humble opinion, something was definitely better than nothing.

But it was not going to be nothing tonight, he resolved. Tonight he planned to pull out all the stops and emerge triumphant. To do so, however, a little preparation time would be needed before Clare arrived, which meant breaking the speed limit back to his apartment and leaving her to follow on by herself. This involved a risk that, left alone, Clare might change her mind and not show up, but the free spirit within him said take the chance. Nothing ventured, nothing gained. Smiling a devastating devil-may-care smile, the spider pressed down on the accelerator and sped off to ready his web.

Jake's web was number 25A in the Mandarin apartment complex, a sprawling two-story structure built around a large swimming pool on the side of a hill, just under the imposing cross that overlooks much of Hollywood's residential and entertainment districts. Both the pool and the cross lit up at night, and even though Jake used neither for its intended purpose, he enjoyed having them outside his window. In particular, he liked the way blue highlights from the pool passed through the translucent paper window blinds in his bedroom and cast rippling patterns over its ceiling and walls. The effect was almost as sexy as those colored lamps with the rising and falling blobs of goop that caught his eye in novelty stores. On several occasions he had nearly bought one, but he had always backed off with regret on the grounds that it could never be fitted into the carefully assembled decorative scheme of his apartment.

Jake took great pride in his apartment. Guided only by instinct and retrospective screenings of 1950s Hollywood sex comedies, he had transformed it into a swinging California bachelor's pad in much the same way as, on first arriving in Los Angeles from New York, he had cast aside his staid Ivy League wardrobe and plunged enthusiastically into open-neck shirts, double knits and costume jewelry. But whereas certain limitations of size, shape and facial structure had governed how far he could go in making himself over, the unfurnished apartment presented no such drawbacks. Its bare rooms and anonymous style provided him with a blank canvas on which he could create to his heart's content. Accordingly, he had covered the walls with rush matting, put down carpet in a matching basket-weave pattern and, with this basic groundwork in place, set about creating.

.He therefore had only himself to blame when, on bursting into the living room a bare five minutes ahead of Clare, he tripped over the zebra-skin rug that provided a central focus to his decorative scheme, sprawled across the oversize African drum he had installed in place of a coffee table, and narrowly avoided cracking his head on one of the bamboo stools ranged against his cane-fronted bar. Luckily, he was in too much of a hurry to worry about possible injury. Picking himself off the floor, he restored the drum to its original position, flattened out the zebra and, at the touch of a switch, activated a battery of ceiling-mounted spotlights. Out of the dark jumped hollow-eyed tribal masks, glowing on walls above crossed spears and blowguns; a softer glow illuminated the acrylic-fur-covered modular sofa units grouped along two adjacent walls, and narrower beams of light picked out carved antelopes and gazelles grazing peacefully on the shelves of a bamboo étagère. At the same time, a concealed stereo system began to throb out a jungle beat, mingled with the exotic sounds of a tropical forest.

Satisfied with the mood he had created, Jake dashed through his bedroom into the adjoining bathroom, where he brushed his teeth and gargled before returning to the bedroom to straighten the pillows and comforter on his king-size water bed, pull back the mosquito netting draperies that hung from a palm-thatched canopy over the bed, and turn on the small television set in the corner of the room. He then threw his jacket and shirt aside, donned a red velour pullover with a flatteringly open neck, and removed his watch and glasses. It only remained for him to lower the blinds in both rooms, knock back a quick brandy, help himself to a refill, and determine how best to be discovered when Clare arrived.

When Clare at last made her way from the distant parking spot she had chosen in order to deceive any passing acquaintance who might recognize her car, she found Jake's door ajar and Jake himself on the floor, arranged around a pair of tom-toms, which he was playing with rapt attention and closed eyes. Wincing once again at Jake's African trappings, she announced her presence by stretching out one arm and intoning, "Hail, Great White Chief!"

Jake managed an almost convincing start.

"Hi, babe," he said, keeping his eyes slightly hooded and grinning that nice lopsided grin he had. "Want a drink?"

"Thanks." Clare sat down on a modular unit. "After that first movie, I deserve one."

"How about a pousse-café?" Jake suggested in what he hoped was a casual tone. "Specialty of the *maison*."

"I don't know. What is it?"

"Colored layers. Very pretty. You'll love it."

A light dawned for Clare. "Is that the awful thing with eight different kinds of liqueur?"

"Four. Plus grenadine."

"Nice try, darling. I'll have a vodka and tonic."

Jake snapped his fingers in time to the stereo drums as he made his way to the bar. "Isn't that a bit dull?"

"It'll do just fine. And go heavy on the tonic, please. This place always makes me feel that I need the quinine. When are you going to let me rip everything out and bring you back to civilization?"

"I'm thinking about it."

This was true. Jake had decided that when Clare had slept with him seven times in a row without saying "Don't be silly" or going home in the middle of the night he might safely consider letting her do her thing with stainless steel and gray flannel. So far, his present surroundings seemed in no danger.

23

"There aren't any bubbles," Clare remarked when Jake presented her drink.

"Sorry, the tonic's a bit flat."

Clare took a sip and choked. "Flat!" she gasped. "It's still in the bottle. Stop playing games and give me something I can drink."

Resigning himself to spending longer on preliminaries than he had planned, Jake dumped a respectable amount of mixer into the glass and brought it back, together with another neat brandy for his own consumption. He then resettled himself with the tom-toms on the floor in front of Clare, who looked at him suspiciously.

"Why are you crouching down there?" she asked, drawing her feet back against the sofa unit.

"I'm going to serenade you while we talk." It struck Jake that it would do no harm to demonstrate a little restraint while weaving a spell of seductive enchantment with his drums. Also, he could enjoy a good close look at Clare's excellent legs and trim ankles. He took a long swallow of brandy.

"How did you like *Mrs. Miniver*?" he asked.

"Not bad." Clare sipped her vodka and tonic. "What were you doing in the men's room with that hoodlum?"

"Nothing. A little business. Which scene did you like best?"

"Your 'secretary' said something about a murder." Clare crossed her legs, and the resulting soft whisper went pleasantly to Jake's head. He found himself beating the tom-toms at a slightly more rapid rate.

"Just a long-lost client. I was thinking of asking a few questions about it." Jake let the last of his brandy trickle down his throat and savored the resulting explosion. "I think *Mrs. Miniver*'s a *great* movie," he added.

"I hope you're not going to do anything silly."

"I'm just sitting here, playing my drums."

"I mean about this murder thing. Nothing dangerous."

"Don't worry. You know the bit I like best in *Mrs. Miniver*? The bit where she faces up to that German parachutist. All by herself in the house."

"Because I thought I saw something sticking out of your pocket when you came out of the men's room, and if it's what I think it is, you could get yourself into a lot of trouble."

Jake had begun to wonder if Clare might not possibly require a more dramatic approach than anything he had so far employed. In the warm glow shed by three stiff brandies, it seemed worth a try.

"Are you listening to me, Jake?"

"Sure. A lot of trouble. Walter Pidgeon away saving England. No help for miles and her so brave—"

"You're not brave, Jake. Do stop with those drums. Of course, it's none of my business what you do, but you could make an awful fool of yourself."

"Blowing a lock of hair aside as she stands up to that ravening beast, wanting God knows what from her."

"A bottle of milk, if I remember correctly. And Jake, you have to think how *I'd* look—"

"Lovely, my dear, as always. Lovelier-er than the lovely Greer herself. *You* could be Mrs. Miniver—"

"Don't be silly, Jake."

"The magic words!"

"What are you talking about?"

"Nothing." Jake felt pleased that Clare had walked into his trap and put the question of redecorating his apartment back to square one. "What was I talking about? Oh, yes. Why don't *you* be Mrs. Miniver, and *I'll* be the beastly Hun?"

"You shouldn't have had that brandy. It always goes to your head."

"Like the bubbles in your tonic and vodka," sang Jake. "Come on, Clare. You're all alone in the house. Frightened but brave."

"Jake, I can't stay long. I wanted to speak to you about our arrangement."

"Later. And I'm the sex-mad soldier with only one thing on my mind and it isn't a bottle of milk."

"If you take one step toward me, I'm going home now," said Clare, feeling about on the sofa for her scarf and shoulder bag.

"Only one thing, Clare, and it's *you*. I've been in the army a long time. I may be a rotten Nazi, but I'm a man and I need a woman. So I fix you with my penetrating look—"

"Not one step, Jake."

"Slowly I stalk . . ."

"I'm warning you."

"Vee haff vays—"

"You asked for it!"

25

"OW!"

From his new position flat on the floor, Jake got one final glimpse of Clare's ankles as they marched to the door and then turned.

"Jake, I've been thinking for some time now that our arrangement isn't working out for either of us and that maybe we should call it off. Now I'm certain of it. Thanks for making up my mind." The door opened. "I'm sorry I hit you, but if it's any consolation, I think Mrs. Miniver would have done exactly the same thing under similar circumstances."

The door slammed and, much to the relief of Jake's neighbors, the sound of jungle drums was heard no more about the Mandarin apartments that night.

Six

Having spent a miserable wide-awake night, Jake ushered in the dawn, word perfect in a litany of self-hate. He had behaved like a fool and deserved everything that had happened to him; he was boring and inept as a lover and would never manage to hold or satisfy a woman; he was overweight and plain; he was a failure in both his professional and private lives; he was silly and stupid and vain and now he was paying for it. If he hadn't tried to dazzle Clare by taking off his glasses, maybe she wouldn't have hit him so hard, or even at all.

He was a coward, too. Clare had said as much last night. That's why he had changed his mind about helping Arnie: he was afraid. As he ran through these gloomy thoughts, one of the sun's first rays slipped under his window blind and raised a metallic glint among the folds of his discarded jacket. It was the handle of Baron's automatic. Jake shivered under the covers. He was afraid of that, too. Well, he told himself, here's one thing I can take care of right now. Hastily, to prevent second thoughts, he got up, seized the gun, and carried it back to bed.

He was amazed how comfortable it felt in his hand, solid and reassuring, with his forefinger falling naturally on the trigger. It had a pleasant weight, too, balanced so that he could hold it firm and steady when he faced his unknown opponent. Jake narrowed his eyes, held the gun in a two-handed grip as he had seen done in the movies, and took aim along the barrel at the dial on the television set. Quite suddenly, an overwhelming desire to pull the trigger came over him. He knew that if he did, the dial would magically acquire a neat round hole in its exact center. It was a matter of willing and sensing the path of the bullet. Either you had the knack or you didn't, and Jake knew he had it.

Maybe I could do it after all, he thought.

Maybe it wouldn't be so bad spending a few days out of the office, getting about, talking to people, using his brain, and all the time playing a secret part: the gimlet-eyed private detective with a fedora pulled down over one eye and a cigarette dangling from his lower lip. It might even be worthwhile buying a hat and taking up smoking.

Then they would all see. Clare would realize how she had misjudged him, Miss Murphy would regard him with awe, and even Baron would have to admit that he wasn't just any old sixty-forty jerk. If things went right, he might even see himself in the papers and on television. There might even be a reward bestowed on the brave citizen who, at great risk to life and limb, had rounded up the killer of his fellow man. Looked on in that light, it seemed the most natural thing in the world to do, almost an obligation.

By the time he reached his office, Jake had convinced himself that he was launched on a holy mission. He eased himself through the door with a movement almost feline in its supple grace and paused, conscious of exuding that special aura of casual assurance granted only to those hiding a secret purpose in their souls and a hot Walther PPK automatic in the glove compartments of their cars.

"Hi," said Miss Murphy, who was reading a current detective novel by way of doing research. "What happen to you eye?"

"Just a little accident."

"She slug you, huh? Man, that chick is bad news."

"You shouldn't be learning your English from Baron."

"He some teacher. You want to take over?"

"Forget I mentioned it. Get Arnie Siganski on the phone." Jake steeled himself to run his first risk. "And coffee," he ordered.

Miss Murphy took it like a lamb, and in short order Jake was sitting back in his chair, feet up on the desk, with a mug of coffee in his hand. Miss Murphy made good coffee. The telephone rang to announce Arnie on the line.

"Arnie? Jake Weissman."

"Oh, hi, Jake. You found out anythin'?"

This was not the rush of gratitude Jake had expected.

"I haven't started yet," he said rather irritably. "I want to come and see you, get some background details. In half an hour. All right?"

"Sure," said Arnie. "I ain't goin' nowheres."

Jake stopped on his way out of the office.

"Murphy," he announced, "I'll be gone for the rest of the day. Keep an eye on things. And if anyone calls, take a message and tell them . . ." As the idea dawned, Jake treated Miss Murphy to his slow, sexy smile.

"Tell them I'm out on a case."

Arnie lived in Santa Monica on the second floor of a duplex apartment building fronted by a mixture of lawn and garden and hemmed in on its left-hand side by a concrete driveway that provided access to garage space in the rear. A brick path laid between the driveway and the garden led past the front door of the ground-floor apartment and came to a halt at the bottom of a wooden staircase cantilevered out from the side of the building.

Acting on instructions, Jake followed the path and climbed the stair. Since the main door of Arnie's apartment stood open, he tried tapping on the edge of the outer screen door. This produced no result. After a second ineffectual attempt at attracting attention he opened the screen door and went inside.

The room in which he found himself was pleasantly furnished in a

28

neutral, unassuming style. On his first glance about, Jake took in the beige wall-to-wall carpeting, a sofa and two upholstered chairs covered in a textured brown fabric, a heavy glass-topped coffee table and some occasional tables to match. A stone fireplace faced him from across the room, a stained glass lantern hung from a looped chain over his head, and to his right the sliding doors of an enclosed balcony overlooking the front garden held back a thick jungle of greenery that allowed only a filtered subaqueous light to enter the room. A wooden hat rack on the wall beside the fireplace displayed a variety of quaint headgear— Jake made out an aluminum construction worker's helmet, a jaunty straw boater, a French sailor's cap, a bowler hat and an enormous sombrero—while a collection of tiny glass and pottery owls absorbed most of the space on the table next to the sofa.

After taking all this in, Jake noticed a button set into the face of the front door, which was hinged back against the inside wall. He was about to push it when a voice floated out from somewhere inside the balcony foliage.

"I wish you wouldn't go all floppy like that," it said.

Jake straightened his posture and was about to reply, but the voice continued.

"I know you guys miss him just like I do," it said in a plodding, patient tone, "but he's gone, and now you're just gonna have to get used to me. I promise I'll really try. I'll water you, and I got plant food here in case anybody feels hungry, and I know if you just give me a chance we'll all get along real well. So don't you go droppin' your leaves or turnin' yellow on me. Be brave, and try not to feel so sad, and—well, gimme a chance. Okay? And I'll talk to you, too, just like he did. A lot." A sigh and a sniff interrupted the monologue. "I sure as hell ain't got nobody else to talk to."

Jake jumped to push the door button, which produced two flat but penetrating musical notes.

"Anybody home?" he called.

The plants on the balcony began to thrash about until Arnie's round face appeared amidst a forest of bamboo.

"Hi," he said, carefully edging through the bamboo stalks. "I was just lookin' after Bobbie's plants. I don't think they like me."

"Plants are funny," replied Jake. "They go into shock whenever there's a change in routine, but they usually come around. Just give

29

them a little time and they'll start brightening up whenever they see you."

"Yeah?" Arnie had his doubts but was willing to put them aside for the moment. "It was real good of you to come all this way. Can I get you somethin'? Coffee, tea—beer?"

"I had coffee in the office, but I'd like another." Jake felt the need for something to relax the interview.

But instead of relaxing, Arnie turned bright red. "Gee, I just remembered. I was sayin' what Bobbie always said—but I don't know how to make coffee."

"Don't you drink it yourself?" asked Jake, to whom a morning without coffee was like an extended session of sleepwalking.

"Sure," said Arnie. "But I can't get the machine thing to work." He led the way into the kitchen and pointed at it. "I tried it once," he explained. "I put water into that glass pot and the coffee into the basket and plugged it in, but nothin' happened."

It was time to take command. "Where's the coffee?" asked Jake.

Arnie looked embarrassed again. "Well, it's kind of crazy, but Bobbie always kept it in the freezer."

"It stays fresher that way. Now look. You see these cup markings on the pot? Well, you fill it with as much water as you want, then you pour it into the top here . . ." Jake proceeded to give Arnie a lesson in the art of handling an automatic drip coffee maker and allowed himself a small moment of pride when it produced a successful brew.

Arnie was impressed. "Hey, that's not so hard. I bet I could do it too. Now if I could only learn how to cook . . ."

"Read one of those cookbooks." Jake had no more kitchen hints to offer. "It's all in there. Now, let's get down to business. Tell me something about Bobbie."

Arnie thought hard about this for a moment, then, "He was the most wonderful person in the whole world," he said. "That's his picture beside you."

On the small table next to the sofa, in the middle of the owl collection, a colored snapshot in a stand-up plastic frame laughed out at the world.

"Bobbie din't like pictures of hisself around the apartment," Arnie explained. "He thought it looked like, you know, blowin' your own horn. But since he—now that he ain't here, I put out a couple."

Jake studied the picture. It had been taken at the beach, and Bobbie was leaning against what looked like the metal frame of a set of swings, backed by an expanse of yellow sand and, beyond that, a high surf. He was wearing flip-flops, white pants, a pink polo shirt and a gold chain, and his sunglasses were pushed up onto a mop of—probably natural, thought Jake with a twinge of envy—yellow curls. He was certainly no he-man, but even from the confines of a slightly grainy photograph under a thick sheet of plastic, he projected a sparkle and relaxed confidence that made Jake feel he had been wrong to sign him up and then forget about him. Bobbie just might have had something.

"Did you ever see him act?" he asked.

Arnie cheered up. "Yeah, a couple of times at this place on Melrose where they do plays for kids on the weekends. Once he played a great big frog, hoppin' all over the stage, and the other time he was a funny doctor who kept losin' his glasses. He didn't get paid or nothin'; he just liked to get up there and make the kids laugh. And me, too, except when he was the frog and got lost in the city and couldn't find his way back to the pond. Then I cried. But some of the other kids did too, so it was okay."

"And friends?"

"Oh, everybody liked Bobbie. But, you know, we din't have no real friends. I'm on the road a lot and Bobbie don't—din't like goin' out by hisself. . . . And then when I got back we din't need nobody else but us." Arnie looked a little abashed. "I guess we was kinda selfish and we always thought that sometime, well, that we'd get sort of tired of bein' alone and then we'd start goin' out more. But we never did," he finished simply.

Jake sensed that his investigative technique could use some sharpening up. At this rate, he was never going to get a jump on the police.

"So Bobbie never went out by himself?" he tried.

"Not much," said Arnie. "Maybe to Safeway or the bank while I was away. But he always said he just stayed at home and I know he wouldn't lie to me. Not that he had to stay in," he went on hastily. "He had his own car. But mostly he liked me to drive, so we'd go and stock up at the market and Thrifty's and maybe a couple of times a month I'd drop him off at that theater place for a while."

"You mean the Quest?" Jake asked.

"Yeah, that's it. He liked to see what they was doin' and he knew a

31

few people there and he helped in the box office. So I'd drive him over and then go read some comics in the car and then come back."

"You never went in with him?"

"Nah. Those theater people, they kiss and yell and talk so fast I can't keep up. So I'd make like I had somethin' else to do and then when I come back he'd be waitin' for me on the sidewalk and then we'd go home."

Jake hesitated for a moment, knowing that the next part was going to be difficult. It would be more comfortable for both of them if he could get an answer to his next question without setting Arnie off on a crying jag, but with or without tears it had to be asked.

"Now Arnie," he said in what he hoped was a quiet, firm voice, "I want you to tell me exactly what happened to Bobbie, when it happened, and how you found out about it. Just take your time and tell me everything."

Arnie closed his eyes and took a deep breath; after a moment, he opened his eyes again, breathed out, gave Jake a reassuring smile and began.

"A week ago last Sunday," he said, speaking slowly and carefully, "I was drivin' back from Vancouver—that's in Canada," he put in politely, in case Jake's geography happened to be weak, "and I got to the depot in lots of time to get home for dinner, just the way Bobbie likes. Well, I drove home and I even stopped off for some flowers for kind of a surprise, like, but when I got here there wasn't nobody home, nothin' on in the kitchen, and the whole place seemed, well, kind of empty." He stopped for a second and passed a hand over his forehead. "Anyhow," he continued, "the first thing I thought was maybe I done somethin' wrong and made Bobbie mad at me, mad enough to go away somewheres, but then he never walked before, even when we'd had a kind of fight, so then I thought maybe he's left me. I thought maybe all those times I been away he's been makin' out with some other guy and now he's gone and moved in with him."

Arnie took another gulp of air and blinked again. "Jeez, I almost passed out right then and there, like sometimes at the gym when I push too hard, but then I thought he'd leave me a note—he'd always leave me a note—and I looked around and there wasn't no note. There was food in the fridge, though, chicken and stuff and a bottle of wine like he always had in when I got back, so I begun to feel better

32

and I went into the bedroom and there was all his clothes and his electric razor that he'd never leave behind and I knew then that he was gonna come back."

Arnie smiled in relief at the memory, but the smile faded. "He din't though," he said sadly. "I waited for him and din't eat nothin' so's we could have maybe a hamburger out when he come home, but he din't, and I finally went to bed but I couldn't sleep because I kept waitin' to hear his key in the lock. And all next day, all next day I just waited and thought maybe someone was sick and he was called away, but he din't have no family, or maybe he'd had a accident and was layin' there with nobody . . . oh shit." Arnie blew his nose and wiped his eyes. "Sorry," he mumbled. "Anyways, I started feelin' crazy and I din't know what to do, so I put on the TV and watched the soaps and the game shows until the news come on at six. I wasn't payin' a lot of attention because I was kind of lookin' without seein' nothin' while I thought of—you know, but all of a sudden they was showin' this picture, like somebody drew it, of this guy they'd found dead in the Hollywood Bowl parkin' lot. They din't know who he was, but I did. It was Bobbie, except they got his hair wrong, but I knew it was Bobbie, so I called this number they gave and a couple of police come and took me downtown and made me look."

Here Arnie raised a tear-stained face to Jake. "Well, it *was* Bobbie." He hiccupped, then carried on. "And this time I thought they was gonna have to hold me up for sure. Not because it was the first time I'd ever seen anybody dead, but because of the way he looked. He din't have a hair on his head, or no eyebrows or nothin'. And where his hair used to be there was all these little round burns where some- body'd . . . oh Jesus. . . . And they wouldn't show me, but they said he was like that all over. And I told them who he was and everythin' I could think of, and all over again the next day, and that was it. They sent me home and din't tell me nothin'. I called over and over, but still they din't tell me nothin' and they acted like it wasn't none of my business."

He was calmer now and breathed more easily. "None of my busi- ness, and me the only person he had in the world who loved him. But you know what I think? I think them sons of bitches ain't doin' one fuckin' thing to find out who killed my Bobbie, so that's why I come to you. I'll pay you a hunnerd bucks a day, two hunnerd, whatever you want, and two thousand more if you find the shit who killed my Bobbie and tell me his name and where to find him and you don't have to do nothin' else except be sure you're right. I'll take it from there."

There was a pause, then Arnie managed a weak smile. "I ain't never had so much to say in my whole life. That's all there is. Let's have a beer."

◆━━◆●◆━━◆

Seven

◆━◆▸◆

J ake was having a busy day. His session with Arnie had gone better than he had expected, and he was now headed downtown to interview the two police officers who had discovered Bobbie's body and the detective who was handling the case. When he had called the police department before leaving Arnie's, he received the strong impression that the department did not welcome inquiries by the public into their investigations. But Jake had put forth a convincing case for his interest as Bobbie's agent with legal responsibility for his affairs, and the appointment had been granted.

On nearing the central police station, which he had often passed on his way to the Music Center arts complex but never entered, Jake parked his car and followed directions to an enclosed courtyard in front of what looked like a raised loading dock with a series of glass-windowed doors opening onto it. The yard was occupied primarily by police cars in which a constant supply of identical-looking members of the Los Angeles Police Department arrived and departed, frequently with handcuffed members of the public in tow. Feeling rather like a brown-suited interloper at the entrance to a nest of blue-clad ants, Jake lingered for a moment, expecting to be challenged by a worker. When this failed to occur, he followed the flow of traffic up a set of stairs at one end of the platform and, by peering through the window of each door as he came to it, eventually found a central office where he asked for officers Harrison and Santana.

Officer Santana had been called out, but in a large room farther down the platform Jake found Officer Harrison standing beside a prosperous-looking gentleman, arms handcuffed behind his back, who faced a large black metal box fitted with a short length of plastic tubing, several buttons and a black readout screen where three red zeros glowed like a winning slot machine combination.

Officer Harrison had invested in a gleaming motorcycle jacket to set off his gleaming black boots and tight blue breeches, the latter made even snugger by a tendency on the part of Officer Harrison to spread a little around the hips. Although indoors, he had kept on his aviator-style sunglasses, through which he regarded the three zeros on the black screen with hostility.

"There's somethin' wrong with this machine," he announced, pounding on it with a clenched fist. "Try again."

Obediently, the handcuffed gentleman leaned forward, took the plastic tube between his lips and, after Officer Harrison had pushed a reset button to clear the screen, blew heartily into the tube. The screen responded instantly with another negative reading.

Officer Harrison produced a high whinny of frustration from somewhere in the back of his sinuses and pulled the offender, who was now beginning to wear an expression of smug relief, over to another metal box.

"Okay," he said, "blow into this, and this time gimme some air and hold it until I tell you to stop. Stop," he growled, when the three zeros reappeared. "Boy, you sure are lucky."

"I told you I wasn't drinking," said the vindicated civilian in an aggrieved tone. "I just swerved because I thought the car in the next lane was going to hit me. You should have pulled *him* in."

"Yeah, yeah," said Officer Harrison, tearing up the booking form he had been preparing and throwing it viciously into a nearby wastebasket. "Just go sit over there and somebody'll take you back to your car."

The harassed driver looked astonished. "But I'm late for a meeting. I want to get back to my car now!"

"Tough," said Officer Harrison, making a poor attempt at suppressing a smile. "My partner isn't here, and I gotta go talk to some jerk who thinks the police can't do their job right. I'll take you back when I'm through."

"Then at least take these handcuffs off."

Officer Harrison beamed at him. "Sorry. Not till we get back to your car. Regulations. Now just sit." Quite restored to humor, he began heading toward a side door, whereupon Jake spoke up.

"Officer Harrison?" he asked politely.

The police officer halted and looked back at Jake over his shoulder. "Yeah," he admitted.

"I'm the jerk you have to talk to."

Officer Harrison was unrepentant. "Oh yeah." Flexing his shoulders, he hitched up his belt and walked over to Jake with a stiff-legged swagger. "What can I do for you?"

Standing with his neck bent back to look up into Officer Harrison's dark sunglasses, Jake experienced a strong sensation of déjà vu, which he immediately associated with Baron in the men's room of the movie theater. Officer Harrison, however, had a mustache and longer sideburns.

"I think you were one of the officers who found the body of Robert Lang on the sixteenth of this month in the Hollywood Bowl parking lot," said Jake in as efficient a manner as he could muster.

Officer Harrison caught sight of himself reflected in a nearby window and altered his posture slightly to produce a more flattering line. "Yeah," he said. "Me and my partner."

"The parking lot isn't used much, now the concerts have stopped," Jake pointed out. "How did you find him? Was he just lying out on the blacktop?"

"Nah, he was pushed under some bushes goin' up the hill on the east side of Highland. A couple called in about it around nine at night, and we answered the call. I guess they'd pulled in to make out or smoke a joint, but what with all the fuss about the body I didn't get a chance to check on them."

36

"What was the condition of the body when you found it?"

Officer Harrison tore his attention away from the window. "Look, buddy, this is police business, and I got work to do. If you get a kick outta gory details, why don't you go buy a dirty book? They even got 'em with pictures."

Jake's temper began to slip. "Officer Harrison," he began, "I am Mr. Lang's agent and, in view of the fact that he has no family, his sole legal representative. I am also a taxpayer of this city, to whom you as a public servant are responsible. I have a right to know the details of my client's death, and I have a right to get them without any snide insinuations from you."

"Okay, okay. Keep your shirt on." Officer Harrison took off his sunglasses by way of a goodwill gesture, put one foot up on a nearby chair, and leaned forward on his knee. "You don't know the kind of nuts we have to deal with here. If you want the details, sure, you can have 'em. We found the guy under the bushes, like I said. He didn't have any clothes on and he didn't have a hair on his body either. He was covered with little round burns. Somebody had a real good time with him."

"Was anything found with him?"

"Not that we could see, but we left the real search for the experts. You'll have to ask them."

"And his car?"

"Nothin'. We didn't know who he was until we got a call from his friend."

"Mr. Siganski."

"Yeah. The Incredible Fruit. Boy, what a waste! When I think about a big guy with a great build on him like that bein' a faggot, I could just puke." Officer Harrison shook his head at the injustice of nature.

"About Mr. Lang . . ." Jake reminded him.

"Oh, yeah. Well, that's about it. They came and took him away, interviewed the people who found him, let them go, and then me and Santana got back on patrol. Pretty dull stuff."

"Not to Mr. Lang," said Jake. "Now I have to see a Detective Rosa."

"Sure, this way," volunteered Officer Harrison, apparently suffering some pricks of conscience about his earlier rudeness. "Hey, you!" he called over to the handcuffed driver, who was twisting himself into contortions in an attempt to get a look at his watch. "Just hold on a minute. I'll be right back."

"Sorry to take up your time," said Jake, as they walked back to the main building.

"That's okay," replied Officer Harrison. "I was goin' to lunch anyway. A man's gotta eat."

Casting a backward thought to the unhappy driver and his missed meeting, Jake allowed himself to be led through a maze of corridors, presented to a preoccupied receptionist behind a narrow counter, and left in a vacant interrogation room to await Detective Rosa. His image of what type of person to expect ranged through the familiar faces from film and television; however, as the minutes passed and his clear conscience gradually took on the weight of the oppressive room and the many guilty persons who had passed through it, he began to visualize a sadistic ogre who would throw him into a hard wooden chair, train a glaring white light on his eyes, and ask him to describe his movements on the night of the fifteenth. It came as a great relief, therefore, when the door opened and in walked a short, trim man with crisp black hair, a full mustache and sympathetic brown eyes.

Impeccably turned out in a tan lightweight suit, an off-white shirt with a dark striped tie, and smooth brown oxfords, Detective Rosa gave Jake a friendly nod and sat down, ready to answer questions. Jake explained his reasons for being there in terms milder than he had used with Officer Harrison, and asked for a progress report. Having taken an immediate liking to Rosa as the first man he had met in several days who did not make him feel like a pygmy, he was disappointed when Rosa shifted uneasily in his chair and confessed that they had made no progress at all.

"I know that big guy he lived with thinks we aren't doing anything because of some sort of moral disapproval," he said, "but there aren't any leads, and quite frankly I don't believe we'd be justified in spending much more time on the case than we have. It's a sad thing to have to say, but what we have here is probably one of those situations where we're never going to find out who did it. Some guy gets bored with his sex life at home and starts looking around for a good time, a bit of excitement on the side. And he finds it."

"What happened to Mr. Lang doesn't sound like anybody's idea of a good time," remarked Jake.

"No accounting for tastes," said Detective Rosa tolerantly. "Whatever turns you on."

"Being tortured to death?"

"Oh, that wasn't what killed him. He was playing games. Somewhere along the way he let somebody cover him all over with that stuff they sell in drugstores to dissolve hair. Or maybe he did it himself. And he died of an overdose of heroin and cocaine. What we don't know is whether he got it in several injections or all at once. If he was lucky, he was high as a kite through the whole thing; if not . . ." Detective Rosa shrugged. "Well, he had a great few seconds at the end."

"And that's it?" Jake was appalled. "Whoever did that to him just dumps him out on the street like garbage and gets away with it?"

Rosa gave Jake a patient smile. "Look," he said. "What can we do? This is a one-off job: things go too far, a guy dies, the other guy panics, and we get to clean up the mess. Now, if we had a mad killer here and started finding bald bodies all over the city, then sooner or later the guy would make a mistake and we'd get him. But just once, an accident—well, Mr. Weissman, if you feel like killing someone, that's the way to get away with it."

"Have you talked with anyone at all?" asked Jake.

Another shrug from Rosa. "Nobody much to question. Lang kept pretty much to himself, except for that Mr. America he lived with, who was fifteen hundred miles away when it happened. Not that something like this would be his style at all. More the bare hands type, or not knowing his own strength. I sure wouldn't like to find myself up against him."

"But you are," said Jake, "in a way. He says that Mr. Lang wasn't the promiscuous type and he thinks that you're putting an obvious construction on the circumstances of the case so you can take the easy way out and drop it."

Rosa grinned. "He said all that?"

Jake was not in a mood to be laughed at.

"Not in so many words," he said, and immediately regretted sounding pompous. "But that's the way he feels, and I can see his point. After all, he knew Mr. Lang better than anyone else."

"Nobody knows anyone as well as he thinks." This time Rosa wasn't laughing at him. "That's why husbands are surprised when their nice

little wives suddenly run off with other men, and why wives are surprised when their nice little husbands come after them with guns.
Everybody sends out signals, but it's amazing how often they're ignored, even by people a lot smarter then Mr. Lang's boyfriend. No
offense."

Jake began to feel depressed. "One thing I forgot to ask Mr.
Siganski," he said. "Mr. Lang owned a car. Was it missing?"

"Nope. Safely tucked away in his garage at home. No prints. Looks
like he was picked up by whoever did him in." Rosa's watch sounded
a triple-beep alarm.

"Or whoever it was put the car back." Jake got up. "Did you interview anyone at the Quest Theatre?"

Detective Rosa got up too. "Yes, Mr. Weissman, we did. But there's a
limit to how much we can do. Just while we've been talking there could
be a dozen major crimes taking place somewhere in greater L.A., maybe
even a murder or two. We're short on manpower and we can't always
spend as much time on things as we'd like, particularly when we can't see
much chance of coming up with any useful information. But the case isn't
closed. We're keeping our eyes open. Just leave it to us."

They were now standing in the corridor outside the interrogation
room.

"Any objections if I do some looking around myself?" asked Jake.

Rosa had obviously shifted his mind ahead to more pressing matters. "Be my guest," he replied. "Just don't get into any trouble. We've
got enough on our hands already. Can you find your way out? Good.
See you around."

He disappeared, and Jake, after several wrong turns and backtrack-
ings, finally got himself headed back toward his parked car. He still
had three blocks to go when a familiar sound of heavy footsteps with
metal taps caused him to look back. It was Officer Harrison, carrying a
bag of sandwiches from a take-out restaurant. He nodded amiably at
Jake.

"How'd you get on with Rosa?"

"Not bad. He couldn't tell me much."

"Nothin' much to tell. Why are you so interested in that dead guy
anyhow? What'd he do?"

Jake wondered if passersby might think he was being arrested. He
waved a hand in the air to demonstrate otherwise.

40

"He was an actor. I was his agent, like I said."

"You mean like for the movies?"

"Well, television mostly."

"Oh yeah? You handle anybody I'd know?"

Jake began to feel embarrassed. "I don't think so—unless you're a fan of the Kwik-Sudz dancing detergent box."

Officer Harrison's face took on an expression that, had he chosen to remove his sunglasses, might have passed for respect.

"No kiddin'—you mean there's a guy in there?"

"A girl, actually."

"How much would someone like that clean up for jumpin' around in soap suds?" He whistled when Jake told him. "Boy, that must be one happy detergent box," he said enviously.

"As a matter of fact, she's miserable," Jake informed him. "She wants to play Shakespeare. For free," he added bitterly as he stopped beside his car.

Officer Harrison spat into a nearby patch of grass. "I saw Shakespeare once," he remarked. "Personally, I'd rather watch the Kwik-Sudz commercial."

Having at last reached an area of mutual agreement, they parted, with friendly feelings on both sides.

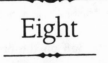

Eight

When he got home late in the afternoon, Jake made up his mind to telephone Clare and grovel. Much to his surprise, she was graciousness itself.

"Don't apologize, Jake dear," her voice came warmly over the receiver. "It wasn't your fault. If anyone's—mine."

Jake hastened to contradict.

Clare refused to listen. "No, no. I've failed you, and I blame myself entirely."

"You haven't failed me, Clare."

"Yes, I have. Don't try to be kind. What you need is someone who can give you a direct animal response. Someone who can meet you at your own depraved level and submit to, how shall I say, semi-rape."

"Oh, come on, Clare."

"Or possibly worse, if given your head. One never knows in these matters. So what I think you really need, Jake, is a person more experienced than I, and possibly more accommodating. You might have to pay."

"Clare!"

"And if you find yourself short of cash, you can always come to me for a loan. Otherwise, you won't call me again, will you?"

The line went dead. Jake stared at it, stunned, for several seconds and then hung up. He had mismanaged things badly. At the very least, he should have sent flowers first, then a letter, and then, perhaps, have called. On the other hand, she would probably have thrown out the flowers, torn up the letter, and given him the same telephone response. At least he knew the worst, all at once. There was also the possibility that she might regret her harsh, and, Jake felt, unreasonable, treatment of him and call back.

The telephone rang. It was a sweet moment that Jake prolonged for as long as he dared. Finally, he picked up the receiver and said hello in what he hoped was a crushed and wounded voice.

"Jake?"

It was Bill Walters from 36B on the other side of the swimming pool.

"Hi, Bill."

"You got a cold?"

"No, I was just thinking of something else. What's up?"

"Have you anything planned for the next few days?"

"Not yet," said Jake, hopefully.

"Well, Betty and I have to go east for six or seven days and we wondered if you could feed Hector while we're gone."

Jake's vision of a social weekend collapsed into rubble. "Sure. No problem. I've got some cat food from last time."

"That's great. Maybe when we get back you, Clare, Betty and I can have an evening together."

"Sounds good, but there may be a problem."

"Little spat?"

"Well . . ."

"Worse?"

"Maybe."

"Well, look, old buddy, don't worry about it. These things work themselves out. Come see us when we get back, and we'll talk."

"Okay. Have a good trip."

"Thanks. And thanks about Hector. Just leave your screen open and we'll push him through the window when we go. See you next week."

Jake hung up. It looked like a lonely weekend ahead. The telephone rang again. Jake's heart leapt. This time for sure, it told him. He waited out one ring, two, three—

"Hello?"

"Jake?"

"Arnie."

"It din't sound like you. How ya doin'?"

"Fine. Just fine. What's up?"

"I just kinda wanted to know how you got on with the police."

Jake began to feel weary. "Nothing much. They were quite pleasant, and I made contact, but that's about all."

"Oh." Arnie sounded very low. "Well, that was it, I guess. Sorry I bothered you."

"That's okay."

There was a moment of indecision, then Arnie got out rather hesitantly, "You doin' anythin' tonight?"

Jake wondered if Arnie, too, had a cat. "PBS is showing *Meet Me in St. Louis* at nine," he said cautiously. "I think I'll watch that."

"One of them serials made in England?" asked Arnie.

"No, it's a great old Hollywood musical. If you haven't seen it, you should watch."

"I seen some of those with Bobbie. I liked them. The thing is, I gotta get out of this apartment for a while. I was thinkin' of goin' to the bars, but it's been a long time, and I never liked them in the first place. All that smoke and noise."

This struck a responsive chord in Jake. He wondered if an invitation

43

to Arnie might get in the way of their detective-client relationship but decided that it would be better than spending the evening alone. It would also be nice to watch the movie with someone who hadn't seen it six times already. God knows there weren't many of them around.

"Why don't you come and watch the movie over here," he suggested. "Then you can go on wherever you like after."

"Gee, thanks. I'd like that."

Warmed by Arnie's obvious pleasure, Jake threw caution out the window. "If you want to come over around half past seven, I'll make dinner," he offered.

"Hey, sure!"

"You're not a vegetarian, are you?" Jake began to wish he had left matters as they were.

"Don't worry. I can eat anythin'. Even what I make myself."

"Okay. See you about seven thirty." Jake gave Arnie his address and hung up. Fortunately, he had a casserole of some sort left in the freezer by Clare at a happier stage in their relationship. Rice would be healthful, if Arnie was into health foods, as he probably was; then a large or even an extra-large salad, just to be on the safe side, plus beer, and he would be home free. It would mean, the thought suddenly occurred to Jake, he would have to start cooking for himself tomorrow, or eating out, but that was a problem for later. He could always join Hector in a can of cat food.

Promptly at seven thirty the door bell chimed the opening notes of "The Indian Love Call." On the other side of the door was Arnie, wearing his usual jeans and keys, a white sweatshirt and a red face. He was clutching a bouquet of multicolored flowers, which he thrust at Jake.

"I know you don't give guys flowers," he said, growing even redder. "But Bobbie said always take somethin' when you go out to dinner, and I couldn't think of nothin' else. What's so wrong with flowers anyway? Everybody likes flowers."

"Well, I certainly do," said Jake, conscious nevertheless of looking faintly ridiculous. "Thanks very much. Come on in."

Arnie jangled in, taller than ever in high-heeled boots, and stood transfixed by Jake's African fantasy.

"Sit down," said Jake. "I'll just put these in some water."

He had a disturbing image of himself in a picture hat, being gracious with a flower basket, but was saved from an excess of gentility by the fact that his meager supply of containers and kitchen equipment included nothing that might serve as a vase. Finally, he poured the last of his morning grapefruit juice into a glass, rinsed out the empty bottle, refilled it, and stuck the flowers in. The narrow neck of the bottle made them stand rigidly upright in a tight cluster, but otherwise the effect was not unpleasing. Jake carried his arrangement ceremoniously into the living room and placed it on the bar.

"I never seen nothin' like this before," said Arnie, still entranced by the room. "You do it all yourself?"

"More or less," answered Jake. "It was the first time I ever had an unfurnished place of my own and I sort of got carried away."

Arnie looked wistfully about. "I wish Bobbie coulda seen it. He was always readin' magazines about how to do up rooms, but he never really got a chance to let go like you done here. You gotta be straight to get away with a place like this."

Having poured a couple of beers, Jake handed one to Arnie. "I never thought of it like that," he said, hoping to see the end of the subject.

But Arnie was not one to let go of a good topic. "What about your mom and dad? What do they say about it?"

Jake smiled at the thought. "No problem. My father doesn't like to travel and my mother thinks everything west of the Hudson is Indian territory. So they stay in Manhattan, and I visit them."

Arnie nodded to acknowledge the satisfactory nature of this arrangement. "Well, Bobbie din't have to worry because he din't have no family, but he knew I did, so he played it safe. Frat House Modern, he called it. I like this better."

There was now a chance for a conversational detour. Jake jumped at it.

"Do you get to see your family often?"

"Oh, sure," answered Arnie. "They live just outside of Bakersfield and I get to call in sometimes on my way back from a job. They only been to see us twice, though. I guess they din't take to Bobbie much."

"Have you told them what happened to him?"

"Yeah. I had to talk about it with somebody. But in the end I chickened out and said he'd had a accident. They said they were sorry and Mom wanted to know if I'd met any nice girls lately. It din't make me feel a hell of a lot better."

45

"My mother always asks that too," Jake confessed. "I think it's just something that comes out automatically when ladies have sons over twenty-one."

Arnie took a drink of beer. "The police or somebody called today. They're lettin' me have him tomorrow."

"You mean—?"

"Bobbie. I guess they done everythin' they want and checked that he din't have no other family but me."

"So what arrangements have you made?"

"Oh, Bobbie done all that already. He said he wanted to be cremated, and last year he picked out the place and planned the service and everythin'. Parkhill Memorial Chapel. So it's all set up for eleven, day after tomorrow."

"Are you asking anybody?"

"No. There ain't nobody to ask, except maybe you, so I thought I'd rather just be there by myself and get it over with fast. You don't think that's bein' a coward?"

"No," said Jake, much relieved. "It's whatever suits you." His conscience gave him a nudge. "But if you change your mind and want some company, give me a call."

"Thanks." There was a short pause while Arnie inspected a nearby tribal mask. At last he said, "It's nice of you to have me over like this. I guess you got a girlfriend you could be with."

"I did have," said Jake. Honesty seemed the best policy under the circumstances. "But I kind of blew things last night. So I'm on my own too." He raised his beer to Arnie. "Thanks for the company."

Arnie's answering smile sagged into one of his worried looks. "When does it stop hurtin'?" he asked.

Jake hesitated for a second, wondering if honesty required him to confess that none of his romantic involvements had lasted long enough or achieved a sufficient depth of feeling for him to answer such a question. "Well," he said, "it depends."

Arnie considered this, nodded, and waited for more specific words of wisdom. Just as Jake had despaired of delivering any, the kitchen buzzer came to his rescue. "Food!" he cried, leaping to his feet. "Let's eat."

After dinner, they watched the movie, billowing softly up and down on opposite sides of Jake's water bed. Before climbing aboard and

46

almost catapulting Jake onto the carpet, Arnie had thoughtfully removed his boots, so that whenever his mind wandered during the more familiar parts of the film Jake found himself admiring the luminous whiteness of his guest's sweat socks. Were they new? he asked himself, and, if so, could Arnie be getting around the problem of clean clothes simply by throwing the dirty ones away? Or, he wondered, did Bobbie and Arnie know something about soaps and detergents not revealed to his, Jake's, laundry service. He decided to delay asking until the unthinkable time when he started washing his own clothes.

The film over, Arnie pulled on his boots and began his departure. "It's been real nice," he said, "I thought I was gonna have to go on to a bar, but now I don't feel like it. I guess I just needed to get out."

Here they were on common ground again. "I know what you mean," Jake told him. "I've got to get back into circulation myself, but I can't face it. All those hours hanging around, waiting to score."

"Oh, that ain't what bothers me. I can usually get in and out with someone in five, six minutes." Arnie brought this out in all innocence as a simple fact of life, never imagining the sharp attack of envy it aroused in Jake. "It's just that I don't want nobody but Bobbie."

"That'll pass too." Jake spoke absently, still dealing with the thought that he would willingly part with his soul for the ability to go into a bar and emerge five minutes later with the lady of his choice, starting tonight. "Have a safe trip home."

"That's the worst part." Arnie stopped in the doorway and scratched his head. "Sometimes I think I'm goin' nuts."

"You mean lonely?"

"Well, that too. But I meant like havin' a screw loose. Sometimes when I get home there's somethin' funny about the place." Arnie looked abashed. "Do you believe in ghosts?"

"No. Have you seen one?"

"Nah. It's just that sometimes when I get in everythin' seems the same but different. You know—like I think maybe I left a drawer open and it's closed, or I din't stack my T-shirts too neat and they're all piled up straight the way Bobbie used to. Or I din't close the bathroom door, or maybe I did—I just ain't sure anymore, so I wonder if there's somethin' wrong up here." Arnie did a double knock on his skull.

47

Jake had a thought. "When they found Bobbie, was there anything lying around that belonged to him?"

"They din't say there was."

"His keys?"

"Uh-uh."

"Then he left them at home?"

"No. He always put them and his change in a bowl by the door. But there ain't nothin' there now." The light dawned. "You think maybe whoever killed him kept his keys and is comin' back to the apartment?"

"I think you'd better consider the possibility. And get your locks changed tomorrow—on Bobbie's car, too, if you can."

Arnie shook his head. "Gee, that's sick. Why would anybody want to go prowlin' through my place? I ain't got nothin' that nobody'd want."

"Maybe Bobbie had."

"Like what?"

It was Jake's turn to shake his head. "That's what we'll have to find out. If you really think someone is searching your apartment, you'd better tell the police about it. And use the chains on your door at night."

"Yeah, I will." Arnie regarded Jake solemnly. "You know, things look a bit different now than they did when I come to see you yesterday. Maybe I better just pay you for your time so far and call off the deal."

Jake surprised himself. "Don't worry," he said. "I'm not taking any chances. And I'm not taking your money either, unless by some weird accident I really get on to something and find out what happened." He smiled. "At the moment, I'm doing this more for me than for you, so you don't owe me a penny yet. Just take care of yourself."

"You too." Arnie hesitated for a second to consider the propriety of his next move, then forgot about caution and crushed Jake's face to his chest in a warm bear hug.

Before Jake had recovered from the surprise of this, Arnie had lumbered off. A tinkle of keys and a "See ya" floated back from across the courtyard as Jake gingerly felt his nose for possible damage and, for the first time in years, engaged the safety chain on his door.

He then opened the window screen for Bill and Betty's cat and, fully aware of the inconsistency of his security arrangements, went to bed.

Nine

J ake awoke without opening his eyes, aware that he was not alone
in his bedroom. The daylight that passed through his paper blinds
and closed eyelids told him that it was morning, and the echo in
his mind of some foreign sound told him that it would be wise to
feign sleep and lie very, very still. Jake feigned sleep and lay very, very
still.

Suddenly the noise that had awakened him repeated itself, an un-
earthly sound, as of an infant under torture. Jake opened his eyes and
brought them to focus on a point beyond the end of the bed, where
the curved top of a brown tail appeared like a furry periscope.

"Hello, Hector," said Jake.

The tail retracted.

Jake wiggled his feet under the sheet. "Puss, puss, puss," he called
in his most ingratiating manner.

There came a brief trill from somewhere out of sight, then a young
Siamese cat made a four-point landing on Jake's feet, which it attacked
with gusto, rolling over on one side and kicking heartily with its rear
legs. This game went on for some time until Hector became bored and
decided to bring it to an end with a carefully calculated nip through
the sheet.

"Ouch!" said Jake.

Hector gazed at him with round blue eyes.

"That hurt."

Hector waited patiently for fresh developments.

Since the next move was being left to him, Jake attempted to suggest a more subdued entertainment. He patted his chest enticingly.

"Puss, puss, puss."

Hector immediately pretended to lose interest and turned his attention to a small spot on the ceiling. Jake, who knew how to play this game as well as Hector, gave his chest another pat and pretended to go to sleep. Having established his position as a free and independent individual, Hector now condescended to reestablish contact. He climbed onto Jake's stomach, marched upward on hard pile-driver feet, and settled comfortably on Jake's chest. He then placed a cold nose on the underside of Jake's chin and breathed.

Jake reached up and rubbed Hector behind the ears before running his hand down the soft arched back and twitching tail. He was rewarded with a deep contented purr.

"I suppose you want your breakfast."

"Yah!"

Having brought up the subject, Jake became aware of a need for some breakfast himself. This was unusual, since he normally required only several cups of coffee to get himself away in the morning, saving the indulgence of a Danish pastry or a doughnut for later on in the office. All became clear when he glanced over at his clock and was astonished to discover that he had seriously overslept. It was quarter past ten. Which, thought Jake, might be all very well for a hard-living, hard-drinking private eye but was no good at all for an agent who ought to be in his office. Withdrawing a cordless telephone from its own special compartment in the padded headboard behind him, Jake pushed buttons and waited.

"Hello, Jake Weissman office."

"Murphy, it's Jake. I'm going to be in late this morning. Or maybe not at all."

"What happen, Teddy Bears? You have big night?"

"I was working," lied Jake. "Ouch!"

Hector, feeling neglected, had begun to knead the sheet over Jake's chest in a subtle ploy that combined affection with apparently accidental retribution as the occasional claw made its way through the sheet into Jake.

"What was that?" asked Miss Murphy.

"Nothing. Anything happen in the office yesterday? Ow!"

"Hey—you still fooling around in bed?"

"Certainly not. Quit that!" Hector had switched tactics and was now idly making pinpricks in Jake's chin with one lazy paw.

50

"It sure sound like it."

"I don't care what it sounds like. It's just Hector. All right, that's enough—get off!"

"So I right all along. You like the boys."

"Hector's a cat."

"Mm-hm."

Jake held the telephone out to Hector, who was giving himself a bath on the corner of the bed, where Jake had toppled him. "Say something, Hector." Hector stopped for a moment, regarded Jake with glazed eyes, then went back to his washing. "Come on, Hector. How about breakfast? Don't you want your breakfast?"

Hector tucked his nose under his tail and pretended to fall asleep.

"Rotten cat," said Jake, and then into the telephone. "He isn't talking right now. He's having a nap."

"He have big night too. Naughty Teddy Bears."

"Not funny, Murphy. I'm babysitting a Siamese cat. Now what about the office?"

"Nobody come in, but we get a casting breakdown from the Born Again Musical Company for *Greenwillow*."

"They're a good bunch. I'll go through the files this afternoon and send them some names."

"I do that already. And I send Vicky March up for TV commercial."

"Hey! I'm supposed to be the one who makes those decisions."

"They want somebody right away. And who else you got who can play young, pretty, blond, blue-eyed mother, age twenty-nine to thirty-two? Anyhow, they hire her and she think you one red-hot agent."

"Murphy, I apologize. In you I have a true treasure."

"You bet. Also we get form letter from Quest Theatre. They want to cast for children's Western musical. No money."

"No money, no helpee. Scrap it."

"Uh-uh."

"Uh-uh what?"

"You not thinking. I call them up and say maybe we help, but first you got to check them out. Look around. Ask questions. See who knew Bobbie Lang. Yes?"

"Yes. I apologize again. I'll get right on that. So I probably won't be in at all today."

"That's okay. You want anything done?"

"No. Yes." If only he had had even one cup of coffee, his brain would be working better. "Send some flowers from the office to Parkhill Memorial Chapel in Santa Monica. To get there before eleven tomorrow morning. Arnie's having Bobbie cremated there."

"And you go?"

"He said he didn't want anybody."

"Maybe he say now. But that one, he got a soft heart. He need somebody tomorrow."

"Murphy, did you ever see *Pinocchio* when you were a little girl?"

"Sure."

"Well, stop playing Jiminy Cricket. I can operate my conscience by myself."

"Fine. So I see you tomorrow in Santa Monica."

"Who gave you the time off?"

"It better be you. You think I work Saturday for what you pay me?"

"My God, is today Friday?"

"Too long in bed make you soft in the head."

"Okay, okay. Have a nice weekend. And don't forget about the flowers. Not too expensive."

"I pick them myself. Have fun with Hector."

The line went dead and Hector, sensing that the time had now passed when his vocal talents were required, set up a loud imperious wail.

Jake got out of bed. "Rotten cat."

By way of revenge, he put his coffee on first, with Hector howling and arching around his ankles, before making a move to open the tempting tin of chicken liver cat food he had set out on the counter in full view of Hector's anxious blue eyes. In return, Hector sat on the back of Jake's chair while he was trying to enjoy his first cup of coffee of the day and, under the sly cover of grateful adoration, puffed heavily chicken-liver-flavored breath into his left ear. Jake decided to skip his second cup and get to work.

The Quest Theatre was located on the stretch of Melrose Avenue known as Theater Row, where it shared one of the district's smaller blocks with a neon-lit glass and chrome ice-cream parlor. Unlike its glamorous neighbor, with which it had nothing in common but a party wall, the Quest looked anything but theatrical. It was a two-story building of no particular distinction, whatever character it may once have possessed in a previous existence as a store or warehouse now obliterated by a layer of gray stone-speckled stucco that covered all three of its external walls.

Of these walls, only the one facing Melrose made any attempt at achieving anything approaching an architectural style. Here, a row of peeling wooden greenhouse windows let light into the ground-floor lobby, while outside the building they scattered flakes of dried-out white paint over two scrubby night-blooming jasmine hedges that flanked a red-painted door set into the exact center of the wall. A wooden sign above the door announced the name of the theater in irregular painted letters, and above and to the right of this two sashed windows provided the only break in an otherwise solid expanse of stucco on the second story. Around the corner, four similar second-story windows overlooked more hedge and, beyond that, the narrow side street where Jake parked his car.

As he walked back toward Melrose, Jake noticed that the back of the theater facing onto the rear lane had no windows at all, only a high, wide service entrance fitted with twin sliding doors to permit the carrying in and removal of scenery and large properties. Over the years, however, this utilitarian wall had managed to achieve an exuberant character all its own as the outdoor painting of many different sets in as many different color schemes had covered it with a random mural of multihued splashes. Even as Jake paused to appreciate this pleasant effect, the mural was being added to by a pair of teenagers, one small and thin, the other taller and somewhat stout, dressed in identical plaid shirts and denim overalls. Both were applying buttercup yellow paint with overloaded rollers to a number of tall panels propped up against the side of the building. Becoming aware of their audience, they cheerfully waved at Jake with their dripping rollers, spattering more paint about, and then went back to work with renewed vigor.

The first object to catch Jake's eye when he reached the front of the theater was a large poster board propped up near the curb, just opposite the red door. It was made of white-painted plywood and it incorporated a series of metal hooks so that thin wooden panels, each announcing a current attraction, could be hung up, withdrawn, or rearranged according to the whims of the public and the producer. Jake walked over to it and read:

HANK & HAZEL HARVEY PRESENT

The Quest Theatre Repertory Company
in
A Season of New and Classic Entertainments

This was permanently lettered on the plywood board itself and much faded by sun and age. Below it hung the more freshly painted horizontal panels, with titles large in red and comments smaller in black:

WOMAN ALONE
by
Yolanda Meltzer
"A . . . psychological drama." (*L.A. Times*)   Tues.–Thurs. at 8:00

THE IMPORTANCE OF BEING ERNEST

A Wilde and crazy classic.   Fri.–Sun. at 7:30

BEL AIRS

A late-nite musical revue.   Fri.–Sun. at 10:45

THE MAGIC POND

Our popular children's musical.   Sat. & Sun. at 2:00

Coming Soon: SHOOTOUT AT SHILOH

An inspirational musical for children of all ages
by
Yolanda Meltzer

54

When he had digested this information, Jake passed through the red door into the lobby, a wide, shallow room with a flagstone floor and an overhead jungle of yellowing plants suspended in macramé nets. A variety of ancient seating units, ranged about the walls, spoke of visits to secondhand shops and nocturnal collecting tours around the city's more affluent back lanes. There were wooden kitchen chairs, plastic stacking chairs, a revolving office chair and even, at the far end of the room, an impressive but sprung leather-covered sofa, given pride of place between two cascading spider plants, each on a metal stand. An overall dusting of dead leaves from the hanging plants gave the room an air of eastern autumn, very much at odds with the brilliant California sunshine that streamed in through the unwashed windows.

Across the room from Jake, a flight of three stairs led to a wide passageway with, on the left, a pair of doors marked CLOAKROOM and KEEP OUT respectively and, on the right, a box office window. Jake climbed the stairs and presented himself at the window, which at first glance appeared to be unattended. He was just about to move on into the house when a mechanical sound from deeper within the room prompted him to lean forward and investigate further.

The sound that had caught Jake's attention came from an old electric adding machine on an improvised desk made of a plywood panel set across two filing cabinets located in the near-right-hand corner of the room. Seated at the desk on a rickety swivel chair, the operator of the machine faced a jumble of paperwork that included a heavy accounting ledger, two spiral-bound notebooks, a stack of bills, several multicolored bundles of ticket stubs held together with rubber bands, and a three-ring binder filled with pages of tear-off checks. Her back was to Jake, but from time to time, as he suppressed an initial impulse to speak and instead remained quietly watching, she turned slightly, entered some figures on the calculator, checked the answer on its printout tape, and returned to her paperwork.

Once again, Jake began to enjoy his role as private investigator. His motives to investigate had never been so strong, his powers of observation had never seemed so acute. And what he observed, he liked: a mass of light brown hair loosely pinned up and glinting red and gold in the light of the overhead lamp; a graceful neck arched over the ledger; long, narrow fingers tapping the keys of the calculator; a side-glimpse of high cheekbones and long eyelashes; and the line of a strong, slim back visible through the folds of a loose cream-colored blouse with wide sleeves, which the wearer had rolled up above her elbows. Brown slacks and straw espadrilles hooked behind the crossbar of the chair completed a picture that, in the otherwise dimly lit room, seemed to shine with its own golden light.

Having waited so long to speak, Jake was in no hurry to break the silence. It occurred to him, however, that to be caught eavesdropping would probably produce a bad initial impression and that what he needed now was a sophisticated, amusing introductory remark to simultaneously announce his presence, break the ice, and capture the lady's heart. When his search for this magic phrase produced only a sense of frustration and a light sweat, he had no choice but to fall back on banter.

"There's a spelling mistake on your sign outside. 'Earnest' has an *a* in it."

"Thanks." The object of Jake's interest was absorbed in erasing an incorrect entry in the ledger.

"I guess people tell you that all the time."

"No. Just about every half hour. Sometimes they make special trips in from their cars."

"Then why don't you change it?"

"Are you kidding? That's how we sell half our tickets." And, at last swinging around to face Jake, "What can I sell *you*?"

Wide green eyes, an amusingly upturned nose, a full humorous mouth: the front view was better than the back. Only the knowledge that his credit would never run to it prevented Jake from ordering every ticket in the house. On the other hand, it wasn't a bad line.

"How about every ticket in the house—if you'll have dinner with me tonight."

"All right." Those long, narrow fingers made a quick calculation on the machine. "That'll be nine hundred eighteen dollars for ninety-nine seats. Plus dinner at Bernard's."

Jake gulped. "I don't suppose you'd settle for two seats and a Big Mac?"

One delicate eyebrow turned itself into a question mark. "As long as I don't have to occupy one of those seats."

56

"Does that mean you can't recommend this establishment's entertainment—or its chairs?"

"I don't think I want to commit myself on that. Do you really want a ticket, or was there something else?"

"There was something else. Are you Hazel Harvey?"

A quick laugh, then, "No. Mrs. Harvey won't be in today, and Mr. Harvey's out too. Can I help?"

"Maybe." Jake began at the beginning. "My name's Jake Weissman. I'm a theatrical agent. We got a casting breakdown from this theater sent to the office the other day, and my secretary told someone that I'd be calling in to have a look at the place. I don't send my clients off into the unknown."

"We're not exactly unknown. The place is kind of tacky and it's had its ups and downs, but we have a certain reputation. Last year one of our productions got nominated for an L.A. Drama Critics Award."

"Winning isn't everything."

"Not when you're up against a couple of Mark Taper goodies and a Pulitzer Prize winner from Broadway. Can I show you around?"

Jake tried not to sound overly eager. "If you aren't too busy."

He was rewarded with a broad, warm smile. "As a matter of fact, I'm *very* busy, but I need a break. Balancing these books needs a combined Einstein and Light-fingered Louie; and since I don't fall into either category, the whole business gives me a headache and takes three times longer than it would if the people around here bothered to keep proper records."

While she was speaking, Jake's guide blocked off the box office window with a cardboard panel bearing the message GONE OUT. IF YOU WANT A TICKET—YELL. She now emerged into the lobby, locking the office door behind her.

"The 'Keep Out' door behind you leads to the dressing rooms and backstage," she said, "and the stairs behind the office here go up to the lighting booth, a storage room and Mrs. Harvey's apartment. I'll just run up and turn on some lights. The house is right through there."

She pointed to a curtained arch opposite the stairs and then disappeared. Jake proceeded through the curtains and emerged at one end of a wide low corridor with, on his left, a shoulder-high wall. Although the light here was very dim, he could make out a gap halfway along this wall where it was bisected by a central aisle, and by keeping one hand on the wall and edging forward gingerly in case of any unforeseen changes in floor level, he managed to reach the aisle and look into the gloom toward the stage.

"I can't find the main switch," came a voice from above, followed by a triumphant "Aha!" as six metal-shaded ceiling lights came on.

Like all such spaces, this one looked its worst under the harsh glare of its house lights, which, once Jake's eyes had adjusted to the change in brightness, threw into cruel prominence every chip and crack in the walls, every tear and fray in the seat covers, and every variation in shade and finish that had resulted from the use of several different types of black paint to cover every major surface in the room. Then the house lights dimmed, the stage lighting came up and, in a graceful transformation, the room lost its tattered, patched-together look and took on an air of warmth and mystery. At the touch of a switch it had become a theater.

Still standing at the back under the lighting booth, Jake counted the seats: nine rows of six on the left and nine rows of five on the right for a total seating capacity of ninety-nine—the maximum a theater can have and still qualify for lower salaries and other concessions made by Actors' Equity. Only the last five rows were mounted on stepped platforms, so Jake moved forward and sat down in a fourth-row aisle seat to see what kind of view it offered of the raised stage. Thanks to careful placement of the seats in the rows ahead, the sight lines seemed good, and there was a pleasant feeling of intimacy and expectation, as if at any moment something exciting might happen.

"Well, what do you think?" The girl from the box office was sitting in the row behind him.

"Somebody did a good job. I get the right feelings."

"Me too."

They sat for a moment and looked at the stage, which had been set up with an ornate tea table surrounded by three small period chairs for the first act of The Importance of Being Earnest. Behind the furniture, four free-standing canvas-covered flats, painted to represent wood paneling draped with red velvet hangings, provided a note of Victorian opulence that was augmented by two potted palms (artificial) placed one on each side of the proscenium opening. The general effect, although sparse, suited the restricted acting area and had more style, thought Jake, than might have been expected.

"Nice set," he commented.

"Yes. They came up with a winner this time. Unfortunately, the designers around here usually don't last for more than one production—and sometimes not even that."

"How come?"

"Oh, you know. They say, sure they can mount a show for two hundred dollars, and then they find out they can't, and there isn't any more money, and they have to do everything themselves and—well, you get the picture. The good ones stick it out and do the best they can. The bad ones fade into the night about halfway through rehearsals. We've had some very strange-looking sets."

Jake shifted in his seat to look behind him. "You haven't told me your name yet."

"Sorry. It's Ginny. Ginny Warner."

"Any relation to the brothers?"

"I wish. No, I haven't any film connections. And Warner is my husband's name."

Jake's world crumbled into fine ashes and blew away on a hot dry wind. "You're married?"

"Separated." Ginny laughed as renewed hope appeared in Jake's eyes. "And divorced sometime next month."

"I can't say I'm sorry."

"Neither can I. It wasn't exactly the marriage I'd dreamed about in high school."

"What happened?"

Ginny looked back toward the stage. "Oh, it's kind of a boring story now: boy meets girl, boy marries girl, boy meets guru. And then it was off to the consciousness-raising sessions, and first it was no meat, then no sex, then no job, and finally no me. Now he's off on a farm commune in the Valley. I just hope they all stay there and don't do anything crazy."

"You could always have him kidnapped back again," Jake suggested without enthusiasm.

"Not a chance. By the time Hal was ready to move out I'd have paid his pals to cart him away. No thanks. I've had enough of married life for a while."

All this was most satisfactory. Jake felt he could risk getting down to a little business. He started off with, "How long have you been working here?"

"Just under a year. I needed a part-time job when things started going funny with Hal, and I just fell into this. The pay's rotten, but the place becomes addictive—like a soap opera. You want to stick around and see how things turn out. Except, like the soaps, it never comes to an end."

"I wonder if you knew a client of mine who used to work here: Bobbie Lang."

Ginny looked surprised. "Used to work? I thought he still did. He comes in a couple of times a month and gives me a holiday from the box office. Have you got him into a new show or something?"

"I'm afraid not." Jake hadn't pictured himself as the bearer of evil tidings. "Actually, I haven't seen him for years. And now he's dead."

Ginny's eyes grew wider. "Oh, that's awful. He was so nice—and so young. Was he sick?"

"No, somebody killed him. They found his body in one of the Hollywood Bowl parking lots about ten days ago."

Even in the half light reflected from the stage, Jake could see the color leave Ginny's face. Two tears formed and were brushed away.

"I hate that," she said. "I really hate that. What a rotten thing to happen." She produced a handkerchief and blew her nose. "I don't know why I feel so bad. I didn't even know him very well. He was always coming when I was leaving, or the other way around. It's just, you never think of anyone you've met ending that way. He had a friend, didn't he?"

"Yeah: Arnie. Great big guy. They lived together. Did you ever meet him?"

Ginny put her handkerchief away. "No. He never came in. I just saw him sometimes when he dropped Bobbie off or was waiting outside to pick him up. He always seemed to be there, like a nice big dog. Is he very upset?"

Jake twisted himself around in his seat so that he could lean back against the armrest and look at Ginny without having to strain his neck. "He's okay now."

"That's good. Whenever I saw them together, I couldn't help thinking that if my marriage had worked that well I wouldn't be trying to balance accounts in a crazy theater and my husband wouldn't be wandering around somewhere with a tin cup and a shaved head."

"A shaved head?"

"Yes. It makes them feel holy. Why?"

"Just something I thought of. Is that all they shave?"

Ginny managed a laugh. "I don't know. Their chins, I guess. That came after my time. What a strange question."

Jake smiled back at her. "I'm surprised you didn't know about Bobbie. Surely the police must have been around here."

"They probably were, but I've been away for the last couple of weeks. Visiting my parents in Chicago. Do I have an alibi?"

"Oh, I don't know. Suspect in Chicago tells parents she's going out for a day's shopping, catches a morning flight to L.A., does the deed, flies back in the afternoon, and comes home with a few packages bought the day before. And an alibi. Just a routine job for your average killer."

A light of suspicion came into Ginny's eyes. "Are you with the police or something?"

"No. Nothing like that." Jake felt like a fraud. "It's kind of silly, but I promised Bobbie's friend that I'd—well, look into things for him. He thinks the police aren't interested, and he's right. The only trouble is," he confessed, "I don't know the first thing about being a private detective, and my image doesn't fit the part. I haven't got steely eyes, I don't smoke, and I can't slouch. How can I get people to take me seriously?"

At this moment, the armrest on which Jake was leaning detached itself from the iron chair frame, tumbling him backward into the aisle. For a shocked moment, he lay there with his feet in the air while Ginny stared at him, both of them too astonished to react. The moment was broken by a distant titter.

"You might have made sure I wasn't hurt before you started laughing," said Jake plaintively as he checked his spine for damage by sitting up carefully.

"It wasn't me," replied Ginny, doing her best to keep a straight face.

A second laugh was cut off in mid snigger, followed by a soft thump and the sound of scuffling.

"It's the twins," Ginny explained. "They spend all their spare time under the stage with the old props and costumes. Not to mention the mice and spiders." Raising her voice, she said, "I thought you two were supposed to be outside painting flats."

"We're having a break," came a righteous voice from beneath the stage.

61

"If there's anything left to break," added a second voice, followed by more muffled hilarity.

"It's better to pay no attention to them when they get like this," said Ginny. "Is there anything else you'd like to see?"

Catcalls from under the stage: "Take it off, Ginny!" "Let's see 'em, Ginny!"

Clearly the time had arrived to suggest a move back to the lobby. But before Jake could open his mouth to do so, there came from the dressing room area a sound of heavy footsteps and a loud male voice.

Ten

"Hell's bells," said the voice. "Ain't I told everybody a thousand times not to waste the stage lights? Who's out there anyway?"

Ginny stood up and went to the edge of the stage. "It's me, Mr. Harvey," she called. "I was just showing someone around."

After a further moment's suspense on Jake's part, Hank Harvey appeared onstage: a slim weather-beaten man of about sixty-five, with iron gray hair cut short on the back and sides, a full mustache curling down over his upper lip, and the palest gray eyes Jake had ever seen. He wore a red checked shirt over long-sleeved underwear, narrow blue jeans held up by a silver-buckled belt, and western boots with stacked heels that thumped resoundingly on the wooden floorboards as he crossed the stage, shading his eyes against the glare of the ceiling-mounted spotlights to peer out into the darkness of the house.

"A theatrical agent," Ginny added, gesturing toward Jake, who had followed her down the aisle. "Jake Weissman."

Hank Harvey's face softened into a network of lines and creases. "Well, now, that's a whole different story." He reached down to shake hands. "Glad to know you, Jake. Good of you to drop by."

Jake took the strong dry hand offered him and immediately regretted the move. "I'm glad I did," he said, straining not to yelp as his knuckles cracked under Hank's hearty grip. "It's the first time I've been here."

"Son, you don't know what you been missin'." Hank released Jake's hand and squatted down on his heels. "We got the best damn little the-ay-ter in town, bar none. Just you come around some night and see what we can do."

"Mr. Harvey's our star performer," said Ginny loyally, while Jake surreptitiously kneaded his hand back to life. "He used to be in the movies."

Hank looked pleased. "Yep," he said. "I was a stuntman, and a good one, too. But it stood in my way, 'cause I wanted to act and they never let me. I guess they figgered actors come easy but how many damn fools is willin' to let theirselves get drug behind a runaway horse?" He let out a dry laugh. "I fooled 'em, though. They'd got me on to teachin' the newcomers and doin' odd jobs, when I saw this place for sale. It was out of use then, but I said to myself, 'That's for you, Hank boy. Here's where you start actin'.' So I took out the money I'd put by and I bought it and fixed it up and now I'm doin' all the things I wanted to forty years ago. Took me that long to work out if you can't get what you want one way, you better try another."

"I'll remember that." Jake had his hand back in working order. "What are you playing in now?"

"This one right here." Hank indicated the set of Algernon Moncrieff's morning room. "I don't have time to fool around with no crap, so I'm stickin' to the classics."

Jake ran through the cast of *The Importance of Being Earnest,* but could only think of one minor character in Hank Harvey's age bracket. "Which part?" he asked.

"Well, it ain't Lady Bracknell," Hank said, with a guffaw. "I guess I could have had a shot at Algy, but I'd set my sights on Earnest. You can't go wrong when you got your name in the title. Guess what I'm gonna tackle next."

While Jake hesitated between *Waiting for Godot* and *Harvey,* Ginny gave up for both of them. Hank became confidential.

"I ain't told no one about this yet, so keep it under your hats. Here's a clue." He rose to assume a contemplative pose and began to declaim in round tones, "'Tew be or not tew be—'"

A squawk from beneath the stage ended abruptly in a smothered gurgle. Hank paused and looked expectantly at his audience.

"Hamlet!" cried Jake, sensing that a guess was required.

Hank stamped a heel in delight. "You got it! Yessir, just the other day I said to myself, 'Hank, boy, there ain't no use hangin' around the shallow edge; you gotta jump right in the middle.' And I come up with this great idea, too: Hamlet does the ghost! Here, I'll show you." He took up a position over to one side of the stage and fixed his eyes on a point in space some twelve feet away. "'Where wilt thou lead me?'" he roared. "'Speak; I'll go no farther.' Gaah!" Clutching his throat in a strangle grip, he spun about, reeled to the other side of the stage, and croaked, "'Mark me,'" in a sepulchral voice before staggering back to his original position to answer, "'I will,'" in a normal tone. "Gaah!" he shrieked again, as a second seizure contorted his features and twirled him off to a new location, from which he moaned a hollow "'My time is come.'" Then, passing a hand over his forehead, he awoke from his trance to utter a pious "'Alas, poor ghost.'"

"Get the idea?" he asked, leaving the Elsinore battlements and returning to the edge of the stage. "The old guy speaks through Hamlet like that kid in *The Exorcist.* Pretty clever, eh?"

"And think what you'll save on salary and costumes," Jake pointed out.

"You can say that again!" Hank winked to show that he had already considered that advantage. "And remember what I said—don't go tellin' Hazel or anybody about this. I want to hit 'em with it myself."

"How will it fit into our running schedule?" Ginny wanted to know. "Are you going to close *Earnest*?"

Hank's pale eyes widened. "Hell, no! That's the whole point—I'll be doin' comedy and tragedy back to back, and them dumb critics'll *have* to notice me." He narrowed his eyes and squinted into the banks of overhead lights. "A lotta them spots has burned through their gels. I better get out the ladder and put in some new ones."

"Maybe not just now," Ginny suggested. "There's a rehearsal for *Shootout* soon, and you know Yolanda."

"Oh, yeah." Hank stroked the stubble on his chin. "I don't want a run-in with her yet. See, I was thinkin that now she's got this new show comin' up, it might be a good time to close *Woman Alone*."

"WHAT!!?"

The outraged shout came from the back of the house, where, dramatically posed at the end of the center aisle, stood a figure that might have been plucked from the 1960s by some time warp and set down that very moment in the Quest Theatre. She was covered from neck to ankle in a layered assembly of blouses, pullovers, jackets, scarves and overskirts, all murky in color and rough in weave; a curtain of straight dark hair hung over her face in a sheer drop to her waist; and she carried a black guitar case. Looking neither left nor right and apparently navigating by some inner radar, she marched down the aisle on sandaled feet to address the unhappy Hank.

"*What* was that you said?"

"Now, Yolanda . . ."

"Did I really hear that you want to close *Woman Alone*?"

Hank shoved his hands into his back pockets and started to shuffle his feet. "Well, not *want* exactly. But you've had a pretty good run—"

"Run?" Yolanda hurled a loose scarf end around her neck so that it fell obediently behind her right shoulder. "I haven't even *started* to run. People are just beginning to discover me. I'm finding my audience."

"Seems to me if you ain't found your audience in three months—"

"Two and a half!"

"And bein' as how you're busy with the new show . . ."

"You can *not* close *Woman Alone*!"

Hank stroked his chin again. "Well, I guess I can if I've a mind to. This here's my the-ay-ter."

"And mine, too!" By this time, Yolanda had walked over to a temporary set of steps and made her way onto the stage, where she faced Hank on his own level. "I'm the voice of the future. I've earned my place here. And if you think I'm going to let myself be pushed out just so you can do another of your pathetic so-called classics—"

"*Pathetic!*"

"—you've got another thing coming. I was promised a free hand here and I intend—"

"Now just a dang minute—"

As the angry voices rose higher, Jake fled the house and joined Ginny in the lobby.

"Poor old Hank," he said, plumping down in a chair beside her. "His big secret didn't stand a chance."

"Not a hope." Ginny brushed a stray lock of hair out of her eyes in a gesture that reminded Jake achingly of Greer Garson in *Mrs. Miniver*. "He should have known better, though. Around here, even the floors have ears—and the ears usually belong to the twins."

Jake recalled the two dissimilar figures waving their paint rollers out in the alley. "They don't look much like twins," he observed.

Ginny smiled. "Maybe they just adopted each other at an early age. I wouldn't be surprised."

"Eccentric adolescents."

"Eccentric's the word. Lately, Tina's been turning herself into the Marlboro Man, and Tim's come up with a smart little skating outfit he swears Sonja Henie wore in *Sun Valley Serenade*. He'll model it for you at the drop of a hat."

Resolving never to drop a hat within a mile of the Quest, Jake remarked that the twins didn't seem like Hank's kind of people.

"Far from it. They're on Hazel's side."

"Meaning?"

"Power games." Ginny gave the phrase a dramatic reading. "They all have different ideas on how the Quest should be run, but the twins support Hazel in trying to get Hank to stop putting on plays that he can't handle as an actor; and in return Hazel supports the twins in backing their discovery, Yolanda. Which means that nobody much supports Hank," she ended rather apologetically.

"Poor old Hank," Jake repeated.

"Of course, he does own the theater, so he has a strong hand. It seems to balance out."

For some time now, actors had been drifting in from the street and passing through the lobby on their way to Yolanda's rehearsal. As a final group disappeared through the door into the dressing room, Hank emerged wearing a tired expression and mopping his brow with a blue bandanna.

"Sometimes I really miss the good old days," he informed them, "when all I had to do was go out and crack up a car or fall over a cliff. That was peanuts next to what I have to go through here."

66

"How did you make out with Yolanda?" Ginny asked.

Hank grinned ruefully. "Oh, I told her if she didn't like the way I ran things here she could pack up and go somewheres else. Now I'll have Hazel and her gang down on me before I can get my second wind." He regarded Jake sternly. "You married, son?"

Jake confessed that he was not.

Crinkles formed around Hank's eyes. "Then why don't you ask this nice young lady here for a date? She needs to go out more. If I was a few years younger, I'd ask here myself."

"Why Mistuh Hahvey!" Ginny fluttered an imaginary fan. "You wicked man!"

"Hell, if I was single and *his* age,"—Hank jerked a thumb in Jake's direction—"I'd've had you roped, tied, and hitched at the altar by now."

"I don't work that fast," Jake protested. "I just met her half an hour ago."

"Have you asked her out yet?"

"Yes."

"What did she say?"

"She hedged."

"Keep workin' on it." Hank waved to them both. "I gotta go buy some amber gels for them lights. If you see Hazel, tell her I'm comin' by tomorrow mornin' to put them in. See you."

As Hank headed out to the street, Jake turned what he considered to be his irresistible quizzical look on Ginny, who purposely misinterpreted it.

"They're separated," she said. "Hazel got the apartment upstairs and Hank lives in a room somewhere off Franklin."

"That isn't what I wanted to know. Are you having dinner with me tonight?"

"I'm sorry, I can't."

Jake resolved to take Hank's advice and keep working on it. "Tomorrow, then."

"Uh-uh."

"If there's someone else, don't spare my feelings. I can take it."

"There's someone else."

"I can't take it!" Jake collapsed back in his chair, sending off a puff of dust and a small scattering of dried leaves. He gazed up sadly. "Throw him over. Come out with me."

"I couldn't do that to Cal. He's pretty insecure as it is."

Jake stood up. "You don't want to get mixed up with someone like that. He'll play the insecurity for all it's worth until both of you are screwed up. I know. I can do it myself."

Ginny stopped teasing him. "Cal is my son," she said. "He's five years old. He lives with Hal's parents in Pasadena while I'm working, and he spends weekends with me. Which means he's coming home tonight and I can't wait to see him and that's why I'm not available for dinners."

Jake refused to give up. "Maybe not on weekends, but how about the rest of the week? When do you get back here?"

"Monday—maybe Sunday night, if Hazel wants out of the box office and I can get a baby-sitter."

"I'll come by. In the meantime, there's a service for Bobbie tomorrow at eleven at the Parkhill Memorial Chapel, Santa Monica. Arnie isn't expecting anybody, but there'll be at least a couple of us there if you want to show up."

Ginny shook her head. "I would, but not with Cal. I'll tell the Harveys though, and I hope you'll tell Arnie how sorry I am about Bobbie."

"I will." Jake resigned himself to leaving. "And I'll be seeing you soon. Don't forget: I have to solve a murder, and now I've got a great reason for hanging around here."

"So that's it." Ginny made Jake's afternoon complete by tossing her hair out of her eyes again. "I'm just a pretext."

Jake pulled out his best Humphrey Bogart impression. "Sure, sweetheart," he drawled, heading for the door, "But, like I said, a great one."

The door swung shut behind him and he sauntered happily back to his car, where the twins had left a large cardboard sign propped up against his windshield to proclaim the message JAKE LOVES GINNY in buttercup yellow letters.

"They could be right," Jake told the sign as he tossed it into the back of the Thunderbird. Excited by the thought, he drove home in a daze and swam three lengths of the pool to inaugurate a new regime under which he would gain muscle, skin color and a more vital physical aura while losing inches around the waist. Then, thoroughly enervated by the unaccustomed exercise, he heated up a frozen dinner and joined Hector in falling asleep in front of the television.

Eleven

The Parkhill Memorial Chapel took Jake by surprise when he pulled into its parking lot the next morning. He had expected something in the stately California Tudor or Spanish adobe style, with dark woods, heavy carpets and thick curtains. Instead, he discovered a plain modern building with polished terrazzo floors, ceilings of pale slatted wood, and tall windows overlooking an attractively landscaped interior courtyard. Filled with light, plants and broad comfortable Italian furniture, it showed what the Quest Theatre lobby could make of itself, given the income from a steadier, more lucrative line of business.

Arnie, too, received a surprise that morning. Neatly turned out in a blue blazer and slacks, he entered chapel B under the impression that he was to be the sole member of the congregation, only to find a party of six already assembled there. In addition to Jake and Miss Murphy, the latter smart and subdued in a blue linen jacket and skirt, the group included Miss Murphy's Baron, appropriately funereal in an undecorated motorcycle jacket and matching black leather jeans; the twins, outfitted from their understage wardrobe in black tailcoats, white shirts with black string ties, black denim jeans and paint-spotted sneakers; and, straining at the seams of a poppy-printed navy blue nylon pants suit, a tall, full-figured lady whom Jake correctly assumed to be Hazel Harvey.

After Arnie had asked everyone how he or she was doing, shaken hands all around, and said thanks for coming, a hidden organ wheezed out the first few bars of "We'll Meet Again," and the service began. Jake noted with gratitude that Bobbie, in making his own funeral arrangements, had chosen not to be present himself, although his influence on the proceedings became clear from the moment a lithe young minister, clad in what appeared to be an ecclesiastical sweat suit, bounced up to the lectern and began his sermon. Brief, informal and tied to the dogma of no recognizable religion, it tripped lightly over the familiar topics of life and the loved one before settling into its main theme, which, while never specifically named, struck Jake as hovering remarkably close to the edges of reincarnation.

At this point Jake's mind wandered off to speculate on who or what Bobbie might be expected to return as, then wandered back to find itself less interested in picking up the thread of the sermon than in studying the small congregation listening to it. Only Arnie and Miss Murphy seemed to be giving the words their full attention, Arnie leaning forward with his elbows on his knees and Miss Murphy sitting straight and alert beside Baron, who, having worked himself down onto his spine, appeared to be considering whether or not he could get away with putting his feet on the back of the empty pew in front of them. The twins periodically nudged one another and traded meaningful looks, each in the hope of setting the other off on a course of helpless giggles. Hazel Harvey sat bolt upright, fast asleep.

Or perhaps she's just listening with her eyes closed, Jake speculated, since she gave no sign of nodding or slipping back in her seat. As he studied her more closely, Jake realized that he had underestimated her age by about twenty years on his first distant view. She was not, as he had thought, in her late forties, but rather well into her sixties.

Seen in profile from six or seven feet away, Hazel Harvey did not show to advantage. Her red hair, long at the back and teased into a French roll in the front, was either a wig or suffering from the effects of too much dye and lacquer; her eyelashes could be called hers only by right of purchase; and no amount of makeup, however thickly applied, could conceal the pouches under the eyes, the surrounding web of fine lines, or the loose chin and neck. Only her undulating figure, although plainly owing much to inner buttressing and restraint, still gave an approximation of something that must, Jake concluded, once have been spectacular.

A change in tone and rhythm signaled that the sermon was coming to an end. Hazel Harvey opened her eyes and automatically reached forward to a point in midair, where a cigarette might have been resting had she been somewhere else at some other time. Jake turned his attention back to front center.

"And so we say farewell and bon voyage to our dear friend and loved one, Bobbie Lang," said the young minister, who appeared to equate death with a slightly extended pleasure cruise, "in the certain knowledge that the Great Mystery will see us all reunited both in this world and the next. May the Force be with you." He beamed at them. "And have a good day."

To the strains of "Someday I'll Find You," they all filed out into an open lobby designed to permit the smooth departure of the bereaved (Jake recognized what must have been Bobbie's white Datsun parked in a porte-cochère at one end) and to display whatever flowers had been sent. While the minister spoke privately with Arnie, who had come through his ordeal quite calmly, Jake inspected the flowers. These comprised a spray of white dahlias and yellow iris from Arnie, another of daisies and tiger lilies from the Quest, and something resembling a king-size bath mat made of roses and carnations.

"That's from you," murmured Miss Murphy into Jake's ear, confirming his worst fears. "Nice, no?"

"Very," replied Jake, stifling an impulse to point out that Bobbie had died, not come in first at Santa Anita. "Can I afford it?"

Miss Murphy patted him on the cheek. "Don't worry. I get from my uncle. Cheap."

"Murphy, you're—"

"I know. A treasure. When you want to dig me up?"

A prickling sensation on the back of his neck, coupled with a strong smell of Lenox leather oil, informed Jake that they were no longer alone.

"You remember my boyfriend Baron?" asked Miss Murphy brightly.

Jake turned around and stared into the mirrored glasses that Baron had reassumed after leaving the chapel. "Hi. How ya doin'?" he said, taking a leaf out of Arnie's book.

"Well, if it ain't Mr. Sixty-Forty," observed Baron, who had an uncomfortable habit of standing so close that Jake could never focus his eyes on him with any degree of comfort. "Shot anybody yet?"

"Not yet. But I'm making progress in other directions." Jake fingered the lapel of his prize lightweight suit. "Hundred percent. Wool. Italian."

Baron gave no sign of being impressed. "You ever tried leather?" he asked, hooking his thumbs into the back pockets of his glistening jeans.

"No. No, I haven't."

"You should. Dames love it." Baron made a trial prod in Jake's stomach with an exploratory forefinger. "Lose a few pounds and you might start really makin' out."

"Yes. Well." Jake wished that he had never pursued the topic of apparel.

"When you think you can handle it, I'll give you the name of the guy who makes mine."

"Thanks." The minister had left, the twins were talking with Arnie, and Hazel was at last free to be approached. "Look, there's someone I have to speak to. See you later." Jake made his escape.

Hazel was rummaging through a small drawstring handbag as he approached her. "Hazel Harvey, isn't it?"

"It sure is." Hazel expended a few calories batting her eyelashes. "Do I know you?"

"No, I'm Jake Weissman. I'm—that is, I was Bobbie Lang's agent. I called in at your theater yesterday."

"Oh, yeah. The kids told me." Hazel gave up on her handbag and pulled the drawstring. "I guess you could tell it was me because I'm with them, huh?"

Jake admitted this was the case.

"Reason I asked is because sometimes someone with real sharp eyes recognizes me from my movies."

"You were in the movies?"

"About a dozen. I could never keep track. You don't have a cigarette, do you?"

Jake noticed that Hazel's hands were shaking slightly as he apologized for not smoking.

"That's okay. I should quit anyway." Hazel let out a deep whooping laugh. "That'll be the day. They'll know I'm dead when they don't see smoke coming out of me. What?"

Jake repeated a polite query as to Hazel's film career.

"Oh, that. You seen any of them Esther Williams movies they used

72

to make? Well, I was in all but two. Swimming around in the background, you know?" Hazel let out another laugh. "It was a natural for me. With these boobs, I knew I'd never drown. Oh, yeah. Those were good days. We had a real career splashing around Esther. Never out of the goddamn water." Hazel lowered her voice at this in case they were still on holy ground. "The dopey thing was, we was kept so busy we never knew what movie they had us working on. We just showed up, put on the rubber roses, and made circles underwater, fell off swings, any dumb thing those fags—sorry. No offense. Oh. Well, you can't tell these days. Anything those guys could think up to do with us. And when we'd finish one number, they'd rebuild the set around the pool and we'd start rehearsing another."

"What was Miss Williams like?" asked Jake, an unashamed star worshipper.

"Oh, a doll. A real doll, wet or dry. We thought the world of her. What the hell, she kept us working for ten years." Hazel pulled her purse open again, and then shut it. "A real lady, and always nice to us in the chorus. Look, I gotta have a cigarette." She called over to Tina and Tim. "Hey, kids, let's split. Nice meeting you, Mr. . . . ? Oh, yeah: Jake. Come on over to the theater some day and we'll talk some more."

Jake went through his routine again. "Thanks, I'd like to. We got a casting breakdown for your new show, *Shootout at Shiloh,* and I wanted to get a little more detail on what you need."

Hazel looked puzzled. "Casting? We finished that a couple of months ago. We open next week, if we can get the set finished on time. That goddamn designer—" She broke off. "Anyhow, what the hell, we're always working on something new. Come around tomorrow. We got a kid's birthday party booked into the matinee and I gotta be there. You'll get a kick outta it."

Jake promised to drop by and watched as Hazel teetered away on very high-heeled sandals, supported by a twin on each arm. They crossed the street and let themselves into a vintage Hudson sedan that, with its generous curves, massive structure and shocking-pink paint job, presented an accurate reflection of its owner. Jake wondered how the strange trio would sort itself out for traveling and was amused when Hazel took the driver's place behind the wheel while the twins settled themselves regally in the back seat.

73

Miss Murphy and Baron had already left, so Jake walked over to join Arnie, who was standing by Bobbie's car, clutching a brown metal canister under his left arm and patiently waiting to say good-bye. He was prevented from speaking, however, by a sudden roar and screech as Hazel pulled away from the curb and took off at high speed, trailing a cloud of smoke from her exhaust pipe.

"Some car," said Jake, when conversation again became possible and they had watched the Hudson shrink to a vibrant pink dot in the distance.

Arnie nodded. "Yeah. That was my Bobbie's favorite color."

Jake took the opportunity to comment that the service had gone very well.

Arnie looked pleased. "Bobbie sure knew how to do things up right. I just wisht he coulda been here to see it." He regarded the canister sadly. "But I guess in a way he was."

A blue vinyl adhesive label on the side of the container carried the legend ROBERT LANG in raised white letters.

"You feel okay?" asked Jake.

Arnie thought for a second. "I guess so. I'm kinda hungry." His ears reddened. "I'd like to buy you lunch, but you prolly got somethin' else to do."

Jake assured him that his time was his own, and by common consent they strolled across the street to an outdoor taco stand where they were soon munching excellent burritos at a small round table under a dilapidated sun umbrella, Bobbie occupying the seat between them. Exercising the caution necessary to eat the tortilla-wrapped bundles without getting a mixture of meat, vegetables and sauce on their trousers kept the two men silent in a pleasantly companionable way until Arnie had finished two burritos to Jake's one and was taking a short rest before beginning a third.

"Jake," he began, "I just heard somethin' that's got me kinda worried."

Jake had suspected something of this nature. "What's the trouble?" he asked.

Arnie felt the foil wrapping of his remaining burrito to make sure it was still keeping warm. "You remember that minister guy who spoke to us back there in the chapel? Well, he talked to me some more after, and he knew my Bobbie."

Jake expressed interest.

"And he said my Bobbie used to give him money, you know, like a con—a con—"

"Contribution?"

"Yeah. Anyhow, he said Bobbie used to give him pretty big con— well, those things, and he wanted me to do the same."

"You don't have to unless you feel like it."

"Oh, I know that. What's worryin' me is, where did my Bobbie get the money?"

Jake had not been expecting this. "Didn't you give him any of his own, or have some kind of arrangement?"

"Jeez, yeah." Arnie's eyes became very round in his effort to make Jake understand. "I'da given him anythin' he wanted. Anythin'. He signed almost all our checks and I wouldn'ta cared what he did. But he never spent much on himself, even when I ast him to, and I never seen nothin' big took outta the bank. And somethin' else." Arnie put on as much of a frown as his good-natured face could form. "Them people at the chapel, they told me all of Bobbie's funeral had been paid for already, when he come to see them just a little while ago. Jake, I know I ain't real bright or anythin' like that, but I think,"— Arnie checked for eavesdroppers and gripped the edge of the table with his two huge hands—"I think there's somethin' funny goin' on."

With these thoughts off his mind, Arnie released the table and placidly returned to his burrito, leaving Jake free to ponder what he had just been told and inspect more closely the metal canister on the seat next to him. As he did so, a trick of his imagination altered the letters on the label to spell out his own name. Jake quickly put this morbid image out of his mind; nevertheless, he was unable to prevent himself from thinking fondly back to his dim, dark, musty and, above all, *safe* office, so well hidden at the bottom of its airshaft, and wondering if perhaps it might still not be too late to return there, lock the door, and live long enough to go bankrupt in peace.

Twelve

B ut today was Saturday, and Jake did not go back to his office. Instead he drove home and spent the remainder of the afternoon adding to his tan, on the theory that if he could not immediately become thin and muscular he could at least look healthy. He then swam four energetic lengths of the pool before staggering indoors, gasping and dizzy, to take a long restorative nap.

Nine o'clock that evening found Jake wide awake, fed, and wondering what to do with his Saturday night. Food, music and television had all failed him, and he felt irritable and restless as a soft breeze made its way into his living room, ruffling the beards on his tribal masks and bearing a scent of flowers from the climbing vine outside his bedroom window. It also bore the distant call of Hector, now paying court to the charming white Persian cat who lived in an apartment facing the lane and who had already made it as clear as possible that Hector appeared nowhere on her list of eligible suitors. Undeterred, Hector balanced precariously on a branch of a large tree on the opposite side of the lane and sang of undying love in affecting tones.

Jake lay on his back in bed, swaying slightly with the ebb and flow of his mattress, and gazed up at the thatched canopy overhead as bitter thoughts regarding the difficulty of life and the sad plight of the single unattached male ran through his head. He had consulted his list of friends to call, but all were firmly paired off into couples who would therefore already have made plans for weekend merrymaking that did not include the company of a third party. He had even swallowed his pride and called Clare again, only to hang up when a male voice answered the telephone. That girl sure knows how to twist the knife, he thought. And she hadn't wasted any time.

Still, he hadn't let the grass grow under his feet either. He had a good feeling about Ginny—more than good—but she was not to be seen until tomorrow or Monday, and even then she was not the sort of girl with whom one could expect to go too fast too soon. It would all take time. And what, wondered Jake, now bouncing up and down on the edge of the bed, what about tonight?

Obviously, Ginny was worth waiting for. And surely he had enough strength of character and self-control, not to mention inner resources, to spend a pleasant evening alone at home without turning into a nervous wreck. He went into the kitchen and ate some yogurt. This was bad. If he stayed in, there was a strong chance he would eat his way through all the junk food in the house and put on weight and become fat. No. The thing to do would be to go out, have a quick drink, and then come home again. That would keep him occupied, nothing would happen, and he would sure as hell sleep a lot better. Self-control didn't come into the picture. It was simply a matter of using up animal energy.

At ten o'clock, ready to depart in search of his quick drink, Jake inspected himself in a full-length mirror. He was confronted by a devastating figure in a pale green summer suit accessorized with a white belt and white shoes and set off to great advantage by a bottle green satin shirt, unbuttoned to mid chest, the better to display a developing tan—unfortunately still in its bright pink stage—and several gold chains of varying thickness, length and design. Turning sideways, Jake surveyed his stomach with a critical eye. It looked flatter. Even the rimless glasses played their part, adding a twinkle of intelligence to a face that, Jake had to admit, might otherwise have belonged to just another handsome Hollywood stud. Not, of course, that it mattered at all how he looked, because he was just going to call in at a few of his favorite bars and then come right home again. Making a mental note to check into the possibility of contact lenses, Jake dimmed the lights, turned the stereo down to a soft level, set out his bongo drums (because, after all, one never knew), and sallied forth into the night.

Some four and a half hours later, down from his tree and in need of sustenance, Hector called in at Jake's kitchen to check his bowl, just in case something might have materialized there in his absence. Finding it empty, he wandered into the bedroom, where he discovered his friend fast asleep on top of the bed, alone and fully dressed, except for the white shoes. Hector was pleased. If Jake was merely taking a nap, he might be in the mood for a late night snack. He jumped up on the bed and sat down on Jake's sunburned chest. This evoked no response except for a loud snore. Hector applied his cold nose to a convenient patch of rosy skin, following up with a few delicate claw pricks. Jake snored on. Clearly there would be no food for quite some time, so Hector curled himself up on a free pillow, leaving Jake to sleep off the effects of many brandies and to wake at noon with a painful hangover.

Even before he opened his eyes, Jake knew that the bedroom was twirling around him and occasionally executing a neat loop-the-loop. Opening his eyes made things worse, so he closed them again and, following a tip picked up from a magazine last New Year's, placed one foot on the floor. The room promptly ceased its gyrations and came to a halt. Jake began to feel slightly better, until the throbbing cloud that enveloped his head was pierced by a harsh, grating wail. Having missed both late-night supper and breakfast, Hector wanted food.

"Don't do that." Jake tried for a commanding tone, but could only produce a whisper.

"Yah!"

"One minute. Then I'll do anything."

"Yow!"

"Hector, please."

"Yrrr!" Hector landed on Jake's chest and glared at him with accusing eyes.

The telephone rang. Jake uttered a moan of anguish and started up in bed, toppling Hector onto his back and setting up a series of rocking undulations in the water-filled mattress that threatened to bring on an attack of seasickness. When the waves and his equilibrium had both subsided a little, Jake had to make up his mind whether to die or to answer the telephone. He picked up the receiver.

"Hello," he whispered.

"Jake?"

Jake winced and held the receiver a foot away from his ear.

"A piece of him."

"I can't hear you."

There was no help for it. Jake brought the receiver back to its normal position, taking the precaution of wrapping his fingers around the earpiece. "A piece of him," he repeated.

"Are you all right?"

"No, I'm not. Who is this?"

"It's Ginny. What's wrong?"

Jake began to realize that he had made the right choice in deciding to live.

"Oh, nothing." And in his best Rosalind Russell manner, "Auntie's hung."

"Shall I call back when Auntie feels better?"

"I'll never feel better. You wouldn't like to come over and feed me custard and nourishing broth?"

"No, but you're not far off. I haven't been called in to work tonight, so I wanted to ask you for dinner. But if you're feeling fragile . . ."

"Who feels fragile? Just give me the time and place."

Ginny gave him the address of an apartment in the Silver Lake district. "And come about eight, if you don't mind dining fashionably late. I'll have Cal fed and into bed by then, so we won't have to have a nursery meal."

Everything was clear now. The unsuccessful night, the consequent hangover—all were part of some happy plan organized by a kindly fate. Insofar as anyone with a pronounced greenish cast could be said to glow, Jake glowed.

"Sounds great. I'll be there with bells on." A particularly severe throb rocked his head. "Make that muffled bells."

"If you have a relapse and can't make it, I'll understand."

"Don't worry. I'll make it." Jake hung up. "If I have to crawl there on my hands and knees. Whoopee!"

And with that glad cry, which he instantly regretted, Jake leapt out of bed, steadied himself against a convenient wall, and set a course for the kitchen, where he swallowed aspirin, made coffee, and, after a brief episode involving a particularly revolting flavor of Hector's favorite cat food that sent him back to bed breathing heavily, began to feel capable of facing what remained of the day.

Although he had planned on reaching the Quest Theatre by two o'clock, in order to take advantage of Hazel's invitation to attend the children's matinee, Jake did not get there until nearly three. The lobby was deserted, so he ascended the three steps to the next level and proceeded into the auditorium, where *The Magic Pond* was reaching its exciting conclusion before a packed house of two- to ten-year-olds and their heavily outnumbered parents.

Into a rudimentary woodland setting of some hanging foliage and two large papier-mâché stumps tiptoed an actor in a bright green frog costume with matching underwater flippers on his feet. He held a finger to his lips and came downstage to plead with the young audience in an apprehensive whisper.

"You must help me," he said. "The wolf is coming, and if he catches me, it'll be"—he shuddered—"frog's legs for dinner. I've got to hide. But where? Where can I hide?"

"Behind the stump," came a few adventurous voices from the audience.

"Where?"

"BEHIND THE STUMP!" This time a full chorus smote Jake's tottering constitution like an anvil blow.

"Oh, that's a wonderful idea! But if the wolf asks, you won't tell him where I am, will you?"

"NO!"

Jake propped himself up against the back wall.

"Promise?"

"YES!"

The frog hurried behind one of the stumps just as a ferocious wolf in a shaggy top and overalls came growling onto the stage. The wolf slunk down to the front of the stage and glared at the children, several of whom quailed visibly.

"All right," he snarled in a rasping voice. "I know that frog is here someplace. And when I catch him I'm going to bite him and chew him and eat him all up!" A whimper arose from a small boy in the front row. "Now, where is he?"

The frog bobbed up behind the stump to make a renewed plea for silence in dumb show.

"Where is he?"

"BEHIND THE STUMP!" sang out some seventy bloodthirsty voices.

"Which stump?"

"THAT ONE!" Seventy eager fingers pointed, just as the frog managed to run behind the second stump.

The wolf looked behind the first stump and then scowled malevolently at his informants.

"Liars! There's no frog here."

A jumble of voices indicated that the frog had shifted his hiding place.

"Well, I'll look. But if he's not there, I'll never believe any of you again."

The frog skipped back to his original hiding place, the wolf bore down on the wrong stump, the children screamed, and Jake sped back to the lobby where a voice hailed him from inside the box office.

"Hi there, Jake-y boy," it boomed. "Just the man I want to see."

Jake stopped and looked through the ticket window. There at what he had come to think of as Ginny's desk sat a clown in full gaudy circus garb: a voluminous red and yellow costume with pom-poms, topped off by a curly blond Harpo Marx wig, a red conical hat, and a lot of white makeup on which were painted raised eyebrows, starry eyelashes, a red nose and an enormous red smile, outlined in black.

"Swell service yesterday," continued the clown affably. Jake agreed and approached the window until he could finally make out through the heavy paint and balloonlike coverall certain unmistakable contours and features that could have belonged only to Hazel Harvey. For some reason, this discovery produced in Jake an attack of acute embarrassment, as if he had opened a door without knocking and discovered Hazel engaged in some private pursuit not intended for general display. Hazel, however, appeared perfectly at ease and disposed to chat.

"Some getup, eh?" she chuckled. "Always wear it when we have birthday party groups in. The kids love it, and it shows the parents who's in charge. Whoo!" Hazel gave her head a shake, then beamed at Jake. "Did I say I wanted to see you?"

Jake replied that she had.

"Did I say why?"

"Not yet." Jake smiled encouragingly and looked about for the bottle from which he suspected Hazel had been helping herself a little too liberally.

"Damn." Hazel thought for a moment. "It was something important. Oh, well, what the hell. It'll come to me. I'm not thinking too good at the moment, after what happened to Hank and all."

Jake's internal antennae began to quiver. "Something happened to Hank?"

"You mean nobody told you? Yesterday morning when we were at

81

the funeral. He was putting gels on the house spots and the ladder fell over."

"Is he. . . ?"

"Kaput. Cracked his neck over the back of a seat. The doc said he went just like that." Hazel tried to snap her fingers, oblivious to the fact that they were encased in white cotton gloves. "He's over at that Parkhill place right now. I liked their style."

"Who found him?"

Hazel managed a pained expression under her clown's makeup. "Yolanda Meltzer, wouldn't you know? She had the police, ambulance, everything but the fire department milling around here when we got back from the service. Wouldn't be surprised if she pushed the ladder herself. God, what a day! Hi, there, sweetie. What're *you* up to?" This last was addressed to a small blond girl in a frilly pink party dress who had stopped outside the open box office door to stare at Hazel in fascination.

"Looking for something?" Hazel moderated her usual hearty voice to something approaching a normal level.

"Bathroom," came back the whisper.

"Straight ahead and then that way." Hazel pointed. "You need any help?"

"No." The little girl scampered away.

Hazel came over to the ticket window to look after her. "Jesus, aren't they something at that age? Fucking shame they have to grow up. God, I love kids! We never had any. I forget—did you ever meet Hank?"

"Just once, the other day."

"Lousy actor, but what a stuntman! A real artist. It was worth the price of admission just to see him get shot off a roof. Nobody could fall like he could—graceful as a leaf. And what a beautiful man when I married him. Like one of them marble statues." A tear slipped down Hazel's painted cheek. "'Course, that didn't last forever, and now he's gone for good."

Jake made sympathetic noises while Hazel attempted to blot her cheek with a tissue.

"Yeah, well, he went the right way. Funny, when you think of all the falls he did on purpose." She sniffed. "Oh, well. At least we won't have to do any more of that fruity crap he wanted to act in. 'A *hand-*

bag?'" She gave a creditable imitation of an imitation of Edith Evans's famous delivery. "You need real style for that, and money to back it up. The twins said he wanted to do *Hamlet* next. Over my dead body, I said. Well, that's another worry out of the way, but I guess I'm stuck with *Woman Alone*. Ninety minutes of whining by Who-Cares-About Yolanda Meltzer with no story, no laughs, no other characters and, Jesus God, no intermission."

"Smart move," said Jake, "if you think your audience won't come back for a second act."

"You're telling me," sighed Hazel. "And now she's written this musical for kids, poor little buggers. The twins say it's great, but I say it sucks, and if I had any guts I'd scrap the whole mess. A Western version of David and Goliath, yet, and—yes! *That's* what I wanted to see you about. You said you're in casting: you got any giants on your list?"

"You can't find a Goliath?"

"Oh, we found one all right. But yesterday after rehearsal the big bozo went and pranged his car into a palm tree on Sunset, and now he's in the hospital in a body cast. Lucky to be alive, they say, but we open Wednesday and we need a giant."

Jake said he was pretty sure he didn't represent anyone that large.

"Come on, Jake. Don't play cute with me. What about your big friend from the funeral yesterday?"

Jake sorted out the pros and cons in his head. He wasn't anxious to get Arnie involved in a potentially dangerous situation; on the other hand, here was a fine opportunity to get a foot in the door of the Quest Theatre.

"He isn't an actor," he said dubiously.

"He doesn't have to act."

"And I don't think he could handle much in the way of lines."

"What lines? All he has to do is say 'Aargh' and be big. Any dope could do it." Hazel let out one of her resonant laughs. "Hell, if you were a couple of feet taller, I'd offer the part to you."

"I'll see what I can manage." Jake tried not to sound huffy and failed.

Hazel came out of the office and put her arm around his shoulder.

"Now don't take that personally, Jake. You're a nice little guy." Jake stiffened. "I mean, nicely average. Who wants to be seven feet tall?"

83

She paused for a second. "I wonder what that kid's still doing in the john. I better check. Go have a look at the end of the show."

She waddled off toward the washrooms at the end of the main lobby, leaving Jake to make his own way back to the house. He had waited too long, however. His progress was interrupted by a wave of children who burst out of the curtained doorway making enough noise to overwhelm even the most aspirin-numbed brain. Jake again recoiled against a wall and closed his eyes. The pounding in his head had almost vanished when he heard himself addressed by a young female voice.

"Are you a daddy?"

Jake opened his eyes and found himself confronted by a member of the cast, several of whom had followed the children and their parents into the lobby and were now mingling with them. The young actress facing Jake was dressed in a white pinafore with striped stockings and black patent leather shoes. She had pigtails, painted-on freckles and a lollipop, and she appeared to be about twelve years old.

"No," said Jake. "I'm a friend of Mrs. Harvey's."

"Oh." Apparently this was disappointing news.

"Sorry."

"That's okay. It's just that my friend Kathy"—she pointed out a similarly dressed urchin, who was gazing up at a real father with adoring eyes—"and I, we like to pick out the dishy daddies and get them all upset. You'd be surprised at how many guys go for the little-girl look. Once Kathy sat on someone's knee and he got all sweaty and red, just like you are now. My name's Laura."

Noting with relief that the face under the freckles, the bust under the pinafore and the hand that shook his own all belonged to someone of adult years—he guessed eighteen or twenty—Jake lost his blush and began to relax. He introduced himself to Laura and asked if she had ever worked with Bobbie.

"Oh, sure. He played opposite me in this show. He was great. Were you and he—?"

"No," Jake interrupted quickly. "I was his agent for a while."

"I was real sorry to hear about what happened to him. We missed him in the show when he stopped doing it, and around the theater, now that he's not coming in. He was so funny and nice to everybody, even Hazel when she was rotten to him."

84

"Hazel didn't like him?"

Laura took a lick at her lollipop and made sure they weren't being overheard. "Hazel's a bit old-fashioned. She just can't stand gays, which is kind of a handicap in this business, and she really hated the way he did such a good job in the box office—" At that moment, her attention was captured by a genuine dishy daddy, who wandered by in a slightly dazed condition. "Excuse me. I've got to catch that one before Kathy grabs him. Nice meeting you. Come and see me work sometime. I could use an agent too."

She hurried away just as Hazel billowed up, her clown makeup beginning to run but otherwise still going strong.

"You look like hell," she said. "Want to come upstairs for a drink or something?"

The noise and crush of people had begun to take their toll on Jake in his weakened condition. He took a rain check on Hazel's offer and began to make his departure.

"Okay," Hazel conceded, "but don't forget about the giant. We only have two more rehearsals, and we'll need him tomorrow. Will you call me?"

"I'll call you." Jake started edging away. "Nice seeing you again."

"Good seeing you, Jake. Oh, look, there's Yolanda! Don't go— you've got to meet Yolanda. Biggest bitch in L.A. *Yoo-hoo!*"

Hazel waved sweetly across the lobby to the familiar multilayered figure, now with her guitar slung over her shoulder. After a moment's hesitation, when she appeared to deliberate whether to stay or ignore Hazel's call, Yolanda slapped across the lobby on thonged sandals and allowed herself to be introduced to Jake, whom she gave no sign of having seen before.

"Jake is a famous agent," warbled Hazel, who was clearly beginning to regard Jake as a useful addition to her theatrical family.

"Then why haven't I heard of you?" Since almost all of Yolanda's face was hidden behind her screen of hair, Jake found it difficult to form a clear idea of her features, her age or just how rude she meant her opening question to be. He gave her the benefit of the doubt.

"Mrs. Harvey's being kind," he said. "I'm a transplanted New Yorker, and I'm not famous at all."

Yolanda tossed back her hair to allow a fleeting glimpse of large gray eyes, a thin pointed nose, and a clear pale complexion decorated

85

with freckles that, unlike those on Laura (who had now backed her red-faced dishy daddy into a corner), were perfectly genuine. She patted Jake's arm sympathetically.

"Yes," she said, giving Jake's arm a final squeeze before releasing it. "They're all running here from the East, deserting the sinking ship of Broadway."

"Yolanda's so quaint," explained Hazel. "She hates the commercial theater."

"I don't hate it. I despise it—writing to please the lowest common denominator, to sell the greatest number of tickets at the highest price. That's not what theater is about."

"Sounds good to me," murmured Hazel.

Yolanda shook back her hair again to give Hazel a pitying smile. "Of course it does, Hazel dear. So does ice cream and cake to these children. But no one can survive on a diet like that. The body needs good, solid nourishment, like nuts and grains and lentils, and so does the mind. That's what I believe, and that's what Mother Guitar here"—she gave the instrument in question a fond pat—"and I are trying to provide for those with the capacity to assimilate it."

In the heat of her delivery, Yolanda had almost vanished again behind her hair, leaving only the pink tip of her nose to indicate which way she was facing. This convenient pointer now turned toward Jake.

"In my work," continued Yolanda, "particularly in my recent monodrama, *Woman Alone,* I feel that I have pushed beyond the narrow frontiers of our hidebound theatrical tradition and brought new life to a stagnant art form."

She paused to allow a comment from Jake, who remarked that such a breakthrough couldn't have come easily.

Yolanda nodded. "It didn't. I had to cast away restraint and open myself and my music to my audience, holding nothing back. I had to reach deep into my living guts and spill them out, raw and quivering, onto the stage."

A literal picture of this unpleasant image floated unbidden into Jake's mind, bringing with it a sharp attack of nausea.

"Unfortunately," Hazel cooed, "there aren't too many theatergoers willing to pay money to see guts quivering on the stage."

Jake opened his mouth to announce his immediate departure, but was interrupted by Yolanda.

86

"Hazel hates my work," she stated without resentment. "Just like Hank did. She doesn't understand it, any more than he understood his responsibility as a producer and theater owner to provide a platform for voices like mine, crying the way toward the future."

"But not the way to the box office, Yolanda, dear."

Yolanda tilted her head back and closed her eyes. "You are trying to make ripples in my well of tranquillity, but you will not succeed. I don't want commercial success—"

"Just as well." Hazel nudged Jake in the ribs with a well-padded elbow.

"—and if that's all this theater means to you, then you should give up and hand it over to someone who knows how to make it socially useful."

"Such as you?"

Yolanda's eyes remained closed. "In the words of the great Brecht, 'Things belong to those who can make best use of them.'"

Hazel's eyes narrowed and her mouth tightened under its painted smile. "Don't worry, sweetie. I know how to make best use of this place. And now that it's mine, I just might let some developer tear it down and make room for some nice big health food boutique. You just make sure that turkey show of yours is ready to open on Wednesday."

Yolanda opened her eyes and gave Hazel another patient smile. "You find me a giant and we'll be ready."

"I'll get one. And you remember something: I'm in charge now, and if this show doesn't click, you're out on your ass." Hazel turned back to Jake, who observed that beads of sweat had broken out on her forehead. "I think my own well of tranquillity needs some topping up, so I'll just . . ." She looked about vaguely. "I'll be talking to you. Rehearsal's at one tomorrow."

After making a false start in the wrong direction, Hazel stopped, looked about her in mild surprise, and then retraced her steps, giving an absentminded wave as she wandered off. Jake watched her turn the corner past the box office, wondering if he should offer her a supporting arm up the stairs. But then he heard her negotiating the steps with a reasonably steady tread and felt free to make the most of his time alone with Yolanda.

87

"I hear you were the one who discovered Hank Harvey yesterday," he began.

Yolanda pulled her hair back to give him the full force of a cold look. "Yes," she said. "I came to use the piano for half an hour and there he was, sprawled over the back of a seat." She looked away. "I thought he was drunk or something, but then I got closer and . . . he wasn't."

"That must have been terrible for you." Jake thought it wise to drop in a little understanding. "What time was this?"

"About eleven thirty. Why?"

"I'm doing a little private investigating. To help the police," he added untruthfully.

Yolanda looked at him with suspicion. "I've talked to the police already."

"You called them right away?"

"More or less. I was so upset, I didn't know what to do, but when I ran out of the auditorium some of the kids from *The Magic Pond* were coming in, and they suggested calling the emergency number, so we got everybody."

Jake smiled approvingly. "It must be a comfort to know you acted quickly. I mean, if he *had* still been alive . . ."

Yolanda repositioned the strap of her guitar to sit more securely on her shoulder. "Hank Harvey was an idiot and a liability to this theater," she said coolly. "It would *not* have been a comfort to save his life. Now it's time for my meditation before rehearsal. Good-bye."

She disappeared into the auditorium, leaving Jake to escape at last into the fresh air.

It was a beautiful afternoon, warm without being oppressive, and beginning to take on an orange glow as the sun started to make its descent into the Pacific Ocean. Jake suddenly thought how pleasant it would be to sit on some quiet beach, or better still in some quiet bar overlooking that beach, and watch the sun go down. But he was too far away from the ocean, the hour was too late and—he cheered up immediately—he was due at Ginny's for dinner at eight. On second thought, even more enjoyable than watching the sun go down would be to miss it entirely by taking an afternoon nap. With this attractive prospect in mind, Jake headed back to his car, which he had left parked in the lane behind the theater. If he hurried, he could count on a good three hours in bed before getting ready to go out again.

This modest dream was not to be, however. As he turned into the lane, he realized with dismay that he would have to pass Tina and Tim, who were seated comfortably on the ground with their backs against the theater wall and their legs sticking out in front of them. They were sharing a joint. Still hoping to pass unnoticed, Jake thought of himself as invisible and put on speed.

"Hi there."

"Hi."

The two greetings, spoken almost simultaneously, acquired a force that could not be ignored. Jake mustered up a pleasant expression and faced up to his first encounter with the twins.

"Hello," he said. "I see I don't rate a sign on my car today."

A smile spread over Tina's broad face, which looked like a benevolent moon under its short Dutch bob. "Did you like it? Tim wanted to paint it right *on* the car, but I stopped him."

"I did not!" Tim's thin face turned red and he punched Tina on the shoulder with a small fist.

"Did too!" Tina punched him back.

"Ow! That hurt!"

Tina ignored the reproof and pointed at the fat half smoked joint between Tim's fingers. "If you don't want any more of that, you might pass it around."

Tim took a defiant puff, held his breath, and offered the joint to Jake.

"No, thanks; not on top of a hangover. I just heard about Hank Harvey."

"Yes." Tim finally took a breath. "We missed everything."

It was now Tina's turn to exhale. "If we'd just got back sooner, we could have been the ones to find him. It isn't fair!"

Jake risked a shot in the dark. "Hazel seems to think that Ms. Meltzer might have given Hank's ladder a bit of help falling over."

The twins looked impressed.

"We had a different idea," Tim said.

Tina dug an elbow into his side. "Don't tell him!"

"Why not?" Tim moved out of elbow reach. "We can have ideas too." He looked up at Jake. "Yesterday we all ate breakfast together in the place next door, and then Hazel went off to get the car. She keeps it in a garage up the street and she *said* she had to get help because the door was stuck, but she was gone so long . . ." He faded off delicately.

89

Tina, however, had no such inhibitions. "We thought she might have stopped in at the theater and done the job herself."

This startled Jake. "But were she and Hank on such bad terms?"

"Oh, no!" The twins spoke this together, then Tim took over. "But Hank ran the theater pretty much his way, and his productions lost so much money. It drove Bitch Hazel crazy."

Jake raised an eyebrow. "Bitch Hazel? I thought you and she were supposed to be such buddies."

"We are." Tim handed the last of the joint to Tina for a final toke. "But she doesn't know shit about theater, and sometimes she gets difficult and that pisses us off."

"Especially when she had Bobbie on her side," Tina murmured.

"I got the impression Hazel didn't think too much of Bobbie," said Jake.

"She didn't." Apparently on the verge of dozing off, Tina opened her eyes again. "But when we discovered Yolanda and *Woman Alone,* Bobbie told Hazel it was a load of crap and that's just what she wanted to hear because she was jealous that we'd discovered a genius and she hadn't. Lucky for us Hank hated the show too, so she had to put it on just to get back at him. Anyhow, that's the only time she and Bobbie were ever on the same side about anything."

"Life at the Quest seems complicated," Jake commented.

"Well, we couldn't do much with Hank." Tina hugged knees that, even allowing for the thickness of her denim overalls, could only be described as chubby. "But we can handle Hazel."

Tim got conspiratorial. "She's not stupid, though. She owes money all over the place, but she could write a book: *Ninety-nine Ways How Not to Pay Your Bills.* You've got to admire her."

"So that's why you stay here. You admire her."

The twins looked shocked. "Oh, no," they said in unison, and Tina carried on, "we love her."

"She's our pet," Tim informed him. "If it weren't for us looking after her, she'd go under just like that." He snapped grubby but delicate fingers.

"What do you mean by 'pet'?" Jake asked.

"Well, she's not really a *friend,*" explained Tina slowly. "But she's always there, and she makes us laugh, and we feel responsible for her."

"And sometimes we tease her," Tim giggled. "We've got a new game—"

"Oh, don't tell him," Tina interrupted, becoming coy and putting her hand over Tim's mouth.

"It's called—stop it, Tina!—it's called 'Spot the Star', because she lets us—"

"She lets us dress her wigs for her," put in Tina, not wishing to be left out of the limelight.

"And she doesn't care *how* she looks—"

"So we've been changing the styles from one old movie star to another, bit by bit so she doesn't notice."

"Can you guess who she is now?" asked Tim, between screams of merriment.

"Betty Grable!" shrieked the twins together, before Jake had done more than conjure up a brief image of Hazel's current confection.

"And tomorrow," Tina gasped, "tomorrow we're going to begin—"

"Shirley Temple!"

The twins collapsed in helpless laughter. Sensing that he had got as much out of them as he was going to, Jake took a moment to let them recover, then said good-bye and began to move on.

"You'd better have a look at your left front shock absorber," Tina called after him. "Your car's low on that side."

Jake stopped and inspected his pride and joy. The Thunderbird looked as always.

"I can't see anything," he said.

"If Tina says it's low, it's low," Tim cautioned him. "She knows what she's talking about."

"I'm a qualified mechanic," Tina explained, not without a note of pride in her voice. "*And* an electrician."

"She wanted to be a football player, but they wouldn't let her into the locker room."

"Shut up, Tim."

"Either that or a construction worker."

"Be careful."

"Or a lumberjack."

"All right for you! Want to know a secret about little Timmy?" Tina called to Jake, who was beginning to ease off toward his car. "He's glad Bobbie's dead—"

"I'm not!"

"—because he wants to get Bobbie's boyfriend into bed with him!"

"You traitor!"

"He says he dreams about being ravished by him." Tina laughed, easily fending off an attack by Tim with one arm. "Dressed up like a cowboy in a Stetson and chaps!"

"Fucking fat dyke!"

"Crybaby!"

Jake left them pummeling each other and sped home, his head whirling. Sure enough, the car did seem to be riding a little heavily. Terrific—another big bill that he couldn't pay. Maybe he should ask Hazel for a few of her tips—or persuade her to write that book on how not to pay bills. It should have the makings of a best seller, he thought gloomily.

Thirteen

Talking Arnie into appearing on stage hadn't been easy.

"Oh, Jeez, no, Jake. I couldn't do that."

"Only for a while, Arnie. Until they can find someone else."

"I just couldn't."

"You don't know. Maybe you'd like it. And you'd be getting out of the house and meeting new people."

"I don't wanta meet new people. Specially not actors. I'd hafta kiss them and say 'darling.'"

"Not unless you wanted to. Really."

"Please, Jake, don't ask me. I don't like to say no, specially to you, but I get so scared in front of people, and these days I just wanta be by myself for a bit. Anyways, I gotta get back to work pretty soon."

"Okay, Arnie. I understand. It's just that it would have given me a chance to hang around the theater more, and"—here Jake had played his trump card—"I thought you'd like to do something for Bobbie."

There had been a long pause, then: "Okay, Jake. Whatever you say."

"Thanks, Arnie. It won't be so bad; you'll see. Be at the theater around twelve thirty tomorrow. I'll meet you there."

"You mean you're comin' too?" Relief had come flooding across the telephone line.

"Sure. That's what this is all about."

"Gee, you're a good friend, Jake. I'd do anythin' for you."

"So long, Arnie."

Now, still feeling like the lowest kind of heel, Jake pulled his convertible up opposite a wire mesh fence at the street number Ginny had given him, scattering seven or eight local urchins who were playing catch with a baseball up and down the hillside street. Picturing the Thunderbird, just back from a paint job, with its beautiful new surface scratched or its trim stripped away or, at the very least, its windshield smashed by a well-aimed hardball, Jake hailed the largest boy in the group, who lounged over to him.

"Hi," shouted Jake, raising his voice above the shattering rock music that came blaring out of an enormous portable stereo set on a nearby lawn.

"Hi." The youth leaned against a front fender. "Nice car."

"Yeah. And I'd like to keep it that way. How'd you like a dollar to keep an eye on it?"

"Five bucks and I'll keep two eyes on it."

"Two."

"Okay. Can I sit in it?"

Since the top was down, Jake had little choice in the matter. "Sure," he said unhappily. "Be my guest." And taking what might have been a last look at the expensive new paint job and polished trim in their pristine condition, he unlatched the gate of the mesh fence, climbed four concrete steps, and set off up the garden path.

As Ginny had explained, she lived on the second floor of a small building set toward the rear of a hillside lot, on which had also been built a white stucco private house. Jake toiled up the path, past the house and through a large vegetable garden where an elderly gentleman in a straw hat was pulling weeds.

"Evening." The man nodded at Jake.

"Evening." Jake pointed at the trim white outbuilding facing him. "Mrs. Warner?"

"She expecting you?"

Jake felt himself under review and was glad he had sacrificed flash in favor of a good cotton sportshirt, a light cotton sweater and well-pressed jeans.

"Yep. I've got an invitation." He brandished a cellophane-wrapped bunch of pink roses and white carnations, purchased on the way over.

"Well, she's old enough to know her own mind. Up the steps and ring the bell." The man went back to his weeding.

Ginny seemed delighted with the flowers and, unlike Jake, had an attractive glass vase to put them in. She was shocked to hear about Hank.

"I feel like such a messenger of doom," Jake said gloomily as Ginny wiped her eyes. "Every time I see you I have another death to announce. It isn't the way I'd planned to start off a fun evening."

Ginny placed the vase with its flowers on the low glass coffee table opposite Jake. "I'd rather hear it from you than go into the theater tomorrow not knowing. And we won't let it spoil the evening. That won't help anybody. Can I offer you a drink?"

"Something gentle. What have you got in the soda line?"

"Everything: regular, sugar-free, caffeine-free, and if you want flavor-free, you can have Perrier and lime."

"The last, please. From now on I'm drinking for health."

While Ginny disappeared into the kitchen to open bottles, Jake made himself comfortable on a chintz-covered overstuffed sofa and inspected his surroundings. Although the long low living room–dining room showed every sign of having been furnished on a tight budget from local garage sales in a manner neither chic nor exotic, Jake felt happy there. The well-worn furniture, the crammed bookshelves stacked on plastic milk crates, the braided rugs on polished floors, and the row of windows with their folding yellow blinds half raised to offer an aerial view of the neighbors' rooftops all spoke to

94

him of home and family in a way that African masks and drums did not. A round dining table covered with a yellow and white checked cloth and set for two made him realize he was hungry, as did, in quite a different way, the half open bedroom door visible on the other side of the entrance hall.

Jake's thoughts had just tiptoed off on an excursion into the bedroom when they were called back by the appearance in the hall of a small barefoot figure clad in striped cotton pajamas. With the flipper of a large plush penguin clutched in one hand and a sagging elastic waistband held fast in the other, the figure marched up to Jake and glared at him from beneath a fringe of straight blond hair trimmed in a line above the eyebrows. It spoke in a clear accusing voice.

"You're not my daddy."

"No. I'm Jake. Are you Cal?"

"Yes."

"How are you?"

"Fine." Not having come prepared to indulge in social niceties, Cal took a second to shift gears back to the main purpose of his visit. "I hate you," he announced.

"That's too bad. Why?"

Before Cal could frame an answer to this, Ginny emerged from the kitchen carrying their drinks on a small tray. She set down the tray and pointed a finger at her son.

"You're supposed to be in bed."

"It's too early. I can't sleep. Why is *he* here?"

"It's not early at all, and you know perfectly well why he's here." She turned back to Jake. "This is Cal, in case you haven't introduced yourselves. Cal, this is Mr. Weissman."

Cal regarded Jake with a cold eye. "My daddy's bigger than you."

"Cal!"

"That's okay." Jake reached forward and took his mineral water, bringing himself closer to Cal's eye level. "I'm afraid lots of people are bigger than I am."

"My daddy's got an electric razor."

"Ah, well now, so do I."

"And a camera."

"So do I."

"And a gun."

"Me too."

Cal, who had freewheeled into the realm of fantasy, stopped short with his mouth open and gazed awestruck at Jake.

"Can I see it?"

Ginny saw that the moment had arrived for her to step in.

"Your father does not have a gun. Now would you please say good night and go to bed?"

"It's not fair! You didn't read to me."

"We discussed all that. You agreed that I could make it up when you come next Friday."

"I changed my mind. I want it now."

"Cal, dear, it's too late. Mr. Weissman and I want our dinner, and I've still got some things to do in the kitchen. Now, stick with our bargain: double time on Friday."

Warned by an ominous trembling of Cal's lower lip, Jake raised his hand to take the floor and offered himself as a substitute reader. Ginny looked doubtfully at Cal.

"Isn't that nice of Mr. Weissman? How about it?"

"Do I still get double time on Friday?"

"I don't see why you should, but all right."

"Okay. Come on." Summoning Jake with a jerk of his head, Cal turned about and started retracing his steps.

Jake followed him through the hallway into a narrow bedroom that looked out onto a grove of trees behind the house. Despite its small size, Cal's room had been ingeniously laid out to provide a considerable amount of usable space, with built-in shelves, a table, two chairs and, in one corner, a raised bunk bed set above a low base that incorporated a child-size clothes cupboard, an open storage chest and an access ladder. Cal tossed his penguin up onto the bed, got a firm grip on his pajama bottoms, and began to climb the ladder.

"That's my daddy," he said, pointing to a poster-size photograph on the wall opposite the end of the bed, mounted next to an equally large version of the same subject executed in brightly colored felt markers. Both were lit by a small night-light set on top of the table.

Jake studied the poster. Enlarged from a snapshot taken in some amusement arcade, it showed in grainy detail a sunny-faced young man, blond like Cal, with light-colored eyes and a wide smile that revealed a set of even white teeth. He was a perfect example of a type that Jake envied and disliked in equal measure.

"He looks very nice," he said, nobly putting baser thoughts aside.

"Yeah." Cal had reached the top of the ladder and was crawling up to the head of the bed. "But he never comes to see Mom and me, so I guess he doesn't like us anymore."

"I'm sure he does." Jake had found an open book on the table and was now sitting in a small armchair. "He's just found something he has to do, and he can't get away."

Cal yawned and rubbed his eyes. "That's what Mom says, but I don't think she means it. Have you really got a gun?"

"Yes, I really do."

"Can I see it some time?"

"Maybe." Jake already regretted his boasting. "Guns are dangerous things. I keep mine locked up. Are you under the covers?"

"Yes." The springs under the bed stretched rhythmically as Cal bounced up and down.

"Okay." Jake adjusted the light and inspected the book. It was *The Wind in the Willows* and it had a bookmark inserted at chapter six. "Here goes: 'Chapter Six,'" he read, "'Mr. Toad. It was a bright morning in the early part of summer; the river had resumed its wonted—'"

"What's 'wonted'?"

"Normal. 'The river had returned to its normal banks and its accustomed pace—'"

"What's 'pace'?"

"Um—speed." Jake got the message that Ginny must have subjected the text to some fast editing as she went along, so he began again: "'The river had returned to its usual level and speed and the hot sun seemed to be pulling everything green and bushy and spiky . . .'"

A few minutes later, when she looked in to announce dinner, Ginny found her son fast asleep in bed and Jake in a similar condition slumped back in his chair, mouth open and head resting against the wall under the picture of her soon-to-be-ex-husband. In any comparison that she might have cared to make between the sprawling sleeper, who just then let out a light snore, and the fresh-faced laughing young man in the poster above him, Jake could hardly have emerged as a winner. He did, however, have one advantage over his adversary: he was there—a fact not lost on Ginny, who after many painful months of breakup and separation from Hal found it an unexpected pleasure to be in her son's bedroom waking up a man with a storybook on his lap to announce that dinner was ready.

97

Several hours later, having been fed a superlative meal followed by the best coffee he had tasted that year, Jake considered and regretfully put aside the possibility of making a pass. But the groundwork had been most enjoyably laid, and he sensed that a future meeting on his own territory might yield rewards satisfactory to both Ginny and himself.

"This has been a great evening," he said, finishing his fourth cup of coffee and standing up to leave. "I still feel stupid about falling asleep on Cal."

Ginny put down her cup and stood up too. "He's used to it," she said. "I do it myself all the time, and I can tell you from experience that he fell asleep before you did. Otherwise you'd have been wakened up smartly and told to go on. Cal has a deadly aim with Percy the Penguin."

"He's a nice kid."

"I think so. But he misses his father, as you heard."

"Does he never see him?"

Ginny bit her lip. "No. I've written and written, asking him to visit, just for Cal's sake. But he's never answered or shown up." She ran her hand back through her hair in a hopeless gesture that went straight to Jake's heart. "I don't know. Maybe it's for the best now. He doesn't look like that picture anymore—he might just frighten Cal. But I wish he'd try."

Jake sensed some of his groundwork slipping away. "It sounds like you still miss him a bit yourself."

Ginny shrugged. "Sometimes I wonder. I say I don't, but then I think if we could just go back . . ." She smiled. "But we can't. And in a few weeks we'll be single people again, so that will be that. Thank you for coming. You're the first person I've had over since the split-up, and I've enjoyed it."

Jake made a short formal bow from the waist. "I'm honored. I've enjoyed it too."

Ginny ducked her head, then met his eyes. "I'm sorry I haven't . . . That is—oh, hell, it's so dumb, but I still feel so married. I guess I've just been alone too much. Will you come again?"

"Whenever I'm asked." Jake leaned over and brushed a light kiss on her cheek. "But I'll ask you first."

Ginny put her hand to her cheek and blushed. "Good night."

98

Running lightly down the outside stairs, Jake felt pleased with him-self. He was even more pleased to find his car still in one piece, with solid tires and no dents. He drove home in a more optimistic frame of mind than had been granted him in many months.

A bare fifteen minutes later, back in his parking space at the Man-darin, he sat frozen behind the steering wheel of the Thunderbird in a state of shock. From a tree on the other side of the lane, Hector let out a long mournful wail. Jake desperately wanted to do likewise, but instead rifled once more through the sickeningly familiar contents of the car's glove compartment. Maps, Kleenex, chamois cloth, old sun-glasses: all were there. The gun, however, was not.

Jake closed his eyes and tried to make a mental list of all the places where someone could have had access to his car during the past few days. They seemed endless. In addition to its present location, the car had been parked outside the downtown police station, Arnie's, the Quest Theatre, the Parkhill Memorial Chapel, several supermarkets and the flower shop on Cahuenga before ending up outside Ginny's, where any of the kids who had been running about in the street might have got into it. The very thought sickened Jake. Could some of those kids now be playing with a loaded gun? And would any of them admit it if Jake were to go to the police and ask them to conduct a house-to-house survey? The answer, he knew, was no—unless the worst hap-pened and the gun went off, in which case it would most certainly be traced back to the owner of the flashy red convertible that had been parked outside Mrs. Warner's. Jake opened his eyes and fled indoors.

Anyhow, he thought as he got ready for bed, going to the police would accomplish nothing. The gun would never be found. Moreover, as it was unregistered and he had no licence, he would only bring down the wrath of the law on himself and Baron by reporting its loss; and the gun, which could have been stolen in any of a dozen places, would remain as lost as ever. Anyone who had gone to the trouble of picking a locked glove compartment and stealing a gun was not likely to be the type of person who would hand it over sweetly, even if Jake or the police knew whom to ask. The thief was probably just some petty criminal who had taken a chance looking into a sporty car for something to sell. Unless, of course, he had a more specific objective.

Lying wide awake in bed, Jake broke out into prickly beads of sweat as three thoughts he had been trying to suppress pushed themselves ruthlessly forward into his caffeine-activated mind. The first was, could he himself now be under surveillance by whoever killed Bobbie, and perhaps Hank as well? If Arnie had been correct in his guess that someone was searching almost imperceptibly through his apartment, then perhaps that same stealthy person had used the same talents to open the locked glove compartment. And if this were the case, might it be a warning, a cool hint dropped by a killer who might be starting to tire of the clumsy amateur bumbling about in his wake, and who might be tempted to get rid of this annoyance if it ever came too close? This was Jake's second worry. His third was that sooner or later Baron would discover the loss of his gun and that this, too, could prove fatal.

These gloomy thoughts produced a restless night, and it was not until the sky had started to lighten and Hector had long returned from his arboreal vigil that Jake's beleaguered mind began to shut down. Gradu- ally, while the early morning birdsong seemed to recede farther and farther into the distance, his sense of awareness softly contracted into a small core of being, located somewhere in the center of his chest. And as the last birdcall faded away, all physical sensation faded too, leaving Jake floating in a disembodied fashion a few inches above himself and the bed. He hovered like this for a moment; then his last spark of consciousness flickered, went out, and released him into sleep.

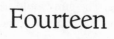

Fourteen

Three hours after he had drifted off to sleep, Jake once again lay wide awake in bed suffering from an attack of nervous agita- tion. This time his unsettled state was caused not by a guilty conscience but by a new alarm clock.

The clock had been purchased some weeks ago in response to a promise on the box that Jake would be awakened each morning by a "cheerful birdlike chirp." To one who shied away from loud noises and jumped like a rabbit when subjected to any sudden report, this small miracle of modern technology seemed to offer a whole new outlook on the difficult business of starting the day. No more would he find himself waking half an hour early in order to disarm the fire alarm bell in his old clock before it went off and shattered his peace of mind for the morning; instead, he would be eased gently into consciousness by something he imagined would resemble an electronic exultation of distant larks.

What he got was more along the lines of a whooping crane, better suited to announcing a nuclear meltdown than quarter past eight in the morning. So Jake had reverted to his preventative strategy of early waking and spent the extra time before having to get up in regretting the overhasty disposal of his old clock and the unnecessary expense of the new one. On this particular morning, having been taken by surprise in a stupefied condition, he concentrated on lying quietly with his eyes closed, waiting for his rattled brain to regain its equilibrium and his pounding heart to resume its normal action.

Jake got through the next hour and a half on automatic pilot and managed to arrive at his office door without having once raised his eyes above half mast level. However, when he opened the door and stepped across the threshold into the reception area, his heavy eyelids snapped open as if on springs.

For a moment he stood transfixed, convinced first that he was experiencing a hallucination brought on by too much alcohol and too little sleep, and then, more rationally, that he had blundered into the wrong office. By squinting, he was able to read the gold letters on the door, which reassuringly spelled out his own name. It was his office, sure enough, but his office transformed. On the floor, covering the cracked linoleum tiles, lay a pale green shag rug, dotted with specks of black and white. The area where three plastic stacking chairs had once waited to receive clients was now occupied by a black-vinyl-covered sofa with seat cushions upholstered in lime green nylon fur. A lace net curtain on the room's single narrow window obscured its dismal view of a grimy brick wall, while beneath the window a ruffled chintz skirt concealed the rusty metal shelving unit upon which the familiar coffee maker still stood. Matching ruffles surrounded Miss Murphy's desk, now partially given over to a collection of small pottery animals in assorted colors, a large vase filled with red and white plastic roses, and a stereo radio that was serving up mariachi band music at high volume; and on the wall behind the desk hung two posters from the Mexican National Tourist Council, large framed photographs of Baron and John Travolta, and an oval mirror surrounded by a plaster garland, each painted flower of which incorporated a sequin in its center. The sequins reflected glints from the leaded-glass facets of a star-shaped lamp hanging over the desk, and the mirror gave Jake a rear view of Miss Murphy's head, which was otherwise hidden behind a glossy hairdressing magazine that featured on its front cover an equally glossy young couple, both with identical metallic blond hair and smouldering expressions.

Jake crossed the room and turned down the radio. Miss Murphy emerged from behind her magazine and greeted him with a radiant smile.

"Teddy Bears! You come back!"

"What have you done to my office?"

Miss Murphy surveyed her handiwork with a pleased expression. "I bring the woman's touch. Pretty, no?"

Jake rubbed his tired eyes with one hand and then looked about again. Nothing had changed. He moved both hands behind his back where he could clench them unobserved.

"It's very, very . . ." He hesitated and was lost. "Very colorful. And lively."

Miss Murphy smiled and waited for more.

"And of course I appreciate all the trouble you've gone to—"

"No trouble." Miss Murphy went over to the window and poured out coffee into a ceramic mug. "When I move out of my apartment, I just bring some things here." She handed the mug to Jake, who was then able to read his name written on the side. He had never owned a mug with his name on the side.

"Thanks," he said. How could he fire someone who made such good coffee or who had just—

"You gave up your apartment?"

"Sure. How can I afford apartment on the lousy salary you pay? So I move in with my sister, but I spend most time with my boyfriend Baron, or here, to be alone."

"I see."

"Good idea, eh?"

102

"Well." Jake flapped his arms up and down against his sides as if preparing to take off. "Yes. But you won't be alone here a lot. I'll be coming back to the office full time pretty soon."

Miss Murphy became excited. "You find out who kill Bobbie?"

"No. But I will. Or someone will. And then there'll be people coming to see me. Clients and actors and writers and producers . . ." He petered out.

"And you think maybe they think you got kind of crazy office?"

"Well. Yes."

"Forget it. The more crazy you get, the better they like you. Trust me." Miss Murphy looked critically at the rings surrounding Jake's eyes. "You eat this mornings?"

"I don't think so."

"Go sit. I bring you breakfast." Miss Murphy pulled aside the curtain on the shelf unit to reveal a bread box, a small assortment of jars and cans, and an electric toaster oven.

"Everything but the kitchen sink," croaked Jake weakly, as he headed into his office. "And a refrigerator."

The apartment-size refrigerator sat on a low table in the far corner of the room, next to a wheeled clothing rack on which hung an assortment of dresses, skirts, coats, blouses and sweaters. Shoes for these outfits rested on metal slats set into the base of the framework.

Jake sank down into the chair behind his desk. Like Miss Murphy's, the desk wore a fabric skirt, although one with a more subdued pattern of mustard-colored autumn leaves. Cushions on the leather-covered sofa and the imitation-leather-covered clients' chairs echoed the same shade of mustard, and Jake noticed that the top of his desk had been used to accommodate the overflow from Miss Murphy's collection of pottery animals. Three small donkeys glazed in ice cream shades of pink, blue and green, respectively, stood on a stack of papers, letters and, doubtless, bills, all waiting for his attention. He sighed.

Before Jake had time to do more than clear away the donkeys, Miss Murphy breezed into the office carrying a white plastic tray on which were arranged fresh coffee in an oversize red mug, three pieces of toast on a matching plate, a plastic rose in a glass bud vase, a folded napkin, two knives and two spoons. To these she added a glass of orange juice, a jar of raspberry jam, a dish of butter and a container of yogurt from the refrigerator before depositing the tray in front of Jake, who regarded it with astonishment.

"Murphy, that looks great—but I'm supposed to be on a diet."

Miss Murphy gave him a pat on the head. "Don't worry about diet," she said. "You eat good breakfast, you do good work, make money, *and* lose weight, all at once. Trust me." She headed for the door. "I read in beauty magazine."

Miss Murphy was wearing a short flounced dress of peasant design, and as she clicked out of the room on high-heeled sandals, Jake could not help deriving a certain satisfaction from the fact that his new secretary, in addition to her other attractions, had the best pair of legs since Betty Grable, with ankles that made—well, even Clare's, for instance, look positively utilitarian. This unkind thought cheered Jake up considerably, and after clearing the tray of everything edible, he set to work on his backlog of mail.

It was not as bad as he had expected. In addition to the inevitable bills, there were a few incoming checks for clients who had appeared in television commercials and, in one case, an unexpected miniseries rerun. When deposited in the bank, Jake's commission from these would cover some of his more uncomfortable bills, as Miss Murphy had tactfully suggested in a short memo, accompanied by the appropriate outgoing checks, filled in and ready for his signature. There was also a contract to be read for an otherwise unexceptionable client who, much to Jake's surprise, had obtained a small but not insignificant part in a new play at the Mark Taper Forum. After Jake had waded through this, dictated his comments on it to Miss Murphy, and selected several more clients whose photo-résumés should be submitted for the upcoming production of *Greenwillow,* he congratulated himself on doing a good morning's work.

On his way out to meet Arnie, he found Miss Murphy sorting through a pile of eight-by-ten glossy photographs, each representing a different young lady wearing an enticing expression and the currently popular exploded hair style. It seemed as if all the photographers in town had rushed out in a body to invest in powerful wind machines.

"How'd you like to take Baron to a first night on Wednesday?" he asked. "Nothing glamorous, but there's an admirer of yours in the cast."

Miss Murphy continued her sorting. "I got lots of admirers," she said coolly. "Which one you mean?"

"Your pal Arnie. He's filling in as the giant in *Shootout at Shiloh* at the Quest."

Miss Murphy stopped sorting. "Why you let him do that?"

"Why not? He's the only giant I know, and he's giving me a reason to spend time at the theater."

"What if somebody hurt him, like Bobbie?"

"Nobody's going to hurt him." Jake felt neglected. "If anybody's going to get hurt, it'll probably be me."

"That's okay then." Miss Murphy went back to her eight-by-tens. "We come and watch."

"Just so long as you don't go asking for a refund if I survive."

"You mean we got to pay? Forget it."

"It's on me." Jake drew himself up to his not very imposing full height. "I'll put it in my will in case I don't make it to Wednesday."

Miss Murphy gave him a fond smile. "You look so cute when you go like that."

"Like what?"

"I don't know how you say. Tight-ass?"

"Thanks, Murphy."

Miss Murphy waved her hairdressing magazine at him. "When you get thin, maybe you like to go blond like this. My sister do it for you cheap."

"No thanks, Murphy."

"Blonds have more fun."

"I'm having a ball right now. So long."

Miss Murphy blew Jake a kiss as he made his exit; but, being too intent on achieving a relaxed John Wayne walk, he failed to notice.

In the lobby of the Quest Theatre, where autumn seemed to hold perpetual sway, Jake found Arnie pacing to and fro amidst the hanging baskets and fallen leaves, jingling his keys nervously.

"Somebody oughta talk to these here plants," he remarked while shaking Jake's hand. "They look pretty sick. Do I hafta do this?"

"Not if you really don't want to. I just thought—"

"I know, I know."

"For Bobbie."

"Yeah." Arnie took a deep breath. "Okay, where do I go?"

On their way into the auditorium, they met Hazel and Tim descending the stairs from Hazel's apartment. As a couple, they could hardly have presented a more striking contrast. Tim, wearing semitransparent white pants, a T-shirt that had been cut off and fringed at midriff level, and a suggestion of eye shadow, became radiant at the sight of Arnie. Hazel, enveloped in a purple muumuu, looked drawn and ill under a hairpiece that had begun to show just a hint of the famous Temple ringlets at each side. Inhaling deeply from a cigarette in her right hand, she steadied herself against the wall with her left as she peered shortsightedly at Jake through diamanté harlequin spectacles.

"Is that you, Jake? I can't find my contacts and I don't see too good through these damn glasses. Who's that with you?"

Cut off in mid speculation as to why Hazel, who had disliked Bobbie, seemed to get on so well with Tim, Jake introduced Arnie and explained that he was the new Goliath.

"Oh, yeah, I remember." Hazel moved closer and gazed up at Arnie with eyes that seemed to be fighting against the weight of their heavy artificial eyelashes. "My, you are a big one, aren't you?" she asked admiringly, giving one of Arnie's massive biceps a trial squeeze.

"Yes'm," mumbled Arnie, beginning to back up across the hall in an agony of bashfulness.

"Work out, do you?"

"Yes'm."

"Well, that's real good. You sure got the results. I like a man with a build, and believe me I've seen the best." By way of lascivious punctuation, Hazel took a deep drag on her cigarette and collapsed in a fit of coughing.

"Mrs. Harvey was a swimmer in the movies," Tim supplied helpfully, when Hazel had been patted on the back and more or less restored to normal.

"Aw, he's too young to know anything about that," said Hazel, wiping her eyes with a tired ball of Kleenex. "But I had a good figure too in those days." She moved in closer to Arnie. "Every guy in Hollywood had the hots for me."

"Uh . . ." By this time, Arnie had been brought to a halt with his back against the wall.

Jake took pity and stepped in. "I guess they must be looking for Arnie at rehearsal by now," he suggested.

Hazel gave him a sharp look. "Don't worry, I'm not after your pal's body. What does he want with an old bird like me when he can have, well—"

"Anybody he wants," murmured Tim, moving smoothly between them. "Hi. My name's Tim. I was at the service last Saturday."

"Oh, yeah. How ya doin'?"

"Just fine. Come on with me and I'll introduce you around. How often do you have to work out to keep all those beautiful muscles?"

"Uh, every day," said Arnie, casting a backward glance of despair at Jake as he allowed Tim to lead him away.

"My God! That's too much!"

"Not if you wanna get big."

"You look big enough already."

They passed through the curtained arch into the house so that only their muffled voices floated back to Jake and Hazel.

"Aw, I can build up a lot more if I really push myself. In three months I'm gonna be *huge*."

"I can't wait. Everybody, look what I've got! Here's our new giant. Isn't he *lovely*?" Tim's voice disappeared in a general hum of conversation.

Jake turned to Hazel. "I don't feel good about this. That poor guy hates being here."

"What the hell, it won't kill him." Hazel took a final pull at her cigarette, looked about for somewhere to dispose of the butt, and ended up by tossing it on the floor. "We need some more ashtrays," she commented, grinding out the still glowing ember with the toe of a rather shredded gold lamé slipper. "*If* we ever make any money again."

Jake felt he ought to be in the auditorium, giving Arnie moral support, but Hazel too seemed to be in need of some propping up. "Business not so hot?" he asked.

"Business lousy." Hazel fumbled vainly in her pockets for a cigarette. "We always used to do okay on weekends, and in the collection box after I made my curtain speech. You ever hear me do my curtain speech? Well . . ." She gave up her search. "Say, you haven't got a— no, that's right, you don't. Well, it's the usual crap about 'Hope you enjoyed the show, tell your friends, nonprofit organization, hard to make ends meet, put your contributions in the box on the way out.' All that stuff. But it used to work. Now . . ." Hazel leaned back against the wall and closed her eyes for a moment. Then she opened them and straightened up. "Well, I guess things are tough all over," she continued more cheerfully. "But I'll bet we'd be getting on better if we had

107

that fairy back in the box office. It sure was a dumb thing to do, bumping him off."

Jake's stomach muscles instantly tied themselves up in a knot. If ever there was a time to be cool—"It sure was," he agreed. "So why do it?"

Hazel gave him another of her quick, sharp looks. "Now isn't that the sixty-four-dollar question?" she asked sweetly. "I've wondered about that myself." She had another fit of coughing. "I better go upstairs and lie down. I don't feel too great. You go keep an eye on your big friend. See you later."

But before Hazel could turn and begin to climb back upstairs, her attention was caught by a small black boy of eight or nine who had just come into the lobby and was now standing motionless at the base of the steps leading up to the box office. He had a coiled length of rope in one hand, and he was hoping that by remaining perfectly still he would not be noticed; however, as soon as Hazel's eye fell on him, he lit up with a wide smile and came bounding up the steps.

"Hi, Miz Harvey. Look what I can do." And with a brave air of careless nonchalance mixed with nervous concentration, he adjusted a slipknot at the end of the rope and began twirling the resulting noose into a perfect airborne circle, first horizontally over the floor, then vertically in front of himself, and finally horizontally again over his head. "Pretty neat, huh?" he asked, letting the noose fall over his shoulders. "I been workin' at this all day, real hard, nonstop, and before I knowed it—"

"—you were late for rehearsal again." Hazel frowned down at the budding Will Rogers. "You know what I told you yesterday. You *have* to be on time for rehearsal, or we'll just let you go and give the part to some other lucky little boy." She turned to Jake. "Kevin here is our David, but we have *lots* of little boys who are just dying to get up there onstage and sing and dance and get to shoot a giant."

"Aw, hell, how can I shoot a giant when we ain't got one?" asked Kevin in an aggrieved tone. "We still ain't rehearsed the end, and now that big turkey's got hisself all banged up in the hospital."

"If you'd got here in time, you'd know that we've found a *wonderful* giant, a friend of Mr.—er, Jake's here, and even bigger than poor Carl."

Kevin looked unconvinced. "I hope he's smarter. What a dope! No lines to remember," he explained to Jake, "and he still always come in at the wrong time and fall over things. Man, that poor dude has more accidents in a day than other folks do in a year. Except last Saturday wasn't no accident."

Jake's inner workings went into spasm again. "What do you mean no accident?" he got out in what he hoped was a casual manner.

"Kevin, they're waiting for you," began Hazel.

"Shit, everybody know about it," broke in the irrepressible Kevin. "Ol' Carl, he driving home after rehearsal, *vroom, vroom*"—here Kevin did an impression of old Carl behind the wheel—"and the road go left and he go straight ahead—kaBOOM!—into this big ol' palm tree and totals the car and damn near hisself."

"Thank you, Kevin, we all know that." Hazel was again leaning on the wall with her eyes closed. "Now I'm sure Ms. Meltzer is looking for you."

"Okay." Again Kevin addressed Jake. "But if this new guy's a friend of yours, you better look out for him, because the way I hear it that wasn't no accident. Someone go foolin' around with his steerin' wheel and brakes so poor ol' Carl, he turnin' this way and that and pumpin' up and down on his brakes and that car still run into that tree. Ka-BOOM! If he been goin' just a little faster, he be dead by now."

Hazel opened her eyes. "Where did you hear that?"

"I hear lotsa things." Kevin made his eyes round and innocent. "I hear the cops when they come Sunday mornin'."

"Well, you heard wrong." Hazel glanced nervously at Jake. "That's just a silly story, so stop spreading it around. Now go on in and see what they want you to do."

"Hey, don't come down on me! I just thought this guy oughta know—"

"Kevin!"

"Okay." Kevin gathered up his lasso and marched off toward the house. "But don't say you ain't been warned."

With the coast clear, Jake exploded. "Hazel, I can't believe what I just heard. What the hell are you playing at? You get me to railroad Arnie into taking this part, and now I find out that the guy who had it before was sabotaged. What's going to happen to Arnie? No, never mind. I'm pulling him out right now and sending him home."

Hazel flapped a hand soothingly in Jake's general direction. "Don't get all worked up, Jake. Kevin's got a vivid imagination. Hell, he's a sharp little liar. You can't believe what a kid like that says; and even if it were true, what's it got to do with your pal? Take my word for it, he's safe as houses."

"That's easy to say—"

"Look, he doesn't know anybody here. He's just come in to play a little part in a dopey kid's show. Who's going to have it in for him?"

"I wish I knew. Who had it in for Bobbie and Hank?"

"Hank was an accident. Bobbie's a whole different story."

"So tell it to me."

"Jake, I feel rotten. I gotta go to bed."

Impulsively, Jake put a hand on her arm as she started up the stairs. "Hazel, if you know anything, you should tell me. Or the police."

Hazel jerked her arm away with such force that she careened back against the wall. Gathering herself together, she glared back at Jake. "Get offa my back, will you? I got enough problems without having to put up with every two-bit, half-pint agent who wants to come in here and start throwing his weight around. If you're so worried about your fag friend, then take him home. Just don't come whining around me. I got enough worries. Everybody thinks I don't know what's going on here, but I do. Well, what are you waiting for? Fuck off!"

And with an extravagant gesture of dismissal that almost sent her reeling back down the stairs, Hazel grasped the folds of her muumuu with one hand, took a secure hold on the banister with the other, and began her slow ascent, punctuated with regular gasps and the odd groan.

Jake watched the departing figure until it was out of sight, wondering what he had done to provoke such an outburst. That he had touched a tender nerve, he had no doubt; but as to the nature of the nerve, he had no idea. The only thing he felt sure of was that Hazel most certainly knew something that would be of use to him and that he had better pry out of her as soon as possible. He was trying to work up sufficient courage to follow her upstairs and pursue the matter further when Tina materialized at the entrance of the house.

In her usual working attire of plaid shirt, overalls and work boots, Tina presented a formidable figure to Jake's increasingly wary eye. He estimated that inch for inch and pound for pound she could wipe the floor with him, if it ever came down to hand-to-hand combat. Come to think of it, Hazel too had it all over him in terms of height and weight. He was surrounded by amazons. But these sudden physical qualms subsided as quickly as they had flared up, partly quelled by the benevolent sparkle in Tina's eyes and the amused expression that animated the very feminine features of her round face.

"You better come and watch," she informed Jake. "Meltzer's having trouble getting through to Arnie. The situation has possibilities." Whereupon she vanished behind the drawn curtains, leaving Jake to pull himself together, put down a swarm of nagging worries that had begun to dance like gnats around his already guilty conscience, and follow her into the theater.

◆━■━◆

Fifteen

◆━◆

Walking in on a rehearsal brought out in Jake the same feelings of insecurity that arose when duty compelled him to visit a client backstage. Despite his status as a recognized, possibly even necessary member of the theatrical community, with every right to look in from time to time on the doings of those he represented, he still felt like some intruder who, blundering into the midst of an ancient mystery, might at any moment be discovered, denounced, and torn limb from limb, or at the very least firmly ordered out of the theater. The fact that nothing of this nature had ever happened did not prevent Jake from experiencing an acute attack of anxiety as he stole quietly into the house, tiptoed over to a remote back-row seat in a shadowy corner, and slowly eased himself into it.

When the seat failed to collapse noisily under him and no one made a pointed announcement to the effect that the rehearsal would not continue until all outsiders had left the theater, Jake began to unwind and attend to the situation before him. The signs were not encouraging. Standing on one side of the stage, red of face and sweaty of body, an unhappy Arnie faced a group of four actors arranged in attitudes of fear and apprehension on the opposite side of the stage. Yolanda Meltzer surveyed this tableau from a third-row-center seat. Tension had pulled her shoulders so close together that they almost met behind the canopy of hair that fell over them, and from his vantage point at the back of the house, Jake caught the flash of stage lights on white knuckles as Yolanda gripped the back of the seat in front of her.

"No, Arnie dear. That's still not quite right." Yolanda spoke in strangled tones of repressed emotion, bringing up the words from the depths of her chest. "It has to be louder. *Much* louder. You are Goliath Jones, the biggest, meanest, cruelest, most terrifying gunman in the West. So you have to *sound* terrifying. Subhuman. Like an animal." Yolanda took a grasp of air and raised the pitch of her voice a little. "Now I want you to try it again. It isn't difficult. Just relax and let go. Like this: AAAARGG!"

Arnie paled and took a step backward. His round blue eyes became even rounder. Yolanda recovered her equilibrium and spoke encouragingly.

"There. There's nothing to it. Now let's have a really loud roar. AAAARGG!"

Arnie closed his eyes. "Arg," he said, weakly.

"AAARGG!"

"Arg."

"No, Arnie. Try looking ferocious. Make a terrible face. Look at this: AAARGG!"

"Oh, Jeez."

"Come on, we haven't got all day. Give me something *fierce!*"

Arnie took a deep breath and pulled his eyebrows a quarter of an inch closer together. "Arg."

"AAA—oh, my God," croaked Yolanda. "My throat feels like sawdust. Tina, be a darling and get me a Coke from next door."

A sulky murmur came from backstage.

"Did you say something, Tina dear?"

"I want to stay and see what happens," came the reply.

112

Yolanda threw her head back and stared at the ceiling. "So do I, so do we all, but we're not holding our breath. We will all be as you left us when you get back. I guarantee it. Now go!"

"Bitch!" This was followed by the slow tread of heavy work boots and the slamming of a door.

Yolanda continued her inspection of the ceiling. "I don't know what I'm going to do. I really don't."

"Let *me* show'm, Miz Meltzer!" Kevin bounced onto the stage with his twirling rope neatly coiled over one shoulder. "I kin show *anybody* how to roar. Look, Arnie, you just git a bunch of spit in the back of your throat and start your tonsils shakin' and let go." Whereupon Kevin let go. The sound seemed impossibly loud to be issuing from such a small source.

"Stop!" cried Yolanda, her hands over her ears. "That went right through me," she added, when Kevin cut himself off in mid roar.

Kevin looked pleased. "That's what my mom says. She says she kin hear me five blocks away. Maybe we'd get to the shootout sooner if *I* roared backstage," he suggested hopefully.

"Thank you, dear. I know you mean well, but I don't think the audience could take that." Yolanda slumped her head back again. "I know I couldn't. Now just go back there and be patient."

"Shit. The way things is goin' around here, it looks like I ain't never gonna plug that sucker." Kevin kicked the stage with the toe of his sneaker and marched off.

The pianist, who had been sitting through all this in a posture as upright as her instrument, with hands in her lap and a cigarette between her lips, now removed her cigarette, coughed hesitantly, and said, "Nanda," in a faint whisper that could barely be heard above the animated chatter that had broken out onstage.

Yolanda carefully raised her head to avoid any sudden surprises from a crick in the neck and looked toward the piano.

The pianist gave a nervous smile and continued. "I've had a little idea. I mean, nothing, really—"

"QUIET, EVERYBODY!" Shouted Yolanda, producing an instant silence onstage and an acute attack of hand fluttering at the piano. "Miss Hruska has an idea."

All eyes turned toward the piano bench, as its occupant took a miserable look behind her to assess the possibilities of flight and then

113

began to toy nervously with the piano lid. "Well—" She stopped to clear her throat. "It really isn't anything. I mean, I was just thinking that, maybe, well—"

"Oh, Kitty, do get on with it!"

"I was just thinking that if Mr. Siganski isn't up to roaring, then perhaps I could do it for him on the piano. Like this." She executed a rising and falling arpeggio on the lower register of the piano.

Yolanda sat up. "Do that again."

The effect was reproduced.

"I like it!" Yolanda stood up and ran over to the piano. "I love it! Kitten, you're a genius!" Kitty smiled modestly and gazed up at Yolanda with reverent eyes. "An absolute genius. What would I do without you? Everybody"—Yolanda had now taken up a center aisle position, the better to address the stage—"everybody, here's what we'll do: instead of Goliath roaring, the piano will do it for him, and he'll be even more terrifying because *he'll never make a sound!* Arnie, what do you think of that?"

Every eye turned toward Arnie, who thought for a second and then asked, "Does that mean I can go home?"

"No, it doesn't. We're going to go through the whole finale again. Unless you want to do the end of act one. Do you remember when you come on there?"

"When the girls scream."

"Good. The girls scream, you walk on, we hit you with a red spot, and curtain. I think we'll be all right there."

Arnie looked uneasy. "Nobody said nothin' about hittin' me."

"With a red *light*. You won't feel a thing. Now we're going back to the finale. Arnie, you're offstage over there. Boys, upstage left. Girls, downstage a bit to the right of them. Good. All right, here we go. Who's *that?*"

In glancing behind her, Yolanda had caught sight of Jake huddled down in his shadowy corner. She glared through the gloom in his direction, while Jake rapidly assessed his chances of leaving the theater unrecognized before being thrown out. There were no chances at all, so he was forced to smile, wave, and say "Me" in his most relaxed professional manner. "Jake Weissman. We met yesterday."

Yolanda leaned forward and squinted. "Oh, yes, the agent. Nice of you to drop in."

Jake experienced a sudden thrill of surprise and pleasure as if he had succeeded in executing a dangerous spying maneuver. He permitted himself to relax a little more.

"I don't usually allow an audience during rehearsal," continued Yolanda, putting Jake's defense system back on alert. "Are you here on business?"

"Just keeping an eye on my client," said Jake, with an airy wave toward the stage, where all the actors began looking about eagerly to see which among them had been keeping an agent under wraps. "Mr. Siganski," he added, to forestall the question trembling on the tip of Yolanda's tongue.

"He has an *agent?*"

"Oh, yes." Jake began to enjoy himself. "Mr. Siganski is very much in demand." Another question hovered in the air. "All kinds of things. Commercials, industrials . . ."

"But not theater?"

"Not yet."

"Well!" Yolanda began with a small explosion, then paused, changed her mind, and began again on a softer note. "Well, we're getting ready to do the big shootout finale"—a shout of "Yay" came from Kevin backstage—"where I have achieved a synthesis of the tonal mode that represents the youth and innocence of David"—("That's me!" from backstage)—"with the atonal style that I have used in the rest of the score, including my own part as Narrator. Now if everyone is ready,"—the actors, who had begun chatting again, pulled themselves back into position—"we'll begin from 'When will this killing ever cease?' Kitty, dear, let's have the death motif."

Kitty obliged with a series of doom-laden dissonant chords that made Jake wince and slide down in his seat, and the action proceeded along the following lines:

GIRL 1
(Clasping hands beneath her chin and singing earnestly in what, to Jake's untutored ear, sounded like a series of unrelated notes plucked at random from a variety of scales)
Oh, when will this killing ever cease?

GIRL 2
(Ditto) Did we bring our children into the world for this?

115

BOTH

To be gunned down in the street like dogs!

MAN 1

The sheriff has hightailed it out.
Who can save us from the terrible Goliath Jones?

At this point, with a grinding of stylistic gears, Kitty modulated into a melody expressive of youth and innocence that brought Jake back up in his seat and Kevin, as David, onstage at a run.

DAVID

(*Taking up a foursquare center position and belting out in a piercing voice:*)
Hey, man
I can.
Gimma a chance and I'll do the job.
Don't fret
No sweat
I'm gonna plug that eight-foot slob!

Here Kitty pounded out the "death motif" again to bring Yolanda, with closed eyes and an ethereal expression, into the proceedings as Narrator.

NARRATOR

(*Intoning hollowly to her own dirgelike accompaniment on Mother Guitar*)
And the people all said:

MEN

Beat it, kid,
You're just a little boy.

NARRATOR

And the people all cried:

GIRLS

Go home, David.
You can't kill a man with a toy!

116

NARRATOR

And the people all laughed:

ALL

Ha, ha, ha!
Ho, ho, ho!

Kitty now produced her pianistic roar, causing everyone except David to recoil in the attitudes of fear and apprehension witnessed earlier by Jake.

GIRL 1

What was that?

GIRL 2

It's past noon. Big G's comin' fer the shootout.

MAN 1

Bad news!

MAN 2

Yeah, let's split.

GIRLS

But who's gonna take him on?

MAN 1

Not me!

MAN 2

Not me!

NARRATOR

(*Very solemn, with a dash of piety*)
And an innocent shall save them from the forces of evil.

DAVID

Hey, man
I can—

NARRATOR

And the lamb shall devour the lion.

                            DAVID
Don't fret
No sweat—
(*A louder rumble from Kitty.*)

                            MAN 1
Scram, kid! Save yourself!

                            MAN 2
Here's Big G now!
(*An even bigger rumble. General terror. A dramatic pause.*)

                            NARRATOR
(*In a particularly patient voice*)
Goliath, that's your cue.

                            GOLIATH
(*Peering around the edge of the proscenium arch*)
You mean I'm supposed to come on?

                            NARRATOR
Yes, please. Mark over there says "Here's Big G now!" and then
you swagger on.

                            GOLIATH
I was waitin' for the girls to scream.

                            NARRATOR
No, dear. That's the end of act one. We are now at the end of act
two. The finale. Where you meet David. That's Kevin here. You
remember that? Where you draw your gun?

                            GOLIATH
(*After a moment's thought*)
Oh, yeah. Where you yell, 'Draw!'

                            NARRATOR
Exactly.

                            GOLIATH
Except I ain't got no gun.

                            118

DAVID

(Joining in)
Yeah, me too. How can I plug him if I ain't got no gun?

NARRATOR

We're getting guns. *(Calling offstage)* Tim, where are the guns?

TIM

(Calling back)
I've got two for tomorrow.

NARRATOR

There. We've got guns. Now can we get on with this? From
'Here's Big G now!'

MAN 2

Here's Big G now!

NARRATOR

And I want to see Goliath swaggering onstage looking *mean!*

After a short pause, Goliath sidled onstage, cast a panicky look in
Jake's direction, and came to an abrupt halt, standing rigidly to attention.

KITTY

(From the piano)
Did you say something Nanda?

NARRATOR

(Through clenched teeth)
No, keep playing.

(Another rumble)

DAVID

(Springing to life.)
Hey, Big G, you're three minutes late!
I'm takin' you on—

GIRL 1

David, don't!

119

Not with that peashooter!

DAVID

(Triumphantly producing a clenched fist and a pointed forefinger)
—with my Colt thirty-eight!
(Sensation onstage!)

NARRATOR

Goliath, draw! Your end is near!

Looking very pleased with himself, Goliath followed David's example and pointed a forefinger at him.

NARRATOR

David, shoot! The way is clear!

DAVID

BANG! *(Aside to Goliath)* That's where you fall down.

With barely a moment's hesitation, Goliath overbalanced on his heels and tipped backward like a felled tree. The crash was impressive.

ALL

(Singing happily)
David, David,
How did you learn to shoot so straight?
David, David,
You and your!—COLT!!—**THIRTY-EIGHT!!!**
(General rejoicing and a shower of hats. David with one foot on Goliath's chest, grinning proudly. Tableau.)

"And hold it," droned Yolanda. "And curtain." The curtain closed. "Applause, applause, applause. Curtain opens." The curtain opened. "And hold it. Now break for bows."

The cast lined up along the front of the stage and made small bends from the waist as the curtain closed behind them.

"Fine," said Yolanda. "Tomorrow I'll set the full bows when we have all the cast. Where's Goliath?"

Everyone looked about vaguely as Yolanda heaved a large sigh and called, "Curtain open!"

The curtain parted to reveal the prostrate form of Arnie, still flat on his back on the stage.

"Oh my God!" said Girl 1, whom Jake now recognized as Laura from yesterday's matinee.

"Is he dead?" whispered Girl 2, her friend Kathy.

They all clustered around Arnie.

"I didn't do it," protested Kevin, to no one in particular. "I just said 'Bang!'"

Kathy knelt down by Arnie's side. "Well, anyway, he's still breathing."

"He must have hit his head."

"Lift his legs."

"I thought you weren't supposed to move people."

"That's just, like, in traffic accidents."

"Try rubbing his wrists."

Tim wandered onstage. "I can do mouth-to-mouth."

"Don't you wish!"

"He's coming to!"

Arnie opened his eyes and gazed in a puzzled fashion at the toes of his sneakers hovering mysteriously above him. The two boys holding his legs up now lowered them to the floor.

"Are you okay, Arnie?" asked Laura, who had been delegated a wrist to rub.

"Sure," said Arnie. He turned his head sideways and looked over to Yolanda, who was sitting with bowed head, her forehead resting in the palm of one hand. "Did I do good?"

Jake slipped out of the theater as silently as he had come in.

Sixteen

J ake entered a lobby that appeared to be deserted until he passed
the box office window and saw Ginny inside, reading at her desk.
Sensing Jake's presence, she looked up and closed her book.

"How's the rehearsal going?"

"It's over." Jake propped himself up on the ledge of the ticket window. "Arnie just knocked himself out in his death scene."

Ginny looked alarmed. "Is he all right now?"

"Oh, yes. It was the best acting he did all afternoon."

"That doesn't sound promising."

"I never made any promises. How's business?"

"As usual. Slow."

"Can I have a couple of tickets for Wednesday? My secretary's
bringing a friend to Arnie's debut."

Ginny made a note on one of the seating plans in front of her and
handed Jake a pair of tickets.

"On the house. Compliments of Mrs. Harvey."

"Thank Mrs. Harvey for me."

"Not on your life." Ginny lowered her voice. "The word is out: she's
having one of her bad spells. It pays to keep away."

"I saw her just a while ago. She'd been hitting the bottle."

"I don't know what she does, but it can get bad. Tina and Tim are
the only ones who can handle her."

"They're welcome. Are we having dinner tonight?"

"Can't. I'm a working girl."

"Even working girls have to eat. I'll pick you up at five and get you
back at six."

"I'm not dressed."

"You look great." She was wearing white jeans and an oversize yellow sweatshirt that fell off one shoulder. "In fact, better than great. We'll go to Hampton's and eat through the salad bar."

"Really, Jake. I have to stay here. That's what I'm paid for, and with Hazel out of action, maybe—"

Ginny broke off as Yolanda came striding into the lobby with Kitty at her heels. Catching sight of Jake, they made a small procession over to the box office.

"Your client is a rotten actor," Yolanda announced. "I don't believe he could do even a commercial to save his life. He's ruining my oper—my musical," she corrected herself.

"I'm really very sorry about that." Jake put on his smoothest manner. "Please feel free to call in any other giant you happen to know of."

"You know damn well it's too late for that," mumbled Yolanda, searching a well-chewed thumbnail for something to nibble on. "I don't know what to do with him. He can't fall down properly, he can't roar, he's probably got muscles where his brains should be. He can't even frown!"

Kitty paused in the middle of attempting to light a cigarette unnoticed. "He's not that bad, Nanda. With makeup and a costume and lighting . . ." She faded off.

Yolanda was not to be soothed. "*And* he can't remember his cues. Look," she said, thrusting a thick blue binder into Jake's hands, "here's a script. Read it through with him a few times. And please, *please* teach him how to fall."

"I don't know how to fall," replied Jake, truthfully.

"It's easy. You just bend forward a little and then tip back on your—your—"

"Ass," said Kitty helpfully.

"Backside. There's nothing to it."

"Then why don't *you* teach him? You're the director."

"I haven't time. Kitty and I have an appointment at the Temps Perdu Coffeehouse to interview the author of their new play."

"It's called *Tender Relations*," Kitty explained. "All about incest and cannibalism in Manhattan. Nanda wants to turn it into an opera."

"What a subject!" said Ginny, who had come up to the ticket window to join in the conversation.

A spark of animation leapt into Kitty's otherwise placid eyes.

"Nanda can make *anything* wonderful," she said defiantly. "If people would just let her get on with it."

Yolanda gazed thoughtfully off toward a distant horizon. "I see the play as a challenge," she mused. "A grain of sand on which to construct a pearl. Raw clay that my music can bring to life by adding an extra dimension, a new level of tenderness and horror."

"And a few laughs wouldn't hurt," added Jake lightly, bringing down on himself a pair of icy stares from Yolanda and Kitty. "Has anyone seen Arnie?" he asked hastily, to change the subject.

"Tina and Tim took him away to check on wardrobe," Kitty volunteered in a distant voice. "He says he can bring his own boots and jeans, but they want him to try on the chaps they made for Carl."

"Anyhow," said Yolanda, in tones of distaste, "can I take it that you will get your . . . *client* into shape for tomorrow?"

Jake caught the barb in her voice and turned stubborn. "No. I don't have time either. I'm taking Mrs. Warner out to dinner."

"But I have to work tonight, Jake," said Ginny, taking a wicked pleasure in watching Jake flounder. She smiled innocently at him. "Don't you remmember?"

"There you are." Yolanda wrapped the subject up briskly. "You can go over everything with Arnie when you get home."

"I don't go home with Arnie." Sensing Ginny beginning to laugh in the safety of her office, Jake climbed onto his high horse, which rocked dangerously beneath him. "We don't live together," he announced grandly.

"Oh." Yolanda looked nonplussed and traded a quick glance with Kitty. "I just thought that, well, why else would you want to represent someone like that?"

"It takes all kinds, Ms. Meltzer. One man's meat." This was not a promising line of development, and Jake wisely abandoned it just as Arnie shot out of the dressing room door into the lobby, closely followed by Tim, who appeared to have acquired a strange pear shape under the pink kimono he kept wrapped about himself.

"Come on, Arnie. You haven't tried the chaps."

Arnie backed away, looking hunted. "They'll be okay."

"They look too short."

"I'll wear'm low."

Tim started to wheedle. "It'll just take five minutes."

"I got a date," stammered Arnie, perspiring freely.

124

"Who with? I'll scratch his eyes out."

Once again, Arnie found himself at bay against the lobby wall. He looked about desperately for help.

"Jake!" The floor shook heavily as Arnie lumbered over to Jake and took a firm grip on his arm. "Jeez, I'm sorry. I din't mean to make you wait so long."

"That's okay," said Jake, who felt the lower part of his arm going numb. "I wasn't—"

"So let's go."

"I was just—"

"Jake's takin' me out to dinner," explained Arnie to his interested audience. "Then we're gonna have a drink with the guys at Boys Town—"

"Arnie!"

"—or someplace. So we gotta run. C'mon baby, let's *go!*"

And before he could protest further, Jake was half carried out onto the sidewalk, pushed into Arnie's small white Datsun, and driven away at top speed.

"I'm real sorry, Jake," said Arnie, as he wove expertly through the late afternoon traffic, wearing a hangdog expression.

Jake sat slouched down in his seat with arms folded across his chest. He stared straight ahead out of the window. "That's okay."

"It was just—he got me under the stage where they keep all these costumes. And there was candles, and then he come out in this dumb little white dress with sparkles on it and blond hair—"

"My God!"

"And I hadda get out and I know I shouldn'ta said that about us goin' to Boys Town, but I couldn't think of nowheres else."

"Don't worry about it. That's what agents are for."

"And the 'baby' just slipped out. I don't want you to be mad at me, Jake."

"I'm not, Arnie. Honest. Where are we going?"

"I gotta bring some clothes tomorrow to wear in the show, so I need my bag I left at the depot when Bobbie din't show and I got worried and forgot it." Without taking his eyes off the road, Arnie fumbled for a Kleenex and blew his nose loudly. "It won't take long; then I'll drive you back to your car when nobody's lookin'."

"Nice bag," Jake commented twenty minutes later, after Arnie had made his way back from the drivers dispatch office and deposited a handsome piece of leather-trimmed soft luggage in the back seat.

125

"Yeah," said Arnie, waving to a security guard, who waved back and raised a heavy steel barricade to let them out of the wire-fenced enclosure. "It was the first thing Bobbie ever give me. It's too good for me, but I like it 'cause it makes me think of him." He turned onto the freeway behind a massive eighteen-wheeler that had preceded them out of the enclosure.

"What's it like driving one of those big things?" Jake asked.

Arnie managed his first smile of the day. "Kinda scary when you first start, but you get used to it."

"I wouldn't," said Jake, who still approached backing up and parallel parking with a certain dread.

"Oh, yeah. After a while it gets just . . . just like you was part of the rig. And then you kinda know inside what it's doin'." Arnie risked a quick look away from the road to see if Jake understood him. "That don't come right away. But when you got it, it feels great."

"Even on a long trip?"

"Sure. But I don't do too many of them. Just up to Canada every now and then."

The soft rocking motion of the car and the warmth of the late afternoon sun made it increasingly difficult for Jake to keep his eyes open. He began to drift into a comfortable state of drowsy torpor.

"How long does that take?" he asked in a flat voice as he dully watched Arnie's collection of keys swinging to and fro on a metal ring suspended from the ignition key in the dashboard. At regular intervals, a glint of sunlight caught a long flat key resting on top of the spring clip Arnie used to hang the collection from his belt loop. The flat key was smooth and silver and satisfying to contemplate, and the flicker of sunlight on it encouraged Jake to lower his eyelids.

"Coupla days, if I drive real hard." Arnie's reply seemed to make its way back from a great distance. "'Course, I don't mind that, 'cause I got a real nice place to stay when I get there. Bobbie found it when he come up with me once. It's cheap, but they feed me good and Bobbie pays—well, he used to, when I got home. They always ask for him, and we was goin' back sometime. . . ."

Hypnotized by the swinging keys and overcome by a need for sleep after his restless night, Jake gave up the struggle to keep awake. His head fell forward on his chest in a series of drooping nods; and as Arnie's calm monotone wove itself into the soothing hum of the car engine, Jake slipped peacefully into dreams of a city of mountains and

126

lights and beaches and cheap hotels run by friendly people with limited English and names like McLean or McLure or—

Jake woke suddenly. They were parked at the side of the Quest Theatre, just behind his own car. He turned and gave Arnie a sleepy grin.

"I must have dropped off. How long have we been here?"

"Five, ten minutes. I din't wanta wake you up."

"Thanks." Jake executed the best stretch he could manage in the confined surroundings. "I didn't get much sleep last night."

"Me neither. I ain't used to sleepin' alone yet." Arnie consulted the face of his black metal sports watch. "You wanta eat dinner out someplace?"

Jake considered the matter. He had several options open to him, the least attractive of which was to spend the evening teaching Arnie how to survive dying onstage. Instead, he could go back into the theater and make another unsuccessful attempt at enticing Ginny out for a meal at the risk of having her regard him as a persistent bore with nothing better to do. Or he could try another night out on the town at the risk of feeling a total wreck tomorrow. Or he could go home and spend an exciting evening in front of the television with Hector. Or—

"Sure," he said, and immediately felt ashamed of his grudging acceptance when he saw how it lit up Arnie's round serious face. "Anywhere you like. Then we'll go back to my place and I'll give you a lesson on how to get shot. There's nothing to it. You just lean forward a little and then tip back on your ass."

<hr />

Seventeen

<hr />

"What happen to you?" asked Miss Murphy when Jake hobbled into the office the next morning.

"You have nice times with Hector?" she suggested as

she carried a mug of coffee into Jake's office just in time to catch him carefully lowering himself into his chair with a wince and a groan.

"Hello," said Miss Murphy, waving a hand up and down in front of Jake's eyes. "Anybody home in there?"

She stroked Jake's cheek, then ran her hand back over his ear and through his hair. The pulse point on her wrist gave off a warm scent: spicy, with a hint of musk.

"You want breakfast?"

Jake turned his head to speak and found himself staring down the front of Miss Murphy's extremely low-cut blouse, where far too little in the way of material was fighting a losing battle to restrain Miss Murphy's far superior forces. Jake's reaction was not lost on Miss Murphy.

"Or maybe you want something else."

"Murphy," said Jake hoarsely, "don't do this to me. I spent all last night falling on my ass and I'm in pain and I'm deprived and I'm ready to pop. So unless you want to pull down those window blinds and clear my desk and join me on top of it, you'd better keep your distance."

"Why, Teddy Bears," exclaimed Miss Murphy, who had already backed a step or two away. "I thought you all worn out with Hector."

"Hector's a cat, Murphy. I need a woman, and I can't hold out much longer."

Miss Murphy began a slow smile that gradually achieved full-blown radiance.

"Birds do it," continued Jake passionately. "Bees do it. Even Klein across the way does it. Let's do it, Murphy."

"Oh, Teddy Bears!" In one fluid movement, Miss Murphy joined Jake on his side of the desk, twirled him around in his chair, and plumped herself down on his lap. Jake's grunt of agony was interpreted as rapture. Miss Murphy began covering his face with kisses.

"Oh, Teddy Bears," she repeated, deftly removing Jake's glasses. "I know all the time you want me," she whispered, just before inserting her tongue into Jake's left ear.

"Murphy, the blinds!"

"Who care?" cried Miss Murphy, artfully shifting her weight on Jake's knee in a way that brought exquisite satisfaction. "Oh, my sweet, brave Teddy Bears!"

At this point, the décolletage of Miss Murphy's blouse, having fought the good fight, surrendered gracefully by retreating to a point beneath her lower ribs. The effect was stunning.

"My God," breathed Jake, plunging into this lush new territory.

"Oh, yes," gasped Miss Murphy, who had succeeded in unbuttoning Jake's shirt and was now alternately kneading his chest and embracing his head. "Oh, Teddy Bears, take me. We no care what happen. We go together. What's wrong? Why you stop?"

"What do you mean 'we go together'?"

"Nothing. Kiss me."

"And calling me brave," continued Jake out of the corner of his mouth, which was once again clamped against Miss Murphy's.

"Nothing. Forget I say." Miss Murphy began planting kisses on his eyes.

"Murphy, tell me the truth."

Miss Murphy began to pout. "Oh, Teddy Bears . . ."

"The truth, Murphy." Jake got a hand on each of Miss Murphy's shoulders and gave her a shake.

"Well," began Miss Murphy, hiccupping when Jake shook her again. "Well, my boyfriend Baron, he say he kill me if I have the sex with you."

Jake was touched that Miss Murphy should think him worth dying for. On the other hand—

"You said something about going together."

"Then he kill you."

"Oh, shit." Jake's racing blood now slowed down to a walk. "How's he going to find out?"

"He ask me."

"Couldn't you lie?"

"Sure I lie, but he find out anyway."

"How?"

"I get rash here." Miss Murphy indicated an enticing area between her breasts that now failed to kindle quite the same fire in Jake.

"You wouldn't lie to me, would you?"

"You see any rash?"

Alas, there was not a single mark on the smooth, honey-colored skin.

"Get up, Murphy."

"Maybe he no kill us. Maybe he just beat up a little."

"We'll never know." Jake raised his eyes to the window and met the

129

envious gazes of Messers. Klein, Klein, and Smith, who were lined up at the window of their conference room on the other side of the air shaft. "You'd better pull your blouse back up," he added, as Klein, Klein, and Smith reluctantly tore their eyes away from Miss Murphy and pretended to be watching a passing jet.

"You mean we never going to make love?"

"Not until Baron stops getting jealous or you stop getting your rash."

"You one big coward." Miss Murphy straightened her skirt and prepared to return to her own desk.

"Cowards live longer, Murphy. Now let's have the mail and some fresh coffee. This has gone cold."

"I know how it feel," said Miss Murphy, marching out of Jake's office.

Moments later, Jake's mail was slapped down on his desk. Coffee, however, did not follow, and a deep chill that had nothing to do with air conditioning seeped under Jake's door from the outer office.

Jake managed to get through a coffeeless morning and even accomplished a respectable amount of work without the help of any stimulus beyond that provided by pride and a stubborn nature. Having checked over a couple of contracts, approved them for signing, made up a list of clients who should be sent off to certain forthcoming auditions, and had a satisfactory conversation with a friendly casting director who agreed to consider one of Jake's more talented clients for a minor role in a multipart television space epic, he felt that he had earned a reward before lunch. He picked up his telephone, obtained an outside line, pushed buttons, and made a firm resolution to allow a maximum of six rings.

On the ninth ring, he got a click and an out-of-breath "Hello."

"Ginny?"

"Jake! Just hold on a minute, please." There followed the sound of deep breathing.

"I feel like I've tapped into a filthy telephone call," said Jake, becoming aroused for the second time that morning.

"Sorry. I was just getting my key in the door when the telephone rang, and I ran up the stairs with my grocery bags."

"Then let me make it worth the climb. I didn't do very well with my dinner invitation yesterday. What are my chances for tonight?"

"Up to an hour ago, wonderful." Ginny now had her breath back and was able to speak without gasping.

"That sounds bad."

"I hate to keep on saying no, and I don't want you to give up on me, but I really can't help it. My in-laws called this morning to say they'd like to come into town tonight and see me. They sounded a bit odd and wouldn't say why, so of course I told them to come."

"Do you think something's wrong?"

"Oh, maybe it's just the divorce coming final and they want to talk me out of it."

"How about lunch, so I can argue the other side of the case?"

"That's out too. I've got to do some cooking for tonight, then get to work early and ask Hazel if I can leave by seven or so." Ginny sighed. "She won't like it, but we're closed to set up the new production tonight, so there won't exactly be crowds at the box office."

The time had come to give up graciously. "I'll see you later at the theater, then," said Jake. "I'm coming to hold Arnie's hand."

"How did the falling lessons go?"

"Just like Ms. Meltzer said, there's nothing to it." Jake shifted uncomfortably in his chair. "Of course, I can barely sit down, but I think we've got the problem licked. He also knows his cues. I even tried to get him to say 'aaarghh' with conviction, but that was going too far."

"Yolanda will love you."

"I doubt that. I don't think she even likes me."

There was a brief hesitation, then, "Well, I like you, Jake. See you later." And Ginny hung up.

Jake had just a few seconds to savor the small glow of satisfaction kindled by Ginny's good-bye when his door opened and Miss Murphy made an aggressive entrance.

"What that woman got that I don't got?" she demanded.

"Stop listening to my telephone conversations."

"What else I got to do out there?"

"That's your problem. Keep off my line." Jake began sorting out some of the pages lying on his desk.

"Why you like her better than me?"

"Maybe because she doesn't have a hoodlum boyfriend who makes death threats."

Miss Murphy considered the matter. "How about I tell Baron to get lost?"

131

"No!" said Jake quickly. "Don't do that. Leave things the way they are."

"How about I sleep with you and tell Baron I fall in poison ivy?"

"No," Jake said again. "Really, Murphy, it wouldn't work. I shouldn't have made that pass at you, but you're a very attractive woman, and I had a weak moment, and I'm sorry. I was wrong. What we need here is a nice, quiet, professional relationship, so let's try and keep it that way, okay?"

"I get the turnons when you go all red like that."

"Well, you'll just have to learn to live with it. And oh, yes—" Jake fumbled in his pocket and produced the tickets Ginny had given him. "Here are those seats for tomorrow's opening. Have you told Baron about it?"

"He say bor-ing. I go with you."

"No, you won't. Tell him it's about this overgrown thug who terrorizes a whole town. He'll eat it up."

"But—"

"If anyone calls, I'm having lunch at the Blue Parrot. Then I'm going to the dress rehearsal at the Quest. See you tomorrow."

And in order to forestall any further discussion with Miss Murphy, Jake shut the office door firmly behind him, sped past two dark-suited Japanese businessmen waiting for an elevator, and ran down five flights of stairs to the ground floor lobby, where he was forced to sit for several minutes until his heart stopped pounding, his breath returned, and his legs felt capable of carrying him down the street to the Blue Parrot Café.

In the past, it had been Jake's custom to recover from difficult mornings by treating himself to lunch at the local Brown Derby. Although no longer a preserve for spotting film personalities in their natural habitat, this living embodiment of Hollywood's legendary heyday nevertheless offered an irresistible opportunity to combine good food with a nostalgic trip back to a more formal past, where in Jake's star-struck imagination ladies still lunched in furs and hats with veils, attended by gentlemen who still dressed like their fathers in suits with wide shoulders and floppy trousers. But these elegant ghosts no longer dined on Vine Street, now that their favorite meeting place had closed its doors to the public and, in an appropriately cinematic final gesture, burned itself down to a gutted shell.

132

Jake mourned this sad event as an act of malice aimed at him personally and refused to take comfort when a new Brown Derby appeared on the corner of Hollywood and Vine, occupying space that had once offered refreshment to the public under another famous name. Somehow, he could not imagine sharing a table with Greta Garbo at Howard Johnson's. It all seemed very unfair, and Jake kept his sense of loss honed to a fine edge by a system of protest based on the shaky premise that if he could no longer exorcise his difficult mornings at the restaurant of his choice, he would give in to them utterly by patronizing the worst eating place he could find. So far, he had found nothing worse than the Blue Parrot.

It was therefore with a sense of gloomy satisfaction that Jake entered the unprepossessing establishment and found its dark brown atmosphere, stale odor and plastic décor unchanged since his last experiment in self-mortification. Also unchanged was the unappetizing menu, encrusted here and there with desiccated samples of past daily specials, which had its usual effect of reducing his appetite to zero. While attempting to select something other than dessert that would allow him to get through the afternoon without having to go home and lie down, Jake became aware of a popping sound in his left ear. The sound issued from a wad of gum in the jaw of a bored waitress, whose yellow smile button informed any interested reader that its wearer's name was Gloria and that she wanted him to have a good day. After executing a few more virtuoso pops, Gloria heaved a sigh and shifted her weight from one foot to the other.

"You gonna make up your mind?" she inquired. "Or should I come back next week?"

Jake hastily decided on a chef's salad and, as he watched Gloria march off to the kitchen to collect it, began to wonder if perhaps the time hadn't come for him to stop sulking, abandon his protest, and find a decent place to have lunch. His answer arrived with suspicious speed in a wood-grained plastic bowl where a few damp strips of pressed turkey, boiled ham and processed cheese rested limply on a mound of chopped lettuce awash in salad dressing. On one side of the bowl, an underripe strawberry and a slice of dry orange made an inadequate gesture in the direction of subtropical bounty. Jake removed this offering, carefully buried the turkey, ham and cheese under a layer of lettuce, and ordered dessert.

A man could starve in this place, he thought, as his fork failed to make even a dent in the petrified slice of pecan pie that Gloria had dropped off in his general vicinity. He made a few more stabs in an attempt to dislodge a pecan or two, but each glistening kernel clung limpetlike to its rocky setting. Abandoning his twisted fork and all hope of food, Jake contemplated the pristine triangle under his nose and wondered how the original pie had ever been divided. They must have jumped it as it came out of the oven, he decided. Either that, or someone in the kitchen had a buzz saw.

Coffee arrived. It was hot and drinkable but too late to lift Jake's spirits. Not for the first time, he closed his eyes, slumped down in his unpadded chair, and longed to be back at the Brown Derby amidst the sprays of white foliage, chandeliers, soft banquettes and framed caricatures that decorated the warm little world it had been his pleasure to inhabit four or five times a month for the duration of a leisurely lunch. His favorite location had been a corner overlooked by the likenesses of Greer Garson and Walter Pidgeon, whom he imagined having intimate little lunches together, perhaps in that very corner, laughing at a choice bit of studio gossip or accepting a call from Louis B. Mayer on a white telephone brought to their table by a smiling, star-struck waiter.

Jake still regretted that he had never discovered whether, in the unlikely event of his being called during lunch, a telephone would have been brought to him too. It seemed the height of debonair sophistication to make a light excuse to one's companion—"Sorry, Greer darling; I don't know *how* they find me"—and then accept one's fascinating call over a hallowed line that had once vibrated to the ruthless tones of Harry Cohn or a Warner brother. He imagined that such a call, had it ever come, would have initiated a turning point in his career, a step up to the big time, since none of his regular contacts would have had the nerve to come riding in to the Brown Derby on a white telephone. Nothing less than M-G-M, he mused, or ABC, or a client catapulted to megastardom, or—

"Your name Jake Weissman?"

Jake snapped his eyes open. Gloria had crept up behind him on silent rubber-soled feet.

"You got a telephone call," she announced, adding "over by the counter," as Jake, whose mind still lingered in a more exalted sphere, waited blankly for the white telephone to appear on his table.

Jake reluctantly returned to the Blue Parrot and started to blush. "I don't know *how* they find me," he said, in what he hoped was a convincingly debonair manner. Gloria rolled her eyes and returned to the kitchen.

Doing his best to convince himself that the call of a lifetime could just as easily make its way over a humble instrument, Jake walked over to the cashier's counter, near which the receiver of a pay telephone swung slowly to and fro at the end of its metal-wrapped cord. This was humble indeed, but the important thing was to keep on hoping. Jake picked up the receiver.

"Hello?"

"Jake, is that you?"

Jake stopped hoping.

"Hi, Arnie. What's up?"

"I gotta see you. Are you comin' over to the theater?"

"I'm just on my way. What's wrong?"

"Can't talk on the phone." Arnie's voice wavered. "Please, Jake, I gotta see you now. I'll be in my car in the alley. Can you make it?"

"Sure. Ten minutes."

"I'm real worried."

"It's okay, Arnie. Take it easy. We'll talk."

"Thanks, Jake. See you."

Arnie hung up, and Jake, invigorated by the prospect of some new development that might help raise his investigation off the ground, headed quickly out onto the street in the direction of his car. Halfway to the parking lot, however, he remembered that he had neglected to pay for his uneaten meal and was brought to a halt on the sidewalk by a crisis of conscience, in which opposing inner voices conducted a battle as to whether he should follow the path of honesty or give himself the rich satisfaction of carrying on to his car and allowing the Blue Parrot to whistle for its money. At last, a third voice joined the argument, pointing out that Gloria knew his name and, in the absence of a tip, would doubtless take great pleasure in turning him in to the police.

Jake turned on his heel and retraced his steps.

Eighteen

When Jake pulled into the alley behind the Quest, he found Arnie's Datsun, with Arnie inside in a state of seige. Tina and Tim, dressed in their painting overalls, had propped themselves up against the car, one on each side of the driver's window, and were engaged in animated conversation, more with each other than with Arnie, who sat huddled up behind the steering wheel clutching his overnight bag to his chest with both arms. He looked red and hounded, but cheered up when Jake got out of his car and joined the little group.

"Well, here's Mr. Weissman at last," boomed Tina, giving Jake a roguish look.

"We thought you'd never come," said Tim. "Poor Arnie's been just pining away."

"Wasn't," muttered poor Arnie, staring straight ahead and getting redder.

"I don't know how you do it," Tim remarked to Jake, while keeping a calculating eye on Arnie's rising blush. "I keep throwing myself at him and he won't even talk to me, when all you have to do is whatever it is you do, and his little heart goes all fluttery."

"Doesn't."

"I guess he just wants to try someone older," sighed Tim. "Or rounder—ow!" he yelped as Tina, who had moved over beside him to make room for Jake, drove a hard elbow into his side. "Stop doing that!"

"Don't listen to Tim," Tina confided to both Arnie and Jake. "He always goes too far. What you get up to together isn't any of his business."

Jake was getting used to this line of teasing. "We don't get up to anything," he said, glad that no one had seen them doing backfalls the night before. "Arnie and I have a good agent-client relationship."

Tina smiled brightly. "I'm sure you take care of him very well."

"Or maybe Arnie takes care of Mr. Weissman," giggled Tim, jumping clear of Tina's fast elbow. "How about it, Arnie—do you take care of Mr. Weissman?"

"Oh, Timmy, shut up!" said Tina, trying not to laugh too. She turned to Jake. "We want Arnie to come and show what clothes he's brought, but he won't get out of the car."

"I gotta talk to Jake," mumbled Arnie.

"It won't take long," Tim began to coax. "Then we can make the alterations before tomorrow."

"I ain't goin' under that stage again."

"Arnie's afraid of me," observed Tim to Jake.

"I ain't."

"He won't even get out of the car. He just wants to sit there and hug his security bag." Tim looked closer at the article in question. "Not your style at all, Arnie. Far too chic. I bet Bobbie gave you that."

"So what if he did?"

Tina stepped in again. "You should just slap Tim down when he gets like this," she advised Arnie. "I do."

Arnie made a head-to-toe assessment of Tim. "If I slapped him down, he wouldn't get up again."

Tim rolled his eyes. "Promises, promises."

But Tina clearly felt that her physical prowess had been slighted. "I bet you're not that much stronger than me," she said huffily. "Let's try some Indian wrestling." She placed a well-developed right arm in position on the ledge of the open car window. "Come on—I dare you!"

Arnie hunched down in his seat. "I ain't wrestlin' with no woman."

"What's that got to do with it? Come one—one, two, three!"

"I hate to break up this party," Jake interjected, "but I came here to talk with Arnie before rehearsal starts, and you two obviously have some painting to finish." He indicated several cutouts of giant cacti propped up against the wall and partially covered with a bright green shade that matched the latest splashes on the twins' overalls.

"Oh, there's no hurry," drawled Tim. "The rest of the set won't be finished in time anyway."

"It never is," explained Tina. "The Harveys are so cheap, there's only one designer left who'll work for them."

"Wet Set Willie," said Tim.

"'Do you want it done now or do you want it done right?'" they mimicked together.

"But we'll leave you two alone anyway," Tina said graciously. "Come on, Tim. We know when we're not wanted."

"Do we?"

"Yes, we do."

"Why does nobody want us?"

"Maybe you should put on some muscle."

"Maybe you should take some off. Ow!"

They wandered away punching each other.

Jake walked around to the other side of the car and got in beside Arnie.

"Tina was right," he said kindly. "You shouldn't let yourself be bullied or teased if you don't like it. Tell them to beat it when they start bothering you. Get mad a little."

Arnie gave Jake a hangdog look. "I can't do that," he said apologetically. "I can't get mad."

"You were good and mad last week in my office."

"That was different. That was for Bobbie."

"Well, stick up for yourself. Stop being a doormat."

"Okay, Jake. Whatever you say."

Suspecting that he had somehow been outmaneuvered, Jake decided to get on with business. "What was it you wanted to see me about?"

"Oh, yeah." Arnie, who had begun to relax a little after his encounter with the twins, now tensed up again. "It was somethin' that happened at home just before I called you."

"Not somebody in your apartment again."

"How'd you know?"

"Arnie, I *told* you to get the locks changed."

"I did!" Arnie protested. "Honest to God, Jake, just like you told me, but listen: I went to the gym this mornin', and when I got home I was climbin' the stairs outside when I remembered I forgot this bag in the back of the car from last night, and I knew I was goin' to need it. So I clum down again and went back to the garage to pick it up. And when I was there . . ." Arnie paused for dramatic emphasis and to catch his breath. "When I was in there I thought I heard footsteps comin' down the stairs fast, so I run around to the front of the house, but when I got there, there wasn't nobody around."

"Maybe your downstairs neighbor?"

"No," Arnie pressed on. "That ain't the end. When I'd looked around, I went upstairs again and put my key in the lock—and the door just swung open on its own. And I *know* I locked it when I went out."

"Anything missing?" asked Jake.

"No."

"Or out of place?"

"Uh-uh."

Jake had no further suggestions to make. "Well, somebody seems to want something from you. But if nothing's missing, we can't know what—or who."

Arnie looked surprised. "But that's why I called you, Jake," he said. "I do know who."

Jake's heart did a backflip. "Arnie, this is the moment where the witness always gets shot in the movies, just before he spills the beans. Tell me quick—who was it?"

"It was Miz Harvey."

"Hazel?" Jake tried and failed to picture Hazel as a housebreaker, skipping up and down stairs. "You saw her?"

Arnie hesitated. "Well, almost."

"What's 'almost'?"

"I seen her car. When I got inside and started huntin' around—you know, to see if anythin' was gone—all of a sudden I heard this engine start and wheels skid and I run to the front window and seen that big pink car of Miz Harvey's headin' down the street like a bat outta you know where."

"But you didn't see who was driving?"

"Yeah!" Arnie thumped the steering wheel, causing a small earthquake inside the car. "It was some guy in one of them English hats. You know, like we got hangin' up at home."

"A bowler?"

"Yeah, that's it. And sittin' beside him was Miz Harvey. Nobody else got hair that color, or wears them things with flowers all over."

"Well!" Jake's head swam from this unexpected revelation. "Hazel the Housebreaker. I wonder how she got in." His eye moved to the dashboard ignition lock, where the shaking car had set Arnie's key collection swinging to and fro. "I didn't see you wearing your keys at rehearsal yesterday. Did you have them on you?"

"Not exactly." Arnie began to look sheepish. "I knew I was goin' to have to fall and I din't want to land on all them sharp points, so I put them in my jacket pocket."

"And you left your jacket. . . ?"

"In that dressin' room place."

"That's it, then." Jake ran his hand back through his hair to aid his thinking. "You were hanging around the stage area all through the rehearsal. She could've taken the keys, got them copied, and put them back in your jacket any time during the whole afternoon."

"I'm sorry, Jake." Arnie was back to looking miserable again. "That sure was dumb of me."

"It wasn't your fault." Jake gave him a reassuring smile. "You couldn't have known."

Arnie brightened. "Anyhow, she din't take nothin'."

"Nothing that we know about."

"Well, there ain't much that I'd miss. Except maybe this." Arnie looked down at his bag. "Because it was the first thing Bobbie give me. And maybe . . ." Here Arnie stopped and produced one of his blushes. Jake was just about to change the subject by suggesting they go in to the theater when Arnie began again. "And maybe this," he said, fishing down into the bag and coming out with a small blue box. "I brung it back for Bobbie, but he ain't around now, so I was wonderin' . . ."

He paused again while Jake did his best to think of something to forestall what he imagined to be the inevitable next words. Nothing came to mind.

"I was wonderin' if maybe you'd like it," Arnie finished simply.

Jake took the proffered box and opened it. On a bed of white cotton batting lay a miniature jade owl with a gold ring set into the top of its head.

"It's for wearin' on a gold chain like you got," explained Arnie. "It's a owl. Bobbie liked owls."

One look at Arnie's eager yet hesitant expression told Jake that there could be no question of a refusal. "So do I," he said, "and this one's—" He picked up the delicate little object to examine. It was smooth to the touch, carved with great care and had an inner glow at the heart of its semitranslucence. "—a real beauty," he finished admiringly. "Thanks very much. But you're sure you wouldn't like to hang on to it as a—a memento?"

"Naw," said Arnie, now very pleased with himself. "You really like it?"

"Yes, I do," said Jake sincerely. He unfastened the catch on one of the chains around his neck. "I'll put it on right now. There," he said, after the owl had been threaded on and the chain replaced. "How's that?"

"Real nice." Arnie beamed with delight. "And it'll be good luck for you. The lady in the store said so."

"Isn't that quaint?" said Tim, who had returned to the car without being noticed by either of its occupants. "I hate to break up *this* party, but they're calling for Mr. Siganski onstage."

"Okay, I'm comin'," said Arnie reluctantly. He waited until Tim had resumed his painting, then collected an off-white Stetson hat from the back seat and squeezed himself out of the car. Jake got out too, following Arnie's lead in making sure the door on his side was locked.

Arnie stared at the paint-spotted back of the Quest Theatre. "I don't wanna go in there," he said.

"I know." More than ever, Jake felt like a louse.

"I'm just doin' it for Bobbie."

"I know."

"And I guess for you, too, Jake."

Jake opened his mouth to make a reply, but before he could think of one, Arnie had tossed over his bunch of keys with a "Hold these for me, will ya," and clumped off into the theater. Tina and Tim, having finished painting their cacti, followed in his wake like a pair of Lilliputians on the heels of Gulliver.

Nineteen

Instead of using the back entrance, Jake went around to the front of the building. He was hoping to find Ginny alone and in the mood for a chat, but a whisp of smoke curling out through the box office window told him she had company. Before he could approach the window, the hoarse voice of Hazel Harvey stopped him in his tracks.

"God damn it, we *can't* be in that bad shape," came the foghorn croak, followed by a spell of coughing.

"Business hasn't been too good lately," observed Ginny, when Hazel had recovered and blown her nose.

"It's been lousy. But it's been that way for months, and we always managed to make ends meet. What the fuck's gone wrong?"

There followed a rustling of paper, then Ginny's voice: "I've been checking back, and we seem to have made most of our money on collections from the audiences after the shows."

"You mean after they've sat through one of our crummy shows they feel like coughing up *more* money?" Jake heard the snap of a cigarette lighter and a long intake of breath. "That's crazy."

"I know it seems strange, but look here—"

"Honey, I can't even *see* those figures, let alone understand them. Jesus, I wish we had that fag back. We did okay when he was around."

"I hope you don't think that I—"

"Oh, shit, no, honey. It ain't your fault. Maybe now and then Hank kicked in something I didn't know about." A chair scraped against the floor. "I'm getting antsy in here. Let's go get us a coffee or a drink . . ."

Jake ducked under the box office window and hurried into the house.

Much had been accomplished since his last visit. The Victorian splendors of *The Importance of Being Earnest,* which had given an air of solid respectability to yesterday's rehearsal, were now gone, and in their place was an open wooden framework of rustic columns and beams. Members of the cast milled about the stage in various articles of western attire, while Yolanda reigned over all from a raised platform precariously built into one end of the wooden framework. Behind all this, an elongated skeleton of a person, whom Jake took to be the notorious Wet Set Willie, busily sketched out a panoramic street scene on a canvas backdrop that had already been roughly painted in with shades of pale blue for the sky, brown for the buildings and yellow for the street. When the green cacti appeared, they would add a welcome bright touch.

"Have we got everyone we need for the opening?" asked Yolanda, keeping a tight grip on a nearby column as she teetered nervously on her sky platform.

"Kathy's still in wardrobe," answered the ever-present Laura.

"Here I am," called out a breathless Kathy as she ran in wearing a poke bonnet and a calico skirt very much too long for her.

Yolanda regarded her with dismay. "Is *that* what you're going to wear?"

"Tina says she's got a jacket for me, but she can't find it right now, and Tim's going to take the skirt up later."

"Oh, that's all right then. You look *lovely*. Is Goliath here?"

"Tim's making him up," volunteered one of the boys.

"No, there he is," said Kathy, pointing offstage.

Yolanda peered carefully over the edge of her platform. "Send him out here. I want to see how he looks."

There followed a pause while everyone waited expectantly. Nothing happened.

"Come along," snapped Yolanda. "We haven't got all day. I want to run through the whole show, then we've got to do the lighting. *If* we have a set to light," she added significantly.

"I heard that," said Wet Set Willie, whose matchstick limbs and jerking movements reminded Jake of a praying mantis. "You know what this place is like. You're lucky to have as much as there is."

"Yes, Bill dear, and it's going to be just *lovely*. But you *promised* we'd have everything by today."

Willie stopped painting and wiped his hands on his filthy sweat-shirt. "I'm doing the best I can," he said in an aggrieved voice. "With precious little help. Where are my goddam cactuses?" he yelled into the wings. "Why does everyone pick on me?" he wailed to the theater in general. "Do you want it done now or do you want it done right? I heard that!" He whirled around as the tail end of a titter floated through the canvas drop. "And what else don't you like about the set?" he asked, turning back to Yolanda. "There's got to be something, so you might just as well tell me now and be done with it."

"Now don't get upset," said Yolanda in her most soothing manner. "I just wanted to make sure everything was under control. And you know I just *love* the set."

"Well, thank God for that," sniffed Willie, somewhat mollified.

"Although . . ." Yolanda began unwisely.

Willie froze. "Although what?"

"Well, nothing, really."

"Although *what*?"

"Well, dear, it's this platform."

"What's wrong with it? It's the best part of the set."

"Of course it is, and I just *love* it. But I get dizzy whenever I look down."

143

"So don't look down." Willie picked up his paintbrush and prepared to return to work.

"But don't you think it's just the tiniest bit too high?"

"I gave you what you asked for. You said you wanted it eye level."

"Yes, dear. But I suppose I meant mine, not yours."

"What's the difference?"

"About two feet, I should think," said Yolanda, in a nervous attempt at light humor.

Willie dropped his brush. "Are you making fun of my height?" he demanded, glaring at Yolanda over the edge of the platform, which was indeed just level with the bridge of his nose.

"No, dear, certainly not."

"Because if you are, I quit."

"Now Willie—"

"And don't use that name. I know what you all call me behind my back!"

"We don't!"

"Don't what?" asked Willie craftily.

"Call you—well, anything. And don't worry about the platform. I'm sure I'll get used to it eventually."

"I *could* drop everything and cut the whole set down."

"No, no."

"It would only take a couple of days."

"*No,* no."

"Or I could scrap the whole thing and do something else."

"Bill, dear—"

"That would take about a week."

Jake, who had started off in Willie's camp through dislike of Yolanda, now felt that the battle was becoming too one-sided and accordingly shifted his sympathies to the underdog. He had now become so involved in the impromptu drama onstage that he barely noticed a voice whispering his name from somewhere in the house. When the whisper was repeated, he turned in his seat to find Arnie sitting directly behind him.

Arnie was wearing his western outfit and the pair of painted-canvas chaps made for his unfortunate predecessor. He was also wearing his high-heeled boots and the white Stetson, which he had pulled down over his face until the brim almost touched his chest.

"Hi, Arnie." Jake found it disconcerting to be staring into the crown of a hat where there should have been a face. Clearly Arnie had a problem, and it was up to his agent to find out what it was. Jake decided that a direct approach would save time. "Why are you wearing your hat over your face?" he asked.

"I hate what he done to me," came from behind the hat.

"Who?"

"That Tim," said the hat.

"Let's see."

"I feel so dumb."

"Take off the hat."

"Promise you won't laugh."

"I promise."

Arnie took off the hat and, despite a resolute attempt to lock his features into an expression of polite interest, Jake's eyebrows rose. Tim had done his work well. Above the collar of Arnie's freshly ironed checked shirt sat the head of a monster, whose hollow eyes, deeply etched lines and cruel dissipated mouth were perfectly set off by an ashen complexion, a three-day stubble and a mass of lank, greasy hair. Only by concentrating very hard could Jake make out Arnie's own apprehensive features submerged beneath the horror, like a faint image on a photographic double exposure.

"It's very good, Arnie. Really." This was true.

"I din't think I'd hafta look so bad."

"But that's what the part calls for. You're supposed to be a horrible person."

"I don't wanta be a horrible person. What if somebody I know sees me?"

"He'd never recognize you."

"Yeah?" Arnie still looked mean but sounded hopeful.

"Absolutely. It's a fabulous makeup job."

"Maybe if I don't look in the mirror again."

"That's the idea," said Jake heartily. "Just forget about everything except what we went through last night and you'll be a sensation."

"Where's our Goliath?" Having placated Willie, Yolanda was gathering her forces together for the run-through. "Oh, there you are!" she exclaimed as Arnie pried himself out of his seat and shambled down the aisle. "Don't you look *lovely*! Good work, Tim. Now Arnie, I want you to stand out of the way over there on the side and wait until it's your turn to come on. You *do* know when to come on, don't you?"

"Yes'm. Me'n Jake worked on it last night."

145

Jake caught the double giggle from backstage.

"Splendid. All right—first act beginners, please. Kitty, dear, let's have the end of the overture."

Kitty crashed out doom-laden chords on the piano while Yolanda, teetering carefully on her platform, plucked Mother Guitar from a peg on the railing behind her, shook her hair away from her face, and settled into a comfortable playing position. When the overture came to an end, she twanged a few exploratory notes on the guitar and sang the following through her nose:

> "Oh, hark to a tale of the old, old West
> That's been sung 'neath a wanderin' star
> Wherever a cowpoke plucks on the strings,
> On the strings of Mother Guitar."

Conscious of being stabbed in the lower back by something sharp and hard, Jake slid down in his seat in a vain search for comfort. Yolanda continued:

> "Oh, the Stranger was big, and bad, and cruel
> And the Little One pure as the Morning Star.
> Oh, hark to their tale as it comes from the strings,
> From the strings of Mother Guitar."

Jake shifted about again, then gave his attention to the stage, where Kevin, as David, was being scolded by his stern but loving parents for wasting time at target practice with his air pistol when he should have been attending to his chores on the farm.

Much to Jake's surprise, the rehearsal went well. No major hitches occurred, no lines were forgotten, and the show itself proved to be less inept than he had guessed from his brief glance through Arnie's script. Also, to his great satisfaction, Arnie made both his entrances on cue and executed his death fall to perfection, earning an admiring "Right on!" from Kevin.

As soon as he had made sure that Arnie had survived to the end of the rehearsal without suffering any major damage, Jake felt that he could safely grant himself a walk into the lobby, leaving others to carry out the business of setting curtain calls and giving postrehearsal notes in his absence. No sooner had he stood up, however, when a region just above his right buttock that had slowly become numb over the course of the run-through exploded into a dull throbbing ache of exquisite painfulness. Fishing into his rear pants pocket, Jake discovered that what he had taken to be a loose spring in the theater seat was actually Arnie's bunch of keys. With these transferred to his shirt pocket and his new bruise announcing its presence at every step, Jake hobbled off into the lobby to see how Ginny had weathered her financial session with Hazel.

She was bent over her makeshift desk in much the same attitude as when he had first seen her, doing sums on the calculator.

"How's it going?" he asked.

"Not so good." Ginny pushed her hair back with both hands, causing Jake to forget all about his aching rear, and turned to him with a dazed smile. "We haven't been making enough money to meet expenses, but our attendance hasn't been any worse than usual, so I'm trying to find out how we managed before when we can't now. If you see what I mean." She managed a short laugh. "I've been staring at these columns of figures for so long I'm getting dizzy."

"Can I have a look?"

"Sure. Come on in."

Although indifferent at arithmetic, Jake was willing to try anything that would get him past the box office window and into the office itself. Once there, standing close to Ginny, he became acutely aware of the warmth that bridged the space between them and, like Ginny, had difficulty concentrating on the rows of figures.

"I think I've found where most of the money has been coming from," Ginny said, turning back a few pages, "but I don't know what it means. Look: usually in the first weekend of each month, and sometimes in the third, we've done very well from the collections they take up after the shows. See? On this Friday they got over three hundred dollars, and then six hundred for the two Saturday shows and the same on Sunday. Then it drops back to peanuts for the next two weeks, but starts right up again over here. And the same here, and here. . . ." She worked through to the end of the accounting records, then began turning back again. "So for the past few weeks we've been sinking into the red, when before we had all those lovely times in the black."

"Or green," Jake pointed out, referring to the color of the entries for the good times in question. "How did you know when you were going to start making money?"

147

Ginny smiled. "I didn't, of course. Those are Bobbie's entries. I guess he liked green ink."

"You mean Hazel was right when she told me the theater always did better with Bobbie in the box office?"

"It looks like it. I—" Ginny stopped abruptly and stared open-mouthed over Jake's shoulder. At the same time, warned by a stirring of the hairs on the back of his neck, Jake turned to see who had joined them in the office. Like Ginny, he gaped.

Without her wig, Hazel seemed a shrunken travesty of her usual flamboyant self. The wet red lips, the heavy foundation makeup base, the generously applied rouge and the long eyelashes were all there, but transformed into a grotesque mask by the thin spikes of close-cropped gray hair that surmounted them. As in an optical illusion, when a hidden picture materializes out of the elements of some other, quite different image, so the faded hair and pale scalp seemed to pull Hazel's true features up through the thick layer of makeup that tried to conceal them. One by one, each wrinkle, line, pouch and fold made its presence known, until there stood before Jake not the Hazel Harvey he had seen only yesterday but some ancient stranger, with a face that would have looked more at home above her clown's costume than the embroidered Chinese wrapper she now wore as she leaned against the doorframe, panting from the exertion of coming downstairs. Her eyes were half closed, and the remains of a cigarette hung from the corner of her lips.

"Well," she said in a dry rasp that affected Jake like a fingernail drawn down a blackboard. "So this is what the mice get up to when the cat's away."

"I was just helping Mrs. Warner," Jake explained.

"Yeah, I figured that," Hazel drawled. "You were helping each other—to *my* money."

"Now just—"

"Shut up!" snapped Hazel. "Such a cozy little arrangement, but you got greedy, didn't you? First *she* starts slipping a little out under the table for her phony skinhead husband, then she wants a little more, and more, and now you want to dip in so you can play around with your big boyfriend."

"You have no right—" began Jake again.

"Balls!" shouted Hazel, in a sudden passion. "You all think I don't know what goes on here, but I do! It just took me a little while longer to catch on to the pair of you. Well, I've had enough. Hear me? Do you hear

148

me?" she demanded again, as Yolanda, Kitty, the twins and most of the cast began drifting into the lobby to discover the cause of the shouting.

"Oh, yes," continued Hazel, "you're a lovely bunch, you are, and you've fucked me up good and solid, but I know what you're all up to. You think you're so smart, but I know a few little things that I wouldn't mind telling."

"Hazel—" said Yolanda.

"Eat shit!" Hazel drew the back of her shaking hand across her face, sniffed, and carried on in a lower tone. "Eat shit, all of you. I'm tired of being used and spied on and fucked up. But I'm not going to take it anymore." She put one hand on the doorframe to steady herself and used the other to point a trembling finger at Ginny. "You! You're fired! Pack up and fuck off." Pleased with the phrase, she barked out a short laugh, then turned to Yolanda and Kitty. "And you two can do the same. Pack up and fuck off. What do I need with your crummy shows? They're shit! Get that? Shit! So you can all go home. There ain't gonna be no show. Not tomorrow, not anytime!"

A concerted gasp rose from the cast. With Yolanda apparently struck dumb, Kitty tried to emulate her soothing technique.

"Mrs. Harvey, you don't mean that."

Hazel had closed her eyes and dropped her head back against the doorframe, but she came alive again with great energy. "Who says I don't?" she demanded loudly. "I mean everything I goddamn say. And if I say I'm getting out of this fucking place, you better believe it. I'm closing those fucking doors and selling this fucking building, and you know what I'm going to do then? Have me a fucking *ball*! You hear that? A *ball*! Old Hazel's gonna stop carrying all you deadbeats and take herself off and live it up. Hey there!" she yelled as Arnie came charging into the lobby with a desolate expression on his freshly scrubbed face. Hazel lurched across the passageway toward him. "Hey there, you big dumb hunk. How'd you like to go straight and spend some money with old Hazel?"

Arnie stared down at her in horror.

Hazel coquettishly brushed a few stray whisps of hair away from her forehead. "Oh, maybe I don't look so good right now, but just let me get myself fixed up a bit, and we could really take off. What do you say?" Being unable to reach his shoulder, she threw an arm around Arnie's waist.

Arnie swallowed. "You stole my bag," he said faintly.

Hazel blinked. "How's that?"

149

"My bag," said Arnie miserably. "That Bobbie give me. It ain't where I left it."

"So what?" Hazel stepped back a pace, lost her balance, and avoided a fall only by colliding with the wall on the opposite side of the passageway. "Come on with me and I'll buy you another. I'll buy you a dozen. And if you don't wanna come with me, fuck you. I'll find someone else." She surveyed her audience. "Who wants to have a dirty holiday with old Hazel? Who's got the biggest dick?" She began a laugh that, as usual, deteriorated into a cough.

Taking advantage of this pause, Tina approached Hazel and laid a hand gently on her arm. Hazel wrenched violently away.

"Don't you touch me. I don't want anybody to touch me except him." She pointed at the unhappy Arnie, who was edging away behind the other members of the cast. Hazel tossed her head and smoothed the wrinkled wrapper down over her hips. "But he don't want me because I ain't a crummy little fag. Ain't that a good one? He don't want me, you don't want me. Nobody wants old Hazel." She let out a little laugh, collapsed against the wall again, and closed her eyes. "Jesus, I'm tired."

Tina put her hand back on Hazel's arm and this time was not repulsed. "Hazel, come on upstairs and lie down."

"I'm nobody's baby now," sang Hazel in a high, thin voice.

"Yes, you are," Tina reassured her. "We all love you."

"No, you don't. Nobody loves Baby."

"I think we should go upstairs. It's Baby's bedtime."

Hazel looked at Tina shyly from under her eyelashes. "Has Baby been bad?"

"You're just tired. You'll feel better in the morning."

Hazel put on a wicked little smile and twisted her toe into the floor. "Naughty Baby doe bye-byes," she lisped.

"That's right." Tina put her arm around Hazel and started her along the passageway toward the stairs. "Say 'Night-night, everyone.'"

"Night-night," Hazel said obediently, then stopped short as she turned and caught sight of Kevin, who was standing at the bottom of the stairs, trying to look inconspicuous. "What are you doing here, kid?" she asked in her normal voice.

"Nothin', Miz Harvey," said Kevin, looking up at her with frightened eyes. "I'm just goin' home."

Hazel stroked the top of his head. "That's right, kid," she said. "You go home to your mommy. Don't come back."

She moved on and started climbing the stairs, still supported by Tina. Suddenly she halted.

"Where's *my* mommy?"

"I don't know, dear," said Tina patiently.

Hazel's lower lip began to tremble. "I want my mommy," she whined. "You find her."

"All right, I'll try. After you go bye-byes." Tina once again got Hazel moving upward.

"And I want some cocoa."

"All right."

"With a marshmallow."

"Maybe."

"And then candy."

"We'll see."

A door closed upstairs and their voices could no longer be heard.

Twenty

After a suspended hush while everyone downstairs waited in vain to hear more from upstairs, a flurry of activity broke out in the lobby. The actors wondered if indeed they were out of a job; Yolanda and Kitty conferred anxiously with Tim; Arnie fled back to the safety of the dressing room area; and Jake, on discovering that his arm had strayed around Ginny in the excitement of the moment, made plans to keep it in that position for as long as possible.

"What was that all about?" he asked.

Ginny appeared stunned. "I'm not sure. But I've got a feeling that no one's going to care very much if I go home early tonight—and stay there."

"Everybody! Everybody, listen." Yolanda was calling for attention. "We've all witnessed a very distressing scene, and I know all your hearts go out to Mrs. Harvey, as does mine. But Tim assures me that he has seen her like this before, when she has, um, overindulged, and that she'll be her old self tomorrow. So . . ." She paused while an outbreak of chatter threatened to drown her out. "Quiet! Quiet. Thank you. So I just want to inform you that I intend to ignore Mrs. Harvey's unfortunate, um, attack and carry on as planned. We'll have a dinner break, then be back at seven for a full dress rehearsal at eight. Any questions?"

"What's our schedule for tomorrow?" someone asked.

Yolanda parted her hair and threw it back to reveal a maternal smile. "Tomorrow I want you all to get a good rest while we drudges finish work on the set and the lights. The call is six thirty for a vocal warm-up and then curtain at eight. Now go eat."

The conversational hum died out as the cast headed for the street. Tim went upstairs in search of Tina, leaving Yolanda and Kitty to whisper together in the lobby.

"It looks like you aren't fired after all," said Jake to Ginny, who had gently disengaged herself from his arm and was collecting her bag and some last-minute groceries prior to setting off for home.

"I don't know whether to be pleased or not," she said, rummaging in her bag for car keys. "I'll never find anything else as flexible. On the other hand, it seems like I may not get paid. Can I afford this job?"

"Don't worry about that." Yolanda appeared in the office doorway. "I didn't want to say this before all the others," she said, switching to a more confidential manner, "but Kitty and I feel that, much as we may all love her, dear Hazel has finally gone right round the bend, and it's up to me—that is, all of us—to keep the theater going and to make a success of it, as Hazel would have wanted. After all"—she lowered her voice even more as Kitty joined her in the doorway—"the Harvey management hasn't exactly been what one would call efficient, and threatening to throw me out is just the last straw. But if we ignore that little outburst and put our shoulders to the wheel and pitch in and pull together"—here Jake experienced a strong temptation to start

152

humming "Land of Hope and Glory" to provide the right inspirational background—"then I'm sure we'll all weather the storm and emerge victorious with a strong repertoire and happy audiences."

"What about money?" Jake inquired.

"That will come too," Yolanda assured him. *"If,"* she added, turning to Ginny, "if we can count on everyone sticking to their guns and not deserting. Can we count on you?"

"Not tonight. But I'll be back in the trenches tomorrow." Ginny looked away as Jake tried to catch her eye.

"Splendid!" cried Yolanda, who appeared to be zeroing in on her finest hour in true Churchillian style. "Good show! I knew you weren't a quitter!"

"No," said Ginny rather sadly, as she gathered up her things. "Unfortunately."

"That's the spirit! Now, Kitty and I are off to a really *super* vegetarian restaurant for a nut cutlet. Who wants to join us? No takers? You'll be sorry when your veins clog up! Bye-bye."

And with that cheerful message, Yolanda sailed off on a cloud of rosy prospects while Kitty remained behind for a moment.

"Nanda hates me smoking these things," she said, dabbing out a cigarette in a bent metal ashtray filled with Hazel's red-tipped butts. "Do you think she's right about Mrs. Harvey? Will she forget that awful scene she made, or could she really throw us out?"

Jake shrugged. "If this afternoon is any indication, Mrs. Harvey could do just about anything."

Kitty's mouth trembled. "It isn't fair," she said. "Just when Nanda thought she'd finally found a home for her work."

They all turned to gaze out of the lobby windows toward the sidewalk, where the subject of their concern was serenely executing a few mild deep-breathing exercises.

"I wouldn't worry about Yolanda," remarked Ginny. "She can look after herself."

"Oh, no!" Kitty's eyes grew round with alarm. "*I* look after Nanda." Her expression softened to an apologetic smile. "But that isn't what you meant, was it? And you're right." Her smile broadened to include Jake. "Nanda can do *anything.*"

"My impression is that Nanda feels ready to take on World War Two single-handed," said Jake as he and Ginny emerged from the theater and caught sight of Yolanda striding off at a brisk pace, with Kitty doing her best to keep up behind.

"She *was* laying it on a bit thick," Ginny laughed.

"Frightfully gung-ho and all that."

"Frightfully." Ginny gave Jake a peck on the cheek and got into her car.

"I say," exclaimed Jake in his best Ronald Colman manner, "you're a damned fetching little thing. Pity you have to dash off."

"It's beastly, I know. But Mummy's waiting tea for me. Such a bore."

"We *will* meet again?"

"I expect so."

"Promise me." Jake became intense. "The Three Bells at two."

"I can't. It's Cook's day off."

"Very well, the Two Bells at three."

"But Geoffrey's getting so suspicious!"

"Damn Geoffrey! Who do you love—him or me?"

"Oh, Nigel!"

"Fiona!"

Carried away by the moment, they indulged in a long kiss through the car window.

"The Station Café," Ginny whispered, when they came up for breath. "Platform one at four."

"I'll be there, my darling." They kissed again.

"Make that platform four at one," murmured Ginny.

"I'll find you anywhere."

"My God!"

"What is it?"

Ginny pointed. "Geoffrey!"

Arnie had just come out of the theater. Jake stood up and spoke from the corner of his mouth.

"He's not wearing his spectacles. He'll never recognize us."

"Hey, Jake," called Arnie.

Ginny started her car. "I must go. The tea will be stewed."

"Ghastly stuff, stewed tea."

"Toodle-oo."

"Cheery-bye."

Nigel watched Fiona drive off, then walked across the street to join Geoffrey.

154

"I din't want to bother you, Jake, but you got my car keys."

"So I have, old chap. Here you are, right as rain."

"You feelin' okay?"

Jake made a fast trip back across the Atlantic. "Sure. What was that you were saying inside about your bag?"

"It's gone. *She* took it." Arnie jerked his thumb back at the theater.

"You sure?"

"It must be her. She couldn't get it at my place, so she swiped it here. She's crazy!"

"Tim thinks she'll be okay tomorrow," Jake reassured him. "I'll talk to her."

"Yeah?" Arnie shed his cares in perfect confidence of a happy outcome. "Gee, you're a real friend, Jake."

"All part of the service."

"You comin' to the dress rehearsal?"

Jake patted him on the back. "You don't need me now. I'm going home to do some thinking."

Arnie put on a serious expression. "I think sometimes," he said modestly.

"It's harder than it sounds."

"I'll say."

When Jake walked around to the back of the theater, he found that another message had been left on the windshield of his car. This time the cardboard read JAKE LOVES ARNIE in bright green letters. Jake removed the sign, tore it in two, and drove off. Some hours later, returning to his car after rehearsal, Arnie discovered the two pieces and took them home to stick back together.

About the time Arnie was hunting through Bobbie's desk for some adhesive tape, Jake pulled into his parking space at the Mandarin in a grumpy mood. Instead of going home when he left the theater, he had decided that constructive thinking could be carried out just as productively in several of his favorite bars, even if it meant having to interrupt the workings of his brain from time to time in order to repel, gently but firmly, the many young unattached females who would doubtless find his air of intellectual concentration impossible to resist. Now he felt bitter, because not only had his thoughts been allowed to flow without any interruption whatever, but even in this atmosphere

155

of enforced solitude they had been unable to form themselves into anything that resembled a constructive idea. In his present humor, he would have found considerable satisfaction if he had been able to say something rude to Hector in his tree, but even that harmless pleasure was denied him. Hector had vanished from his amorous lookout, leaving the grateful occupants of the Mandarin to slumber in peace.

Once back in his apartment, Jake stripped for bed and took advantage of his unclothed state to stand backward in front of the full-length mirror in his bedroom and inspect the area that still offered a throbbing reminder of Arnie's bulky key collection. At that very moment, possibly due to some extra degree of mental receptivity brought about by his convoluted pose or to the genuine satisfaction of discovering a rich study in purple and green blossoming on his hindquarters, Jake took delivery of the idea he had been searching for. He picked up the telephone and called Arnie.

"How did the rehearsal go?" he asked, when they had got past the initial hellos.

"Okay," Arnie replied. "Except I forgot I had my keys in my back pocket and I fell on 'em."

"Welcome to the club," said Jake with feeling.

"It's turnin' blue back there."

"Wait a couple of hours and you'll want to frame it. And while we're on the subject," continued Jake, getting down to business, "that long flat key on your ring—the one that probably did all the damage: where did you get it?"

"Bobbie give it to me to wear on my ring."

Jake's heart jumped. "It looks like the kind that opens a safety deposit box. Did Bobbie have anything like that?"

"Yeah. He took one at the bank here when we opened an account for the two of us."

"And do you have access to the box? Can you get into it?"

"Gee, Jake," the answer came back slowly, "I never tried."

Jake's mouth became dry as blocks of neat green figures, like those from the Quest accounts book, began to parade tantalizingly past his inner eye. He swallowed. "Arnie, this is very important. Were you with Bobbie when he signed for the box?"

"Yeah. I remember that. We hadda go downstairs."

"Good. And did they ask *you* to sign when Bobbie did? On something like a little file card?"

There was silence on the line, then Arnie's hesitant voice: "I—I *think* so. I don't remember things like that too good."

"Okay. You're doing great. Now, here's what we have to do." Jake's mind was skimming ahead of his conscious thoughts with an exhilaration that had nothing at all to do with the drinks he had consumed during his thinking sessions at the various bars. "First of all, have you told your bank about what happened to Bobbie?"

"No!" Arnie sounded shocked. "Should I?"

"Maybe later, but not yet. As long as they think he's alive, then you can get into the box. So as soon as you can tomorrow, I want you to go and see what's in it. They'll let you take it into a little room by yourself, and what you're looking for are papers—receipts, records, letters, notebooks, anything like that. Have you gone through his papers at home?"

"He din't keep nothin' here."

"Okay. Then especially look for a savings account book. And bring everything home with you."

"Will they let me?" Arnie sounded dubious.

"Sure. No problem. If it's a jointly held box and they have your signature on file, you can take everything. But if they find out that Bobbie—that he's dead, they'll seal it until they get some kind of legal clearance. We can't wait for that."

"Is somethin' wrong?"

"I don't know. But if Bobbie kept his financial records in that box, maybe we can find out."

"What if I din't sign that card after all, or the key don't fit?"

"Just say you have another box somewhere else and you got mixed up. Do you want me to come with you?"

"Naw. I'll do it on my way home from the gym."

"Fine. And you better take your gym bag or something with you to carry the papers out in."

"Okay. You want to meet sometime?"

"Sure. When will you be home?"

There was another silence while Arnie considered. "Well, it's legs and neck tomorrow. How about my place at three?"

"That's fine. I'll be there."

Jake's attention was deflected from Arnie's next remark by the sight of Hector, who had staggered into the bedroom and now sat looking

157

up at the bed in an uncertain, defeated manner. "Sorry." Jake pulled his mind back to the telephone and Arnie. "I didn't quite catch that."

"I just said if you don't mind waitin' till three, I can make lunch. I got a whole fridge fulla tuna fish and cottage cheese."

"That's what you're living on?"

"It's good stuff. All the guys at the gym eat it. High protein, low fat—"

Lured by the prospect of a soft spot to spend the night, Hector visibly gathered his last energies and made a leap at the bed. He landed short of the mark, however, and had to haul himself awkwardly over the edge.

"—it don't need no cookin," continued Arnie, "and it's great for muscle definition."

"Maybe I'll just get something in the office," said Jake, who had no muscles worth defining. "To save time. But thanks anyway." He watched as Hector, spread-eagled on top of the bed, took one exhausted look around the room and then dropped his head on his front paws. "I better go now. I've got a cat here who's acting funny. See you tomorrow."

They traded farewells and hung up. Jake sat on the bed and inspected Hector.

"All right," he said to the apparently unconscious cat. "What's wrong with you?"

Hector half opened his eyes and closed them again.

"Have you been in a fight?" Jake explored with one finger behind Hector's triangular brown ears. "Are you feeling okay?"

Hector rolled over on his back in an abandoned attitude and started purring. The message was clear.

"So that's it: you made out," said Jake, not without a small stab of envy. "Congratulations."

Revived by a light stomach rub, Hector turned right side up and became prim, folding his front legs neatly under his chest. "Yah," he said.

"I suppose you intend to spend the whole night there, right in the middle."

Hector turned his eyes into narrow slits and looked smug. For an instant, Jake imagined him squinting through the rising smoke from a half-spent cigarette and was reminded of Hazel Harvey.

"Okay," he conceded. "Just don't come waking me up at five in the morning."

But it was Hector who barely stirred and Jake who jumped awake when the telephone rang at eight.

<h1 style="text-align:center">Twenty-one</h1>

"Jake," said Ginny, "I'm sorry to call this early, but I have to ask you a favor."

"Sure. Anything." The words emerged in a semicroak.

"Did I wake you up?"

"Are you kidding? I've been up for hours." Jake cleared his throat to get it into working order. "I just haven't done any talking. What's the favor?"

"It's just that I—I'm leaving right now to go out of town, and I haven't been able to get hold of Hazel or anyone at the theater to tell them I won't be able to come in until tomorrow or maybe the next day. So I wondered if you could try calling later, or tell them when you go over there."

"No problem. Is everything okay?"

"Yes." Ginny hesitated a little. "Well, the thing is . . . Hal is leaving the commune. He wants to come home."

"Oh." Something died in the pit of Jake's stomach. "That's why your in-laws wanted to see you?"

"Yes. He's been staying with some friends in Ventura and his parents went to see him there on Monday. They say he's different—more like he was—and he's letting his hair grow. They're so happy, and Cal is over the moon about seeing his father again."

"How about you?"

Ginny gave a small rueful laugh. "Part of me's over the moon with Cal and the rest is scared. I kept hoping he'd write or visit Cal sometime, and that's the most I ever expected: just a little piece of him. Now I'm not sure I can handle the whole thing."

"But you're going to give it a try."

"I have to, Jake. Even if it doesn't work, I'd never forgive myself if I didn't give it the chance. I'm sorry about what—what seemed to be happening with us. But I'm not a quitter, to quote Yolanda."

"Unfortunately," said Jake. "To quote you."

"Be happy for me, Jake. And let's still be friends. I—oh, well. . . . good-bye." The line went dead.

Jake hung up the telephone and sat in bed for a while, staring blankly at his toes under the covers. Although his relationship with Ginny had hardly managed to get even slightly off the ground, he had nevertheless allowed himself to indulge in many pleasant daydreams as to the way things might work out if it had. Beginning with thoughts of rampant sex, he had progressed through the delicious prospect of love into the forbidden zone of marriage, having children, buying a home, trading the Thunderbird in for a station wagon, setting up college funds, and becoming a full-fledged member of the PTA. But Hal wanted to come home, and Ginny wanted him back, and why not? He, Jake, would just have to find someone else and start all over again. Preferably someone loose and unencumbered and anxious to stay that way. He, personally, had always said that he couldn't take the heavy responsibility inherent in a long-term relationship; he should have stuck to that instead of indulging in frivolous thoughts of settling down. Free to pick up and move on as the fancy took him, that's what he wanted to be. Who needed somebody else's wife, already tied down with a kid? A stud like himself, with looks and personal magnetism, could do better than that any day. Jake slid down under the covers and pulled the sheet over his head.

He planned to remain in this position until forced back into the world by hunger or a delegation of concerned friends, but he had reckoned without Hector, who now yawned, stretched, and climbed heavily onto Jake's chest as the first stage in his campaign for break-

160

fast. Feigning an attack of kittenish high spirits, he took a swipe at the sheet where Jake's breathing was making it rise and fall and then began to shift his weight to and fro for a follow-up pounce. Jake knew when his bluff was being called. He pulled the sheet down to his chin and met Hector's steady blue-eyed stare.

"All right," he said. "You win. I'm getting up. But my heart isn't in it."

Preceded by Hector, he shuffled into the kitchen and steeled himself to open a tin of liver-and-cheese cat food while Hector twined about his ankles in an ecstasy of anticipation.

"Mark my words," he announced as he bent over to scoop the contents of the tin into Hector's bowl, narrowly missing Hector's head in the process, "this is going to be a lousy day."

Such is the perversity of human nature that, although Jake seldom if ever took more than coffee for breakfast, on those days when the laws of hospitality compelled him to feed Hector he often came away from the kitchen with the thought that he might indeed have enjoyed a bite of something, had not the thick, rich aroma of Hector's favorite meal left him feeling too queasy to get it down. Sooner or later, however, food would become necessary; and as Jake emerged from the bathroom, showered, shaved, and ready to face the day in an ingeniously chosen outfit that would look equally appropriate at tonight's opening, it occurred to him that with a little careful handling Miss Murphy might be persuaded to repeat her breakfast service at the office. The news of Ginny's decision to return to her husband should do the trick, he thought, as he stood in front of the mirror and admired his reflection in white suit and midnight blue nylon shirt. The effect was so successful that his main worry seemed to be not so much how to get breakfast out of Miss Murphy as how to avoid a repetition of yesterday's passionate scene in his office.

Although, thought Jake, there were worse ways of starting work: it would take the hex off the day; it would clear his head to make room for more constructive thoughts; and even if Baron found out, an abandoned hour with Miss Murphy would probably be worth it. In any case, Baron was probably bluffing. Jake unfastened another button on his shirtfront, adjusted its long-pointed collar to lie outside his jacket, and tore himself away from the mirror.

161

Just before leaving the apartment, Jake remembered his commission from Ginny. Having neglected to ask her for the necessary telephone numbers, he resorted to the directory and tried first Hazel's private number, then the Quest Theatre without getting any response.

"To hell with them," he told Hector, who was seated in the middle of the zebra rug washing his whiskers. "La Murphy awaits."

But by the time he had backed the Thunderbird out of its parking slot, his conscience had begun to send out reproachful signals: if he really intended to submit to Miss Murphy's advances, God knew when he would be ready to think about making that telephone call; the Quest was short of money and couldn't afford to assume there was someone in the box office when in fact there wasn't; it was his responsibility to deliver Ginny's message before falling into Miss Murphy's arms; and at most it would only postpone this encounter by twenty or thirty minutes. Poised to turn right on Cahuenga, Jake gritted his teeth and turned left.

Ten minutes later, Jake walked into the Quest lobby, where he was struck immediately by its improved appearance. Someone had at last swept the fallen leaves away and given the plants a much needed watering, to judge from the moist scent in the air. There was no one in the box office, and in the house only Wet Set Willie, splashing more paint on his canvas backdrop. The cactus cutouts, now looking more solid thanks to painted-in shadows, thorns and flowers, stood propped up against the front of the stage.

"Hi," Jake called. "Have you seen Hazel anywhere?"

"No," said Willie shortly as he took a vicious swipe at the canvas with his brush.

"Yolanda Meltzer?"

"Don't make me laugh. She was supposed to get here half an hour ago, but she's probably still in bed. They're probably *all* still in bed." Willie turned around to glare at Jake, at the same time pointing upward with his dripping brush. "Tell me something—do *you* think this platform's too high?"

"Well . . ." began Jake, who knew this was a loaded question. Luckily, Willie did not expect an answer.

"All last night, nothing but pick, pick, pick. 'Bill, dear, I have this feeling it's going to collapse'; 'Bill, dear, my ears are popping.' She can't understand—it's a matter of *proportion*! Who gives a damn if her ears pop? It's the look that matters. Who are you, anyway?"

"I represent one of the actors," Jake replied.

"Oh," said Willie. "Well, I guess we all have our problems." And he returned to work, leaving Jake to wander back into the lobby.

Clearly, the only way to avoid wasting time was to leave a note. Jake was just beginning to write on the back of a leaflet—"Are you on our mailing list," it asked—taken from the ledge of the box office window, when he felt something drop on his head. Reacting to an instinctive fear that whatever it was might be alive, he leaned forward rapidly and brushed his fingers over the top of his head. His fingertips came away wet. Jake was just concluding that the liquid was probably water when another droplet fell on the floor in front of him, where a dark patch of dampness had already begun to spread over the threadbare carpet. He looked up.

The ceiling over that part of the lobby consisted of interlocking grooved wooden planks coated with an enamel paint that, whatever its original color, had weathered down to a dirty gray-brown shade. As Jake watched, a small bead of water formed between two planks, swelled, and dropped into the center of the wet patch on the floor.

Jake was now torn between two thoughts: a wish to head for his office without getting involved in any of the Quest's maintenance problems, and an unpleasant mental picture of how bad the mess upstairs must be to have worked its way through to the floor below. Finally, prompted by the certain knowledge that this image would plant itself stubbornly in the center of whatever bliss he might find in Miss Murphy's arms, he set off to investigate, first looking into the auditorium to enlist Wet Set Willie's aid. But Willie had vanished, and he had no choice but to proceed on his own.

At the top of the stairs, Jake discovered a small landing, with two doors set into the wall on his left and a narrower door in the wall directly facing him. A hand-lettered sign on the nearest door identified it as leading to the lighting booth; the door beyond that had a gold star nailed to its top panel, and the narrow door at the end of the landing carried no identification whatever. The carpet on the landing was so saturated that when Jake stepped on it a small trickle began overflowing onto the top step.

Treading as lightly as possible across the sodden surface, Jake approached the narrow door, outside which the water buildup seemed to be heaviest. After a pause to overcome an irrational sense of embarrassment mingled with apprehension, he tapped on the door. No one stirred or answered, so he knocked again. After a third try, he gently turned the doorknob and pushed, but the door refused to open.

His next option was to try the door with the gold star. Like the plot of some fairy tale, thought Jake. But which Hazel, if any, would he find: the lady or the tiger? He was not ready for another encounter like yesterday's; nevertheless, he executed a bold knock and waited again, uncomfortably aware of the water that had begun to seep through the thin soles of his favorite Italian shoes. After one last knock, he tried the door handle and was rewarded with success. The door to Hazel's apartment swung open, releasing a wave of stale cigarette fumes overlayed with a cheap synthetic fragrance of roses.

Jake sensed at once that he was standing on the threshold of a large room, although he could see very little of it, owing to the fact that heavy velvet drapes had been pulled across all the windows. Stepping inside, he experienced the squelching sensation of more water underfoot, and as his eyes became used to the dim light that squeezed around the edges of the curtains, he began to make out more details of the room: deep red walls covered with framed pictures and photographs; a white spinet piano; an overstuffed sofa and matching chairs upholstered in some plush white fabric; and a low kidney-shaped wooden table bearing a cut glass vase of silk roses. It was here that the larger-than-life fragrance originated. Off to the far right, Jake could just make out a dining-kitchen area, and in the far left corner of the room there loomed a king-size bed, surrounded by canopies of white satin.

Most unwilling to draw back the hangings, Jake cleared his throat and tried a "Hello. Anybody home?"

Nobody answered, so he moved farther into the room to a point where he could see the bed through an opening in the draperies. Its sheets, printed with gigantic red roses, were rumpled but unoccupied. As he turned back toward the door he had just entered, Jake noticed a horizontal shaft of light making its way through a gap beneath another door in the same wall, a door that by all the laws of architectural logic had to provide access to the flooded area that, by the same laws, had to be Hazel's bathroom.

He also noticed glinting in the reflected light from the landing three framed glossy photographs hanging one above the other on the narrow wall between the two doors. In the top picture, Esther Williams posed laughing before a slightly out-of-focus group of bathing beauties, of which one could be recognized as Hazel; the picture below this showed a black-clad body that Jake took to be Hank Harvey tumbling backward in midair over a wooden balcony; and the bottom picture was of a young Hazel, standing beside a swimming pool in a wet white bathing suit with her hair lacquered about a spray of artificial flowers. Jake noted with appreciation that her figure suffered not at all in comparison with Miss Williams's, and then, without giving himself any time to reconsider his next move, he quickly opened the bathroom door.

Strong sunlight entered the room through a plastic dome, spotlighting a massive bathtub built into an alcove immediately to Jake's left. At first he was dazzled by reflections from the white porcelain, the green tile walls, the pond of water covering the cracked tile floor, and the elaborate display of gold-plated hooks, rails, knobs and faucets, one of which, in the shape of a rampant dolphin, calmly disgorged a flow of tepid water into the bathtub. Faceted bottles, jars and a large mirror added their own highlights to the room, where, as it seemed to Jake when his eyes gradually became accustomed to the brilliant light, the only nonreflective surfaces belonged to a pair of dull white kneecaps protruding like twin islands from the miniature lake that slowly flowed over the edge of the bathtub. At the bottom of the lake, with closed eyes, open mouth and Technicolor makeup still intact, Hazel rested comfortably on her back. She wore a faded pink bathing cap to which, long ago, someone in the M-G-M costume department had fastened a cluster of rubber daisies, and she appeared to be very much in her element.

Only the ghastly thought of where the water on the bathroom floor had come from prevented Jake from collapsing into it; and, when a sense of equilibrium returned to his reeling head, only the lack of anything to eat since dinner the night before stood in the way of his being sick on the spot. Instead, he was able to avert his eyes from the tub itself and, reaching blindly across the threshold, turn off the wall-mounted taps that controlled the dolphin faucet. He then managed to walk slowly downstairs and call the police before having to dash out of the building, where yesterday's meal finally forced its way up and out onto Melrose Avenue.

Twenty-two

The police came, tramping heavily up and down the stairs to Hazel's apartment and making their presence felt overhead by shaking down a fresh scattering of dead leaves onto the floor of the main lobby. They were followed by several people in plain clothes, who ascended the stairs in a bored fashion and then after a time wandered away again. Yolanda arrived with Kitty and the twins and made a scene to the effect that, dead or alive, Hazel would have wanted the show to go on that evening. Hazel herself passed through on a stretcher, wrapped in a blue blanket and a zip-up plastic bag.

During all this, Jake sat in the leather-covered sofa at the far end of the lobby, hardly able to think or do more than stare at the floor. He had been asked to remain for questioning, so he passed the time by watching white watermarks form around his shoes as they began to dry out. Presently another pair of shoes came into his field of vision. They were of a smooth brown lace-up style and they belonged to Detective Rosa, who today sported a beige linen suit with a yellow shirt and a brown patterned tie. Jake, however, was too far gone to notice this outfit or to feel even a twinge of envy for the casually elegant effect he constantly aimed at but, if the hard truth were to be faced, generally failed to achieve. He barely reacted as Detective Rosa pulled over a hard-backed chair, dusted it off, and sat down.

"You don't look so hot," Rosa remarked pleasantly, stretching out his legs and leaning back. "How do you feel?"

"Just like I look," said Jake.

"Tell me the whole story."

Jake told about Hazel's strange behavior of the day before and the events that led him to her bathroom. When he had finished, Rosa closed the notepad he had been writing in, shifted his weight on the chair, and rubbed behind his left ear.

"You certainly hit the jackpot," he said. "Only a week on the job and already you've got your first body."

"Lucky me."

"No, I'm serious. Lots of private eyes spend their whole lives without finding anything more exciting than a lost husband who's skipped out on his alimony payments."

"I'm not a private eye," Jake stated firmly. "And I definitely don't want that kind of excitement."

Rosa smiled. "What about those inquiries you were going to make about that guy we found in the Hollywood Bowl parking lot? Any luck there?"

"Not really." However down in spirit, Jake had no intention of giving anything away about Bobbie's safety deposit box until he had inspected the contents himself. "I think I'd better stick to my regular job."

"Not a bad idea," Rosa agreed. "Leave the dirty work to us. But before you retire from sleuthing, maybe you could give me your thoughts on why we found all that water upstairs when there wasn't a tap running."

"Ah," said Jake.

"There are many possibilities, of course. Mrs. Harvey could have turned the tap on, fallen asleep in the bath, wakened later to turn the water off, then fallen asleep again and just slipped under—always assuming that she had drunk too much or taken a sleeping pill or both. But all that sounds kind of complicated. It seems more likely that someone else—"

"It was me," Jake confessed.

"You don't say." Rosa didn't sound too surprised. "Why did you do that?"

Jake shook his head. "I don't know. My head was going around, and all that mess—I just did it."

"So if we find any fingerprints on those nice smooth taps they'll probably be yours. Good work."

"Oh, God."

"Stop by the station and give us a few samples. Did you go into the bathroom at all?"

"No."

"Or touch anything else?"

"No."

"Well, that's something." Rosa stood up and flexed his back. "I guess I can get over to the office. Thanks for waiting."

Jake stood up too. "Do you think someone killed her?"

"Don't know," said Rosa. "Mr. Harvey on Saturday, Mrs. Harvey on Tuesday—it doesn't look good. But from what you and Ms. . . . ." He flipped open his notepad. "Meltzer: from what the two of you tell me about yesterday, Mrs. Harvey was acting pretty crazy. She could have been drunk, or high on something, and passed out in the bath. If it was murder, how about a motive?"

Jake thought for a moment. "She threatened to sell the theater for redevelopment. But maybe she didn't mean it."

"It's not that great a place," said Rosa, taking in the newly fallen leaves on the floor. "Is it worth killing for?"

Jake shrugged. "Ms. Meltzer seemed pretty passionate about it."

"According to that lady, Mrs. Harvey fired the woman who worked in the box office during her screaming scene." He turned back several pages in the notepad. "What's this Mrs. Warner like?"

"Nice," said Jake quickly. "Very nice. She wouldn't kill anybody."

"Is that a disinterested opinion?" Detective Rosa had obviously done his research thoroughly.

"Well, not entirely," Jake admitted. "But she seemed uncertain about wanting to stay on here even before Hazel fired her, and I'm pretty sure you'll find she was at home all last night."

Rosa sighed. "Then she's the only person who was. This place seems to have been crawling with people until early this morning."

"I guess the dress rehearsal ran late."

"Mm." Rosa consulted his notes again. "Any dope on those two weird kids who came in with Ms. Meltzer?"

"Oh." Jake doubted that he could do justice to the twins, even when his brain was not behaving in a disordered fashion. "Well, I think of them as the Phantoms of the Quest. They're always here, working away, and I got the feeling that they were fascinated with Hazel, maybe because she's—that is, she *was* like something out of a time capsule. They teased her and laughed at her and looked on her as, well, 'pet' was the word they used. But they took care of her and handled her better than anyone else, so I guess they had some deeper feelings too."

"Mother figure?" suggested Rosa.

"Not exactly." Jake began to feel very much out of his depth. "Maybe just the opposite. In a way, they seemed older than Hazel." He gave up. "I don't know. I've only seen them a few times."

Rosa grinned. "Pretty good, for an amateur. They're the only ones so far who seem to be upset about what happened to the old bird."

"I wish we knew what *did* happen."

"Patience, amigo." Rosa slipped his notepad into a jacket pocket. "We'll have more of an idea after the autopsy."

"What about the show tonight?" Jake asked. "Is it still on?"

Rosa waved a hand protectively in front of himself. "It's on, it's on. I had Ms. Meltzer screaming at me about that the minute I came in. This is a show business town. The Los Angeles Police Department will not stand in the way of an opening night." He began to leave, then stopped. "Have we got your telephone number?"

When the answer to this was negative, the notepad came out again and the number was entered.

"Good," said Rosa. "Now what is it I'm supposed to say? Oh, yeah: break a leg."

"The way things are going, I wouldn't be surprised," muttered Jake as Rosa flipped a hand at him and strolled out of the lobby toward a waiting police car. But his conversation with the detective had lifted him out of his slump and he became aware of a need for food. Checking his watch, he was pleased to discover that he had time for a quiet lunch at somewhere particularly special before meeting Arnie. The Polo Lounge wasn't too far out of his way, he had enough credit left on one of his charge cards to cover a meal there, and he needed pampering. Not only that, but he had something to celebrate. Only a week on the job and he had hit the mark where other private eyes had never even come close: his first stiff!

Without warning, Jake's lowered defenses allowed a vivid picture of Hazel's bloated face at the bottom of the bathtub to flash into his mind. He sat down again. When he began to feel like getting up, there was only time enough to stop in at the chic neon-lit establishment next door for a mound of something healthy on a slice of organic bread. Even so, he was forced to leave half of this untouched when his stomach sent up a positive message that it was not yet ready to go to work.

After recovering in the men's room, Jake paid his check, walked back to his car, and headed for the nearest entrance to the Santa Monica Freeway. A lull in the afternoon traffic enabled him to make good time; nevertheless, he was a few minutes late pulling up in front of Arnie's building.

This turned out not to matter, since the apartment appeared to be empty. Neither knocks nor the gong-button on the front door elicited any answer, and the door itself was securely locked. Jake went back downstairs and tried to see up through the balcony windows, but these were too misted over with humidity from the many plants inside to allow any kind of a view.

With nothing better to do than follow Detective Rosa's advice to have patience, Jake returned to his car, moved it back a few yards into a shaded spot under a tree, and settled down to wait. After an hour, with still no sign of Arnie, he had run out of both shade and patience. He tried knocking and ringing again, just in case Arnie had arrived home by some rear entrance; then he went around to the back of the building to see if Arnie's car was in the garage. In fact, the building contained two garages facing out onto the lane, but both were closed and locked.

As a last resort, Jake drove over to Wilshire Boulevard, where he put through a call to his office from a pay telephone.

"Hello," caroled Miss Murphy over a high whirring background noise. "Jake Weissman, Agent to the Stars."

"Nice touch, Murphy. What's that noise?"

"Oh, Teddy Bears! I use hair dryers. Why you no come in today?"

"It's a long story. Any messages? And turn that thing off."

"Okay." Miss Murphy cut the power to the drier. "Some guy call Tuck Larson come in and leave movie script. He want you to read and say if he should take big movie part."

"Larson can't do anything but commercials. All he's got is a body."

"For sure," purred Miss Murphy. "And that's all they want. I read script."

Jake felt obliged to ask what it was about.

"Oh, he play humpy bagger in supermarket and meet this hotsy housewife and they go fock."

"Don't use that word, Murphy. Then what?"

"That's it. The end."

"Ah." Jake got the picture. "We're talking pornography."

"And how!"

"Well, it might be right up Mr. Larson's alley. But if he wants to do it, we can't be involved."

"Why no?" Miss Murphy sounded disappointed.

"It doesn't fit with my Agent to the Stars image."

"Maybe he become a porn star."

"And it's exploitive, Murphy. As a woman, you should sympathize with that."

"I sympathize better when I eat. We got no moneys."

"Also, it's illegal."

"So am I. Why you so stuffy?"

"I'm just an old-fashioned boy. Any calls from Arnie?"

"Nobody call but you," said Miss Murphy in the tone of one who expected no better. "And nobody here but me." She softened her voice. "How about you come now and see what I wear tonight? One look and I have to fight you off."

"Sounds too dangerous."

"Maybe I don't fight so hard."

"And I'm too far away. See you tonight."

Jake cut Miss Murphy off in the middle of something unflattering in Spanish and congratulated himself on a fine demonstration of self-control, not to mention his prudence in avoiding a possibly dangerous encounter with Baron, who was doubtless scheduled to pick up Miss Murphy at the office quite soon. With all his early bravado evaporated by the events of the morning, Jake shuddered at the narrowness of his escape and made a last, futile attempt to reach Arnie by telephone.

As he hung up in frustration, Jake blamed himself for not finding out where Arnie's gym was, picking him up there, and escorting him personally to the bank. Even as he stood on the sidewalk wondering what to do next, he conjured up a clear vision of Arnie doggedly pumping the various irons necessary to the development of his legs and neck, totally oblivious of the time. In any case, there would be no point in trying to find him now, as all the banks were closed and nothing could be done about the safety deposit box until tomorrow.

His sense of duty appeased, Jake returned to his car and managed to find a parking spot close to the Palisades Park, where he sat for a while under a palm tree and enjoyed a chamber-of-commerce view of the ocean and sinking sun. Occasionally he strolled up to the edge of the escarpment to look down at the busy Pacific Coast Highway and the vast expanse of beach beyond. Although it was getting late in the afternoon, there were still many swimmers and sunbathers bobbing about in the surf and dotted over the sand in a random pattern. Every so often, small alterations took place in the pattern, as when a red body would pick itself up and move away or two well-oiled brown bodies on separate towels would make contact and come together. Watching these casual people, Jake envied the ease with which they seemed to pair off and the fact that none of them was likely to have found a body in the bath that morning.

The sun now hovered very low over the horizon, and Jake realized that, regardless of his disturbing memories, he was starving. He considered trying one of the local restaurants on his list of recommendations, but gave up the idea in favor of eating closer to the theater. Accordingly, he headed back to town and, on an extravagant impulse left over from lunchtime, settled himself into the plush surroundings of L'Orangerie, where, amidst the latticed walls, fan-lit doors and restrained palm foliage of the inner patio, he dined rapturously on a concoction of fresh and smoked salmon followed by a soothing entrée of steamed chicken served in its own broth with a garnish of shallot lemon butter.

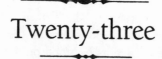

Twenty-three

H aving pampered his jangled nervous and digestive systems into an unaccustomed state of grateful tranquility, Jake ordered a second glass of brandy to accompany his third cup of coffee and settled back with a sigh to savor both in a slow, luxurious fashion. He felt proud of himself. He had survived a truly terrible day without cracking or retiring to bed with a cold compress, he had every intention of staying on the job and showing up for the Quest first night, and it occurred to him that he was now in a rare position of having earned every drop of pleasure that could be squeezed out of his present delightful circumstances.

Of course, it would have been even more gratifying if he could be celebrating something more concrete, such as a major step forward in the case he was supposed to solve. Honesty compelled him to admit, however, that he had made very little progress, or to be absolutely brutal about it, none at all. Jake shifted uncomfortably in his chair, took a sip of brandy, and pretended to take a renewed interest in his surroundings, which somehow seemed to have lost a little of their charm.

And yet, the comforting thought came wafting up with the brandy fumes, perhaps he was being too hard on himself. Perhaps he was trying to do the impossible, looking for a connecting thread where none in fact existed. Accidents happened all the time, and life seldom followed a neat plot line. It could be that the police knew their business better than he when they decided to write off Bobbie's death as an unfortunate miscalculation on the part of some untraceable sex partner. Then, by the same token, Hank Harvey could easily have overbalanced on his ladder, just as Hazel, high on whatever drugs she took, might have had only herself to blame when she slipped into that last, fatal doze.

But it couldn't be that easy. There had been too many deaths too close together, leaving too many unanswered questions. Finding himself still short on answers, Jake shut his eyes, downed some more brandy, and tried to remember the questions.

Why, to start at the beginning, had someone sent him the casting list for Yolanda's play, when casting had already been completed? And who had got rid of Carl, the original Goliath, by tampering with his car? Why did the Quest make more money on weekends when Bobbie ran the box office? And where did Bobbie get the money to pay for his own funeral, not to mention earlier contributions to the presiding minister? Then there was the matter of missing objects: what had happened to Jake's gun and Arnie's bag? Arnie suspected Hazel of taking the bag. Was that what she had been looking for when he saw her being driven away from his apartment? And who was the man in the bowler hat sitting beside her at the wheel?

At this point, Jake found it necessary to open his eyes and drink a fourth cup of coffee in order to subdue a cloud of bees in the shape of question marks that had begun to swarm about in his brain. When at last he felt able to shut his eyes again, it was with a new resolve to order his thoughts along neat methodical lines, not unlike those favored by the detectives in his favorite crime novels. The problem of where to begin presented its usual difficulties, but such was Jake's growing identification with his fictional heroes that in next to no time the words *suspect* and *motive* had materialized in the space recently occupied by the bees.

Jake congratulated himself that, unlike most of his brilliant role models, he had to deal with a case involving fairly straightforward motives and an almost embarrassing shortage of suspects, which should make his game of detection comparatively easy, unless, as a small cautious voice reminded him, he happened to be playing with a list of suspects that lacked a few important entries—such as Hazel's friend in the bowler hat, to name a definite possibility. The cautious voice had a point, but Jake, who had abandoned caution several days ago, chose to ignore it. Lifting his brandy in a farewell toast to all wishy-washy inner voices, he plunged ahead with such materials as he had at hand.

He began with the twins. Tim could have wanted Bobbie out of the way in order to get at Arnie, and in Tina he had a perfect accomplice; as a qualified mechanic, she would have had no difficulty in sabotaging Carl's car. Having made this promising beginning, Jake rewarded himself with a little more brandy and remembered the twins saying that they suspected Hazel of pushing over Hank's ladder when she had left them in the café to get her car out of its garage. Unfortunately, in terms of alibi, her departure had left them free to do exactly the same thing. But why should anyone have wanted to kill Hank? He had threatened to close Yolanda's play, which Hazel and the twins supported, but would they have killed for that? And even if they had, why get rid of Hazel?

Jake's mind now began racing along on automatic pilot, leaving its bemused owner to keep up as best he could. Hazel, too, had tried to stop the play, it reminded him. Could there be a connection? But the twins boasted of having her totally under their control, and from what he had seen, Tina could surely have talked her back into supporting their pet project. But even if she couldn't, what good would killing Hazel do? The theater would close, and the twins, who seemed to have no money and no other home, would find themselves out on the street again.

That left Yolanda. Bobbie had spoken out against her. So had Hank and Hazel. But was Yolanda a cold-blooded killer willing to eliminate anyone who threatened to stand in her way? Yolanda could be irritating in her self-absorption, and possibly she rated her own talents at a level higher than an unkind world might ever grant, but these very qualities seemed to give her a healthy confidence that would make her far too certain of eventual success to consider trying to achieve it by murder. That would be the way of someone quite different; someone with no confidence at all, someone ruthless and dedicated but at the same time so unsure of herself that she felt she could get what she wanted only by eliminating the competition. Someone clever enough to take advantage of whatever opportunity came to hand—an un-steady ladder or a semi-unconscious victim—but otherwise so quiet and self-effacing as to be almost invisible. Someone who killed per-haps not for herself at all but for someone else. Someone like—

"Did you say something, sir?"

Jake opened his eyes and found himself being stared at by a passing waiter and several neighboring diners. He removed his fist from the spot where it had struck the table and did his best to look blandly surprised.

"No, I don't think so."

"I thought you said—"

"Pity," Jake interrupted quickly. "Pity to go, but I must. Could I have my check, please?"

The waiter hurried off and the diners resumed their hushed conver-sations, leaving Jake to massage his hand under the table and rejoice. For he had most certainly hit on the answer. Plain, mousy Kitty, the very last person he would have suspected: it couldn't have worked out better if the butler had done it! And it all made such sense, given a little hindsight. Obstacles vanished from Yolanda's path not because she stooped to remove them but because there was someone behind the scenes doing the dirty work for her. He could still remember the doglike devotion in Kitty's eyes and the urgency in her voice when she had said, "I look after Nanda." It hadn't registered at the time, but clearly she had found her mission in life and was willing to do anything in pursuit of it. *I'd do anything for Nanda*—he could hear her speak the words, but had she ever really done so? It seemed that she had, but it hardly mattered. What counted was that he knew her secret.

Now all he had to do was come up with some proof. It shouldn't be difficult: a few sly conversations with the unsuspecting Kitty, a sudden pounce and presto! he would have a killer all packaged up and ready for delivery to the police. He might even wrap everything up tonight, if he could get Kitty alone for a while, and *then* let that smug bastard Rosa try to laugh at him with his patronizing manner and safe, dull clothes.

Buoyed up by this prospect, Jake knocked back the last of his brandy, paid his check without flinching, and floated beaming out into a velvet evening, where the warm twilit atmosphere seemed a natural extension of the candlelight he had just left. He was still beaming when he wafted into the Quest lobby.

Finding Miss Murphy and Baron presented no problem, since they stood isolated in the center of a wary circle, surrounded by other members of the audience, who pretended to be deep in conversation with each other while inspecting the strikingly attired couple out of the corners of their eyes. Oblivious to this attention behind his mirrored sunglasses, Baron wore his customary motorcycle jacket, chains and cap. In honor of the occasion, however, he had donned a pair of form-fitting black leather breeches set off by gleaming knee boots and, Jake was dismayed to discover, a heavily studded codpiece of more than ample proportions. Miss Murphy matched this sartorial note by sporting a towering hairstyle of upswept curls, tiny high-heeled sandals and a black nylon jumpsuit cut tight at the ankles and constructed with shirred seams that gave her the appearance of a semi-inflated Michelin Man. As a further concession to Baron's favorite style, she wore around her waist a loose studded belt, designed to provide a highly necessary stopping point for the unzipped front of her jumpsuit.

176

Jake attempted to sidle unnoticed around the far end of the lobby, but was stopped in his tracks by a loud cry of "Teddy Bears!" Instantly, the shortest distance between Jake and Miss Murphy was defined by a clear passageway that materialized through the crowd of interested onlookers. Flashing a gracious smile of thanks to right and left, Miss Murphy bore down on Jake and planted a warm kiss on his mouth. Baron followed on clattering steel-reinforced soles, shook hands with a grip more suited to arm wrestling than a normal social greeting and, after giving Jake's white suit a disdainful once-over, asked him when he had started wearing lipstick.

"I keep tellin' her to wear some junk that won't come off," he chortled, as Jake hastily wiped off the residue of Miss Murphy's embrace, "but she keeps on with that greasy stuff."

"Sure," Miss Murphy agreed good-naturedly. "I like to see where I been. You got trouble," she breathed into Jake's ear, employing a vibrant whisper that carried to every corner of the lobby, where it stopped any remaining conversation in its tracks.

"What now?" asked Jake, turning pale.

"Come on boys. Let's go in," suggested Miss Murphy in a bright stage voice for the benefit of the onlookers. Grasping Jake by the arm, she propelled him up the three steps to the area outside the box office, pushed him against a door in the opposite wall, and knocked.

The door opened and a hand shot out. It seized the arm relinquished by Miss Murphy in a demonic grip and yanked Jake sideways into what proved to be an extension of the dressing room area. Here Jake found himself in the clutches of Yolanda, who, enveloped in a cloud of cigarette smoke from a nervously hovering Kitty, seemed to have worked herself into a semi-demented condition.

"What have you done with him?" she hissed wildly. "Where is he?"

"Who?" stammered Jake, for whom things were happening far too quickly. "What are you talking about?"

Yolanda traded a significant look with Kitty. "Don't play cute with me. That idiot you dumped on us, that Arnie." She thrust her hair back in a frantic gesture. "He isn't here and he doesn't answer his phone and"—her voice rose to a wail—"and we're due to start *now!*"

"Can't you get someone ready to go on for him?" Faced with a probable murderer and a possible maniac, Jake cast about for any reasonable solution to the problem, however feeble. "Tim, Tina, anybody? He doesn't go on until the end of act one. Maybe he'll get here by then."

"I've thought of that," snapped Yolanda. "We don't have anyone to spare. Everybody else in the cast is playing three parts already. Tim is all we have backstage, and Tina's running the lights." She glared vindictively at Jake. "You've ruined my opera! I'll sue you! It's all your fault you monster, you, you—"

Yolanda's outburst ended in mid snarl as a new expression, indicative of hope, began to arrange itself on her face. Jake's deepest fears were confirmed when it settled into an ingratiating smile.

"No," he said in the firmest voice he could muster. "Definitely not."

Yolanda ignored him. "Tim!" she yelled.

Tim appeared from behind a curtained area leading to the stage. He looked pale and wore a black band over the sleeve of his white T-shirt.

"Tim," Yolanda hailed him ecstatically. "What do you think? Mr. Weissman has volunteered like an *angel* to be our Goliath. He knows the part backward," she continued, ignoring Jake's feeble attempts at protest, "so all he needs from you is a makeup job and some help with the costume. Start the show right now and you can fix him up when you get that break in Scene Three."

Tim looked dubiously at Jake. "I suppose," he said without conviction.

"Good. Carry on," commanded Yolanda, once again in full command of herself and her troops. "We're *so* grateful," she cooed, turning back to Jake, "aren't we, Kitty? And just remember"—she fixed Jake again with a glittering eye—"if you even *try* and run out on us, I shall personally hunt you down and strangle you with these two hands. I might just do it anyway for what you've done to my show. Understand? Good. Break a leg. First act beginners!" she trumpeted, loping off toward the main dressing area. "Onstage *now!*"

Jake stood dazed for a moment before deciding that, threats or no, his best course of action would be to get out of the theater before someone came for him. But when he turned toward the door, he found his escape route blocked by Kitty.

"Please do it," she begged, reaching out to touch him tentatively on the arm. "Just for tonight. It means everything to Nanda, and I can't bear to see her disappointed."

Jake stared into the humble, pleading eyes behind which he seemed to read a deeper, harder, more dangerous message.

He decided to stay.

Twenty-four

"There!" said Tim, as he added the last touches to Jake's makeup. "You look really horrible."

Staring sadly at his reflection in the dressing room mirror, Jake had to agree. To the hideous face created for Arnie, Tim had added a drooping handlebar mustache and a moplike wig—"To help hold the hat up"—that looked as if it hadn't seen a cleaning for years. Whether real or imagined, Jake experienced a strong sensation of something small and persistent wandering about his scalp, but he was too worried about disturbing Tim's handiwork to risk an exploration. He could only pray that Arnie would show up and rescue him from this nightmare, even as the action rolled forward onstage and his chances of escape grew slimmer by the minute.

"Now we can finish putting on the costume," Tim announced. "Stand up."

This was easier said than done. The resources of the Quest's costume collection had been equal to supplying Jake with a plaid shirt and a pair of old work pants, but the rest of his outfit presented problems. His own featherweight shoes were out of the question, so with nothing suitable in stock he had no choice but to wear the boots Arnie had left behind. Unfortunately, these were twice the size of Jake's feet, making it necessary for him to layer four thick socks over each foot and provide extra anchorage at knee level by means of strings tied through the cloth straps sewn into the inner top edge of each boot. Despite these ingenious remedies, the boots still tended to slip off when he tried to move and to overbalance him when he tried to stand still.

In obedience to Tim's command, however, he stood up and immediately slid several inches down into the toes of his boots. Tim caught him deftly, just as he was on the point of toppling backward.

"Upsy-daisy," said Tim brightly. "Now let's try the chaps and the hat. You know, it could be a lot worse," he mused, when these articles had been added. "Have a look in the mirror."

Jake moved forward a cautious step or two and found that by keeping his legs stiff and sliding each foot forward along the ground, he could manage to make some progress without losing his boots. In this manner he lurched over to the full-length mirror and got his first complete view of himself as Goliath Jones.

It was not an encouraging sight. Although Tim had stuffed many sheets of tissue under the sweatband inside Arnie's Stetson, it still sat uncomfortably low over Jake's eyebrows and ears. And despite generous turnups made to the bottoms of the chaps, they still had to be buckled on just under Jake's arms. These stopgap measures effectively obscured Jake's entire torso, so that only his hat, mustache and arms remained visible above the chaps.

"I look like a walking head," he moaned.

"Well, they wanted an ogre," said Tim consolingly.

"I'm too short for an ogre."

"So they're getting an ogre-ette. Now, where am I going to put the gun belt?"

Another problem arose here, for when the gun belt was strapped around Jake's waist he appeared to be wearing it somewhere in the vicinity of his knees. There was nothing for it but to secure the belt around his chest and wedge the holster under his left arm, where he could reach across and pull out the gun with his right hand.

"Why does this thing have a flap on it?" he asked, as he struggled to open a snap-fastened closure at the top of the holster. "It looks like something a forest ranger might wear."

"Maybe it is," Tim admitted. "We haven't any money to buy proper western ones, so we're having to make do with what we've got. I found two of these downstairs. Try and wedge the top flap open so you can make a fast draw."

"Is there anything special I have to know about this?" Jake asked, gingerly reaching into the holster and withdrawing a metallized plastic gun with a brown plastic handle.

"No, it's just a toy. We've loaded it with a strip of caps, so if you don't get a bang when you first pull the trigger, just keep on firing until you do. It might be a good idea to try out a few rounds in the lane, but I don't think you could walk that far. Anyhow, your entrance is coming up. Let's go!"

Tim raced off toward the stage, leaving Jake to follow at the more sedate pace demanded by his new style of walking. Because the effort of concentrating on keeping his legs straight made his arms behave in the same stiff fashion, he lurched along like a large windup toy or an undersize reject from the Frankenstein laboratories.

All I need is a key in my back and a couple of pins in my neck, he thought bitterly as he teetered along the narrow passageway behind Wet Set Willie's canvas backdrop to take up his entrance position in the wings on the far side of the stage. An actor whom he had heard other members of the cast addressing as Larry was also waiting to go on. He stared at Jake in alarm.

"What the hell are you doing here?" he whispered.

Jake tipped his hat back so that he could see Larry without having to tilt his head. "Arnie can't make it," he whispered back. "I'm filling in."

"Jesus," said Larry. "Nobody told us. Do you know when you come on?"

"When you run in and yell, 'He's coming!' and all the girls scream."

"That's it. Well, here we go." Larry took a deep breath. "He's coming!" he yelled at the top of his lungs, staggering onstage and pointing off in Jake's direction with a trembling arm.

"Aaaah!" screamed the ladies of the company.

Jake's moment had arrived. With beating heart and locked knees, he launched himself onto the stage.

There was a stunned pause while the cast, who had been expecting to see Arnie, stared at him in astonishment and, Jake thought proudly, genuine horror. He decided to glare back at them. This proved to be a mistake, as the action of drawing his eyebrows together allowed the precariously balanced Stetson to slide down over his eyes until it came to rest on the tip of his nose. Thus contracted into a mere hat over a pair of arms and legs, he saw the light on the floor directly under him turn red and heard a piano rumble from Kitty as the ladies of the town pulled themselves together and delivered a series of ragged squeaks.

The sound of the curtain jerking shut was followed by a smattering of bemused applause from the audience and a loud thump onstage as Jake, having slid too far down into the toes of his boots, leaned back to compensate and toppled over like a bowling pin.

"No, no, dear," called Yolanda from her platform. "You're too early. The fall comes at the end of act *two*."

Jake, who had called upon his training with Arnie to survive the fall undamaged, looked up from his reclining position and explained what had happened.

"Oh," said Yolanda, not entirely convinced. "Well, never mind. You did *beautifully*. And the costume suits you too. Can you get up?"

Jake managed to do so.

"Splendid. Now just keep out of everybody's way and we'll get through this performance yet. Oh, I *hate* this thing," she muttered nervously as she began to climb down the wobbling ladder fastened to the edge of her platform.

"I heard that," came the voice of Wet Set Willie from behind the backdrop.

"Willie, *dear* . . ."

Jake pivoted smartly about on one leg and waddled offstage as quickly as he could. In the far corner of the wings, next to a card table where various properties used by the cast during the course of the action were carefully laid out, he found an unoccupied kitchen chair and sat down. Soon he was joined by young Kevin, who had come over to check that everything he needed in the next act was on the table.

"You don't need all that gunk on your face," he announced after giving Jake's makeup a critical inspection. "You be better off cuttin' eyeholes in that there hat."

"I'm just doing what I'm told," Jake informed him wearily. "Don't give me a hard time."

"Shit, I was only teasin'," said Kevin, leaning back on the brick wall that separated the Quest from the ice cream parlor next door. "Don't get all worked up over an ol' walk-on part."

"As Mr. Hitchcock said to Miss Bergman, 'Ingrid—it's only a *movie*.'"

"Yeah," said Kevin morosely, "except in a movie we'd have proper stuff. Look at this dumb holster." He reached over the table and picked up a brown leather holster similar to Jake's and snapped open its top flap. "How'm I supposed to draw fast with this? I look like some dude with a camera. And this stupid *gun*." He pulled out a cheap plastic cap pistol, similar to Jake's.

"Kevin—it's only a *play*."

"Okay, but I'll tell ya one thing: you better listen good when I pull this here trigger, because if some ol' lady cough in the audience you ain't gonna hear the pop. If it was up to me, I'd end this show with a *real* bang."

"I'll pass that suggestion on," promised Jake.

"You do that. And don't sit there lookin' so skeered. You doin' jus' *fine*." With this off his chest, Kevin replaced the despised equipment on the table and wandered off to dispense more comfort and guidance in other quarters, leaving Jake to be shooed back into the dressing room area by Tim and Yolanda, who were busily setting up for act two.

Intermission finally ended and act two began. Left with nothing else to do during the long wait until his climactic entrance, Jake filled in the time by developing a thorough case of stage fright. One by one, the many rich potentials for disaster presented themselves for consideration. The ridiculous appearance of his costume, the difficulty of remaining erect, the ease of falling over—all marched vividly into his imagination and materialized physically in the form of a cold sweat that soaked his shirt, forced its way through his makeup, and ran down his nose. How on earth did I get into this mess, Jake wondered feverishly, and when was he going to set his trap for Kitty, and what had happened to Arnie, and where—

"Hey, come on. This is us," panted Kevin, sticking his head through the curtained doorway. "Don't forget your hat!"

Together they made their way back to the far side of the stage, where Jake tried desperately to stop his teeth from chattering and Kevin rapidly buckled on his holster just as Man 1 onstage was moaning, "Who can save us from the terrible Goliath Jones?"

Kevin gave Jake an encouraging slap on the small of his back, nearly knocking him off balance, and strode singing onto the stage. Jake heard him out to "I'm gonna plug that eight-foot slob" before giving in to panic. He checked that his holster was open and his fly closed; he rebalanced his hat on his ears; he tried to grasp the insides of Arnie's boots more securely with his toes. But what was his entrance cue? Everyone onstage was singing "Ha, ha, ha! Ho, ho, ho!" Then one of the girls said, "It's past noon. Big G's comin' fer the shootout."

Was that it? He took a tentative step forward, but stopped when the dialogue carried on. Presently Kevin began singing again and Kitty rumbled on the piano.

"Scram, kid! Save yourself!" came from one of the men, followed by, "Here's Big G now!" and another rumble.

That was it! Terrified of taking another fall, Jake scuttled out of the wings in a series of ministeps and surprised himself by essaying an "AAARGG!" that emerged as a dry gurgle ending in a squawk.

"Hey, Big G, you're three minutes late!" sang Kevin. "I'm takin' you on—"

"David, don't!" a girl pleaded.

"Not with that peashooter!" cried a man.

"—with my Colt thirty-eight!" trumpeted Kevin, drawing forth his gun.

Although Jake knew next to nothing about firearms, even without his glasses he was quite capable of distinguishing between a toy and the real thing. Furthermore, he had no trouble in recognizing that the muzzle of the gun pointed directly at him belonged not to a cap pistol but to Baron's Walther PPK automatic.

"No," he said faintly, as Kevin took the measure of the weapon in his hand.

"Goliath, draw! Your end is near!" intoned a voice from above.

"No," repeated Jake, beginning a crablike sidle to get out of the line of fire. He could hardly tear his eyes off the deadly black opening in the tip of the gun muzzle as it slowly moved to keep pointing directly at him, but he managed to look up and into Kevin's face with what he hoped was a heartrending expression. Kevin met his pathetic gaze with an ecstatic smile that also, as it seemed to Jake, contained a hint of wicked complicity.

He's really going to do it, thought Jake. He wants his bang and he doesn't care if he kills me to get it. Summoning all his powers of concentration, he attempted to put his entire soul into one final yell, but found himself unable to utter a sound. He tried to fall on the floor, but lacked even the minimal coordination necessary to overbalance.

"David, shoot!" trumpeted Yolanda. "The way is clear!"

184

With his whole attention back on the gun, which seemed to take on the magnified detail of a filmed close-up, Jake saw Kevin's trigger finger tremble, tighten, and then disappear behind a yellow flash, as in rapid succession there came a tremendous crash in his ears, a strange twang and several simultaneous screams. Darkness descended and Jake fell. Thank God it didn't hurt, was his last thought.

"David, David," sang the chorus gamely. "How did you learn to shoot so straight? David, David—"

"Murderer!" came the despairing cry from above.

Every head tilted upward as Yolanda, eyes ablaze, staggered to the edge of her swaying platform.

"*You* did it!" she shrieked, pointing down at Kevin, who had been knocked onto his back by the recoil from the blast and was now sitting where he had fallen, trying to see where the gun had disappeared to.

"*He* did it!" Yolanda screamed, waving a twisted mass of wire and splintered wood at the audience. "That little bastard shot Mother Guitar!"

"You and your!—COLT!!—**THIRTY-EIGHT!!!**"sang the chorus in four-part harmony.

The curtain closed.

Twenty-five

J ake regained consciousness to the sound of applause. Under the impression that the evening had ended with an amusing theatrical twist, the audience was expressing its approval in an enthusiastic fashion. This failed to lift Jake's spirits. He felt sick, the back of his head hurt, and he could see nothing but the blurred interior of Arnie's Stetson, which had been pushed forward over his head when he hit the floor. Closing his eyes again, he tried to decide whether or not he had been shot. An attempt at movement might provide the answer but might also result in considerable pain and loss of blood. It seemed wiser to remain still until help arrived.

"It's all right! They thought it was part of the show!"

The exultant girlish voice over Jake's head could hardly be recognized as belonging to Yolanda. It was followed by a pitter-patter of nimble feet as the rejoicing author-narrator skimmed down her ladder to stage level.

"Tim," she called, "keep the curtain closed. And get out front fast with the collection box!"

What about me? thought Jake plaintively. I'm dying.

Hope rose when rapid footsteps approached him from the left, but fell again when, without a break in stride, they skipped over his inert form and moved away to the right.

"Everybody take a bow!" cried Yolanda from her new rallying point on the other side of the stage. "Out through the side here. Quick march!"

The word *Help* resounded loudly in Jake's mind without actually emerging from his mouth. A small stampede of feet dashed past him and, after a certain amount of jockeying for position, followed Yolanda out in front of the curtain.

Jake began to feel lonely. Help, he thought again, as the audience responded to the reappearance of the cast with increased applause and a few isolated cheers. In the face of total neglect, Jake resolved to risk moving an arm or a finger, but changed his mind when he became aware of footsteps approaching the stage through the dressing room area. He waited.

"Teddy Bears!" wailed Miss Murphy, rushing across the stage. "What they do to you?"

"Never mind that jerk," snarled Baron, tramping in behind her on his steel-tapped soles. "Help me find the fuckin' gun."

"Oh, my poor, poor, Teddy Bears," wept Miss Murphy, who had run out of the auditorium just after Jake fell and therefore missed seeing the corpse of Mother Guitar. She lifted various parts of Jake's costume this way and that in search of a bullet hole. "I don't see no blood," she announced in a puzzled voice.

"Prolly hasn't got any," muttered Baron, stamping about behind Wet Set Willie's wooden uprights and cactus cutouts.

On the other side of the curtain, Yolanda had launched into an appeal for funds. "Our kind of theater cannot exist without your support," she was saying, "and the modest price of your tickets hardly begins to cover expenses. So if you care about alternative theater like ours and want to see it survive, please, please dig down into your pockets and . . ." The appeal followed its familiar course.

Miss Murphy had now removed the Stetson from Jake's face and lifted his head into her lap. "I think he still breathing," she said, just as Baron exclaimed "Here's the sucker!" and zipped the gun away in one of his many jacket pockets.

"Don't just stand around," Miss Murphy blazed at him, meanwhile slapping Jake's cheek's with her fingertips. "Do somethings!"

"Whaddaya want me to do?" Baron asked in an exasperated voice. Nevertheless, so as not to seem disobliging, he planted a thick bootheel against Jake's right hip and shoved. Jake uttered a deep groan.

"He not dead!" Miss Murphy rejoiced. "It's okay—you no kill him," she informed Yolanda and the other members of the cast, now returned from their triumph and ready to take a polite interest in Jake's condition.

"Look," said Kevin, pointing. "He got his eyes open."

"Poor Teddy Bears," said Miss Murphy tenderly, oblivious to the snicker that rose around her. "How you feel?"

"My head hurts," said Jake. "Are you sure I'm not shot?"

"Poor baby, no," crooned Miss Murphy. "You just faint and bang you head."

"Oh, brother," sighed Baron, retreating away from the circle of interest to prop himself up against the side of the stage.

"Then could somebody please get me out of these boots?" Jake asked in a tired voice. "I want to try standing up."

Many hands sprang into action, unbuckling his gun belt, unfastening his chaps, and pulling off his boots. Freed of these encumbrances, Jake took a firm grip on one of the set uprights and hauled himself up. After savoring the pleasure of being able to stand firmly erect on his own stocking feet without toppling over, he suddenly remembered his close brush with a bullet.

"What got into you?" he asked Kevin indignantly. "You might have killed me!"

Kevin gave him a pitying look. "No way," he said. "I know better'n that. I was aimin' over you." He demonstrated. "BAM!"

Jake leapt several inches into the air. "That doesn't make any d-difference." As reaction to his escape set in, he began to shake. "G-guns are d-dangerous," he chattered. "Y-you must be c-crazy. H-h-how d-did you g-get it?"

"I din't get nuthin'!" Kevin protested with wide-eyed innocence, appealing to everyone around him. "It was jus' there in the holster, and I thought somebody'd come up with a good-lookin' gun at the las' minute. Honest to God," he concluded, turning back to Jake. "I din't know it was loaded for real. I was jus' doin' like they said." His chin began to tremble. "Shit, I'm only eight years ol'."

Miss Murphy knelt down in front of him. "It's okay, niño. We know you don't do nothing bad." She gave him a hug. "Now go see outside. I bet everybody wait for autograph."

Kevin rewarded her with a grateful smile and ran offstage, followed by envious looks from other members of the cast who also had near and dear waiting in the lobby.

Larry was the first to speak. "I guess we should call the police," he suggested in a halfhearted voice.

"NO!"

Yolanda, Jake and Miss Murphy achieved near perfect unison, with just a slight echo from Baron. Yolanda, however, took charge of the matter. "No," she repeated in a calmer voice. "I think that would be counterproductive. It's perfectly clear the child was lying. He obviously picked up the gun in some unsavory hangout and tried to show off here without thinking of the possible consequences. Calling the police would only give them the ammunition they need to close the theater—just when we've got a hit on our hands! Now I'm the only one who's suffered from this little incident"—everyone followed her eyes to the mangled remains of Mother Guitar lying in a heap on the stage—"and if I can forgive and forget, then so can you. Unless you all want to be out of a job tomorrow. Right?" she concluded sweetly.

The cast traded dubious looks, then began to wander off.

"Good," called Yolanda after them. "We'll just pretend it never happened. But how can we do it again tomorrow?" she wondered aloud.

Jake opened his mouth to speak, but was prevented from doing so by the arrival onstage of Tim and Tina, who bounced cheerfully in from the dressing rooms shaking weighty collection cans.

"What a night!" Tim bubbled. "Listen to this!"

The cans rattled and rustled in a most satisfactory manner.

Tina, like Tim, wore a black mourning band on her arm. She inspected Jake's face, ashen under its makeup. "Are you okay?" she asked with concern.

"No," said Jake. "I'm not okay." He had received a whispered message from Miss Murphy that the gun was safely back in Baron's possession and with that major worry out of the way felt free to indulge in the luxury of losing his temper. "I'm anything but okay," he rattled on. "I've been humiliated and shot at and ignored and it's a miracle I'm not dead!"

"Now let's not get upset," said Yolanda in the voice she generally reserved for Wet Set Willie and difficult actors.

"Upset!" yelled Jake. "I'm not upset! I'm furious! I don't believe that crap about Kevin for a second. Somebody sneaked the gun into his holster during intermission hoping he'd get lucky and finish me off. Well, as far as I'm concerned, that's it." He stooped down and picked up Arnie's boots. "I'm retiring from the stage! I'm walking out of here while I still can, and if ever I'm dumb enough to set foot in this place again, I deserve everything I get. And you know what else?" he added, collecting the Stetson from the floor behind him. "I'm pulling my giant. I may not be the best agent in the world, but even I draw the line somewhere and I'm drawing it here. This place is a madhouse. It's dangerous and unprofessional, and I wouldn't let any client of mine work here even—even if you *paid* him! Come on," he said to Miss Murphy and Baron. "Let's get out before they start throwing knives."

Satisfied at having made his point with force and clarity, Jake spun about on his four layers of sock and made a dignified, if muffled, exit, grabbing his shoes and clothes from the dressing room, padding past the last few stragglers in the lobby, and not stopping until he had reached his car some blocks away from the theater.

While Jake hunted through his pockets for his car keys, Baron deposited himself on one of the Thunderbird's front fenders and bounced heavily up and down.

"So," he said. "You meant that about pullin' out?"

"You b-bet." Jake had begun to shiver again.

"Maybe you better take this back, just in case." Baron began to unzip a bulging side pocket in his jacket.

189

"G-g-god, no!"

"Teddy Bears, you don't look so good," said Miss Murphy, with concern.

"It's the makeup. I'll be f-f-f—"

There followed a short heated argument in which Miss Murphy insisted on driving Jake's car home and was only dissuaded from doing so when Baron stepped in to point out that she couldn't drive. They finally reached a compromise where Jake would be allowed to pilot himself home, using minimum speed and maximum caution, while Baron and Miss Murphy followed behind to make sure he arrived safely. Even then, Miss Murphy insisted on escorting him to the door, where she dispensed a warm good-night kiss, an invitation to breakfast at the office in the morning, and Baron's telephone number—in case Jake should want to call her during the night—before allowing Baron to send her back to the motorcycle.

Lingering behind for a moment, Baron leaned on the doorframe, scratched under his cap, and said, "It beats me what that dame sees in you. You sure you don't want the gun?"

"I don't want the gun."

"Whatcha gonna do now?"

"I'm going to clean up my face, have a shower, get drunk, and go to bed."

Baron checked over his shoulder and then said, "Hold outcher hand," through the corner of his mouth.

"Huh?"

"I said hold outcher fuckin' hand!" A round white pill appeared in Jake's outstretched palm. "Forget the booze. It'll kill your liver. All you need is this and a glass of water. Have fun."

Twenty-six

When Baron's echoing taps had faded away into the night, Jake closed first his mouth, then the door, placed the white pill in the center of the jungle-drum coffee table, and went off to clean up. An hour later he was back in the living room, seated on his zebra rug in his zebra-striped bikini briefs, attempting to add a tom-tom obbligato to the vibrant strains of "Safari Nights" on the stereo. He had downed most of what brandy remained in the bottle on the bar, but still felt tense and rattled, unable to surrender himself to the native beat. All signs pointed toward a long sleepless night.

Baron's white pill sat innocently on the coffee table drum, primly trying to pull its smooth, polished sides away from the pitted surface of the stretched hide. Focusing his eyes on it more clearly, Jake noticed a shallow incision running precisely across the top of the pill so that it could be broken into two equal parts. From his experience with aspirin—and he was an expert on aspirin, if he did say so himself (Jake drank a toast to aspirin with the last of the brandy)—half a tablet constituted a dose for children. But he was no longer a child. He was a much put upon adult with twitching nerves who couldn't get the beat and who needed help. He carried the pill into the kitchen and washed it down with a gulp of water from the tap.

When the telephone rang twenty minutes later, Jake not only had the beat, he was soaring high above it. He paused to wonder dreamily why he had never before noticed his telephone's particularly melodic note. Obligingly, that instrument granted an encore. After listening raptly to several more rings, Jake formulated the thought that perhaps the telephone might have something to say to him, something that a faint voice in the back of his mind told him he wanted to hear. He picked up the receiver.

"YELL-o," he said, by way of breaking the ice.

"Mr. Weissman?" The telephone sounded upset.

"Jake Weissman here, Agent to the Stars."

"Oh, Mr. Weissman, it's Tim. From the Quest. I'm sorry to call you like this, but I'm so frightened."

A wave of tender paternal feelings, akin to those portrayed so warmly on the screen by Charles Coburn and C. Aubrey Smith, washed over Jake. "And what seems to be the trouble, my"—he hiccupped—"excuse me—my boy?"

"It's Tina." Tim's voice wavered. "She was supposed to take me home in Hazel's car after we finished cleaning up the stage and the dressing rooms, but we had a fight and she went off and now I'm all by myself." A short sob followed. "It's so creepy here. I'm scared."

"Now, now. Don't be upset. Why don't you call home?"

"It isn't a real home," Tim sniffed. "I share a place with Tina, and it's miles away and I don't have any money. Anyway, I won't go back there until she says she's sorry for all the things she said."

Not being able to take on any more problems that night, Jake found his eyes starting to close.

"Mr. Weissman? Are you there?"

"Yes! Yes, I'm here." Jake made a valiant effort to remember the conversation so far. "What do you want me to do?"

"Well, it's a lot to ask, but I have a friend I can stay with who lives near you. But his car's being repaired and he can't pick me up. So I was wondering . . ."

"Sure. I understand. The thing is, I'm not really in good shape to drive right now."

"I can drive. If you could just make it over here, I'll bring you back to your place and walk over to my friend's."

"Well . . ."

"Oh, thanks, Mr. Weissman. And please hurry. I keep thinking about Hazel upstairs and—and I hear noises."

Jake rubbed his eyes. "Okay. I'll—you wait in the lobby and I'll come by."

"Oh—" A squeak of dismay.

"What's the matter?"

"It's just that . . . the water's still dripping in there. Like she was still—"

"Now, Tim."

"And I don't want to stand around on the street. People think you're, you know, for sale."

The problems of youth. "Where, then?" Jake asked.

"Around back, where we paint the sets."

"Fine. Give me fifteen minutes."

Jake hung up and headed for the bedroom in search of clothes. To his surprise, the familiar surroundings seemed to have expanded in size and taken on a life and motion of their own. Walls altered shape in defiance of the laws of perspective and geometry, the ceiling advanced and retreated at its own pleasure, and the floor showed a skittish tendency to tilt when least expected, making it necessary for Jake to sit down on the edge of the bed before attempting to pull on his pants. With this difficult feat of coordination safely behind him, he slipped on a pair of sneakers, fought his way into an old sweatshirt, and was ready to go.

Still the tiny buzz in the back of his head warned of a forgotten something without going so far as to reveal what it might be. Jake checked himself in the mirror: nothing missing except socks, and who cared? He thrust his hands into his pockets: wallet and keys were there. He looked about the room, jingling his keys. In its pigeonhole at the head of the bed, the twin of his friendly living room telephone caught his eye. Keys and telephone . . . The combination clicked. Why hadn't Arnie called? Where was he? Scrabbling in the pocket of his white suit, Jake found his address book and punched Arnie's number into the telephone. After two rings and a click, a faraway voice answered.

"Hello," it said.

"Arnie?"

"This is Bobbie."

Jake's legs gave way and deposited him back on the bed.

"Please don't hang up," continued Bobbie, "because I really want to talk to you. Arnie and I can't come to the phone right now, but if you'll just wait for the beep and leave your name, number and time you called, we'll get back to you as soon as we can. Here comes the beep. You're on!"

Jake hung up and waited for his heart to stop thumping. When he had calmed down a little, he redialed and listened again to Bobbie's voice. It was light and husky with a slight catch, neither obviously masculine nor particularly feminine, and it survived even a poor electrical hookup to come across with a humor and warmth of inflection that once more prevented Jake from formulating a message. On the third try, however, he managed to stammer out a few sentences into the answering machine. He then went into the kitchen and downed a glass of instant coffee made with hot tap water. It tasted vile but provided his system with sufficient stimulus to propel him into his car and over to Melrose Avenue without accident.

There was no sign of Tim in the alley behind the theater. Pulling to a halt opposite some painted canvas panels belonging to the recently closed production of *The Importance of Being Earnest,* Jake shifted into neutral, tapped lightly on the horn, and waited for Tim to appear. The scent of some night-blooming flower floated by on a warm breeze, and an almost full moon cast a soft light over the alley, reducing the paint-splashed walls and service doors of the theater as well as the velvet-draped panels of Algernon Moncrieff's late morning room to a uniform purple monochrome, interrupted by the odd midnight blue shadow. A different type of shadow, however, appeared between the two sliding service doors. Tall, thin and jet black, it came from within the theater. The doors had been left slightly open.

Switching off the car engine, Jake climbed out and walked over to investigate. A short pull on both doors widened the gap between them and sent a shaft of blue light into the theater, which appeared to be quite deserted. This was good enough for Jake. He had taken much longer to get there than the specified fifteen minutes, and it was more than likely that Tim had given him up and wandered off. Or Tina could have relented and returned. His conscience at rest, Jake was just about to roll the doors shut and head for home when his eye came to rest on a vertical band of yellow light that shimmered weakly beyond the front row of seats, somewhere to the right of the stage opening.

"Tim?"

The name came out much louder than Jake had intended. It echoed

194

about the empty house and seemed to blend with another sound as it died out. Jake tried again.

"Tim?"

This time there could be no doubt about it. An inarticulate cry answered him. Jake rested his head against one of the doors and tried not to despair. He had done much that day and lacked the heart to do more. Also, he was fighting a losing battle against sleep. As his eyelids dropped shut, the muffled cry came again, intensified by an added note of panic. Sleep would have to wait. Jake forced his eyes open, pushed the sliding doors farther apart, and stumbled into the theater.

Following a path of moonlight up the corridor behind the last row of seats, Jake crossed to the center aisle, then moved cautiously down it into the deepening shadow. He could see nothing by the time he reached the front seats but managed to turn right and feel his way along the curved edge of the stage until he came up against the side wall, behind which he had nervously waited to make his entrance not so many hours earlier. Here a chink of yellow light escaped into the house through a narrow gap left by a partially open door that led, Jake suspected, to the understage space where Arnie had been given his disastrous costume fitting. From his experience in Hazel's apartment that morning, Jake knew that he must make a move before too many misgivings set in. He pulled the door open and descended toward the source of the flickering yellow light.

The scene that gathered itself together in Jake's numbed brain had the distorted, luminous quality of his earlier experiences at home, and for a moment he was unable to determine whether it belonged to the real world or to some special effect conjured up by Baron's white pill. He was standing on the threshold of a low, cavernlike room, pitch dark at its far end and only dimly lit near the stairs by a cluster of wavering flames that burned in oil-filled jars hung on wires from the underside of the stage. Crowded about this illuminated space, the accumulated treasures from many past Quest productions seemed to press in against the circle of light like ruins in a strange jungle, where irregular columns of torn cardboard boxes struggled up to the ceiling, overloaded shelves sagged under the weight of paint-encrusted buckets and brushes, disintegrating costumes huddled in racks beneath dusty sheets, and a thick scattering of old programs, scripts, posters, set pieces and properties competed for floor space back into the unlit depths.

But these surroundings registered only on the edge of Jake's awareness. His full attention was directed toward the jungle clearing, where the burning wicks in their glass jars revealed a maiden in distress, a sacrificial virgin gagged and struggling beneath a tattered gray blanket on a mouse-nibbled mattress. Although her mouth was obliterated by a square of gaffer's adhesive tape, Jake had no trouble in recognizing the victim. There before him, her red hair tumbling over one pale shoulder, oversize eyelashes wide apart in horror, and beneath her thick make-up, obviously very much alive, lay Hazel Harvey. Too astonished to be frightened, Jake stepped across the threshold of the room. Was this a flesh-and-blood Hazel or a mirage? As if in answer to his question, the scene disappeared in an explosion of light, followed by blackness.

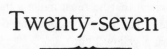

Twenty-seven

"For heaven's sake, what are you doing now?"
"Changing my hair. I don't want to be Hazel anymore."
"Oh, God. Here we go."
"I feel like being a blonde tonight. Blondes have more fun."
"Don't you believe it. I could go for you as a redhead."
"How revolting. But thanks for the thought."
"Well, hurry up. We haven't got all night."
"Stop rushing me. We can't do anything until he wakes up."

"He's taking his time about it."

"Probably because you hit him too hard, you big brute."

"I just tapped him on the back of the head."

"Daddy Bear doesn't know his own strength."

"Hmm." A deep satisfied chuckle. "Well, if Momma Bear doesn't get herself away from that mirror pretty sooon, Daddy Bear's going to kick that cute little skirt right up her ass."

"Ooh, I love it when you talk dirty. Come zip me up."

Jake lay motionless on the mattress, watching through almost closed eyes as Tim gathered the bodice of his spangled skating costume modestly about his chest and presented its unfastened back to Tina for attention. With Hazel's red wig discarded in favor of something blond and curly, Tim had altered his makeup to give himself a rounder face, a smaller mouth and, in a graceful act of homage to the charming star for whom the costume was originally designed, high Scandinavian cheekbones. Tina, on the other hand, favored the soberly formal striped trousers and tight black jacket she had worn to Bobbie's memorial service. These, accessorized with a white shirt, striped tie, bowler hat and toothbrush mustache, made her resemble something between a stout Charlie Chaplin and a slim Oliver Hardy.

Very much in contrast to this carefully dressed couple, Jake wore nothing but several strips of all-purpose gaffer's tape, which sealed his mouth, strapped his arms to his sides, and bound his ankles together. He had made this alarming discovery on drifting back into consciousness some ten minutes earlier, and he now wondered what was going to happen to him and how long he could put it off by playing possum. So far, Tina and Tim had been too occupied with their own personal preparations to pay him any attention, but this period of grace seemed to be coming to an end.

"There!" After some struggling with the fifty-year-old zipper, Tina managed to work it up Tim's back. "That skirt really does something for your legs. Are you ready now?"

Tim assessed himself critically in a long shard of broken mirror propped up against one of the cardboard boxes. "It needs something more. Where's that rhinestone collar I wore last time?"

"I don't know. Upstairs somewhere. And we're not going to hunt for it now!"

"All right. Don't get me rattled. I'll wear . . . I'll wear—this!" And,

197

reaching over to a cloth-covered wooden orange crate near Jake's mattress, he selected one of several gold chains that lay there beside a squat pottery oil burner. A small pendant on the chain, caught by the wavering light from the oil-filled jars overhead, gave off a soft green glow. Although deprived of his glasses, Jake could still recognize Bobbie's owl. He began to sweat.

"Thank you, dear." Tim brushed Tina's cheek with a light kiss after she had secured the chain around his neck. "Now Mother looks quite adorable. Let's see how Baby's doing."

Jake closed his eyes quickly. Footsteps approached. A warm, rough hand felt his forehead and smoothed back his hair.

"Pretty curls.

"Too bad they'll have to go."

"Mmm," Tim agreed. "Now what are *you* doing?"

"Time for another joint."

"Gimme, gimme. Mother wants to *fly*."

Jake cautiously opened his eyes a fraction and watched as Tina laid several fat joints on the crate, selected one, and lit it from the burner, inhaling deeply before handing it over to Tim. They both squatted on the floor, holding their breaths.

"Good stuff," said Tina, the first to exhale.

"Dynamite. How'd you get it?"

"Credit. I told them I had a shipment for them tomorrow."

"Clever Daddy. What'd they say?"

"Said it was about time. Let's have that."

They took alternate puffs in contented silence as Jake, caught in a crosscurrent of acrid marijuana smoke, tried to take slow, shallow breaths so as not to give himself away by coughing.

"Well, now," said Tim, placing the extinguished butt in a metal bottle cap for future recycling. "I feel blond, I feel beautiful, and I feel like some action." He looked over at Jake, who once again snapped his eyes shut. "Do you know what I think, Daddy?"

"No, Mother. What do you think?"

"I think Baby's playing tricks on us. I think he's awake and not letting on."

"Now that's too bad, Mother. Maybe he needs a lick of the old strap."

"Don't you lay a hand on my baby! He'll wake up in his own good time. And if he doesn't, I have a nice long hatpin here that I can insert just . . ."

Jake performed a creditable awakening. Tim twinkled down at him, turning his eyes into jolly half moons. Jake had to admit that the resemblance to Miss Henie was striking. He submitted to being chucked under the chin.

"There he is, the little dickens! Baby's had hims a lovely nap and now he wants to play."

Wanting nothing of the kind and with little to lose by protesting, Jake attempted a brief struggle, accompanied by a yell. The gaffer's tape rendered both miserably ineffective.

"No, no, no." The teasing caresses gave way to a sharp slap on the cheek. "Mustn't do that. Baby be good and pretty soon he'll get his bottle." Leaving the victim with another reassuring twinkle, Tim moved around to the head of the mattress and disappeared into the shadows at the far end of the room.

Jake turned his attention back to Tina, who had just lifted a corner of the cloth covering the upended crate to withdraw a wooden cigar box and a square of glass from an inner compartment. After acknowledging Jake's interest with a friendly nod, she placed the glass down on the cloth next to the oil burner, opened the cigar box, and produced a number of small articles, which she set out in a precise arrangement on the glass. By squinting, Jake was able to make out a metal spoon, a plastic cocktail straw, a pack of cigarette papers, a small plastic bag of green-brown marijuana, an eyedropper, a spool of thread and what he first took to be a short darning needle. But no darning needle came with a thick, round gasket at its blunt end. Jake's eyes widened and then grew wider still when Tim emerged from behind the columns of boxes carrying Arnie's overnight bag. Tim responded with a smile of affirmation.

"Oh, yes. We got it," he said, patting the bag proudly. "No thanks to you."

"Naughty baby," added Tina, accepting the bag from Tim.

"Yes." Tim knelt down beside Jake, modestly spreading the skirt of his skating costume and taking particular care not to scrape the knees of his flesh-colored tights. He ran his fingers lightly through the dark growth of hair on Jake's chest. "Naughty furry baby. But we'll fix that, too." His hand traveled down Jake's chest and over his stomach. Jake

199

arched and rolled over on his side, away from the teasing fingers. Tim laughed. "Isn't that sweet? Baby's shy." The fingers brushed up Jake's thigh and slid between his buttocks. With a sadly inarticulate protest through his adhesive tape, Jake rolled on his back again.

"Oh, Tim. Leave him alone. Come and help me."

"Would you like to rephrase that?"

Tina rolled her eyes in exasperation. "Mother, dear, do put Baby down for a minute and get the hell over here."

"That's better."

Tina handed Arnie's bag back to Tim. "You pushed the stupid bottom in too tightly. I can't get it out."

"Clumsy bear! It needs a mother's touch. Delicate fingertips . . ."

Tim thrust his right arm into the overnight bag, closed his eyes, and began to feel slowly around the edge of its inner base. As last, with a little cry of triumph, he pulled upward to the accompaniment of a loud ripping noise from the inside of the bag. Under Jake's watchful eye, Tim removed the false bottom, finished on one side with a handsome plaid lining material and trimmed on the other with a border of black Velcro gripping tape, and handed the bag back to Tina, who extracted from it two small plastic-wrapped packets, each held shut with several rubber bands. After squeezing both to test their texture, she selected one and commenced to unwrap it with great care. Tim began to do the same with the other packet, earning a sharp look from Tina.

"What do you want with that?"

"What do you think? Mommy likes her candy."

"So does Daddy, but we've got to drive later."

"I can handle it." Tim now had the packet open on the glass square. It contained a crumbling mound of white powder. Taking up the razor blade Tina had laid out, he scraped a small quantity of this onto the glass and began mincing it with fine, rapid chopping movements. "Are you going to have some?"

"If *you* are." Selecting the spoon from her array of equipment, Tina scooped up some white powder from her packet, leaving Tim to arrange his chopped-up crystals into four straight lines on the glass sheet.

"Ready?" he asked, when Tina had put the spoon down, refolded her packet, and snapped the rubber bands back into place.

Tina nodded. Together, they shared the plastic straw to sniff up the lines, one per nostril. A pause followed.

"Whoo!" said Tina at last.

"Whoo, yourself."

After another pause, Tina remarked. "We shouldn't do this too often. We don't want to end up like Hazel." She closed her eyes and chuckled.

"What?"

"I was just thinking how she looked when we pulled her feet up in the bath. Like a big fat sleepy hippo . . . hippopopo . . . hippo-popopo . . ." She dissolved into high giggles, while Jake, forgotten again, made a frantic effort to loosen the adhesive tapes around his arms. In the ensuing struggle, he received an impression that he might have managed to slacken them a little. He used the extra burst of energy brought on by hope to try and loosen them more.

"That was good," agreed Tim, still on the subject of Hazel. "But she was all doped up. It's more fun when they know what's going to happen."

After giving this statement some thought, Tina pulled herself together, put on an owlish face, and nodded in agreement. Tim did likewise, and the two sat with their heads bobbing up and down like a pair of jointed figurines in the rear window of an automobile, until a chance meeting of eyes sent them sputtering into gales of laughter.

Jake, neglected on the floor, continued to work surreptitiously on his bonds. Although unable to risk showing any obvious effort, he kept up a constant outward pressure on the tapes by bracing his hand against his legs and pushing outward with his arms. He began to sweat again.

"Oh, dear." Tim stopped laughing and jerked his head toward Jake. "Baby's getting fretful. He thinks the old folks have forgotten him."

"I've got something that'll make him feel better," said Tina archly, taking up the spoon with its little mound of white powder and holding it delicately over the burner flame.

"Yes, that's what he needs." Tim extracted a wad of facial tissue from the glittering bosom of his bodice and wiped the sweat off Jake's brow. "A nice bottle and a little game before he goes bye-bye."

Jake responded with an outraged noise and a contortion, trying his best to apply more pressure against the tapes.

"What's the matter?" Tim regarded him with an expression of wide-eyed astonishment. "Doesn't Baby want to go bye-bye? Well, he should have thought of that before he started poking his nose into other people's business. Shouldn't he, Father?"

But Tina, intent on her work at the table, only grunted by way of reply.

"Silly old bear," said Tim fondly. "Now, don't waste time doing that," he advised, as Jake strained his arms outward again. "Those nasty things will be coming off in just a minute. It really is all your own fault, you know. You've been a naughty baby, and naughty babies have to be spanked, don't they? So they won't be naughty anymore. We've had to do a lot of that lately."

The corners of Tim's bright red lips turned up in a little smile of satisfaction as he settled down on the edge of Jake's mattress, taking care not to crush the back of his flared skirt. "We're getting quite good at it," he added modestly. "Thanks to dear, *dear* Bobbie, who started everything by being *very* naughty. Do you know what he did?" Tim gave his yellow curls a toss and rolled his eyes in disgust. "Just when we had the business going smoothly and showing a profit, that smug little bastard came and told us that he wanted to pull out! Well! We were so surprised we didn't know *what* to say, but we certainly couldn't let him get away with *that.* So we played a little game with him to make him tell how he got his dumb boyfriend to bring the stuff in, and then we made sure he'd never double-cross anyone ever again. Wasn't that clever of us? And after that, we fixed up poor old Carl to have that auto accident, which was too bad, because he wasn't really naughty at all, but we had to have him out of the show, didn't we? So we could bring in Arnie and get him working for us. And then *you* showed up, you bad boy."

Smiling fondly, Tim ran a teasing finger through the hair on Jake's chest. "We really should have taken care of you right then and there, but how could we know you were going to steal Arnie away from us? Oh, yes, you did!" He tweaked a tuft of hair painfully in response to Jake's violently negative head shake. "You did, and you started *every-thing* going wrong. Without Arnie, we couldn't find the bag with the stuff in it, and pretty soon our supplies ran out and all our little cus-tomers got *very* unhappy, and then Hank had to be spanked before he *ruined* the theater, and then Hazel—well, you saw how *she* got." Tim

202

sighed at the memory and leaned closer to confide in Jake's ear. "She was such a good little pet after we got her hooked and broken in, but when the stuff ran out and we couldn't feed her any more, *what* a change! She started to crack up on us and say *very* naughty things, and even when we found the bag and got her fixed up again, the bitch started stabbing us in the back with all that shit about selling the theater. *Our* theater."

With Tim's face now only inches away from his own, Jake tried desperately to compress himself down into the mattress, away from the staring eyes with their dilated pupils and fringes of smudged mascara. He turned his head away, but Tim hissed on relentlessly.

"Our theater, that we built up from nothing! Do you know what it was like when we moved in? Do you? Just a fleapit, with that hick actor running it into the ground with one flop after another. But we saved it!"

"Tim . . ." With her preparations completed, Tina attempted to interrupt, but Tim chattered on excitedly.

"We saved it, all by ourselves," he continued, reaching over and pulling Jake's head sharply around to ensure full attention. "We worked on it and built it up and slipped in the extra money to keep it running. And pretty soon now, when you're out of the way and we've got Arnie back to work and we don't have to split the money anymore with that fucking little traitor, why, we can buy the Quest for ourselves! That's been the plan all along, and we're just about ready to do it, too. Look!"

Almost before his last words were out, Tim had skipped over to one of the stacked columns and taken down the uppermost box. "Look!" Pulling open the folded top flaps, he lifted the box over his head and tipped it upside down. A cascade of green bank notes tumbled over his shoulders to join the other used papers on the ground.

"Tim!" Tina crouched on the floor to gather up the bills. "Stop acting crazy!"

"Oh, don't be an old spoilsport!" Tim tipped over another box, strewing the contents almost to the bottom of the stairs. "If we can't keep these in a bank, let's have some fun with them. I've always wanted to roll in money; let's roll in money!"

"No!" Tina stood up and glared at him as he lay on the floor throw ing bills into the air. "Do you want to play games with Baby, or do I stop things right now?"

At this, Tim sat up sulkily. "I want to play with Baby."

"All right. Then be good, and I'll let you give him his bottle."

As quickly as it had blown up, the storm passed. All smiles, Tim accepted from Tina a strange instrument, which at closer range Jake could identify as the glass eyedropper, now filled with the melted contents of the spoon and fitted at its tapered end with the hypodermic needle, snugly rammed into place over a collar made from one of the cigarette papers tied on with thread. Panicked by his helpless condition and still clinging to a feeble hope that he might have stumbled into some pill-induced nightmare from which he would awaken at any moment, Jake attempted to speed up his awakening by rolling off the mattress. Tina pulled him back and sat on his stomach.

"It's too bad," she said in awkward apology. "We really wouldn't be doing this, but we need Arnie, and he'll be so much easier to manage when you're not around. You understand, don't you?"

Not a word of this registered on Jake's mind. His total concentration had fixed itself on the makeshift hypodermic syringe that hovered above his head as Tim knelt down beside him.

"Party time!"

Tim expertly pinched up a fold of skin on Jake's arm while Tina leaned forward to pin down his shoulders.

"This won't hurt a bit," she said. "Mother's very good."

She was right. Jake barely felt the needle go in.

Twenty-eight

Although generally not of a philosophic nature, Arnie had long ago formulated a theory that strenuous exercise followed by a brisk shower provided the best specific against thinking too much at times of stress. He had counted on this remedy to see him through the difficult hours before his opening night and was therefore caught totally off guard when a turmoil of conflicting emotions assailed him from the moment he opened his eyes in the morning. For most of the time, his fragile hope of getting through the coming evening without mishap trembled beneath a cloud of apprehension that showed every sign of settling in for the day. Occasionally, however, this same cloud lifted to grant him a brief vision of dazzling success, cheering crowds and a pat on the back from Jake. His head spun.

Arnie tried to put all these thoughts aside as he sweated through his Wednesday gym routine, but without success. No matter how hard he pushed his body, whether taxing his legs to their limit in squatting exercises beneath a massively laden barbell or straining his neck against a stack of metal weights suspended from a leather harness strapped to his head, the unwelcome thoughts pushed back harder, breaking into his concentration and undermining his performance. At last, after straining unproductively against a load far below his normal capacity, Arnie admitted defeat and headed for the locker room.

A reviving shower put him into a more cheerful state of mind, which faded as soon as he caught sight of himself in one of the washroom mirrors. With an eye to putting his best foot forward that evening, he had stopped off for a haircut on his way to the gym, but as usual the barber had gone wild with the clippers. Why do they always wanta make me look like Sluggo in the comics? he wondered, as he ran a hand over the plush fuzz on his scalp. Noticing a tube of hair-dressing cream that someone had left behind on the counter, he wet his head under the tap, plastered down the fuzz with a generous application from the tube, and inspected the result. Slowly, slowly, short spikes of hair righted themselves and stood to attention.

Well, what'd you expect? he asked his reflection. He'd always known he could forget about being a beauty. And if he hadn't been an ugly kid he'd never have started working out. Thank God for the body anyway. Giving the stubborn fuzz a final slap-down, he collected his gym kit and left the locker room. Overhead, the spikes of hair cautiously reasserted themselves in small, stealthy movements.

The clock in the lobby informed Arnie that his abbreviated workout had left him with time in hand. He decided to spend it on a banana-papaya-yogurt milk shake spiked with wheat germ. Accordingly, he took a seat at the health bar, where he was joined by Tony, a friendly rival in size and power with whom he sometimes shared equipment in the weight room.

"Hi, Arn."

"Tone."

"Long time no see. How's it goin'?"

"Okay. You?"

"Okay." Tony broke off to order a tuna salad and alfalfa sprout sandwich with a glass of carrot juice on the side before resuming the conversation. "You're lookin' good," he commented.

"Gettin' there."

"Puttin' on weight?"

"Gettin' there."

"Let's see."

Arnie obligingly pumped up his biceps.

"Jesus, they're *huge*! How much you pressin' now?"

"Bench?"

"Yeah."

"Oh, 'bout five seventy, five eighty."

"No kiddin'!"

"Five eighty-five, when I'm feelin' good."

"Keep that up and you'll have a build like a tank."

Arnie smiled modestly and, under the guise of sucking up the last of his milk shake, inflated his chest. Tony did likewise with his juice.

"Doin' anythin' special tonight?" he asked.

"Not much."

"My girlfriend's sister's in town. She goes for big guys too. Wanna double date?"

"Nah. I gotta see somebody."

"I'm not talkin' dog here. This girl's hot. She'll have your pants off before you can say hi."

"I gotta see somebody."

Tony lowered his voice. "You're not on steroids, are you," he asked.

"Jeez, no."

"No good gettin' big at the gym if you're gettin' small in bed. Haw."

"Haw. Well, I gotta go now."

"Okay. Keep up the good work."

"You bet."

"See you around."

"So long."

Having been taught to tell the truth at all times, Arnie felt troubled when he had to make evasions about his private life. He hoped, therefore, that his visit to the bank would require a simple, straightforward approach and was relieved when his signature underneath Bobbie's on the card file and the presentation of his key gave him unquestioned access to the safety deposit box, which, although of greater than average size, contained only the passports he and Bobbie had obtained last year, their birth certificates, a standard life insurance policy, an accounts book of ever-increasing numbers that suddenly fell from five figures to three in two abrupt drops, and four hundred sixty dollars in cash. There was also an envelope with his name written on it in green ballpoint pen.

As Jake had instructed, Arnie transferred everything into his gym bag before handing the empty box back to the attendant. He wanted desperately to read Bobbie's letter, but not in the bank and not in his car where people passing by on the street would see him bawling. He therefore drove home as quickly as he dared, trying all the while not to think about the letter in the bag on the seat beside him. Once indoors, he forced himself to sit down quietly in his favorite chair beside the table with Bobbie's picture and the owls before opening the envelope. Despite his efforts to remain calm, his hands shook as they pulled out the folded pink pages.

The letter, dated a little over two weeks earlier and written in a hand familiar from a thousand notes and shopping lists, wrung Arnie's heart before he had read even a word. It took up two full sheets and half of another. "Dearest Arnie," it began,

It's funny. This is the first real letter I've ever written you and I'm hoping to God you never get to read it. Partly because if you do then I'll be dead (which I'd rather not be), but mostly because you must never find out what I'm going to tell you if I can just get the words down on paper. Even now, I want so much to tear this up, like the dozens of others I've begun and couldn't finish, and I would too except for one thing.

You see, my sweet innocent darling, there's a chance—a tiny, tiny chance—that if two awful things should happen at the same time, you might get into trouble for something I've done (which is what I don't want to tell you about) just when I won't be able to speak up and take the blame. Of course, this *won't* happen. But if I've learned one thing over the past few years it's that beginnings are easy, but ends can be difficult—or even dangerous. So this letter is kind of an insurance for you (and maybe for me, too, but mostly for you because—well, just because). Anyway, are you all settled down and paying attention? I know you don't like reading, but this is important. Okay, then. Here goes. Read on.

Arnie read on, stumbling over the long sentences, difficult spellings and handwriting that deteriorated as the letter progressed. When he had finished, he began again from the beginning. Satisfied at last that he had grasped the full meaning of the letter, he refolded it carefully, put it in his pocket, and sent Bobbie's picture flying across the room to smash against the wall. He then swept all the owls off the table onto the floor, stamped them into the carpet, ripped open several hats from the collection on the wall rack, and wound up by hurling potted vines and shrubs onto the tiled floor of the glassed-in balcony. It was here, when he paused to look down at the exposed roots and torn leaves lying at his feet, that he started to cry.

Half blinded by tears and heaving with sobs, Arnie repotted the wounded plants as best he could before returning to his chair, where he lay back and let out a series of long, shuddering howls, pausing only to gather strength and breath before giving vent to a fresh outburst. During one of his quiet spells, someone rang the sour two-note gong on the front door and knocked. But Arnie huddled up with his face in his hands and eventually the caller went away.

After an hour the caller returned for another try. Then the telephone rang. Later still, when the fading outdoor light had ceased to penetrate the room, it went off again in a series of shrill tantrums. At last, during a ring that lasted while the illuminated blue readout on the clock across the room counted from 7:39 to 7:42, Arnie walked over to the telephone and stretched out his hand for it, whereupon the perverse instrument immediately fell silent. He continued to reach forward, however, with the idea of putting the instrument out of action by taking the receiver out of its cradle, but one of Bobbie's admonitions ("Don't leave the phone off the hook—you'll be tying up a line someone else might need") entered his mind, and he switched on the answering machine instead.

The thought of Bobbie and what Bobbie had done triggered another bout of weeping, not quite as severe as the first, followed by a craving for food. A bowl of tuna and cottage cheese from the refrigerator satisfied this need, after which he returned to his seat in the darkened living room and stared without thought at the blue display on the digital clock. At 11:53, the telephone gave out a double ring, then stopped as the answering machine took over. This occurred three times before a low humming from inside the machine indicated that a message was being recorded. The machine then fell silent, leaving a small red light burning to announce its waiting message. Tired of watching the bright clock display, Arnie turned his attention to the weaker red indicator light, which gradually assumed the character of an unwinking though not unfriendly eye staring back at him. Off to one side, the clock continued to count off the minutes unnoticed.

On the heels of retching nausea came bliss. Golden warmth and tingling euphoria lapped over Jake like healing waters, into which he subsided with joyful relief. Free of all past and aware only of a radiant eternal present, he lay passive and content on his mattress, lost in wonder at the lovely flames that floated overhead in their glistening containers. Peace, happiness and security were his and would remain so forever in this enchanted cave where he lived a charmed existence with his beloved parents. Parents: the very word conjured up a thrill of adoration for his beautiful mother and his stern, manly father, who together cared for him and kept him safe from the menacing horrors that lurked out there beyond the shadows. Sometimes, too, they would give him wonderful presents, if he pleased them by being good and doing as he was told. Their most recent treat was a cigarette of their own manufacture that sent harsh smoke down his lungs and made him cough. At first he had thrown it away with a sense of betrayal, but when his parents had patiently coaxed him into persevering and demonstrated how to hold in the smoke before releasing it, he began to appreciate the magnitude of a gift that lifted him to a new level of intensified rapture and brought glorious waking dreams.

He seemed to be having such a dream now, for as he continued to gaze upward into the dancing lights, they suddenly gave way to a golden-haired vision of transcendent loveliness, sheathed in sparkling diamonds. But it was not a vision, it was Mother. Smiling down at him, she temptingly offered another cigarette. Jake's languor gave way to an acute craving, but he knew from experience that before Mother made him happy he must do something for her. Taking his thumb out of his mouth, he reached up to her and said, "Mama."

Mother was thrilled. "Oh, what a good boy!" she cooed. "What a clever baby! Daddy, he said 'Mama' all on his own. Come and hear."

A burly mustached figure in formal black loomed over him. Although Jake loved Daddy very much, he nevertheless felt slightly in awe of him. With a view to ingratiating himself, he smiled and said, "Dada." This winsome display melted his father's bluff veneer, and Jake reveled in the praise and caresses that followed. Finally, he received his reward. Drawing the smoke in greedily, he held it for as long as possible, just as his father had taught him, then exhaled slowly and closed his eyes.

By an easy transition, the images of the oil lamps imprinted on the insides of his eyelids transformed themselves first into candles on a crystal chandelier, then into turrets on a luminous airborne castle that shone with a pearl-like lustre against a starry night sky. A silver ribbon falling in soft folds from the castle drawbridge gradually solidified into a path winding to and fro down and down the side of a craggy mountain peak, until it merged with its own reflection in a deep blue lake surrounded by willow trees and bullrush marshes where white herons lived. Treading daintily through the starlit waters, the silent birds stalked and froze in graceful attitudes before taking to the air in a wild flurry of motion that shattered the mountain and castle into a million shimmering particles. These hung suspended in the air for a moment, then collapsed like a falling veil into the depths of the lake.

Jake would have plunged in after them had not the gentle hands of Mommy and Daddy shaken him back to his place on the mattress. They told him it was time for his bath, but he wanted only to return to the lake. His eyes filled with tears and his face began to crumple.

"No," he said, pushing out his lower lip and refusing to get up.

Mommy and Daddy were shocked.

"Bad boy!" Daddy's deep voice scolded. "Bad ungrateful boy!"

"After all we've done for him," wailed Mommy. "He's broken my heart! I can't bear it."

"It's unbearable."

"I'm so unhappy."

"So am I—*very* unhappy."

The unbearable nature of his ingratitude and the great unhappiness it had caused his parents overwhelmed Jake. All his pleasure vanished in an instant, to be replaced by an undiluted sorrow that grew within him like an inflating balloon until it reached an agonizing intensity. Pausing in his attempts to comfort Mommy, Daddy glared at him.

"Look what you've done to your poor mother," he reproached. "She's not strong, and now you've gone and got her all upset."

"And miserable." Mommy buried her face against Daddy's shoulder.

"Oh, no, dearest. Not that. Don't be miserable!"

Racked with a sympathetic misery, Jake hugged himself tightly to prevent the balloon from breaking through his chest.

Daddy continued to comfort Mommy. "Don't cry, my darling, don't cry."

Jake began to cry too. He climbed to his feet and stood weeping in the forlorn hope that forgiveness would come and free him from his terrible desolation. At last it arrived in the form of a kind smile from Daddy.

"There, Mother, Baby's sorry. It's all right now; he won't be bad again. Dry your eyes and give him a kiss."

As suddenly as it had begun, the crushing sorrow lifted. Mommy and Daddy smiled and Jake smiled too. He had learned his lesson. He allowed himself to be led up the stairs and across the stage, stepping hesitantly in the faint light shed by the candles his thoughtful parents had lit before venturing forth from the safety of their cave.

In the dressing room, they set candles down and cut his hair. Scissors snipped about his head and over his body while dark curls fell on the floor around him. Jake shuffled his feet through the soft cloud, then closed his eyes and reveled in the luxury of a voluptuous massage as Mommy and Daddy lovingly spread a sharp-scented pink lotion over his head and arms, around and down his back and chest and up his legs. Finally, after even his eyebrows had been laughingly traced over with the last drops from the bottle, Jake was guided into a warm shower and dried off with rough towels. His skin tingled and he felt happy. Mommy and Daddy were happy too.

"Oh, Daddy, isn't he lovely? Now he's a real baby!"

"Yes, Mother, he does us credit."

"Just the sweetest thing! Come, precious, give Mother a kiss. Mmwa! I could eat him up! Look, sweetheart, look in the mirror and see the pretty baby!"

Jake looked in the direction indicated and was confronted by a pink egg, decorated with ears, nose, mouth and eyes that grew round and wide as he stared in astonishment. Confused, he pointed at the strange being, who pointed back at him. He felt frightened, and when the features in the mirror began to tremble and contort, he ducked his head and refused to look anymore.

His parents laughed and took him back to the cave, where he was powdered, pinned into a folded towel, and set down on the mattress to await what they referred to as his "three o'clock bottle." Thrilling in anticipation, Jake watched with avid eyes as Mommy produced the plastic-wrapped packet and began to melt some of its contents over the oil burner. Daddy swaggered over to her, his hands jammed into his pockets, and spoke in a low voice.

"Mother, it's going to get light soon. Maybe we should just skip to the end of the game."

"And give up the best part?" Mommy tossed her curls in that pretty way she had. "Don't be such an old worrywart. Anyway, it won't take long." She lowered her voice to match Daddy's. "We don't have to do as much as we did to you-know-who." Here they both glanced quickly over at Jake, who slyly pretended not to be listening. "Just enough to mix up the P-O-L-I-C-E."

Jake could make nothing of this cryptic whisper. His only concern was that the promised bottle might be withheld. But Mommy won the day, as he knew she would. Relief replaced concern. He had earned his treat and now he needed it. He stretched out his arm and watched eagerly as the needle slipped under the skin.

Again the incomparable moment. Waves of pleasure surged through his body. Opening his eyes at last, he found Mommy and Daddy seated on the floor beside his mattress. They had each lit one of their special cigarettes, which they drew upon in unison. Strangely, however, even though Jake knew them to be reassuringly near, they appeared small and far away. When Mommy reached lovingly toward him across the void, her arm grew larger as it advanced, inflating itself into a giant hand with a similarly magnified cigarette burning between its fingers. Instinct told Jake that Mommy wanted him to take the long, white cylinder, but he no longer had the strength or will to stir. Nor was he able to do more than watch lazily as the enormous hand, moving in slow motion, lowered the glowing tip onto his chest.

Lying flat, without a pillow under his head, Jake could see neither the exact point where the cigarette touched nor the cruel red circle that formed after it moved away. The pain, when it arrived, was small and somehow remote, like the impassive figures of his parents, who regarded him with faint smiles through the veil of smoke that rose from their cigarettes. Now Daddy's hand made the long journey across the room and Jake's sluggish brain registered another dulled circle on the inside of his left thigh. A third circle stung him on the arm. He began to whimper, then cry, as the circles multiplied.

Twenty-nine

"Managed to read this far, dear, that's the whole story." Arnie had switched on the table lamp and was reading Bobbie's letter for the fourth time, with pauses to wipe his eyes, blow his nose, or hit the table. "One thing led to the next," continued the letter, the way things do. If I hadn't got that part at the Quest, if I hadn't met the twins, if I hadn't got stoned with them and talked too much—if, if. I swear to God, Arnie, I never meant to go back to that dirty business after I met you. Except I hadn't counted on one thing: loving you so much. This may come as a surprise, because I haven't said it very often in so many words, but you know how it is—when you tell them you're in love, that's when they pack up and move on. Even now, I'm so afraid you'll get tired of me and tell me to beat it. You could have anyone you wanted. I can't understand what you see in an aging D.Q. (that's Dizzy Queen, but I know you don't like that kind of talk) who hit her peak five years ago and who can't offer you anything now but more wrinkles as the years go by. Every time I look in the mirror, I wonder when you'll find someone else who's cuter, younger, better in bed—well, no, *nobody's* better in bed. But by the time you find that out, it may be too late.

Arnie groaned and slammed his fist down. How could that son of a bitch be so dumb when he was supposed to be the clever one? The letter slipped from his hand and fell to the floor. Leave it, thought Arnie. I'd like to tear it up. Going over and over it just made things worse. But he retrieved the scattered pages and read on again to the end.

Anyway, that's why I did it. I wanted the money to buy us a future, something solid to work on that will keep us together even after, God forbid, you get fat and my hair starts to fall out. I wanted to give you a dream come true (at least that part has been taken care of) and make you happy and grow old with you. And that's what's going to happen. Then, when you're a very fit 99 and I'm an astonishingly youthful 95 (well, 97, but who cares by that time?), if I've finally run out of things to talk about, maybe I'll risk telling you how I *really* got all that money you thought some rich old aunt left me. By then you'll be too set in your ways to kick me out. And, anyhow, who else will you know who can still give you a surprise when you're 99?

But long before I do that, my dear, perhaps on your birthday this month, I'll tell you something else: how I truly feel about you and how much you mean to me. Then I'll take you outside to see your birthday present, and you'll be so surprised and so happy that you'll never ever think of being without

Your own D.Q. who loves you,

Bobbie

(Or Robert C. Lang, if you have to show this to the police.)

His birthday. He checked the clock. It had started only three hours and six minutes ago and already it was the lousiest ever. With the lousiest birthday present. He looked down at the letter, then tore it into pieces. Let the police arrest him if they wanted to. It didn't matter what happened now, and he'd rather go to jail than let anyone read Bobbie's letter.

A sudden contraction at the back of his throat brought on a shuddering gasp, but by tightening his chest and lying back in the chair, he managed not to start crying again. In an attempt to calm himself further and clear the contents of the letter out of his mind, he turned off the table lamp and closed his eyes. But pictures began to materialize in the darkness. Bobbie on the beach, Bobbie in bed, Bobbie chattering beside him in the car, Bobbie acting out last night's late movie—one by one they forced their way into his head as if he were a prisoner at some awful slide show. Bobbie in an apron covered with flour, Bobbie waving at the front door, Bobbie laughing at him with those people at the theater, Bobbie in a drawer at the morgue. Helpless to shut off the remorseless images, Arnie opened his eyes and looked about wildly for something, anything, to concentrate on. His friend, the red eye on the answering machine, modestly presented itself.

The glowing dot reminded Arnie that if he pushed the right button on the machine, he could summon up Bobbie's voice. It was a tempting thought. Bobbie would be saying something quite harmless and ordinary and this might help blot out the terrible green ballpoint words that waited to pounce into his thoughts the moment he lowered his guard. Glass crunched under his feet as he stood up, walked over to the red light, and pushed down blindly at the first button that met his finger. The machine whirred but remained silent. He pushed another button.

"Hello," said Bobbie. "This is Bobbie. Please don't hang up, because I really want to talk to you. . . ."

215

It didn't help. It made everything worse.

". . . Arnie and I can't come to the phone right now—"

Arnie hit out at another button and cut off the bright voice. He felt sweaty and breathless and he jumped when the machine started to speak again.

"Arnie, old buddy," it said. "This is Jake. Uh—we got through the show tonight, but where were you? I've got to go back to the Quest for a minute, but I'll be right back. Call me when you get in. Toodle-oo. I'm off and away!"

A beep, then a giggle and a different voice: ". . . and I know you don't want to see *anybody* when your muscle man's home, but you might give your girlfriends a ring once in a while just to let us know you're still—"

The tape had reverted to old messages. Arnie picked up the machine, tore its wires out of the wall, and threw it onto the balcony, where it crashed down on the spilled earth. Running to the bedroom, he found Jake's number by the bed, punched it into Bobbie's pink Princess telephone, and waited impatiently as the receiver purred its monotonous *brr . . . brr* into his ear and, far off in Hollywood, Jake's telephone jangled to an empty apartment.

Arnie checked the bedside clock: 3:17. Jake should have been home hours ago. An unsettling sense of unease began to nibble at the back of his mind. Where was Jake?

"Come on, come on," he urged. But the telephone droned on impassively.

Regretting his overhasty smashing of the answering machine, Arnie closed his eyes tight and tried to recall Jake's exact words, which somehow got mixed up in his head with the constant *brr . . . brr* of the telephone and refused to put themselves back into their original order. One thing at least was clear. Jake wanted to hear from him, but Jake hadn't come home. Why not? Arnie thought this over slowly.

Brr . . . brr.

It was too late to be eating out. And the bars had closed over an hour ago. And Jake couldn't still be at the theater.

Brr . . . brr.

Or could he?

Arnie's heart skipped a beat. But why? he wondered. Why shouldn't Jake be there? Maybe they were all having a party after the show. But Jake didn't say that. He said—

216

Brr . . . brr.

Arnie pounded his forehead with his free hand. *Jake said he'd be right back.* And that was three hours ago. Three hours in that place with that creepy room under the stage, and that creepy lady who was dead now, and those creepy people that Bobbie—

Pausing only to slam down the telephone, Arnie tore out of the apartment, down the stairs and into his garage. With the reckless notion of recruiting as an escort any traffic patrolman who happened to stop him, he broke all speed limits into West Hollywood. But his very lack of concern seemed to act as a charm, for when he reached the alley behind the Quest Theatre and jammed on his brakes behind Jake's car, he was still alone.

They had stopped burning him and begun to argue. Their sharp petulant voices reached him through a haze of pain, interlaced with a high keening wail that he could only dimly recognize as his own voice. On one occasion when his eyes flickered open, he caught a glimpse of Mommy melting more powder over the oil burner and Daddy replacing the plastic-wrapped packets in their bag. Then his eyes closed and only the voices remained.

"Can't you shut that goddamn kid up? He's making my head ache."

"He's your child too. Anyhow, this stuff will do the trick."

"Well, step on it. Let's get moving."

"Stop fussing. You'll make my hand shake."

"Are you sure you've got enough in there? He's heavier than Bobbie."

"Sweetie, I've got enough in here to finish off a horse. Why don't you go bring the Hudson around?"

"Oh, yeah. Sure. Get rid of Daddy and have all the fun to yourself."

"Well, why not? It's my turn."

"The hell it is. You did Bobbie."

"You did Hazel."

"I let you hold a foot."

"You fixed Carl's car."

"Big deal. It's my turn to do it with the needle."

"Not fair!"

"Is too! Let's have it."

"No!"

"Or I'll break your arm."

217

"Oh, all right. Take the fucking thing! You can do it all yourself."

"Where are you going?"

"Somewhere. I don't want to play anymore."

Light and heavy footsteps mingled in a scuffle near the door. Far away some glass broke.

"Let me go, you big bully!"

"Now, Mother. Don't fly off the handle. Listen to Father."

"Put me down!"

"Let's make a little deal here." Daddy's deep voice became even deeper and richer. "You give me this one and I'll give you . . ."

"Who?"

"Can't you guess? We won't need him forever, and sooner or later he'll have to be put down."

"You mean—Arnie?"

"He'd last through a couple of days easy. Then you could slip him the big one."

Mommy giggled coquettishly. "You promise?"

"Cross my heart."

"Oh, you're a sweet old bear after all. It's a deal. Now put me down and I'll get Baby all ready for you."

The light footsteps approached Jake's mattress, skipping through the old papers and scattered bills. Jake felt something pass around his arm, just above the elbow. Forcing his eyes open, he stopped moaning and looked groggily at the rolled bandanna that Mommy was twisting tighter and tighter. Further down the arm, thick blue veins bulged up under red blisters.

"Thank you, Nurse," said Daddy. The familiar needle hovered above his arm. "Bye-bye, Baby."

Arnie struggled with the sliding service doors on the side of the theater, bracing his heels and pulling back against the left-hand panel with all his strength. It refused to budge. The moon had disappeared and a distant streetlamp provided the only available light as he pawed feverishly through the discarded litter in a frantic search for anything that could be used as a lever. A metallic glint in the grass beside the wall led him to a short crowbar, but this snapped off in his hand as soon as he thrust it between the doors and applied pressure.

Dropping the severed handle of the crowbar, he ran around to Melrose Avenue, deserted except for the occasional passing car. Although the red front door appeared relatively insubstantial, it, too, held firm when he threw his weight against it. Frustration and a helpless sense of urgency brought forth tears of rage. Stop it, he told himself, stop it. *Think.* But before he had time to shift gears and make that effort, his eyes fell on one of the windowpanes next to the door. Stripping off his T-shirt, he wrapped it around his left hand, smashed the pane, and reached through to the mortise locks on the inside of the doorframe.

Once inside the lobby, he stood still to listen. Somewhere in the building an animal or a child was crying in high, drawn-out wails. Guided by light from the street, Arnie moved up the short flight of stairs to the upper lobby and through the curtained arch into the house. Here all was dark, but the cries seemed louder. And when he had felt his way past the low wall behind the last row of seats to a position where he could look down the center aisle, he saw the vertical strip of yellow light on the right-hand side of the stage.

He knew at once where they had Jake. As he was making up his mind whether to move cautiously or run, the sounds coming from beneath the stage stopped short. He ran. At the partially open door, he paused again to listen.

Tim's voice floated up. "All right, Doctor. He's ready."

"Thank you, Nurse." Could that be Tina? "Bye-bye, Baby."

Arnie threw open the door and hurled himself downstairs.

Like Jake before him, he halted at the entrance to the cave, transfixed by an extraordinary scene just beyond the doorway. Kneeling beside a filthy mattress in the center of a sea of paper money were Tina and Tim—Tina in that English hat and black suit, with a silly mustache glued to her upper lip, and Tim wearing Bobbie's owl and that Godawful wig and spangled dress he knew all too well from a previous occasion. They stared at him in astonishment.

Arnie stared too, not at them but at the mattress, where a strange creature clad only in a pinned-up towel gazed with dead eyes at its own arm, to which a rough tourniquet had been applied. Like Bobbie, the creature was hairless and covered with cigarette burns, but unlike Bobbie, it was still alive, for when Arnie took a step into the room it moved its head slightly and looked up at him blankly. It was Jake.

Arnie tried to speak, but nothing came out. Struck dumb by pity, outrage and a fury far beyond anything he had experienced in his life, he felt his features twisting into unfamiliar contours of rage as his

219

mind whirled in search of some words to express his overflowing emotions. Only one word seemed appropriate. He took a deep breath and let it out.

"AAAARGG!" he yelled as he charged over to the mattress.

"AAAARGG!" he bellowed as his head and shoulders smashed against the suspended lamps, sending a wash of oil over the scattered banknotes, which started to burn wherever the lighted wicks fell.

"AAAARGG!" he roared as he lifted the petrified twins off the floor with a one-hand grip under each chin, cracked their heads together, and sent their unconscious bodies sailing through the air into the side of the orange-crate table. The table overturned, and its arrangement of implements—glass plate, razor blade, thread, spoon and oil burner—all went flying into a nearby costume rack, where oil from the over-turned burner produced first a dark stain across the cotton dustcover and then, when the wick landed, a trail of flame that traveled up toward the underside of the stage and down toward the ancient nets and gauzes on their wire hangers.

"Jake, oh, Jake," sobbed Arnie, kneeling by the mattress, oblivious to the fire that now approached the stacked cardboard boxes and crept across the floor toward the canvas flats and wooden paint shelves. "It's Arnie, pal. Can you get up?"

Jake's eyes wandered to the edge of the mattress, where a half con-sumed hundred-dollar bill was attempting to pass its flame on to the dried-out fibrous stuffing. His mouth worked.

Arnie bent lower. "What, Jake? What is it?"

The faint whisper reached his ear. "Don't. Please."

Arnie looked over his shoulder to check on their line of retreat. The fire was moving toward the stairs, nibbling at scattered scripts, posters and paper money. He turned back to Jake, who had now lost con-sciousness, and squatted down to lift him gently off the mattress. The gathering smoke was thinner near the floor, and he could see sitting next to the smashed orange crate the treacherous bag Bobbie had used to get him to smuggle the dope. He could also see flames beginning to lick against a sequined skirt and a dark jacket cuff. Heaving himself up, he tossed Jake over his shoulder, grabbed the bag, and raced up the stairs.

By this time, smoke had begun to spread through the house, mak-ing it difficult for Arnie to see more than a few feet in any direction. His eyes stung and the thick atmosphere caught his lungs. Shifting

Jake off his shoulder to cradle him in both arms, he bent down as low as possible, followed the center aisle up to the cross corridor, and moved left until he came to the sliding doors. These were secured by two metal bars—No wonder the crowbar didn't work, he thought dizzily—that he had to force back before he could push one door aside and step out into the fresh air and the first light of dawn.

As soon as he had stopped coughing, Arnie inspected Jake. Although still unconscious, he at least seemed to be breathing regularly. Arnie experienced a surge of elation. They were both safe! He almost passed his sense of relief on with a squeeze when he remembered Jake's burns and froze in mid action. Carefully transferring the dead weight of his burden from both arms to just one, he walked around the Datsun, let down the back of its passenger seat, and made Jake as comfortable in it as he could. In the car trunk he found a rug to cover his limp passenger and a grease-stained T-shirt for himself, after which he locked up Bobbie's bag and was just about to wedge himself into the driver's seat when he stopped to take one last look at the theater.

"Serves them right," he said aloud. "They asked for it." He bent down to check again on Jake, then raised his eyes to the dark opening in the side of the building. "Goddamm murderers." Smoke began to drift out of the service door into the alley. Arnie sagged against the side of the car. "Oh, shit!"

Pulling off the soiled T-shirt, he tied it over his nose and mouth and ran back into the theater, where heat and the thick atmosphere immediately forced him to his knees. In this position he crawled back the way he had come until he neared the open door leading to the stairs. Here the heat became worse, but he flattened himself against the floor and moved on with closed eyes and averted head, painful smoke filtering through his improvised mask at every breath. Once over the threshold, he slid otterlike on his belly down the first short flight of steps until he could pull the T-shirt down a little and survey the scene below. Coarse fur brushed his cheek as a frantic rat scrabbled past him up the stairs. Arnie grunted in disgust and struck out with his arm, but encountered nothing. Screwing up his face against the painfully hot air, he opened his eyes a fraction of an inch and peered down through the doorway.

It was a sea of flame. Fire had spread over the entire floor to ignite each stack of cardboard boxes. The mattress blazed, tongues of fire ran along the wooden beams under the stage, and every property, costume or set piece that could burn added its brilliance to the conflagration. In the last bearable instant before he had to shut his eyes, Arnie searched for any sign of the twins, but could make out only a slightly denser concentration of flame in the spot near the collapsed paint shelves where they had fallen.

He had stayed too long. Still keeping as flat as possible, he began to heave himself back up the steps by sheer arm power. In the middle of his first lift, however, he was struck flat by a sudden thunderous crack, followed by a blast of searing heat and an agonizing sprinkle of burning droplets on his exposed back, arms and head. One of the paint cans had exploded. Before another could go the same way, Arnie gathered his last reserves of strength and managed to regain first the top of the stairs, then, through a combination of terror and blind insight, the open door to the alley. Still with his eyes shut, he stumbled over the flats he had tipped over during his attempt to get into the building and collapsed on the ground near his car, alternately choking and filling his lungs with great gulps of air.

At last, as his head began to clear and his breathing came easier, he thought of Jake and climbed to his feet. A wave of dizziness sent him reeling against the car for support. It was when he leaned forward to shake off the faintness that he noticed his arms. The heat from the explosion had singed off every hair and the falling droplets of paint had dotted them with round black patches beneath which blisters were beginning to form. Back in the driver's seat, Arnie inspected himself in the rearview mirror. The offending haircut had vanished, together with his eyebrows and lashes, and more blisters were rising on the top of his head, shoulders and back. He didn't look as bad as Jake, but they now shared a strong family resemblance. The thought pleased him.

"We sure are gonna hand them a laugh at the hospital," he told the unheeding Jake as he unclipped his keys from their place on his belt loop, started the car, and guided it around the theater onto Melrose Avenue.

Behind him, a distant fire siren began to wail.

Thirty

J ake and Arnie sat propped up in their hospital beds like Tweedledum and Tweedledee and for the second time in two days answered questions regarding their active participation in what Jake now liked to think of as the Great Quest Fire. Yesterday's interview had been a brief affair initiated by an anonymous representative of the LAPD and terminated by Jake, who fell into a deep sleep before the young detective had begun to hit his stride. Today he was wide awake and able to present his old aquaintance Detective Rosa with a story that more than made up in simplicity and corroborative detail for anything it happened to lack in the way of strict adherence to the truth.

The interview took place in the private room to which they had been taken after receiving treatment for their burns and in which Jake, on regaining the partial use of his addled wits, had concocted a version of their adventures that combined the double advantage of accommodating the few remaining verifiable facts while, as an added bonus, presenting both Arnie and himself in a highly flattering light. Their term as roommates would end shortly, however, for Arnie was to be allowed home as soon as Rosa had finished with him, while Jake had to stay on until his healing progressed further and he managed to kick a tendency toward painkiller addiction that still puzzled the staff on the ninth floor of the Lila F. Cohen Memorial Wing. Now, feeling tense and jittery, he waited impatiently for the interview to end. He was tired and he wanted to be left alone.

His mistake, of course, had been in telephoning Miss Murphy earlier in the day to explain his absence from the office and request that she order him a new pair of glasses to replace those lost in the fire. Somewhere along the way he had let slip more of his predicament than he had intended, and he had then made things worse by swearing her to secrecy and exacting a promise that she would under no circumstances reveal his whereabouts to anyone or visit him herself.

It seemed as if he had barely replaced the telephone receiver in its cradle when Miss Murphy burst into the room. Having raced directly to his side from her desk without pausing to change, she wore a strapless pink tubular top, matching hot pants and white high-heeled sandals with Joan Crawford ankle straps.

"Oh, Teddy Bears!" she cried. "How you get like that?"

Jake had no choice but to elaborate his story further.

"There!" exclaimed Miss Murphy, shedding tears, "I always say you brave deep down, even when everybody else say no. And I know *you* got to be brave," she told Arnie, taking him by surprise with a warm kiss that turned him almost as red as the lipstick mark left on his cheek. "Thank you for saving my Teddy Bears. Now I got somebody who want to come in and say hello. Pussy Cats!" she called. "Come see Teddy Bears and Mr. Siganski."

Baron sidled into the room with every sign of reluctance and recoiled at the sight of the shining heads and gauze patches sported by Jake and Arnie.

"Jesus," he gasped. "You din't say it was catchin'."

"No, *estúpido*," said Miss Murphy, taking his arm and attempting to draw him farther into the room. "They very brave and have accidents. Wait till I tell you—"

"Tell me later." Baron had become green behind his sunglasses. "I gotta get outta here. Hospitals make me sick." He made a bolt for the door.

"He have to go," Miss Murphy explained apologetically, "Or he vomit. I go too, but I come back tomorrow by myself." She approached Jake's bed and tenderly ran her finger over the nearest visible area of unbandaged skin, which happened to be his ear. "And I make you feel better," she whispered.

Jake's heart executed a quick flip while his imagination ran riot through a scene of extravagant debauchery with himself in the central role of Dr. Kildaire.

"Teddy Bears!" Miss Murphy bent over him. "What happen? You go all white!"

"It's nothing." Jake cleared his throat and thanked his wise doctors for the metal framework that held the thin top sheet, his only covering, a safe distance above his body. "Go back to the office. I'll see you tomorrow."

"You need anything?" Miss Murphy asked in parting.

"Just the glasses." Jake had to clear his throat again. "And no visitors. If anyone calls, you don't know where I am."

Shortly after lunch, Yolanda Meltzer appeared in his doorway, bringing with her a bunch of grapes, a thick manila envelope, and Kitty, now shrunk back to life-size in Jake's estimation after her brief moment as a potential murderess.

"I called your office about a little business matter," Yolanda explained, placing the grapes on Jake's bedside table and pointedly turning her back on Arnie, who was making his slow way through a comic book left by a library volunteer, "and your secretary told me all about the wonderfully brave thing you did. So I just *had* to pay you a visit and shake your hand"—she registered the condition of Jake's hand and rapidly withdrew her own—"and thank you *so* much for filling in so wonderfully the other night in the face of *some* people's unprofessional behavior."

Intent on his comic book, Arnie wet a finger, turned a page, and read on.

"It was a nice show." Jake recklessly added another lie to his growing collection. "Too bad it didn't have a chance to run."

"*C'est la vie,*" Yolanda replied briskly. "I have other fish to fry. Which is why I called you in the first place." She withdrew the manila envelope from under her arm. "I have here a script you might like to represent. It's a musical about Noah's ark."

Spotting dangerous country ahead, Jake remarked that he thought the subject had already been treated musically.

"Not by me." Yolanda fixed him with a cold eye.

"And I'm not really that kind of agent."

By an impressive sleight of hand, the grapes vanished from their resting place on the table.

"Although, of course, I'd be delighted to read it."

Yolanda smiled and the grapes reappeared, together with the envelope.

"I'm sure you'll do very well with it," she reassured him. "I'll call you next week."

"Not that soon. I'll call you."

"I can't *wait* to get together and hear your opinion."

"We'll have lunch."

Arnie, who had been living long enough with an actor to recognize a theatrical brush-off when he heard one, smiled into his comic book.

"Splendid! And if you're *very* good"—Yolanda wagged an arch finger at Jake from the doorway—"I'll let you have a peep at my new work. I call it *Samantha and Delilah: A New Look at an Old Story.*"

"That will raise a few eyebrows on Melrose."

"I see it as a major motion picture with Meryl Streep. But don't tell anyone. Those sharks out there will slit your throat for a good idea."

"My lips are sealed."

"Mum's the word. Come along, Kitty."

Kitty turned back before following Yolanda out of the room.

"Do get well quickly," she breathed. "And *do* read Nanda's script. It's . . . it's better than *Shootout at Shiloh!*" And with a final apologetic smile, she sped off down the hall.

Hard on the heels of Yolanda and Kitty came Betty and Bill. Fresh from her ballet class, Betty whirled into the room like a miniature dervish who had paused long enough to don a glossy magenta leotard and one of Bill's old shirts.

"Darling!" She swept a dazzling smile from Jake to Arnie and back again. "How awful you look!"

"Betty," warned Bill, as he followed her into the room. Considering his fondness for highly colored golf clothes, he cut a surprisingly sedate figure in a plaid Brooks Brothers shirt and tan chinos, with carefully scuffed boating moccasins on sockless feet.

"Well, they do, poor babies. Jake, dear, we got worried when we found Hector at home and you didn't answer your phone, so we called your office and rushed right over because we know how terrible hospital food can be and we wanted to bring you this."

A tin of pâté de fois gras and another of Bath Oliver biscuits joined the wilting grapes on the table.

"Plus something to wash it down with," added Bill, slipping a bottle of Courvoisier under Jake's pillow.

"That nice secretary told us *everything*," Betty informed Jake, "so we can skip right on and tell you *our* news. Bill's going to produce the new Martha Hunter talk show on TV, and we're moving back to New York!"

"No!" said Jake. "What'll I do without you?"

"You'll come and visit us in our *beautiful* apartment on East Seventy-fourth."

"You two really work fast."

Bill put on the lopsided grin that always made him seem faintly apologetic. "It's a great offer, Jake. We'll hate leaving L.A., but I couldn't turn it down."

"I should hope not! Congratulations."

"Thank you, dear." Betty picked up the thread. "And we have another surprise for you."

"I don't think I can handle another."

"You'll love this one. You see, you'll be lonely when we've gone, and we can't keep a pet in the new place, so we're giving you Hector."

"Oh, no!"

Betty looked surprised. "But you love Hector!"

"I never said so."

"Oh, Jake! And Hector adores you."

"Hector adores my bed, food, and the Persian in 12B, in that order."

"How can you say that? Why, when he came in this morning he looked up at me with *tortured* eyes and give this *tragic* wail. He's pining for you."

"Betty, you're the most awful liar."

"Be nice to me, or I'll take back our goodies and you'll have to eat those moldy grapes. Bill, isn't Hector pining for Jake?"

"Well . . ."

"Of course he is. His coat's gone all dry. Jake, why won't you take poor Hector?"

"I don't want the responsibility. I don't want to be tied down. I might want to go away sometime."

"You never go away."

"I was thinking about it just before you came in. How can I visit you in New York if I have to stay at home with Hector?"

"You can board him with his vet and send us the bill. I'll give you the address."

"Definitely not."

Betty frowned. "Jake, I didn't want to tell you this, but if you won't take Hector, we'll have to have him put to sleep."

Jake received a quick flash of Hazel in the bath and broke into a sweat. "God, no!"

"You see? You do love him. Now it's all settled! Bill, I think we should go now. Jake looks a bit ragged. Darling, come see us as soon as you get out. Bring your nice friend. We'll be here for another month. Bye-bye." And she whirled out.

Bill lingered a moment at the door. "Don't worry about Hector. If you can't look after him, we'll find someone else."

Jake shook his head. "It's okay. I'll take him."

"Thanks, buddy. See you soon." He waved, nodded to Arnie, and departed.

Arnie inspected Jake with concern. "You do look kinda funny," he said. "Maybe I should call somebody."

Jake flopped back on the sheepskin pad that helped alleviate the discomfort of not being able to turn over in bed. "No more people," he groaned, adding "I vant to be alone," in a low drawn-out voice that alarmed Arnie even more.

"Maybe I should call somebody," he repeated.

But just at that moment somebody appeared in the person of Detective Rosa, dapper as ever in a mid-gray suit with a thin burgundy stripe and ready to lead them firmly through their movements on the night of the fire.

As the interview progressed, Jake became increasingly uneasy. Intimidated by Rosa's professional manner and relentless note taking, he began to worry that what had seemed so convincing when tried out on Arnie, admittedly not the most critical audience, might not have the same effect on the police. He was therefore both relieved and slightly surprised when Rosa put away his notepad and declared himself willing to buy their story.

"I don't believe it," he sighed, "but I'll buy it."

"What's the matter?" Jake asked unwisely. "You don't trust us?"

228

"I don't trust any two guys who look like Mr. Clean with acne."
Rosa reached for his gray straw hat, hesitated, then dug out his note-pad again. "Let's go around one more time. You got this call . . ."

"From the twins, Tina and Tim."

"At three-thirty in the morning."

"About then. They said they were frightened in the theater and wanted me to drive them home."

Rosa looked up. "According to what they told me, they didn't have a home. They lived at the Quest."

"Maybe I misunderstood." Jake caught himself just in time to sup-press a squirm. "Anyhow, they said they heard noises and wanted to get away from there."

"What sort of noises?"

"They didn't say."

"And where did they want you to drive them?"

"I forgot to ask."

"Crime lost a mighty foe when you decided to retire."

"They woke me up. I was groggy."

"You can say that again. So you got to the theater . . ."

"And I waited outside for a while. But then I noticed the side door was open, so I went in. There was smoke in the house, and I could see firelight coming through the door leading down under the stage."

"At which point you ran downstairs."

"First taking off my shirt and tying it around my face."

"Which is why you have burns on your head and arms and chest. The hospital report says you have them on your legs too."

"I was wearing shorts."

"You wear shorts?" Rosa had his own opinion of Jake's figure and taste in clothes.

Jake read his mind. "Sometimes. When I don't expect to be exam-ined by the police."

"Okay, okay. And downstairs?"

"Very smoky. There were oil lamps and candles burning and the twins were out cold on the floor with a kind of hypodermic syringe beside them. They must have knocked over a lamp or something, be-cause the fire was well under way. I tried to pull one of them out, but the smoke got to me, and I don't remember anything else."

"Luckily, though, you called Mr. Siganski before you took off for the theater and left a message on his machine."

Pleased that his part had arrived at last, Arnie beamed and nodded in agreement.

"Right," Jake continued. "When you're going alone in the middle of the night to a place where people have been murdered, it's a good idea to tell someone about it."

"Always." Rosa continued to make notes. "What people were murdered?"

Jake went cold under his sheet. "Well, I know you don't agree about Bobbie. But I thought Hazel . . . Anyhow, Arnie hadn't shown up for the performance and I was worried about him."

Rosa shifted in his chair to face the other bed. "Mr. Siganski, why did you feel you had to drive all the way in from Santa Monica at three-thirty in the morning?"

"I was worried about Jake."

"You were worried about each other. That makes me feel all warm inside. And when you found him?"

"He was passed out on the floor under the stage, with bits of stuff falling down on him. Then when the explosion happened, I fell over him and the fire was worse and I just had time to pull him out before it got so bad I couldn't go back for the others."

"Okay." Rosa flipped back a page. "*Why* didn't you show up for the performance?"

"I got scared."

"And where were you when Mr. Weissman left his message on your machine?"

"Asleep."

"So how did you get it in time to save Weissman?"

Arnie blinked. "I woke up."

Rosa shook his head. "I guess it does hang together," he admitted. "In a dopey kind of way." He glared at Jake. "I still have this feeling that I'm being screwed, but there isn't much I can do about it when all I have left to work with is a site full of burned evidence and a couple of heroes"—Jake and Arnie traded modest looks—"who come out smelling like roses and looking a lot like the corpse that started all this."

"Except we're alive," Jake reminded him.

"Yeah. Well." Rosa pocketed his notepad again. "Just try and stay that way and don't get mixed up in any more trouble." He retrieved his hat and addressed Jake from the doorway. "It might ease your mind to know that Mrs. Harvey was a heroin addict and she had just given herself a fix before she got into the bath. As far as we can tell, she overdid it and just slipped under. Not a bad way to go. Any questions?"

Jake considered for a second. "Yeah. Who's your tailor?"

Rosa grinned. "I thought you'd never ask." A beige business card sailed through the air and landed on the sheet under Jake's chin. "He's my brother-in-law. Look him up. He'll change your life."

"I already changed it." Jake had to raise his voice as the door closed behind Rosa. "And look where it got me," he concluded bitterly.

Arnie noticed that his friend appeared cast down. "Don't pay no attention to him," he advised. "You dress real good. Like your apartment."

"I always thought so," said Jake. "But people keep hinting that both of us need redecoration." He read the card, then set it down beside the grapes and pâté. "Maybe I will drop in on this guy sometime—just for a chat."

With Rosa gone, Arnie too could leave. Having slid out of bed and into his charred jeans, he was now engaged in tying the laces of his sneakers. "If you're gonna do your place over," he said to the floor, "I'm real handy with a paint roller."

"I won't be doing anything for a while," Jake answered, thinking of his tottering bank balance and impending hospital bill. "But when I need some painting done, you'll be the first to know."

"I mean it," Arnie assured him. "Any time." Half out of his hospital gown, he looked about helplessly for his nonexistent T-shirt. "I ain't got nothin' to wear on top," he informed Jake, handing him the problem for solution.

Jake suggested that he keep the gown on. "Maybe they'll let you borrow it to go home in."

"Oh, yeah!" Arnie's worried face lit up while he tucked the gown into his jeans, then clouded over again as the moment of farewell approached. He stood uneasily at the end of Jake's bed. "Well, I guess I'll be sayin' so long."

"So long, Arnie. And thanks for getting me out of that place."

"Jeez, Jake, it was me that got you into it. And I'm real grateful to you for makin' up that smart story and for not tellin' about Bobbie and me and the bag."

"There didn't seem much point. It's all over with."

"I wish we could get them bastards at the hotel."

"I'll make an anonymous call to the Canadian police. They'll take care of the McLeods."

"Boy, you really got it upstairs." Arnie turned the brightest shade of red he had yet achieved and shuffled his sneakers on the floor. "About the money I owe you."

"Forget it," Jake said quickly. "I made a hash of the whole thing."

"No!" Arnie's eyes became round and earnest. "You did it all, just like I ast. We had a deal."

"Please, Arnie. You don't owe me anything. Let's just say I did it for a friend."

To Jake's horror, Arnie's eyes filled with tears. In their circular blueness, they reminded him of Hector. My God, he thought, Betty's right—that cat does love me! Panic rushed through him, pulling down blinds and slamming doors.

"Can I see you again some time?" Arnie asked, after blowing his nose on an inadequate tissue.

Not two of them, Jake told himself, I can't look after two of them. "Sure, Arnie." The heartiness made his voice loud and false. "Any time. I'll give you a call."

"You know—just, like, to talk."

"We'll have lunch."

Arnie's face froze and Jake saw it. "I mean, I have this place I eat at sometimes," he stammered. "We could . . ."

"Sure," said Arnie. "Sure. Well . . ." He made an awkward offer of his hand to shake, then remembered Jake's condition and dropped it.

"Arnie . . ."

Arnie seemed not to hear. "Sure," he said again, retreating to the closed door. "Take care, now." He fumbled blindly behind his back, found the knob, and was gone.

Alone at last. But instead of being able to revel in his long anticipated solitude, Jake found himself playing host to yet another pair of unwelcome callers. Old friends from early childhood, Shame and Regret, materialized at the foot of his bed, unpacked a little light knitting, and settled down for what Jake knew from unpleasant experience could be a long stay. "I had to do it," he told them. He explained why it wouldn't work. Hector would be as much responsibility as he could handle; he couldn't live up to Arnie's expectations too; it was all he could do to cope with his own life without having to prop up someone else's. "Damn it," he protested, "Why don't they leave me alone?"

Unmoved, his visitors arranged their wool and counted off stitches. Jake wanted to throw something. Only the knowledge that he couldn't afford any extras on his bill—or the bill itself, for that matter—prevented him from doing so.

"Damn it!" he yelled. "Damn, damn, damn!"

"Are you all right, Mr. Weissman?" The composed face of a passing nurse looked in at the door. "Can I get you something?"

"Just out of here," said Jake grimly.

"Not for a while yet, I'm afraid. Oh, look—you've dropped your comic book." She rescued the Incredible Hulk from where he had fallen when Arnie got out of bed and placed him on Jake's table. "Now why don't I lower your head . . ." A motor hummed and Jake felt himself flattening out. "So you can have a nice nap. And before you know it, I'll be back with your dinner." She rustled away, leaving behind a slight scent of chicken soup.

Jake reached over for the comic and looked at the cover. Did Arnie identify with its green antihero? he wondered. He flipped through some of the pages. Arnie and the Hulk appeared to share some points of physique, but Arnie carried off the laurels from the shoulders up. Nowhere did the Hulk manifest anything close to Arnie's mild good-natured expression, nor had he anything to match the hurt look that Arnie had left behind to fill his empty bed and torment Jake's conscience.

Tossing the comic aside, Jake slid farther down in bed and closed his eyes. But sleep avoided him. Not that Jake could blame it. I wouldn't sleep with me either, he thought. Gradually, however, drowsiness crept up on him, melting away his physical discomfort and slowing down his brain. The flow of thoughts that had coursed through his head at flood force now came one by one in single drops. He wondered how long it would take to pay off the hospital bill. He wondered how Ginny's reunion with her husband had turned out. He wondered if Hector would be waiting for him when he got home. And he wondered what Miss Murphy had in mind for tomorrow. He wondered, too, if his life was so full that he could afford to reject someone who looked up to him, however mistakenly, and wanted to be his friend.

Unimpeded by the mental clutter that generally tripped up Jake's waking thoughts, the answer to his last question presented itself in all its obvious simplicity. Jake seized on it with gratitude, and as his uninvited guests packed up and stole away, he drifted smiling into sleep.

Thirty-one

On a winter's day near one of the gates of Paris, Mimi and her lover played out the third act of their ill-fated romance. He confided to his friend that she would die for want of things he could not provide; she, overhearing this melancholy news from her hiding place behind a tree, coughed and wept. Arnie wept too. Cruising north on Interstate 5 with *La Bohème* blaring out at him from a multispeaker stereo system, he shed tears for the unhappy young couple, for himself, and for the vehicle he was driving: a mammoth ten-wheeled tractor unit that, even after more than six hundred miles of travel, still gave off a gleam of newness from its chromium-plated bumpers, fuel tanks, smokestacks, wheels, air horns, mirrors and marker lights, and from the customized red, black and yellow paint job on its cab, where the proud legend A&B TRUCKING, INC. could be read in clear white lettering on each door.

The truck had been delivered shortly after he arrived home from the hospital.

"We were getting worried, Mr. Siganski," said the worried-looking driver. "Mr. Lang was very particular that it had to be here yesterday morning, *with* that bow on it"—he nodded with distaste at the length of pale blue plastic that had been passed through the interior of the cab and tied into a large floppy bow on its roof—"but nobody seemed to be home. And you can't leave one of these things just lying around. Ha, ha."

Arnie had been unable to say more than a few words. He produced his commercial driver's licence and papers on request, signed forms in a daze, accepted the keys, and forgot to say thank you. Left alone, he walked around the outside of the tractor. It stood, a glittering embodiment of all his daydreams, ready to be hooked up to any paying customer's trailer and put on the road. Although boxy and unbalanced in appearance, it struck Arnie as the second most beautiful thing that had ever come into his life. He rubbed a speck of mud off the bumper with his elbow and climbed up the four ladder rungs into the cab. The rich smell of leather-covered seats intoxicated him as it mingled with the throat-catching odors of the padded vinyl ceiling and the thick blue carpet fitted over the floor, the walls and the wide doghouse area between the seats, where a sleek radio telephone had been installed. A CB radio and a stereo system nestled among the dials and switches on the dashboard, and an exploration of the area behind the seats turned up a double bed, television set, microwave oven, miniature refrigerator and a stack of user literature on how to make use of these wonders.

It had all been too much. Arnie lay on the bed and gave himself over to an emotional half hour. When he had recovered and dried his eyes, he climbed down from the cab, went indoors, and returned wearing a light cotton windbreaker over his T-shirt and carrying Bobbie's bag. Within an hour, after making a brief stop at Jake's office, he had piloted the giant truck onto the Hollywood Freeway, heading north.

Now, after an all-night drive, he was approaching the California-Oregon border, with the shadowy bulk of Mount Shasta disappearing behind him, off to his right. Ahead, the long rays of the rising sun slanted across the runway of Weed airport, jumped the highway and spread over the soft rolling meadows that meandered away to his left. A taxiing single-engine aircraft kept pace with him for a short time, then sailed off into the china blue sky, where a procession of white puffball clouds seemed to skim just above the treetops.

Inside the cab, Mimi and her boyfriend decided to part forever. "*Addio, senza rancor,*" sang Mimi.

As always, this phrase, set to meltingly tender music, detached itself and pierced Arnie's heart. He knew what it meant: "So long," Bobbie had explained, "and no hard feelings." No hard feelings. Arnie bit his lip and took an even tighter grip on the soft-wrapped steering wheel. What a dumb tape to have put on, but it was the only one he had at home, and he wouldn't have had that if it hadn't been in Bobbie's bag when he picked it up at the depot the other day. Now they were both singing. *Addio, addio senza rancor.* Sure, easy to say. But when you remembered the smiles and the nights in bed and all the other good times—and then the lies and cheating and those sons of bitches at the hotel.

Mist' Ahnie, Mist' Ahnie, you back! Come in. Sit down. Ian, you take up Mist' Ahnie's bag. . . .

God, it must have been so easy. And him never suspecting for a second.

Hello, you sleep good? Andy, you put lunch in Mist' Ahnie's bag. . . .

And slip in something else while you're at it. The big dumb sap will never notice. But worst, worst of all—

Sweetheart, you're back! Give us a big kiss. Mmm, I've missed that. No, leave the bag. You know I like to unpack for you. . . .

You bet he did. And what else did he like? Making a fool of him? Playing a dangerous game from the safety of home? The money? It must have come to a lot—and all those bucks burned up in the fire, too. Arnie pounded the wheel with his fist. How many customers did it take to make that kind of dough? How many kids turned into users? How many muggings and break-ins and killings?

> *Vorrei che eterno durasse il verno!*
> *Ci lascierem alla stagion dei fior!*

The tape ended and the tractor roared on, skirting mountains, skimming across bridges, plunging down inclines and toiling up others, on into a wild terrain of peaks and valleys, all blanketed with endless stands of evergreen. A thick mist that had been hanging on the mountaintops now sank down to envelop the truck. Arnie wiped his eyes and after a brief hunt for the appropriate switches turned on the windshield wipers and the headlights. These cut through the swirling cloud to pick out just ahead an off-ramp leading to a crossroad, along which, almost without realizing how he got there, Arnie found himself traveling in a northeasterly direction.

An hour later, still submerged in fog and able to see no more than ten yards ahead, he was thoroughly lost, grinding up a steep logging road cut roughly into the edge of an even steeper slope. The road, long out of use to judge by the condition of its crumbling pitted surface, dropped sharply away to his left, while bushes and ferns clinging to the almost vertical cliff swished and slapped against the windshield on his right. Nothing in the way of a turnaround had yet appeared, and to back down the way he had come would be impossible. Arnie pressed doggedly forward.

Slowly, the mist ahead began to lose its dull gray color and take on a faint yellow tinge. It became thinner and yellower and brighter until, with the suddenness of a magician's handkerchief, it vanished to reveal a scene that took Arnie's breath away and brought him to a dead stop.

He had braked on the crest of a hill, at the point where the road widened into the long-sought turnaround, then ran straight ahead down a moderate slope before making a sharp right turn behind the face of the mountain. Beyond the outside edge of the road and far below it, the still waters of a broad lake reflected brilliant blue from the sky and, along its opposite shore, mirrored the conical treetops and soft purple peaks of the mountain range that defined the far side of the valley. Although the sun had not risen high enough to reach the road where Arnie sat awestruck, it had already lit up the distant mountains, bringing into sharp relief every crag and tree—every branch and twig, it seemed—of the picture-postcard scene.

Arnie opened the cab door and climbed out into a heady atmosphere that carried a perfume blended of earth, damp moss, rotting wood and pine sap, with an overlayer of diesel fuel from the tractor. He shivered, glad of his light jacket, and walked over to the edge of the road. On looking down, he took an involuntary step back, for instead of the expected gradual transition down to the water there was a sheer, precipitous drop. His head spun, yet he found it impossible to look away. The dark shadowed water exerted a magnetic attraction that seemed to pull at his brain and draw his thoughts into its black depths. He blinked to break the spell and refocused his eyes to watch a gliding eagle, very small beneath him, become smaller still as it swooped down over the water on a fishing expedition, then disappeared off to his right behind the edge of the cliff.

In a tree behind Arnie, incensed at finding a strange being in its back garden, a chipmunk started scolding in a loud, furious chatter. Arnie looked up to discover his unwilling host trembling with indignation at the end of a pine bough.

"What's all that about?" he asked. "I ain't gonna hurt you."

The chipmunk, unconvinced, continued to express its outrage. Arnie felt happy. He would have liked to shout across the lake and try for an echo, but stopped short, afraid of spoiling the moment. Instead, he walked back to the truck, climbed the ladder into the cab, and descended again with Bobbie's bag under his arm. Squatting on the ground, he unzipped the bag and extracted from it the brown metal crematorium canister in which Bobbie's ashes mingled with the sole remaining evidence of his last drug shipment—a marriage of convenience consummated yesterday afternoon when Arnie, on deciding to transport Bobbie in his own bag, discovered the two plastic-wrapped packets and emptied them into the most secure traveling container he could think of on the spur of the moment. Now, with a thick screwdriver brought along for the purpose, he stabbed a number of holes in the canister and carried it down to the bend in the road.

He stood for a moment on this man-made promontory, noticing how the calm water had increased in blueness and sparkle as the sun rose higher. At last he looked down and addressed the canister.

"Okay, baby," he said. "This is it."

And, taking a firm football grip on the cylindrical tin, he pitched it out toward the center of the lake with all the strength he could muster.

The canister arched up into the air, turning end over end and occasionally emitting a few light puffs of what had once been Bobbie and a modest fortune in heroin and cocaine. At the height of its trajectory, it paused, then plummeted down, growing smaller and smaller until it became impossible to follow with the eye. A tiny white dot on the black water marked where it hit and sank. The sound of the splash died away before it reached the level of the road.

Instantly, Arnie's sense of pleasant solitude turned to desolation. He had made an ending and he felt truly alone. Even the chipmunk, tired of protesting, had dropped him and gone off about its business. Arnie heaved a sigh and turned back to the truck.

It waited for him at the top of the rise, a tamed monster with a ray of sunlight just beginning to graze the top of its open door. In this setting of greens and blues and purple grays, its red, black and yellow streamlined stripes, chromium-plated trim and shining accessories seemed as out of place as a trumpet blast in a library. Regarding it from a distance, Arnie experienced another of the waves of bitterness that had been breaking over him at intervals since the afternoon he had read Bobbie's letter and, in a more intense form, since the moment he had taken delivery of his delayed birthday present. Beautiful as it was, so perfect in design, so majestic even, it nevertheless make him think of matters he would have given much to forget: Bobbie maimed and dead, Jake almost gone the same way, the terrible pair in their fancy dress under the stage, the other lives they had taken and the hundreds more they had corrupted.

And what was it all for? Arnie asked himself. But he already knew the answer. People had died and his world had collapsed just so a pile of money could go up in smoke and he could be king of the highway in his very own custom-designed eight-ton tractor, every ounce of which he hated from the bottom of his heart.

Because he was guilty too, just like Bobbie and the twins. Arnie buried his face in his hands. No matter how you looked at it, it all came back to him. They couldn't have done it without his help; he was the reason Bobbie got involved, and now he was the one left alive holding the dirty bag. But—Arnie looked up—he didn't have to go on holding it. The idea came to him with absolute clarity. If all he had to look forward to was a whole life of feeling bad, with a ninety-thousand-dollar ball and chain fixed to his leg just in case he ever tried to forget what he had to feel bad about, what was the point? Who wanted to live like that? Well, maybe they wanted him to. Maybe they were somewhere now, laughing at the big joke they'd played on him. But he still had a choice. He could fool them yet. He could—

With beating heart, Arnie walked up the hill to the tractor and climbed into the cab. After first switching on the ignition, he rewound the tape on the cassette player for a few seconds, then pressed the Play button.

Ritorna un' altra volta
a intesser finti fior.
Addio, senza rancor.

That was it. Arnie put the gears into neutral and released the brakes.

The tractor inched off the crest of the hill and began to roll. From a barely perceptible movement, it gathered speed, traveling faster and faster until, at the bottom of the incline, it had gained sufficient momentum to hurtle straight ahead into space, neatly clearing the side of the cliff and turning slowly upside down as it fell. In those last few seconds, sunlight glinted off the still-sparkling fuel tanks, a bar of limpid Puccini drifted out into the still air through the open cab door, and the massive machine hit the lake, almost flat, roof-side down.

A vast plume of water rose into the air and an echoing crash resounded across the lake, sending birds wheeling out of the trees in startled flight. A glimpse of red and yellow flashed up through the churning waters, then the echoes died, a few final bubbles broke through to the surface and, as the lake regained its calm, the birds settled back on their perches. The hawk continued to fish, and even the chipmunk abandoned its lookout point to search for fallen pinecones. Except for some tire tracks on the outside curve of the road, where weeds would soon spring up, it was as if nothing had happened.

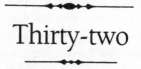

Thirty-two

Jake lay back in his hospital bed and brooded. He had not spent a pleasant morning. Calls to Arnie both today and last night had produced nothing but distant rings, and Jake's conscience, un-eased, now pinched him without mercy. On top of that, he had received a visit from Ginny, who blew into his room like a breeze from the sea, looking beautiful, young and, Jake had to admit, happier than he had ever seen her.

"I called your office," she told him, placing a bowl of yellow roses on his window ledge. "Your secretary seemed very reluctant to tell me where you were. I don't think she likes me."

"It wasn't that," said Jake, who strongly suspected that it was. "I asked her not to let anyone know where I am. I hate being seen like this."

Ginny laughed. "You don't look so bad—and I should know. If you can stand meeting one more person, I'll show you what I mean."

At this point, Hal had come in, grinning under a Dodgers cap, which he removed to reveal a two-week-old stubble. But as a cheer-up device the gesture fell a little flat, owing to the fact that Hal without his hair looked, in Jake's estimation, far better than Jake ever had with all of his. Fortunately, the visit did not last long, since Jake in his weakened condition, could take only so much of other people's happiness at one time. And certainly the couple before him managed to exude a glow of mutual contentment that might have tried a nature even less subject to jealousy than Jake's.

On leaving, Hal presented Jake with his cap and Ginny handed him a copy of *The Wind in the Willows*.

"This is a loan from Cal," she explained. "He thought you might like to find out how it all ends, but you're expected to return it when you come and see us as soon as you're up and around."

On promising faithfully to do this, Jake received a kiss that seemed to carry with it the fragrance of the roses on his window ledge and was left alone with sad thoughts regarding human relationships and his lot in life.

He was still in this morose condition when Miss Murphy arrived bearing his new glasses, six bird of paradise flowers arranged in moss, and a tin of brownies, still warm from her toaster oven. But Jake noticed none of these things.

"Murphy," he gasped. "What have you done to yourself?"

Changes had indeed been made. Miss Murphy stood before him in a simple shirt dress of tawny-colored silk, tied at the waist with a sash of the same material. Cut by some master magician, it flowed over her figure to breathtaking effect and was set off by plain brown leather pumps and a matching shoulder bag, both models of restraint. Her hair, formerly a semicontrolled riot of feral splendor, had been transformed into a mass of curls on top, with the rest pulled back on the sides and allowed to drop down over her shoulders at the back. She wore small white earrings of the same design as her necklace of simple white beads. The very sight of her advanced Jake's recovery by days.

Miss Murphy gave him an amused look and did an about turn. "You like?"

Jake was able to do no more than nod.

"Is my new look for the office," Miss Murphy continued. "And for you." She put the flower arrangement next to the roses and wafted the tin of brownies under his nose. "From Betty Crocker and me. I put in the bit that make you feel better."

Jake's heart fell. He had spent much of the night imagining a variety of ways in which Miss Murphy could make him feel better, but marijuana-laced brownies had not been among them.

"And I got something else," Miss Murphy announced, reaching into her shoulder bag and handing Jake a pink envelope with his name printed on the front in green ballpoint pen.

Jake started to tear it open, but found the top already slit. The folded pink notepaper within had a lily of the valley printed on its upper left-hand corner and carried the following message, written in a round, unformed hand, with many printed letters: "Dere Jake," it said,

I am going away now but I want you to have this because a deals a deal and I want you to have it. It is money I erned myself so you dont have to worry ware it come from.

I will never forget what you done for me Jake. And if you ever need help you just call on

Your friend,

Arnold Siganski (Arnie)

Under the signature were three small X's and the postscript: "Sorry about the paper. Its all we have."

"I find under the door yesterday," said Miss Murphy when Jake had finished reading.

242

Jake checked behind the letter and in the envelope. "There's nothing here. He must have forgotten whatever he was going to put in."

"Oh, no." Miss Murphy shook her head. "He don't forget. I put check in bank before I come here."

"How much?"

Miss Murphy breathed on her fingernails. "Four thousand dollar."

"Murphy! We can't take that. Send it back."

"Silly Teddy Bears." Miss Murphy came and sat by the bed. "You make deals, you get paid. Is no you fault you don't find murderer."

Jake tilted back his baseball cap and threw caution to the winds. "Who says I didn't?" he asked in an offhand manner that would have impressed even the great Bogart. "There were two of them," he added.

"Teddy Bears!" Miss Murphy leapt up in excitement. "I know you do it! I just know!" She bent over to kiss him.

Although changed in appearance, Miss Murphy still used the perfume that sent Jake's blood pumping at twice its normal rate. Consequently, he took some time to open his eyes and register the fact that she had pulled away his upper sheet.

"Murphy—put that back!"

"Madre de díos," whispered Miss Murphy. "What they do to you?" Her large brown eyes filled with tears.

Tired of lying, Jake let his head fall back on the pillow. "They burned me," he said in a small voice.

"My poor brave Jakes." Mis Murphy kissed him again. "You tell me everythings."

"Not now."

"No, not now." Miss Murphy brushed her lips over his forehead and closed eyes, ran her tongue down his neck, and proceeded to plant small kisses here and there on the sound areas between the gauze squares on his chest.

"Murphy . . ." Jake tried to put his arms around her, but was forced to wince and withdraw them.

"Shh." Miss Murphy returned to his mouth, her hair falling lightly on his shoulder. "You lie still." And once again she began to work her way down his chest, where each kiss blossomed into a small rapturous explosion. Eventually, the explosions moved lower down.

"No, Murphy," Jake started to protest. "Don't."

"Shh."

"People come in . . ."

"Trust me."

"No. Please, Murphy," he faltered. "Don't, Murphy. No."

"*Mr. Weissman!*"

Jake, who happened to have his eyes shut at this moment, found himself unable to open them. Neither could he sit up or speak. The two familiar words, barked out in trumpet tones, seemed to have paralyzed his body and seared into his brain a clear, terrible vision in which a starched white figure with an outraged face and a cap of stiffly waved blond hair stood framed in his doorway. Nurse Elsie ("Führer") Durer had this effect on her patients.

By a neat stroke of timing, the image in Jake's mind and its all too solid original, now a step further into the room, chose to speak as one, making up in precision what they lacked in originality.

"What is going on here?" they demanded.

An act of heroism was obviously called for. Jake responded by opening his eyes and mouth, although without having any clear idea as to what he might be going to say. He was never to find out, for the real Nurse Durer silenced any forthcoming response with an imperiously raised hand.

"Don't answer that," she said, apparently addressing a small framed picture of snow-covered mountains to the right of Jake's window. "Who is this person?"

Again Jake opened his mouth to no effect. Miss Murphy took up the conversational ball with a brilliant smile.

"I am great friend of Mr. Weissman," she announced.

"So I gathered." Nurse Durer continued to inspect the mountains.

"My name is Maria Morphy. Dr. Morphy."

Jake's lower jaw, so recently closed, dropped open of its own accord. Nurse Durer's left eyebrow ascended.

"I inspect the bandages," continued Miss Murphy.

Nurse Durer abandoned the mountains and delicately pulled up the sheet Miss Murphy had neglected to adjust.

"You were looking in the wrong place," she observed. "Now I think we should leave Mr. Weissman to get some rest."

"But I no finish!" Despite a brave attempt at standing her ground, Miss Murphy had to fall back before her opponent's relentless advance and considerable weight advantage. "I have to say the good-bye."

"You've said it."

Miss Murphy waved helplessly over a starched white shoulder. "I see you tomorrow, Jake."

"Sorry." Nurse Durer looked almost pleased. "Mr. Weissman won't be receiving any more visitors for a while. Even of"—she inserted a slight hesitation—"a professional nature. I am recommending complete quiet."

"But—"

"As a doctor, you'll understand." The door began to swing to.

"Call me, Teddy Bears," came Miss Murphy's voice from the hall. "Anytimes. I wait for you." And on this pathetic note the door clicked shut.

Nurse Durer turned back to her apprehensive patient.

"Now, Mr. Weissman, what have you to say for yourself?"

Assuming that he was not expected to speak, Jake made no attempt to do so. But his restraint went unnoticed. Nurse Durer had returned to the mountaintops.

"On second thought, I don't wish to hear it. I suspect I may have misjudged the situation. This whole sorry business is probably your doing. No, not a word!" Quelled by a fierce glare, Jake swallowed his protest. "God knows what you must have said to corrupt that poor young lady. In future, no nurse will be allowed in here unaccompanied. I shall personally screen all your visitors. When you are not alone, your door will be left open. Shame on you! I am taking this." The remote control for Jake's television vanished into a starched pocket. "You have had far too much excitement for one day. Really, Mr. Weissman." Nurse Durer turned at the door and shook her head. "We all thought you were such a *nice* man!"

Left to the dicates of his conscience, the smooth-tongued seducer toyed with the idea of self-reproach, but decided against it. Whether due to the faint trace of Miss Murphy's perfume that lingered pleasantly on in the room or the memory of a smile that had flickered on the corners of the Führer's mouth just before she closed the door, Jake suddenly felt happy and hopeful. In this mood, he decided to risk one of Miss Murphy's brownies, which had a nostalgic flavor that reminded him of cocoa and old leaves. It had all been worth it, he told himself. Putting aside his present condition and a few minor blunders that anyone could have made, he had brought his case to a successful conclusion, earned a handsome fee and, in the process, discovered within himself a new Jake that he vastly preferred to the glum loser (however nice) who had spent his days moping about the office.

This improved model was—or would be, when he got back in circulation—smart, dashing and brave. He would return to the world with the kind of bad reputation money couldn't buy, thanks to Miss Murphy and Nurse Durer, who, if she played her part well and denounced him in the right circles, might make the last part of his convalescence far more interesting than the first. Perhaps even now attractive young nurses were lining up two by two, eager for the privilege of entering his den of iniquity. He could almost hear the scuffles and giggles outside his door.

Yes—the new Jake recklessly helped himself to another brownie— there could be no doubt about it. He had seized his opportunities, made all the right moves, and steered his life onto the right track. From now on, he would swing with the best of them and what was more—let Rosa keep his dumb tasteful tailor—he would do it wearing any damn thing he liked. He might hit Vegas for a few really flashy suits. He might try a new hairstyle to match. He might just break a few hearts. The world was his oyster and he could barely wait to get out of this goddamn place and open it. In the meantime, he still had some unfinished business to take care of. Humming a little tune of his own invention, he checked Arnie's number again and reached for the telephone.

The sun now sat high in the sky, and the lake, free of shadow, glistened from one shore to the other. On a patch of grass near where the tractor had gone over the edge, Arnie lay asleep, face down, with his head cradled in his arms. While he slept, the sun reached its zenith and a transformation came over the landscape. The morning breeze died away, the surface of the lake turned to glass, and even the clouds froze in their reflected patterns as the day halted in a breathless suspension of motion before beginning its gentle slide into afternoon. A deep hush fell, and the world became silent and still except for an occasional insect hum or a tiny movement on the scarred ground at the cliff edge, where flattened twigs and shoots were beginning to right themselves.

Wakened by the unfamiliar silence, Arnie yawned, rolled over, and looked back up the hill. Glinting metallic reflections caught his eye near the spot where he had parked the tractor, but these turned out to be only highlights from a heat haze dancing on the crest of the hill. He yawned again and sat up cautiously, as several parts of his body protested the move. Slipping off his torn jacket, he inspected his aching left arm and was relieved to discover that he had nothing worse to show for his leap from the moving tractor than a few cuts and scrapes and a bruised shoulder. A secondary ache in the region of his left hip reminded him that he had fallen once more on his keys.

Arnie rubbed his forehead with the back of his hand as a slight feeling of light-headedness came over him. It must be the air up here, he thought, or all that thinking on an empty stomach. Never before had he thought so hard or so long, but it had been worth it. Starting from the flash of insight that had come to him just before he jumped out of the tractor cab, he had worked it all out: how he shouldn't blame himself for what Bobbie had done, how he could forgive both Bobbie and himself for his own part in it, and how he could still go on loving Bobbie as he had in the past. Because, he had decided, it was always good to love someone, even if you didn't understand them right, even if they made mistakes, even if they didn't love you back in the same way.

That was how he felt about Jake, too. Jake didn't want to know, but it was still better to go on caring for him than to throw away the good feeling. And you could never tell. Even with someone who didn't want to know, there was no law that said you couldn't wait and hope and be there if he ever needed you. Jake was human, after all, and needed help and friends the same as anyone. What it boiled down to, he thought, was trust. Bobbie hadn't had it and neither did Jake. But he, Arnie, dumb old Arnie, he did. And maybe, it came to him, maybe that's better for some people than having brains. Maybe if he trusted enough and waited and worked hard, then someday there might be another rig bought with money he had earned himself, and a way to see Jake now and then, and maybe even another Bobbie. He squinted up at the sun. No, there wouldn't be another Bobbie. But the world was a big place, with lots of people. Somewhere there had to be someone who needed him, someone he could look after and share a life with. He just had to keep on believing that.

Arnie blew his nose, climbed to his feet, and took a last look into the lake.

"So long, Bobbie," he said. "No hard feelin's."

And throwing his jacket into Bobbie's bag, he prepared to make his way back to Interstate 5, where, with a little luck, he could hitch a ride south to Los Angeles. And Santa Monica. And Covina Place. And . . .

With keys ajingle and hopes high, Arnie began to walk.